Barrie Mahoney worked as a teacher and head teacher in the south west of England, and then became a school inspector in England and Wales. A new life and career as a newspaper reporter in Spain's Costa Blanca led to him launching and editing an English language newspaper in the Canary Islands. Barrie's books include novels in 'The Prior's Hill Chronicles' series, as well as books for expats in the 'Twitters from the Atlantic' series, which give an amusing and reflective view of life abroad.

Barrie writes regular columns for newspapers and magazines in Spain, Portugal, Ireland, Australia, South Africa, Canada, UK and the USA. He also designs mobile apps and websites to promote the Canary Islands and expat life, and is often asked to contribute to radio programmes about expat life.

Visit the author's websites:

www.barriemahoney.com
www.thecanaryislander.com

Other books by Barrie Mahoney

Journeys & Jigsaws (The Canary Islander Publishing) 2013
ISBN: 978-1843866466 (Paperback and eBook)

Letters from the Atlantic (The Canary Islander Publishing) 2013
ISBN: 978-0992767136 (Paperback and eBook)

Living the Dream (The Canary Islander Publishing) 2011
ISBN: 978-1450767040 (Paperback and eBook)

Expat Survival (The Canary Islander Publishing) 2012
ISBN: 978-1479130481 (Paperback and eBook)

Message in a Bottle (The Canary Islander Publishing) 2012
ISBN: 978-1480031005 (Paperback and eBook)

Twitters from the Atlantic (The Canary Islander Publishing) 2012
ISBN: 978-1480033986 (Paperback and eBook)

Escape to the Sun (The Canary Islander Publishing) 2012
ISBN: 978-1480033986 (Paperback and eBook)

Threads & Threats

Barrie Mahoney

The Canary Islander Publishing

ISBN 978-0992767105
www.barriemahoney.com

First Published in 2011
Second Edition 2013
The Canary Islander Publishing

Acknowledgements

I would like to thank all those people that I have met on my journey to where I am now and to my partner, David, for his love and support as well as well-honed proof reading skills.

To the children in the many schools where I have worked as a teacher and inspector, for their laughter, openness and natural insight into life.

To professional colleagues in schools throughout England and Wales whose skill and dedication I have been privileged to witness and have so often admired.

Disclaimer

This is a work of fiction. Names, characters, places and incidents either are the product of the author's imagination or are used fictitiously, and any resemblance to actual persons, living or dead, events or localities is entirely coincidental.

Dedication

In loving memory of Pat Huxter

Chapter 1

Two Years Later

The phone rang. It was just after two o'clock in the early hours of Sunday morning and James had only been in bed for a short time. He was already drifting between that comfortable half way stage between sleep and reality. Was it a dream or was the phone really ringing so demandingly in his ear?

"Hello," answered James, drowsily.

"James, Rector here. I am so sorry to disturb you so late at night, or should I say early morning? I am sorry to say that we have an emergency. The school is on fire."

It took James a moment to gather his thoughts. "Rector, did you say a fire at the school?"

"I'm so sorry, James, but yes, sadly. I had a call from Jack Sparrow a short time ago. It was he who spotted it and called the fire brigade. I have just been over there. It looks bad, but there is nothing that we can do until the fire is under control. Thought you should know. I am going back to the school now."

"I'm on my way, Rector. I'll see you there shortly."
James quickly got dressed and quietly closed the bedroom door behind him. The tousled head sleeping at the side of him hadn't stirred.

As James crept downstairs he noticed that Prince, his usually lively Golden Retriever, hadn't even bothered to get out of his basket. Prince opened his eyes wearily and, realising that it was nowhere near time for breakfast, promptly closed them again and gave a deep sigh.

"See you later, boy," James whispered as he closed the front door. "You and I will have a really nice long walk when I get back."

The drive from James' flat to Prior's Hill was a short one from the outskirts of Abbotsford. As he drove down the hill into the picturesque village of Prior's Hill, he could see a plume of thick, black smoke coming from the area of the main school building.

As he got closer to the school he could see two fire engines parked outside, their hazard lights flashing, and a large crowd of villagers standing watching, pointing and shaking their heads outside the main gate to the school building. He recognised many of the faces and most were wearing only pyjamas, night dresses and dressing gowns.

Many nodded or briefly waved when they saw him get out of his car. Later, James would recall with some amusement that several villagers had forgotten to replace their teeth before braving the cool of that mid-September evening.

"Thank you for coming over so quickly, my boy," boomed the Rector, pushing through the assembled crowd and looking genuinely relieved to see James.

"I am so sorry, this must be most disturbing for you and, indeed, for us all. I gather that the fire has now been extinguished, but no one is allowed into the playground, yet alone the building, until it has been checked and declared safe to enter."

"What happened?" asked James, shaken by the sight before him. The thick, black smoke was already creating a burning sensation at the back of his throat.

"Too early to tell. Look, there's Jack Sparrow. Have a word with him. He was the first to raise the alarm."

Jack Sparrow came up to James and shook his hand.

"Good to see you again, young sir, but not like this," mumbled a toothless Jack. "One of me dogs was barking and I went down to see that she was alright and to get a glass of water. It was when I was by the sink that I saw flames coming out of the side window – the staff kitchen window."

James nodded. "What time was that, Jack?"

"Oh, around quarter past one, it must have been. Something woke the dogs and set them off barking."

By now, Anne, James' deputy, was standing beside him. James noticed that she had the good sense to be wearing warm outdoor clothing.

"Hello James. This is dreadful. You have worked so hard to get the school up and running for the new school year. It all looked so nice with all the painting and the new carpets."

"That's the way it goes, Anne," James shrugged. "When will I learn not to plan so much for the future? I was really pleased with it on Friday when I went home. I remember thinking that it was such a pity that it wasn't finished before the new term started. Just the smell of that carpet adhesive to get rid of before the children came back on Monday. We've all worked really hard to get it ready for them."

"James, I was thinking. Do you think it was the adhesive that somehow caught fire? It was solvent based and I remember thinking that it smelled just like lighter fuel when they put it down in that small classroom? Emily said exactly the same thing too before she went home."

"Hmm, it's a thought, Anne. Of course, that's the room with the old gas boiler. I was thinking only a few months ago that we ought to be planning to get it replaced sometime. It must be years old."

"It is, James. It was here when I was a pupil, but I am not telling you how long ago that was." Anne smiled, trying to make a joke and ease the tension.

"Well, you've set me thinking, Anne. It is on an automatic timer, but it has been a very cold week so I guess the frost 'stat' may have cut in last night. Look, I'll mention that to the firemen later. It may just help them to focus on what caused it."

The Rector returned to James and Anne.

"James, the chief tells me that the fire is out. From a brief look inside the building, he tells me that there is severe damage to the kitchen, staff room and the small classroom as well as the first floor rooms. The hall and your two classrooms seem to have suffered mainly smoke damage, but structurally they seem OK. We will know more in the morning."

"What about the library?" enquired James, dreading the reply.

"I asked about that as I know that means such a lot to you, James. It seems that is unaffected. Those new fire doors seemed to have done the job. All that hard work of yours and Tristan's is safe, James."

"So basically, we are one class down, with two others and a hall that will need a thorough clean, no staff room and no staff facilities. As for the upstairs rooms, I guess it was the stockroom and all that paper that helped the fire burn so furiously."

"That's about the size of it, James. You cannot open the school on Monday. I will have a word with Sir Toby and other governors about getting permission from County Hall to close the school for a few days. Goodness knows what we shall do with those extra children. Do you realise that you have doubled the roll since you arrived?"

James nodded. "Yes, ironic, isn't it? County will just have to provide some temporary accommodation for them. We cannot split the class. The infant class is already nudging the limit, and Anne's and mine are over the recommended limit as it is."

"Look, my boy. Best to go home now and get some sleep. We can talk about it again tomorrow. Things always look better in daylight."

James nodded. "Thank you, Rector, maybe I will. I will be over again tomorrow morning. Maybe I can see you then?"

"Only between services, James. Remember it is my busy day!"

"Of course, I had forgotten it was Sunday."

"Yes, I know you had. Maybe you should give us a try now and again, James? You spend all your spare time working, don't you? It's not good for such a young man."

"Maybe I will come to Matins one day. It's just that..."

"I understand, James," replied the Rector kindly, placing his hand on James' shoulder, "It is still early days and it takes time to come to terms with your loss. Remember though that we are always here to help you and look after your spiritual needs."

"James, I am going home now. You are welcome to come in for a hot chocolate before you go home," interrupted Anne, seeing that James was about to be lectured at for some considerable time by the well-meaning Rector.

"Anne, that would be lovely, thank you. I know it is late, but I can feel and taste smoke in my mouth, throat and nose. Are you sure it's not too late for you?"

"No, James. I won't get back to sleep now anyway so we may as well have a drink and then I am going to get on with some lesson preparation. I may fall asleep later. My mind is buzzing with how we get over this next problem at Prior's Hill."

James and Anne said their farewells to the Rector and, by now, most villagers were drifting back to their cottages to resume their abruptly interrupted sleep.

The excitement of the evening, suitably embellished, would remain in the folklore of this close village community for many generations to come. They made their way the short distance down the narrow country lane to Anne's pretty stone cottage.

"Phew, thanks for getting me out of that one, Anne. I know he means well, but our Rector does go on a bit. I do have faith, but since Tristan's death I find it really hard to go to Church by myself. I don't mind going with the kids for school events, but it is still very painful."

Anne led James to the small living room. It was a very pretty, delicately planned room with flowery curtains and chintz covers. James suddenly remembered how Tristan used to tease him about his dislike of chintz.

Anne smiled and nodded. "Hot chocolate alright for you, James? I know just what you mean. When my Tom died four years back I felt just the same. It is true, it does take time, but you never really get over it. We can never forget the people we love and why should we want to? It is part of who we are."

James now realised that, although he had known Anne for nearly three years, he had never been invited to her home before. Indeed, he knew very little about Anne or her personal life, other than that her husband had tragically died early in their marriage. They were always far too busy talking about school and the children.

"What a pretty cottage, Anne. How long have you lived here?"

Anne busied herself preparing the hot drinks in her small, but well equipped kitchen. "You will think this is terrible, James. I was born here – upstairs right bedroom, to be precise."

James laughed. "Never! You mean you have lived here all your life?"

"Yes, my parents lived here and when they died, Sir Toby said I could keep it on. It is part of the Peatwhistle Estate, you see. My Dad used to work for Sir Toby's father, so really he didn't need to let Mum and I stay on when Dad died. He could have let it to one of the other estate workers."

"Yes, I hear that the Peatwhistles are very good to their employees."

"Mostly, yes, but if you cross them then that is a very different matter. You get on well with them, don't you, James? Would you like some chocolate biscuits or should I make some toast? I rather fancy some toast."

"That's a great idea. Yes, toast for me as well please. I like the Peatwhistles. Sir Toby and Lady Lotitia were really good to me when I started at the school and were so supportive when Tristan died. I shall never forget their kindness."

"They have a son too, James. He lives in America, but he never comes home. I haven't seen him in years."

James nodded and changed the subject. "So you went to Prior's Hill School as a child?"

Anne grimaced, "Yes, I'm afraid I did. Even in those days it went through highs and lows, just like you have experienced. Then I went to Ledger's School, teacher training college and then back to Prior's Hill again. I haven't seen much of life or the world, have I?"

James looked at the slightly built, yet attractive young woman who was busily slicing bread for toast.

James had only ever seen her before as his deputy and had been so grateful with the way in which she had adapted to this supportive role, and seen him through his own turbulent year. He now realised that he really knew very little about her.

"One thing that I have learned, Anne, is that there is no right way of doing it. As long as you are happy it doesn't really matter."

Anne fell silent for a moment.

"I was happy, very happy, James. Sometimes I thought I was too happy. I fell in love with Tom – he was my childhood sweetheart. When I went to college he went to work on the Peatwhistle Estate. Later we married and I was asked to apply for the job at Prior's Hill School. County Hall was against it, but the governors, Sir Toby mainly, pushed it through. To be honest, it made a lot of sense for Tom and I to live here with my mum. She was suffering with Alzheimer's. That was terrible for her in the end, but my Tom was wonderful. Did all he could to help her. That was a dreadful period in my life and then…" Anne's voice trailed away.

20

"Great toast, Anne. Thank you," said James, sensing that Anne was reliving, as well as retelling, a very painful part of her personal life. "This is strange. Here we are at three o'clock on a Sunday morning eating toast and drinking hot chocolate." James paused and left Anne to continue her story in her own good time.

"After mum died we had a couple of really good years together and were making plans to buy a home of our own outside the village. Tom was doing well on the estate and we even talked about starting a family. He collapsed at work one day and was brought home. It was then that we discovered that he had cancer."

James nodded. "Yes, I heard it was very advanced by the time you and Tom found out."

"There was nothing that could be done and he slipped away after four months. It was a terrible period, but for most of the time he was without pain and so, for that, I guess I have to be grateful."

"Did he have to stay in hospital for long periods?"

"No, because it was so advanced there was little that could be done, apart from making him comfortable, that is. We made the decision to let him die at home with me and with his friends around him, and in a community that he loved. It was a peaceful end, and I loved him so much. How I miss him."

"You have been to hell and back, haven't you, Anne?" said James quietly. "I never realised. I am so sorry we haven't talked about it before."

"You have nothing to feel sorry for, James," said Anne quietly. "I prefer it like this. In a way you have made sure that I have focussed upon the job and we have all thrown our weight behind you because we can see what you are trying to do. It has been helpful for me to face and deal with these challenges. It has helped me, not to forget, but to come to terms with Tom's death. More toast, James?"

"No, thank you, Anne. I really must get going. Prince will be wondering what has happened to me."

"You've had a rough time too, James, haven't you?" continued Anne, not really wanting James to leave.

"Yes, it's been a bad two years in many ways," agreed James. "I'm alright at school, it's just when I get home again it all comes flooding back. Prince has been such a help to me. Then again, so have the community, the Peatwhistles and everyone at school. They have become like another family to me."

"That's Prior's Hill, James. They are maddening for much of the time, I know, but when it comes down to it they are here for you. That's why I have never left the village. I need that feeling of belonging. You sure you don't want more toast and hot chocolate, I am going to have some more toast. I have a pot of Emily's marmalade in here somewhere as well."

"Go on then," laughed James. "When I get home I am going to take Prince for a night-time walk and then go back to bed."

"He is a lovely dog, James. He simply adores you. Anyone can see that."

"Yes, he is, and I adore him too," agreed James. "Did you know that Bert and Eddie got him for me? They arrived at Doris' and George's one day with this beautiful puppy in Bert's arms and said I had to have him." James swallowed hard as he recalled the pain of those weeks.

Anne nodded. "Yes, I know Bert and Eddie had it all planned after Tristan's death. Isn't Prince one of Bert's sister's dog's puppies?"

James nodded.

"Yes, Bert said that when he first saw Prince his fur reminded him of Tristan's hair. The colour is so similar. He said I had to call him Prince, because Tristan was a Prince amongst men. I shall never forget their kindness either."

"As I recall, that was the beginning of your recovery, James."

"Yes, it was. My days were full of cleaning up sick, pee and vomit," laughed James. "Doris was brilliant, although I don't think George was quite so forgiving of Prince's little mistakes. Anyway, it was Prince that made me see the point of it all once again."

James and Anne tucked heartily into the next batch of toast, accompanied by some of Emily's thick cut marmalade.

"So what are we going to do about the fire, James?"

"Well, I'll be over for a proper look tomorrow afternoon. Maybe you would like to join me, Anne?"

"Well, yes, we ought to take a good look and see what needs to be done. I had a thought earlier. Maybe we could use one of Sir Toby's barns as a temporary classroom?"

"Well, it's a thought, but maybe they are too big? Do you mean the one where we have the barn dances? It would be a nightmare to heat, and this could go on for months."

"No, not that one, but there is a smaller one at the side that we used to use as an outside classroom when we did farm studies a few years ago. I don't think it is used for anything but storage nowadays. I am sure Sir Toby would let us use it. We would need to get a portable toilet or something though? As I recall, it even has a blackboard on the wall. Bert put it up for us."

"Well, it's a good idea, Anne. I don't like the idea of closing the school for repairs. The children have only just started back after a long summer break. We need to keep the momentum going."

"I guess there will be all sorts of rules and regulations about using a non-school building, James, but I am sure there will be a way around it Let's have a look at the barn as well tomorrow. I can ask Sir Toby about it after Church if you like."

"Great idea, Anne. Look, I'll pick you up from here at around midday and I'll treat you to lunch at the Prior's Arms. We can then discuss our strategy. I will also need to call the others and let them know what is happening."

"For goodness' sake, don't forget Emily," laughed Anne. "You two seem to have been getting on quite well recently. I think she rather likes you now."

"In a strange way, I am rather fond of the old thing. She wouldn't be my first choice as a teacher, but she means well and does her best for the children. That means a lot to me."

"I know you like a problem to solve, James, and I think we have a big one here. You seem to enjoy them and you always come through in the end. The thought of it terrifies me, but then that is why you are the head and I am just the teacher."

"Deputy head teacher, if you don't mind, Mrs Armstrong," corrected James, laughingly adopting his most 'headmasterly' tone, complete with raised eyebrows.

"Oh goodness, I know that look," laughed Anne as she led James to the front door. "OK, OK, I take your point."

"Goodnight, Anne. Thanks so much for the toast and the hot chocolate."

"You are very welcome. Goodnight, James. Give my love to Prince."

By the time that James arrived back in his flat, dawn was breaking and Prince decided that, yes, he would like a walk. James had rarely been out of the flat at that time of the day, and certainly not on a Sunday morning. Although it was very fresh outside and there was dew on the grass, it was almost silent.

Prince ran off his lead to a large clump of trees that served as James' local 'forest' and provided Prince with as many 'piddling posts' as he would need. James watched with pride as the young dog chased through the long grass and between the tall pines. After a brisk walk, Prince was back on his lead and the pair walked back home.

"Is that you, James?" yelled a voice from the bedroom.

"Yes, it's us. Don't worry; I had an early start. Just giving Prince his breakfast. I will be along in a minute."

As James was giving Prince his breakfast, the figure of a very sleepy Christian entered the kitchen. The dark haired, muscular young man gave James a hug.

"Where have you been? I woke up ages ago and you had gone. Prince was asleep so I assumed you were in the bathroom. When I woke up again a few minutes ago, you were still missing and Prince had gone too."

"Sorry, I didn't want to wake you. We had such a good night last night and we were late back. I didn't want to spoil it. I had a phone call from the Rector. The school caught fire."

Christian sat bewildered as James told of the early morning events.

"That's terrible, Jay. You have worked so hard this summer. What's going to happen now? You should have woken me up, I would have gone with you."

"You need all the beauty sleep that you can get, Christian!" laughed James. "Yes, I was upset when I saw it, but now we shall have to put it right. I've been thinking, maybe I can get some improvements done while it is being repaired."

"Same old James," laughed Christian, "always trying to get the school better and better. You know what a reputation it has already, I hope. Even the folk in Spotten know about it! I was showing some clients around a property the other day and they said they wanted to be near Prior's Hill, so they could try and get their kids into your school. Spotten is miles away from Prior's Hill!"

James placed a large mug of steaming black coffee in front of Christian. "Well, no one will be coming to us at the moment. We are full as it is, and now we have lost one classroom. It is a real problem."

"Do you want me to come over and take a look? I know a bit about buildings. It might help."

"Thanks, Christian. I would appreciate that. Not today, but early next week would be great. I shall need some good advice, mind." James grinned and ruffled up Christian's tousled hair even more.

"Stop it, Jay. I have just styled it! Now I shall have to do it all over again."

Prince put a large flat paw on the table, looking wistfully at the large bowl of cereal and milk that Christian had poured himself.

"Down Prince," exclaimed Christian. "This dog is getting fat, James. He needs to go on a diet."

"Nonsense. It's just puppy fat. He'll soon walk that off."

"No, I am not kidding, James. You give him too many titbits. I've seen you slide them under the table. No wonder he adores you."

"I just cannot resist those big brown eyes," began James.

"Hmm, is that what you say to all the guys?" teased Christian.

At midday, James' little blue sports car stopped to an abrupt halt outside Anne's cottage. Anne was waiting for him and appeared as soon as she heard the familiar toot of the horn.

"Morning again, James. Do you want to leave your car here and perhaps walk to the pub?"

"OK, Anne. Tell you what. I am a bit early. Why don't we check out the school first and then we can have lunch and talk about what we have found out?"

"Good idea, James. Let me get my brolly, just in case."

Black storm clouds were looming overhead as James and Anne walked the short distance to the school. James unlocked the gate and the first thing that met their gaze was hazard tape and 'Do not enter' and 'Danger signs' fixed to the front and side doors.

James and Anne made their way in silence to the side door at the rear of the building, which had supposedly been unaffected by the fire.

James cautiously unlocked and opened the door, and a strong smell of smoke greeted them. They walked in silence into James' classroom.

At first sight, it looked unaffected, but after rubbing his finger on the walls James could see that everything was covered with a thin film of smoky grime. He opened some of the large windows to let in some air.

"The lights aren't working, James," reported Anne, who had walked into the hall. "Looks alright in here, but my classroom stinks of smoke and just look at all this ash!" she exclaimed pointing beneath the fire door to the small kitchen and the fire damaged area beyond.

"Well, maybe a good scrub would help to sort this out. Don't go any further, Anne. It may be dangerous beyond this part."

James gently opened the fire door from the hall into the small kitchen and was horrified by what he saw. The entire area was burned black, the ceiling and upper floor had given way and James could see daylight through a large gaping hole in the roof. Blackened beams and charred ceiling joists met his gaze.

"It's all gone, Anne. The infant classroom, the rooms above, kitchen and staff room. They have all been destroyed. All that is left is a blackened shell and the open sky. Major rebuilding will be needed to put this lot right."

Anne peered though the doorway. "James, this is dreadful. It is far, far worse than I imagined. Thank God no one was around when it happened."

"Let's get out of here, Anne. The smell is choking me. You don't look at all well either. We both need a stiff drink."

Chapter 2

Pulling Together

The school governors agreed that that Prior's Hill School should be closed for the week after the fire to allow the damage to be assessed, and to make arrangements for accommodating the pupils from the class that had been destroyed.

James had called an urgent staff meeting for early on Monday morning, and this was to be followed by an emergency meeting of the school governors.

The small group of teachers and support staff met together in stunned silence in the infant classroom – a small temporary classroom situated at the far side of the playground and away from the main school building.

Doris handed out mugs of coffee and one of her famous chocolate cakes, which James adored, and sat proudly on a table amidst the circle of chairs that James had arranged earlier that morning.

"Some things never change, Doris," said James, giving Doris a big hug and kiss on the cheek as soon as he spotted her by the sink.

Doris blushed. "This is dreadful, James. Just as you were getting on top of everything here. What are we going to do?"

Suddenly, Doris spotted Prince sitting beside her. The young dog adored Doris, as it was often she who took him for a walk at lunchtimes and was always very generous with her treats.

"Hello, boy. You've come as well today, have you?" Doris bent down to the big dog who gave her a big wet lick on the cheek. "Would you like me to take him for a walk at lunchtime, James?"

"Only if you have time, Doris. He's had a good run already and I'll give him another before I go home."

Doris sat on the floor hugging Prince. James smiled as he noticed that there seemed to be very little difference between the size of either dog or school secretary nowadays.

"Well, Doris, whatever happens I am determined that we will finish better off than when we started. We are not going to be beaten by this little setback, are we?"

"That's my James. I know you will sort it out."

As soon as the group had settled and started drinking coffee and munching large chunks of chocolate cake, James outlined his emergency plans and suggestions for dealing with the crisis that had been thrust upon them.

He made it clear that these were preliminary suggestions only and that anything they decided would have to be agreed by the school governors and County Hall.

As was James' style, it was a succinct analysis of the problem that they faced followed by suggestions of possible ways forward. He sat back, sipped his coffee and waited for the staff to comment.

"That's ridiculous, James!" exclaimed Emily, replacing her near empty mug with a bang on the table beside her. "There's no way that we will be allowed to teach those young children in Sir Toby's barn. Can you imagine all the health and safety requirements and the fuss that will cause with the parents?"

"I'm not suggesting that we do that, Emily. What I am suggesting is that Sue and the top infants move out of the ruined classroom into our classroom and we teach the top juniors in the barn. This way, Class 1 Infants and Anne's class would be largely unaffected. Do you think that would work?"

"Surely County Hall has to provide some sort of temporary classroom anyway?" asked Sue, a tall young woman with rich red hair.

"Yes, I think so, Sue, but I won't know any more about that until after this meeting. Colin Treader, the head at Coombe, says they sometimes do that, but it takes weeks to arrange, as they have to lay pipe-work, electricity and gas. It could mean that your class would be out of operation for several weeks."

"I've only been here two weeks," giggled Sue, "My first job and I'm just getting into my stride with it all, and then my classroom burns down. They didn't tell us anything about that on teaching practice!"

"Hmm, I think I can see what you are getting at, James," said Emily thoughtfully, ignoring Sue's frivolity. "That may well work. We used to use that barn some years ago for farm and environmental studies. Bert and Eddie set it up as an outside classroom for us. It had a blackboard and I seem to remember someone gave us some rather nice tables and chairs."

"Yes, Emily, I remember that as well," replied Anne. "Didn't they come from Dawn Farmer's teashop? You know she opened a cream tea shop next to the farm for passing holidaymakers, but it didn't take off for some reason."

"Yes, it was Dawn. I don't think she ever had any customers. No one but locals ever passed the farm. It was such a silly idea. Anyway, we used to manage quite well in the barn for the odd lesson in those days, James. It was clean and spacious, as I recall."

"Just another thing we must think about," interrupted Doris. "What about toilets and washing facilities? The children cannot keep coming to and from school. I know it's a quiet lane, but an accident could always happen."

"I don't think that's a problem that we can't overcome, Doris," replied James. "I think you can hire those units quite easily. County Hall would have to pick up the bill though."

"And heating?" questioned Julia, the newly appointed infant teacher. "I doubt we would be allowed to use portable heaters. We will need something, though. It is cool in the mornings now and this situation could go on for months."

The group fell into thoughtful silence. Meanwhile Prince sat himself at the side of Emily, giving her a little lick on the hand, which she reciprocated with a hearty pat.

"What about bathroom heaters? You know, those long things that you have in bathrooms. If some of those were put up on the ceilings it would be safe and give off some heat. Would be expensive to run though."

"That's a good idea, Jenny. I know what you mean and I have seen larger units used in some of the out-of-town warehouse stores," agreed James. "I think we are getting somewhere with this."

Jenny went pink with embarrassment, pleased that her idea had met with such a positive response. She had only recently been appointed as a classroom assistant, as well as an additional dinner lady. "You know my Brad is an electrician? I am sure he would help to fit some."

"Thank you, Jenny. If this idea goes ahead, I will have a chat with him."

"I don't like your other alternatives, such as placing the children in another local school until their classroom is rebuilt," sniffed Emily, "Very disruptive for us as well as for the other schools."

"How long do you think it will take to repair the building, Mr Young?" asked Jenny.

"Jenny, do please call me James," smiled James. "I really have no idea. I have this feeling it will not be as straightforward as we think. You see, we are also a church school and so the diocese will be involved as well."

"They wouldn't use this as an excuse to close us, James, would they?" asked Anne, looking worried. "I know they are trying to close a lot of county schools at the moment to save money."

"No, not a chance, Anne. Our numbers have more than doubled in two years and we are full. That really only applies to schools with falling rolls," replied James confidently.

It had been agreed that the governors' meeting that followed the staff meeting would take place at the rectory. James had asked that Anne be invited to the meeting as well, as she could also help to report back to the rest of the staff.

Anne had already asked Sir Toby about the possibility of using his barn and, according to Anne, had said he would be delighted to help in any way that he could.

"I think it's a splendid idea, James," began Lady Lotitia after listening to James' proposals. "The children may also learn a little more about farm life than they seem to at the moment, what?"

"Well, James, thank you for taking us through your proposals," said Sir Toby Peatwhistle, the Chairman of Governors. "They certainly look feasible. I had a meeting at County Hall this morning. They will send out engineers and architects later today, but warned me that it could take some considerable time before the damage is repaired."

"Why is that?" asked the Rector. "Surely the school is insured?"

"Well, apparently not. Not in the sense that we know it anyway. Because County Hall has so many properties they carry their own insurance risk, as this is cheaper than paying individual insurance premiums. However, as we know, the County has financial problems and it could take time to find the funds," replied Sir Toby sombrely.

"So, what happens to the children in the meantime?" asked George Cole.

"Well, of course they stressed that they hadn't seen the damage for themselves as yet. One option would be for that class to be accommodated in a school with an empty classroom in the area, with their own teacher from Prior's Hill. Alternatively, if they could not identify a spare classroom, the children would be split and placed in classes in other local schools, until we are in a position to have them back at Prior's Hill."

"But not with their own teacher, Toby?" interjected Lady Lotitia.

"No, I'm afraid not," Sir Toby shook his head. "I asked if it would be possible to let us have a temporary classroom on our site, but I was told that only happens in exceptional circumstances as it costs too much; it would take a long time to arrange and it would not be cost effective."

"Stuff and nonsense," exploded Lady Lotitia, crossly. "If their offices caught fire, I can assure you that a new temporary building would appear the following day. It is always the children that suffer."

"Hear, hear," muttered the rest of the governors.

"Well, if my colleague governors agree, I propose that we reject County Hall's proposals and that we set up a working group of governors to look at the feasibility of James' proposals instead. With Sir Toby's agreement, using the barn is an excellent idea and would seem to provide an immediate answer to our problems," pronounced the Rector, pompously.

"Oh, let's just get on with it, Hubert," interjected Lady Lotitia. "We don't have time for working groups and such like, what? Those children need to be back at school as soon as they can. What do you think will happen if we remain closed for any length of time? This is stopping parents from going to work."

It was therefore agreed that the Peatwhistle's barn would be used as a classroom and that a small group of governors would be asked to provide James and Anne with all the support that they would need to make it happen as quickly as possible.

George Cole was asked to liaise with the Parent Teacher Association to ask that a group of parents work with Cedric, the school's caretaker, to clean the remainder of the school building and to ensure that the two undamaged classrooms would be fit to accommodate children once again.

"James, you simply cannot do this!" was the initial response from the Local Education Authority adviser when James telephoned him after the meeting. "There are insurance and health and safety issues to be considered."

"Yes and the governors have considered these. It was a unanimous decision, Paul. Maybe you would like to give Sir Toby a call and talk it through with him?"

Paul Jones, an amiable and easy going man by nature, hated conflict of any kind, and the last thing that he wanted to do was to bring the wrath of the Peatwhistles upon both himself and the Local Education Authority. He had experienced the wrath of Lady Lotitia on other occasions in recent years and it had not been a pleasant experience.

"Er, well, James. Let me come over to the school this afternoon and we can talk it all over. I am sure there is a way through this. Have you considered moving the children affected to St. Margaret's until we can get the building repaired?"

"The governors have considered this and a number of suggestions, Paul, but it will break up Prior's Hill school. Besides these children are only six and seven years old. We cannot possibly bus them each day. St. Margaret's is a long way away."

"Well, let's talk about it later this afternoon. Would four o'clock be alright for you?"

After a hasty pub lunch with Anne and other staff in the Prior's Arms, James returned to the school to find that a group of men from the County Premises Department, all wearing hard orange coloured safety hats, were already examining the burnt-out building.

"Don't come in here without a safety hat," yelled one of the men in a blue overall. "This area is dangerous."

"I know," replied James, "I am James Young, the head teacher."

"Oh, I'm sorry, Mr Young, I didn't realise. I'm Tony Storey, County Architects Department. You seemed very young to be the head teacher!"

"James Young," replied James, ignoring the latter comment and holding out his hand to the grey haired man in a suit in front of him. "What have you found?"

"Let's go through to the classroom and leave the others to it. It will take a while yet," replied Tony, looking serious. As they walked through to James' classroom, he continued, "Look, not beating about the bush, this is bad. Already we feel that most of the east wing should be knocked down and rebuilt. The fire has caused considerable damage to the structure of that part of the building. There was certainly some heat created. Do you know what caused it?"

"No, we are still waiting for the fire officer to get back to us. We think it was likely to be the old boiler and the new carpets, but we really don't know for sure. How long is this repair likely to take?"

"That's my point, James," said Tony gravely shaking his head. "We are not talking about a repair lasting a few weeks, but a major rebuild of this wing of the building. It could be a year, maybe longer," he added gravely.

James suddenly felt very worried as the enormity of what was being said to him became clear. "How much will all this cost?"

"Many thousands of pounds, James. It is difficult to say just yet. What with all the financial problems that County Hall has, it could be months before we even get the go ahead to get started with this. We have a Youth Centre in Chine that burned down last year and we are still waiting to get started on that one. As a parent myself, I do know how you and parents will be feeling. It certainly is a sad state of affairs."

The visit from members of the County Premises Department was alarming in itself, but this was to be followed by the promised visit from Paul Young, the schools' adviser, accompanied by Miss Jean Flickersmill, the Early Years Adviser.

Jean Flickersmill was a redoubtable lady, detested as well as feared by many of James' less infant-friendly colleagues, but someone who James had come to respect and sometimes rather admired.

The feeling had become mutual and since Miss Flickersmill had invited James to attend her regular meetings for 'the chosen few' in the county, she had made it clear to James that, although she generally disapproved of men in general and male primary teachers in particular, she was prepared to tolerate him. Both advisers greeted James warmly.

"So sorry to hear the news, James. It really was bad luck after all your hard work," commiserated Paul.

"James, good to see you again. I was so sorry to hear about this and also concerned that you will not be teaching the infants again this year," began Miss Flickersmill.

"Sadly, no. As our numbers have grown, I thought it would provide greater stability for Class 1 if our newly appointed teacher taught them, and I would then teach Class 4 part-time with Emily. If I took the infant class, I would have to use Emily in there for two or three days a week. It just wouldn't be fair."

"Hmm, not on the children anyway," snorted Miss Flickersmill. "Under the circumstances it was probably the correct decision, James. However, I would like to think that you will resume your interest in infant education again very soon."

"Of course. This arrangement will allow me to work with the infants for at least one day each week. I can now help in both Classes 1 and 2 because we have a new probationer teacher, Sue, who will need support in her first year, as well as Julia who is a very experienced infant teacher, but is also new to the school."

"Excellent, James. I can see where you are coming from." James noticed that on this very rare occasion, Miss Flickersmill smiled, admittedly a not very generous smile, but she did at least smile.

"James, this problem with the classroom. From what I am hearing it is unlikely that things will be back to normal until at least the end of the year. Do you really feel that this barn idea of yours will work in the meantime?"

"I don't see why not. The accommodation may be a barn, but it is a large, clean space and if we can get some heating in there it will be perfect. I will ensure that we have at least two adults in there all the time and we can get some portable toilets put in."

"How do you propose to get two adults in the classroom permanently, James? County Hall cannot pay for an additional classroom assistant or a teacher, you know. Financial constraints are upon us all."

"I will use parent helpers. We have more than enough parent helpers in Class 1 at the moment, and I am sure that they will help us out, if they know the reason why we are doing it."

"Yes, we have heard that you are very good at getting parents involved, James. However, might this be just a step too far?" James felt Miss Flickersmill's steely grey eyes boring deeply into him.

"Come and have a look at the barn," said James quickly. "It is only ten minutes' walk away from the school and we already have a group of parents and some of Sir Toby's employees getting it ready."

James, Miss Flickersmill and Paul Jones walked down the narrow lane leading to one of Sir Toby's farms, making polite general conversation as they did so.

James felt a strange link with the past as they walked past Apple Tree Cottage, which was still empty, and where he and Tristan had thought about renting, and the large barn where the annual Barn Dance was held. Many happy, yet poignant, memories came flooding into his mind.

"Charming" enthused Miss Fickersmill. "Quite charming."

"Muddy, very muddy," responded Paul Jones, less than enthusiastically. "I wish I'd brought my boots."

Surprisingly, the barn idea met with the advisers' approval. James was astonished to see Doris and George, as well as Emily and Anne, together with governors and parents brushing, mopping and scrubbing floors, tables and chairs.

Bert and Eddie were busily whitewashing the walls. Even Lady Lotitia's maid, Peggy, appeared with a large tray of tea, coffee and biscuits.

"Me Lady says I am to look after you all well," announced Peggy.

"You've even got Lady Lotitia on your side with this one," whispered Paul. "Thought she would be too busy drowning herself in gin to care," he added cruelly.

James nodded. "Yes, the Peatwhistles have been amazing. This is a strange community, Paul. They take time to get to know, but in a crisis everyone seems to pull together."

"James, I think this is an amazing example of good working community relationships. We must prepare a paper on it sometime. I am sure it will work. Come along, Paul. We need to get on," announced Miss Flickersmill, looking impatiently at her watch.

"Yes, James. We will do what we can to back you. I will support you in getting temporary heating and portable toilets, but the rest is up to you, I'm afraid. Good luck."

By the end of the week, the barn was looking like a real classroom. James and Emily, together with Bert and Eddie, worked hard to transfer equipment, furniture and displays from the school building to the new accommodation.

Electric heaters had been installed and two portable toilet units had been placed in neat cubicles outside the building. It was the first time that James had worked so closely with Emily, and he became increasingly full of admiration for her energy and commitment to the task.

"Thank you, Emily. I really do appreciate all your hard work with this. I could not have done it without you."

"To be honest, I have rather enjoyed it, James. In all my years of teaching, I have never experienced anything quite like this. You certainly know how to get things moving."

"I'll be over to help as much as I can. I have also got a 'rota' of parent-helpers and Jenny will also be on call. I just wish we could have some kind of telephone system over here, but I guess that is asking too much."

"Yes, James, I think you are probably right," laughed Emily.

Meanwhile, back in the main school building, George and Doris, together with Cedric, the school's caretaker, and the Rector's wife June, were leading a team of cleaners intent on thoroughly cleaning and removing all traces of the effects of the fire from the two remaining classrooms and hall.

The school governors had extended the period of closure of the school for a further week, and a letter had been sent to all parents explaining what was going to happen and the reasons for their decision. Doris had telephoned or personally called upon most of the parents during the week and all, but one family, were very happy with the temporary arrangements that James had made.

"Nearly all the parents that I have spoken to are just relieved that the school can remain open, James," Doris reported. "The only problem was the Scott family, you know Geoffrey's parents? They said they would not consider letting their precious son be taught in a barn and are going to move him to Coombe School instead."

"Phew, that's a relief," exclaimed James. "I do pity Colin at Coombe though, having that family on his books, but I am very relieved for poor Emily. She and Geoffrey never saw eye-to-eye since he threw that toy grenade at her. I have never seen anyone turn quite that colour before! This may well be the best solution for us all."

The new week started well, and during morning assembly James told the children all about the fire and why there had been changes. The children sat quietly until James had finished and then Freddy put up his hand.

"Yes, Freddy?"

"Does that mean that we won't be having a Christmas Party this year?"

"No, Freddy. We will still be having one. Why do you say that?"

"The kitchen's burnt down," replied the anxious little boy.

"We still have the main school kitchen, Freddy, and our cook, Mrs Hilary, makes most of the food for our party and your parents and Mrs Cole and the teachers bring some in as well. Don't worry, Freddy, you will still have your party. I promise."

The children cheered and had no further questions on the subject. Emily and Jenny led the eldest children out of the school hall, and to their new classroom in Sir Toby's barn.

"I am amazed at how smoothly this has gone," James commented to Doris during the afternoon break. "I went over to the barn a couple of times and it was working really well and even Emily was smiling! The infants seem happy enough in our classroom and there's lots more space for them now."

"Well, it has been quiet here as well, James," replied Doris. "Both Sir Toby and the Rector called in to see if everything was going alright here. They both seemed very pleased with the response from villagers. I think you have become the hero of the month in the village, James."

"That makes a change, Doris," laughed James, "Do you remember the school stage debacle and the swimming pool incident a couple of years ago?"

"How could I ever forget, James! That was a tough time, wasn't it? Mind you, I think you have calmed quite down a bit since then."

"I must be getting older and wiser, Doris. I am no longer the young upstart in his twenties that you had to train!"

"Well, credit to you, James. You have stuck to your guns and, fire or no fire, this place is really going places."

James had just returned from taking morning lessons in the barn. He and Emily had rearranged their timetables so that James taught in the barn most mornings and Emily took over each afternoon.

It was an arrangement that suited them both well and James rather enjoyed his mornings away from the main school building.

He was very proud of how well the children had settled to their new routine and how responsible they had been in adjusting to their new surroundings. He was surprised when he saw Paul Jones sitting in his office talking to Doris.

"Hello, Paul. Good to see you," said James amiably shaking Paul's hand. "What brings you here this afternoon? Is Miss Flickersmill with you?"

"No, thank goodness," winced Paul, "I left her savaging another local head teacher," he added, less than diplomatically.

"Ah, I see," replied James, who would have liked much more in the way of detail, but thought better of asking a direct question.

"James, I need to speak to you, in confidence, urgently. That is why I am here."

Doris took the hint, made her excuses and quietly left the room, closing the door behind her.

"James, I'll come straight to the point. We have now received an estimate of cost for the repair or should I say for rebuilding the east wing of the school. It is horrendous and I was shocked when I saw it."

"Yes, I gather it is. I think Sir Toby received a copy of the report on Friday, I haven't seen it yet."

Paul nodded. "Sadly there is now serious talk at County Hall about whether or not this school should remain open. I am so sorry, James."

James sat in stunned silence, gradually realising the significance of Paul's words.

"Statistics show that there is spare capacity at both Coombe and Taskers schools. Indeed, there is now excess capacity at Coombe as pupil numbers there are no longer as strong as they were. One possibility being discussed is the merger of Prior's Hill with one of those schools, thus avoiding rebuilding costs here. Indeed, the sale of the land and remaining buildings here would release some much needed cash to County Hall."

"Our roll here is increasing, Paul. We do not have a falling roll. Surely it would make sense to keep Prior's Hill open?"

"If you look carefully at your pupil roll, James, and I have done so, you will see that you have few children that come from the actual village of Prior's Hill. Many of your pupils come from wider afield through parental preference due to, and full credit to you, the good reputation that you have achieved for this school. You have done a wonderful job here and this will be reflected in any future appointment that you may have within the county."

"It sounds to me as if this idea was being discussed long before the fire, Paul. The fire was only a week ago, but your proposals seem well advanced Am I right?"

Paul Jones began to feel himself turning pink. "I'm afraid so, James. We have been looking at the possibility of closing one or more small schools in the area for the last two years. Prior's Hill was being considered, because it had a falling roll. Since your appointment the situation rapidly reversed and I thought the immediate danger of closure had passed. However, the fire has now rather sealed its fate."

"Are the governors aware of this yet?" asked James, suddenly feeling rather sorry for the mild-mannered man seated in front of him.

"No, I have that unpleasant duty to perform in a few minutes. I wanted to see you first to warn you and then I have a meeting with Sir Toby and the Rector. As yet they have no idea of what is being planned for the school."

"How long do you think we have, Paul?"

"Well, the proposal will go forward to the Education Committee next week and if they agree, arrangements will be made to merge Prior's Hill with one of the other schools in time for next September and the start of the new school year."

"The village will be outraged once they hear about this," exclaimed James. "It just cannot happen. This school is at the very heart of our community."

"Yes, and that is what they all say, James. The point is that we cannot afford to keep small schools open. They are not cost effective. There are far too many and they are expensive."

"Well, this one will not be closing without a fight, Paul. I can assure you of that."

Paul nodded and added quietly, "One more thing, James. I know how passionate you can get once you have a 'bee in your bonnet', so to speak. You would be well advised to distance yourself from any form of protest or anything that makes the work of the Education Committee more difficult than it already is, if you see my meaning?"

"Are you threatening me, Paul?"

"Come off it, James, you know me better than that. What I am saying is that Colin Treader, the head teacher at Coombe, will be retiring in the next year or two and you would stand a very good chance of being appointed as the head teacher of the new combined school, if that is the eventual decision. That is, if you behave appropriately and professionally."

"This is appalling news Paul, and your attempts at bribing me with a new job will not work either. I believe in this school and this community. Real people live and work here. The values that this community has are something that money cannot buy. We will fight you every step of the way!"

Chapter 3

Save Our School

The news of the possible closure of the school travelled fast around the Prior's Hill community. By the morning after Paul Jones' visit, everyone seemed to be talking about it. Indeed, the release of this devastating news placed James in a difficult position as he had not as yet had the time to alert staff, other than Doris, whom he had seen immediately after Paul Jones had left the school the previous day.

"This is dreadful news, James. There was talk about it several years ago after the problems that we had with Peter, your predecessor. Parents were removing their children and sending them to other schools. I remember then that Paul Jones raised the possibility at that time. However, after pressure from governors the threat was lifted and you were appointed. Things seemed to be getting better and better until now. I thought that the school's future was secure."

James arranged for an extended staff meeting for lunchtime. All the staff were invited to attend and Doris and Anne agreed to take charge of the children to allow the dinner ladies and kitchen staff to attend as well.

Teachers and support staff entered the outside infant classroom, which was being used as a temporary staff room, in silence. In Doris' absence, no one bothered to make coffee. The silence was broken by Emily, whose dangerous, flashing eyes said it all.

"Why didn't you tell us before, James?" snapped Emily, unpleasantly. "I cannot believe that you have kept this news to yourself."

"Thank you for your trust in me, Emily," replied James quietly. "The first that I heard of it was yesterday after Paul Jones made a surprise visit. By the time that he had left, you had all gone home. He then went to see the governors and they released the news last night. This is the first opportunity that I have had to tell you all."

Emily pursed her thin lips, folded her arms and said no more.

"Surely we must fight this?" began Sue. "I know I have been here only a short time, but anyone can see that this school is vital to the life of the village. Besides, Coombe or Taskers are too far away for young children to travel to by bus."

"I agree," said Jenny. "We need to have a village meeting and get a petition moving. I can organise the petition if you like, James. I know most of the mums through the Wives Group, and I know Doris will help me."

"Thank you, Jenny. That's a good idea. I thought we could have a parents' meeting this Friday. Would you all be able to come as well?"

The staff nodded their heads in agreement. By now the group had started animated conversations with each other. It was difficult to hear what individuals were saying, and James had to raise his voice in order to bring the meeting back to order.

"Look, I really do hope you have all got some ideas about what we can do. Let me write them all down and I can take these to the governors' meeting this afternoon. Now, we already have a parents' meeting and a petition. Did I hear you say a protest march, Julia? What else?"

By the end of the meeting, James had enough ideas to fill the large sheet of paper that he had stuck to the blackboard. The staff were not short of ideas and James was amazed to hear some of their suggestions, as well as their resourcefulness. Anna, one of the dinner ladies, had volunteered her son, Derek, a local printer, to produce posters and leaflets.

Non payment of rates, as well as tying Emily to the railings at County Hall were two of the least helpful suggestions, but even Emily laughed when she heard the latter suggestion from the youngest member of staff.

"In my day, we respected the eldest members of staff. Now here you are volunteering me to be a modern day Emily Pankhurst, Sue! Well, I do have the right name, I suppose."

Emily and Sue's comments provided much needed relief to the tensions of the meeting and the group dissolved into laughter. James had already noticed on earlier occasions that Sue was already helping to 'rub the sharp edges' off Emily, and her youthful, outspoken manner seemed to hit just the right note with this crusty, yet well meaning, teacher. James decided that this was a good time to close the meeting and they agreed that they would all meet again before the parents' meeting.

"How did it go, James?" asked Anne anxiously, as she and Doris returned from the playground. "I was a bit worried about Emily. She was furious when she arrived this morning."

"I know," smiled James, "She started savaging me, but young Sue came to the rescue. Staff dynamics are very interesting, aren't they?"

"It wasn't your fault anyway, James," added Doris. "How could you have told her before today anyway?"

"Well, maybe I should have telephoned everyone last night, but I was in shock myself. I wanted time to think so I went out for a long walk with Prince."

"Any ideas?" asked Anne.

"Well, there are lots of good ideas from the staff. I'll go over them with you both after school if you like. Now on to the governors' meeting. That will be a lively one, I guess."

"I know it is a worrying time, James, but you need to know that, to my knowledge, this issue has cropped up several times before. Remember I was a pupil here, and I recall a similar thing happening then. Nothing ever came of it. It was something to do with the Trust Deed."

James thought for a moment and suddenly banged on his desk. "Anne, that's brilliant! You have just given me an idea!"

The governors' meeting was a surprisingly subdued and reflective affair; James had thought there would be lively argument, protests and plans to oppose the suggestions from County Hall. Instead, there were many detailed questions asked, although the Rector could answer only few of them. Neither Sir Toby nor Lady Lotitia was present and the Rector chaired the meeting in Sir Toby's place.

"Can they really do this to us?" asked Jackie Day, one of the parent governors.

"It seems they can," replied the Rector. "Many schools have closed in the county recently and it seems they have the process 'done and dusted', so to speak."

"But this is a Church school. Surely that gives us some say over the school's destiny?" added Ross Willis, another parent governor.

"I would have thought so," replied George Cole.

"Rector, have you or Sir Toby raised any of this with the diocese yet?"

"Well, that is why Sir Toby and Lady Lotitia are not with us today. Sir Toby is going to County Hall and then he will go on to the Diocesan Office to get more information about what we can do to fight this."

James then outlined his, and the staff's, suggestions for a series of protest meetings, but sensibly omitted the suggestion of chaining Emily to the railings outside County Hall. The governors listened carefully and nodded before the Rector summed up their agreed course of action.

"I propose that we follow all of James' suggestions, but my only caveat is that any protests that we support should be without violence and held with some dignity. We are a Christian community after all, and maybe this is the time to turn the other cheek. Let us pray."

The Rector closed the meeting with a prayer although James was still smarting at the suggestion of "turning the other cheek", when the Rector came up to him.

"Good suggestions, James. Well worth trying, but they do seem to have made up their minds, don't they?"

"This is what worries me, Rector," nodded James. "This is all too convenient. It seems to have been agreed long ago. May I ask, do you have a copy of the school's Trust Deed?"

The Rector thought for a moment. "Well, I will check in the Church safe, but if I haven't, Sir Toby certainly will. After all, it was his great grandfather, Sir George Peatwhistle, who gave the land for the benefit of a school to be built in the village. That was back in the early nineteenth century. May I ask why this interests you?"

James nodded. "I thought it may give us a clue as to where we stand. I spoke to Ray Parsons this morning. You know, the slick lawyer who works in London during the week. I have his lad in my class. He called me this morning after he heard the news and said he would examine it for us and see what the terms were. Didn't there used to be another school before this in Prior's Hill?"

"Yes, there was a Dame school near the village shop. It was one of the first in the county. Sir George was quite a philanthropist in those days and, I believe, started it. He was very wealthy, but gave quite a lot of his money away to start schools in several villages around here. However, the bulk of his generosity went to Prior's Hill in the form of land."

"Sir George sounds quite a good man. This was before all the inheritance laws, so I guess he didn't have to do it."

"Oh, he was, I understand. There were other people in his day, famous people like Cadbury and Rowntree, who realised that their businesses would also benefit if they looked after their people properly, gave them decent housing, schools and such like. It was a similar situation in Prior's Hill and Sir Toby has continued the tradition to this very day."

"Most interesting, Rector. Maybe you should write a history of the village one day. All this needs to be recorded for posterity."

The Rector nodded and smiled. "Maybe one day I will. Meanwhile, I will try and find a copy of that Trust Deed and get it to you, James. By all means let Ray Parsons take a look. We need a slick lawyer at a time like this."

The remainder of the week was a difficult one for James and his staff. The school was still adjusting to having one quarter of its pupils taught in Sir Toby's barn, which was not without its problems.

Much of the week was wet and windy, and James was concerned that he would soon be getting complaints from parents, as the children working in the barn seemed to be returning to the main school building with mud coated on their shoes, socks and, in the case of the boys, their long trousers.

He was surprised and grateful that Emily appeared calm and unflustered about the whole experience, and even gave the impression that she was rather enjoying it.

"I am enjoying it, James. The weather is awful and we could do with some more lights in the barn, but I have seen another side of these children. They are so understanding and co-operative. They know we have problems and they are trying to play their part in helping. We have much more space and even though the weather has been bad, we have been able to look at aspects of farm life in much more detail than we ever could back at school."

James nodded. "I'll see if we can get a few more lights put up. I hadn't thought of that, Emily. What are we going to do about all that mud? I haven't received any complaints from parents yet, but I can see it being raised on Friday evening."

"Yes, I was going to mention that to you, James. Let's ask the parents to send their children to school with a pair of cheap Wellington boots. We can keep them in the barn and use them if it is too wet. They must name them though. We need some clothes pegs!"

"Clothes pegs?"

"To clip the pairs of boots together. I've been in this business a long time, James. This was one of the first tips an experienced teacher told me when I started teaching!"

"Good idea, Emily. I'll get Doris to send home a note today and I will buy some pegs! Yes, it all seems to be going very well and I am very grateful that you have got on with it. This school closure thing is really taking up too much of my time at the moment."

"As I see it James that is essential for the school's survival. I will do what I can to help, but it is up to you and the governors to fight on behalf of us all, I'm afraid."

By half past seven on Friday evening, the school hall and both Anne's and James' classrooms were crammed with parents, governors, staff and villagers. Representatives from County Hall had been invited to attend, but had declined on the grounds that the process was still at the 'consultation stage'.

"What's better than to consult with parents at the consultation stage then?" James had overheard Doris' curt reply to Paul when she had telephoned him to invite him to the meeting.

"I would have thought he would have welcomed the opportunity to put County's case to the parents, James," grumbled Doris.

"Maybe it's because he doesn't have a real case to present, Doris."

Sir Toby opened the meeting, which was intended to be a 'question and answer' session, as well as an opportunity to involve parents and villagers in any protests that would be organised.

A reporter from the local newspaper, Alice Staines, had been invited to cover the meeting and James noticed that she was seated in the back row, busily making notes, whilst a photographer was creeping around at the side taking numerous photos of the large gathering.

Sir Toby gave a clear outline of the problems resulting from the fire, as well as County Hall's response in dealing with the issue. As soon as he mentioned transferring pupils from Prior's Hill to Coombe or Taskers schools, his comments were met with boos and loud shouts of "No" from the gathering.

"This is just not on, Sir Toby. My children are far too young to travel twenty miles each way to a school out of the village," declared Phil Brown.

"Neither of those schools are anywhere near as good as Prior's Hill," added Mrs Flanagan. "They only want us to make up numbers, so they don't get the 'chop' as well. It is they who should be closed and not us. It's disgraceful!"

"This 'ere school is the centre of our village," shouted Mrs Gee, "I cames here and so did Pete and all the kids. Does that mean nothing to those lazy buggers at County Hall?"

For nearly two hours questions were asked, accusations made and arguments flew around the hall. James sat and listened, responding only when he was asked to make a comment.

"What does Mr Young think? He's put the school back to where it should be. What's going to happen to him?"

James responded that his priority was to save the school and, as yet, he hadn't even considered the possibility of defeat, let alone moving elsewhere. There were loud cheers and claps when he said this.

Skilfully, Sir Toby seemed to sense when all that could be said had been said, and decided to bring the meeting to a close.

"In conclusion, I must add that we have only just started this fight to keep our school open. I am in consultation with my lawyers at the moment as well as County Hall and the diocese, and I will inform you all as soon as I have more news."

The villagers noisily left the hall. It had generally been a good-natured meeting, but James could also sense the anger and dismay as they left the hall. Several parents came up to him as they left and shook his hand.

"You've made a big difference to this school and village, Mr Young. We wondered about you at first, but we really appreciate what you are doing for our kids," beamed Mrs Flanagan.

James smiled to himself as he remembered the many occasions when he had to have sharp words with Mrs Flanagan. He sensed that a truce was now in operation between them.

"Thank you. That's really kind of you, Mrs Flanagan. May I ask you to take a few leaflets with you and sign our petition over there?"

Sir Toby walked over to James. "All in all it was a good meeting, James. I am not surprised at the strength of feeling about this matter. The villagers genuinely care for their school. I hope you also noticed the genuine warmth that they also feel towards you? You have gained their trust, James, and it takes a long time in Prior's Hill to be deemed worthy of that trust."

James nodded. "Yes, that came across very strongly, and I was touched. Have you managed to get any further with it, Sir Toby?"

"I would rather not say at the moment, James. All I can say is that my lawyer is taking the matter very seriously and I should know more on Monday. I hear you have been asking to see the Trust Deed. I will let you have a copy next week, but I suspect that you are thinking along similar lines as myself."

"How is Lady Lotitia?" enquired James, feeling that he should move on to lighter matters. "I haven't seen her for quite a while."

Sir Toby paused and said quietly, "Not too good at the moment, James. She sometimes goes through some bad times, since the problem with Giles that we spoke about some time ago. She seems to have withdrawn into herself once again."

"May I call in to see her one day?"

"By all means, James, please do. She is rather fond of you, you know. Give it a few days though."

The first few weeks had taken their toll on James. By the time that Saturday came, James had no energy or wish to do anything other than to take Prince for a long walk over the hills. Prince made do with a series of short walks that James and Doris gave him during the week, but he seemed to know that the weekends were especially for him and that he was entitled to something more strenuous on those precious days off with James and, if he was lucky, with Christian as well.

"Oh Prince, not now. Go away. I'm not getting up yet," was James' response when Prince started pawing the bed and licking his ear. Prince snorted and wandered back to his basket. Two hours later, Prince repeated the process, but this time continued licking James' ear until he had James' full attention. James turned over and glanced at the clock radio at the side of the bed.

"Oh no, eleven o'clock! I have wasted the morning! We are supposed to be going to see Christian for lunch today, boy. You will like that, won't you?"

After James had showered, dressed and given the patient dog his breakfast and eaten his own hurried piece of toast, he and Prince went off on their usual brisk morning walk. They went to the copse that Prince always enjoyed, and James took the opportunity to play throw and catch with the small blue ball that Christian had given Prince last Christmas.

The toy was one of the young dog's favourites, yet the sight of it reminded James of an issue with Christian that he had been putting off for some time.

Since Tristan's death two years earlier, James and Christian had become very close. During those first dreadful months that had been the worst of James' life, Christian had been there for him.

James felt close to Christian from the start, because he knew that Tristan would also have approved of this friendship. Christian was the estate agent who was acting for the sellers of the cottage that he and Tristan had decided to purchase days before that fateful car accident.

Christian had been there for James at the funeral and over the next few weeks until he was well enough to return to work. Indeed, it was Christian who had passed on the final loving comments that Tristan had made about James when he and Tristan had lunch together just an hour or so before Tristan's life was cut short so tragically.

James would always treasure those comments and be deeply grateful to Christian for both his love and support.

James was troubled, because he didn't feel the same way about Christian as he knew Christian felt about him. He liked spending time with Christian, but as a friend and not the partner to be that Christian saw in James.

Christian was a good looking, kind and sensitive young man and when James moved into his new flat, they took it in turns to stay at each other's homes at weekends.

One weekend, Christian would stay with James and the following weekend James and Prince would stay at Christian's. Christian also adored Prince and the feeling was mutual. Prince even had his own duplicate set of toys and a basket in Christian's untidy flat.

On the rare occasions when Prince and James had to be apart overnight, it was always Christian who would look after Prince until James returned.

James now sensed that Christian would shortly be suggesting that they live together on a more permanent basis. Indeed, it was Christian who suggested that James rent the flat that he was now living in, because it was a little larger than his own and had a small garden for Prince. He also often referred to a new property that had just come on the market as "ideal for us."

"Fetch, Prince," yelled James, as he threw the ball even further along the lane leading to the copse. The young dog bounded off in delight, returning shortly afterwards with the ball clasped in his wet, drooling mouth. Yes, he knew that a decision would soon have to be made and, out of consideration, for Christian, the sooner the better.

Lunch at Christian's was not as James had expected. He and Prince arrived, and James let himself in with the key that Christian had given him several months earlier. Prince dashed to his basket in Christian's living room to check that his toys were still there and after much sniffing discovered that they were and settled down to contentedly chew one of them. Christian would arrive later.

He usually had to work on Saturday mornings and James was used to having a little time to relax before his friend burst in full of amusing stories about his latest clients and the latest mortgage woes. James placed the bottle of wine and some food that he had brought for the weekend in the fridge, sighing as he noticed the unwashed dishes, pots and pans in the untidy kitchen.

"Well, Prince, I had better start cleaning this lot up, I guess. Christian will never get around to it, will he?"

As James was busying himself with the washing up, the door opened and in came a beaming Christian holding up two large bags from Marks & Spencer. He put the bags on the table and gave James a big hug and kiss, whilst Prince who was beside himself with excitement leapt around as befitted his age, yelping happily. Christian sat on the floor beside the happy dog who immediately smothered him with big, wet licks.

"That's more than I got from your Daddy," laughed Christian. "Maybe later, James, eh?"

"Let me get you a drink, Christian. You've been working today, but what's with the bags of groceries? You don't cook!"

"I do today. This is a celebration and I am going to cook lunch and tell you all about it over a leisurely drink! Look, I've even got something for Prince to celebrate as well!"

James opened a brown paper bag and gave Prince a large coiled, multi-coloured rope. Prince loved playing 'tugger'. He was a strong dog and usually won the game. Prince enthusiastically grabbed the new toy and trotted off to his basket to chew it contentedly.

James smiled and hugged his friend again, "I am really pleased to see you. What's this news? We usually go to the pub when I come over for the weekend. You sure you can cope with this cooking lark? I don't want food poisoning!"

Christian's boyish young looks turned into a pretend frown, "Look, with the help of Mr Marks and Mr Spencer, I can have a three course meal on the table in one hour. Pour us a drink and let me get on with it. By the way, just go away and play with Prince, will you?"

Christian was true to his word and an hour or so later a delicious meal appeared on the dining table in Christian's living room. He had even bought a tablecloth and napkins especially for the occasion.

After a delicious vegetable soup as a starter, Christian disappeared to the kitchen and later proudly returned with dishes of vegetables and two plates of cheesy vegetable bake.

"You see, you are not the only vegetarian today, James. I am having just the same as you. I thought I may even turn veggie one day to keep you company."

"You don't have to do that," laughed James, "I know how much you like your meat! Now what exactly are we celebrating?"

"Let me top up the glasses again first," insisted Christian.

"I hope we are not driving anywhere after this. We have drunk nearly two bottles already."

"We are not driving anywhere after this, James. I haven't seen you for a week and I have other plans for you," whispered Christian seductively.

James giggled and remembered that this was the first time that he had felt really relaxed since the school fire. He sat and listened to his friend.

"James, I have been promoted! I am now to be the manager of a new branch office for the company. More responsibility, more excitement and, best of all, more money!"

"Well, done!" exclaimed James standing up and hugging Christian. "Very well done. I am not surprised, you have done really well there. Where is the new branch going to be?"

"Er, that's the bad news, James. Actually, it's in Derby. The company wants to expand up north and one of the partners has business contacts there. They asked me yesterday, but I wanted to tell you properly today."

"That's miles away, Christian! When do you start?"

"I think the office is nearly finished, and we will open in a month or so."

"I am really pleased for you. We will miss you."

Silence fell upon the pair and a subdued awkwardness took the place of the previously animated conversation.

"Fancy a dessert, James? I bought one of your favourites."

"I'm full, Christian. That was a brilliant meal. Thank you."

"James, that isn't all my news. I wanted today to be special, because I have something else to say."

James froze in his seat as he realised what was coming next.

"James, I love you. I have always liked you since we all met when you were looking at Lavender Cottage. After Tristan's death, we seem to have become closer and closer, and now I love you. I want to share my life with you. There, I've said it, that's what I've been trying to say for ages."

James sat in silence, a glazed expression on his face. Christian continued, sensing James' awkwardness.

"Do you remember when you first got Prince and we went for that long walk over the hills?"

"How could I forget?"

"Well, remember that you were fooling about with Prince, and you slipped and rolled down that slope right into a cow pat?" continued Christian, beginning to laugh. "Well, that's when I fell in love with you! You looked so helpless and I fell for you there and then. Romantic moment, eh?"

James smiled. "Yes, I do remember, but…"

"What I am really trying to say, James, is that I love you. I want to be with you always and wonder if you would come to Derby with me? I know it's a lot to expect, but maybe now is a good time for you to leave Prior's Hill and head for a fresh start up north. If you don't want to, I can turn the job down and we can stay here together instead. I can find something else."

James looked at the earnest young man desperately seeking an answer from him. Part of James wanted to give a positive answer, yet another voice inside him was holding him back. He didn't want to hurt Christian, but then again he didn't want to lead him on.

"Christian. I like you very much, you are my best friend and I couldn't have got through the last two years without you, but I am not ready for this type of commitment just yet."

"You don't love me, James."

"Christian, I like you very much, but no, I don't think I love you. Not yet, anyway."

"Is it still because of Tristan? Are you still in love with him? Is that the problem?"

"Yes, maybe it is. I shall always love Tristan, but I know he would want me to be happy as well. Christian, I am still mixed up and you deserve better than me. I knew and loved Tristan since we were children, but it was only in the last few months of his life that I ever showed him or told him just how much I loved him. I had wasted all that time. My career is everything to me right now. Maybe I am the sort of person that should not be in a long-term relationship. I just don't know."

Christian sat looking miserable and deflated. "I just don't know what to do. I thought you would want this and be really happy for us both."

"Christian, I am so sorry. I am being honest with you. I owe you that much at least. Go to Derby, it's a wonderful opportunity for you. Maybe Prince and I will come up to see you now and again, and you can come down here and stay with us as you always have."

"It won't be the same, James, will it?"

"Let's give it a try and see what happens. Some space between us may help us both to decide what we really want. We have a good friendship, don't we? Let's build on that and see what happens."

Prince put his large paw on Christian's lap and licked his hand lovingly.

"You see, Prince agrees with me, Christian."

"So, you're not saying no?"

"I'm not saying no, Christian. Just please give me more time."

Chapter 4

Halloween

The following week was a difficult one for James. He had had an awkward parting with Christian and he doubted that things would ever be the same again between them. He had left Christian hurt and unhappy after their Saturday lunch, and James had spent Sunday alone reflecting upon what he had done. Was it the right decision?

Yes, maybe a change right out of the area would have been the right thing for him, but how could he leave Prior's Hill at the time of its greatest need? He had made many friends in the village and would never forget how they had supported him during the worst period of his life.

He liked Christian very much, but James knew, in his heart of hearts, that this was not enough for him. He did not feel the same towards Christian as he had done towards Tristan and whom he would have followed to the end of the earth, if necessary.

James also knew that the possible school closure would test his management and public relations skills to the limit. Somehow he had to present a united front to fight the battle with County Hall, whilst maintaining sufficient enthusiasm and energy to ensure that the education of the children did not suffer during these uncertain times.

He also knew that parents could be very fickle and, despite their promises of endless support, James knew that it would not take long before they 'jumped ship' and moved their children to other schools. After all, who could blame them for putting their own children first?

James was also concerned about the staff. He was proud of the team that he had established and the personalities of the current staff complemented each other so well. It was not a good time, in Sue's case, as a probationer teacher, to be involved in protests against a Local Education Authority with whom she would like to have a future.

Memories were long in this rural county. Julia had a good reputation as an infant teacher in the area and would soon be snapped up by another school. Emily would no doubt retire, but what would happen to shy, retiring Anne?

There was also the question as to what would happen to James? He knew only too well that by standing up to County Hall, despite the promise that Paul Jones had made about being appointed as head teacher of Coombe School, that this would never happen and he would lose any reputation that he had achieved within the county.

No, he would have to move away, but James preferred to leave those thoughts for another day. Meanwhile he had a school to run and this he would continue to do, to the best of his ability.

It was the week of Halloween. This was always an event for which James had very mixed opinions. On the one hand, he knew how much the children enjoyed scary stories about witches, black cats, spells and hobgoblins.

On the other, he was well aware that, as a church school, some may frown upon the celebration of such satanic rituals. Indeed, recent guidelines from the diocese had made it clear that children should be made aware of All Saints' Day, which followed Halloween and for church schools to do their best to ignore, and certainly not encourage, the celebration of evil as part of their Halloween activities.

James had enjoyed all the usual traditional Halloween activities with his pupils in the past and Marion, the head teacher of his previous school, had tended to go overboard herself with Halloween displays and scary events.

James remembered that during his first year at Marion's school, she had dressed up as a very gruesome witch during one of her school assemblies. He smiled as he remembered that this particular dramatic exercise had not gone down at all well with the infant children and, indeed, amidst the screams from some of the younger infants, the overall result was that little Emily Jayne had wet herself and had to be led out of the school hall sobbing, followed by a number of infants who had led similarly sheltered lives in their short existence.

Questions had been asked at the following governors' meeting and future Halloween celebrations had been toned down somewhat since that memorable school assembly. Yes, Halloween had to be dealt with very carefully at Prior's Hill too.

James' main concern was the supply teacher in Class 2. Mrs Doreen Sparkle was anything but true to her name. A dour woman in her late fifties, Doreen Sparkle had decided long ago that teaching was not really her forte. As a spinster who had almost given up hope, Doreen had managed to 'catch' Mr Sparkle some five years earlier at a funeral wake for her aunt, and was now a woman of more than adequate means.

Mr Sparkle, an equally dour man, was much older than his wife, and was content for his new wife to stay at home and look after him in his twilight years. Doreen, on the other hand, had other ideas claiming that she liked to keep 'her hand in', whilst plotting that the supply teaching remuneration would help to pay for the Caribbean cruise that she was planning for the following year.

The Class 2 teacher, Sue Barry, had been complaining about severe pains for several days. James and Anne were concerned and insisted that Sue go to see the doctor that evening.

"Oh it's just stomach cramps, James. It's that time of the month again, I expect. She's complaining about nothing as usual," Emily had grumbled to James in the staff room, when he had asked Emily to cover her playground duty later that morning. "I'll do it, but these young teachers just aren't made as tough as we were."

James was not so sure. Despite Emily's harsh words of disapproval, Sue was not one to make an unnecessary fuss. He was concerned to hear about the pain that she was in and had driven her back to her flat in town and called the doctor. Despite Sue's protests he had also called her parents in Wales, and they had decided to travel from Swansea immediately to be with her. Meanwhile, Doris would stay with her until the doctor arrived.

Later that afternoon, Dr Gordon diagnosed appendicitis and recommended Sue's admittance to hospital for observation and possible appendectomy as soon as it could be arranged. When Sue's parents heard this they immediately insisted that she return home with them to Swansea where she would receive treatment from their local hospital. Sue reluctantly agreed and James was suddenly left without a teacher for Class 2 infants.

"This could go on for a few weeks, James," Emily had announced the following day over coffee. "I wondered myself if it was appendicitis, you know. It is not a good thing for a young woman. It could take her a few weeks to recuperate after the operation. This could really mess up her probationary year."

James caught Doris winking at him from the corner of the room and he just managed to suppress the laugh that was playing on his lips.

"Well, she is in good hands now. Her parents say that they will keep us in touch with what is happening. Doris has sent some flowers to Sue today with our love and best wishes for a speedy recovery. Poor lass, I feel so sorry for her. She has made such a good start and the children adore her. I have been really pleased with her."

"Hmm, well that doesn't get you a teacher now, does it? Who are you calling in to help out?" huffed Emily.

"Well, Doris has been trying all morning. All our regulars seem to be either taken or away. I guess it is the current bug that is going around. I will teach Class 2 myself today, but I am supposed to be at a meeting at County Hall tomorrow. I cannot really miss it as it is all about these new local finance arrangements. I am supposed to be going with Doris."

"Have you tried Doreen Sparkle?" asked Emily. "We went to college together. To be fair, she's seen better days, but her heart is in the right place."

James was not too sure of the enthusiasm or quality of this recommendation, but he felt sure that Emily would not knowingly saddle him with a problem that would have a negative effect upon the children. He liked to think that this was the case anyway.

"Thank you, Emily. If you could give Doris her number, if you have it with you, we will call her and see if she is free."

It was those fateful words that brought Doreen Sparkle to Prior's Hill School the following morning.

James had decided that he would have to be late for his course. Doris would be there and would give his apologies, but he had to meet Mrs Sparkle, show her around the school, explain procedures and class routines as well as introduce her to the children. He knew full well that his deputy, Anne Armstrong, could carry out these procedures perfectly well, but on this occasion, for some unexplained reason, he felt that he should carry out the 'meet and greet' duties himself.

"I don't do dinner duty. I cannot do country dancing because of my ulcerated leg, netball is difficult for me and I can only stay until four o'clock each day, Mr Young," announced Mrs Sparkle within minutes of her arrival.

"That's alright, Doreen," smiled James as he greeted the short, dour-looking woman standing in the front entrance. "I am grateful that you could come at short notice. Let me take you to the infant room. Just follow me."

"Infants is it? Mrs Cole said nothing about that. It's been a few years since I took infants. Emily will tell you that I prefer the juniors. You sure it's infants?"

James smiled. "Yes, I'm afraid it is. Their teacher has had to go to hospital and is likely to be off for a few weeks. There are some really good children in Class 2. They are very independent and their teacher, Sue, has taught them well. You will enjoy it. I am sure."

"I doubt it, but as I said I will do it, I will give it a try," declared Mrs Sparkle as she plopped her rotund form in the teacher's chair and surveyed the scene around her.

"Everything is so small in here. You sure this isn't the nursery?"

James smiled. "No, Mrs Sparkle, these are the six- and seven-year-olds. The furniture is small, because the children are still small."

It was at this point that the Class 2 children quietly filed into the room and sat on the carpet in the reading area. James knew that this was customary for the children to settle quietly on the carpet, where Sue would listen to their news and talk to them about their work for the day. It was a time for sharing news as well as dealing with the usual administration of completing registers and ordering dinners.

"Good morning, children. As you know, Mrs Barry is not well at the moment. She has had to go to hospital and so her Mummy and Daddy have taken her to a hospital near where they live. Scott, please don't pick your nose. It's not very nice."

After a short silence, Sarah Jayne put up her hand.

"Yes, Sarah Jayne?"

"Will she die? I like Miss Barry. I don't want her to die just yet."

James smiled and replied softly, "No, Sarah Jayne. Miss Barry won't die. She will just be a bit sore for a while though, and you must look after her when she returns to school."

"My granny died in hospital," persisted Sarah Jayne.

"So did mine," interrupted Susie.

"Children, Miss Barry will be fine, I promise you. Until she gets better, we have Mrs Sparkle to look after you. Say 'Good Morning' to Mrs Sparkle, children," said James, ignoring Sarah Jayne's waving hand. However, he knew from past experience that Sarah Jayne was highly unlikely to be sidetracked that easily.

"Scott, your nose is still troubling you, I see. Can you get a paper handkerchief from Miss Barry's desk and have a good blow."

"Good morning, children," boomed Mrs Sparkle briskly. "Yes, I will be with you until your teacher returns. I am sure we will have a lot of fun together."

"My granny had an operation. My mummy says that there was a lot of blood," continued Sarah Jayne, demonstrating with her hands the quantity of blood that had supposedly appeared from her granny.

"Right, well that's enough of grannies and hospitals. Let's get on with some work that I have for you," replied Mrs Sparkle, finally standing.

"Did your granny die in hospital?" persisted Sarah Jayne, determined that discussion about hospitals and grannies should continue for a while longer.

"No, dear, she was flattened by a lorry in the High Street. She didn't get to hospital," added Mrs Sparkle, a little unkindly.

A look of horror swept across Sarah Jayne's face and she said no more until break-time.

James left the room hearing the last of a verbal battle between Mrs Sparkle and Sarah Jayne. He was not happy with what he had seen or heard, but he had very little choice.

From what he had just seen from the dour Mrs Sparkle, he decided that he would ask Jenny, the classroom assistant who usually worked in Class 1 with the reception children, to work in Class 2 for the next few days, until Mrs Sparkle had settled and come to terms with her new class.

The subject of Halloween produced much excitement from the teaching and support staff at Prior's Hill. James had gathered that, in the past, everyone had done their 'own thing' and it was totally unrelated to anything that had been planned for in the school curriculum as a whole.

Although James didn't want to put a damper on creative and imaginative activities for the children, he wanted to ensure that it didn't overstep the diocesan and local authority guidelines, particularly as the second day of his course was on Friday – the day of Halloween.

"Well, I don't like Halloween," announced Emily. "Nasty American thing. My advice is to steer well clear of it. All this trick or treating nonsense is dangerous as well. Kiddies going out on their own playing pranks on people. What about the Stranger Danger campaign?"

"Oh, don't be such a spoil sport," countered Anne. "My children have had such fun planning it. We have written witches' spells and poems, made masks and the children have painted some wonderful pictures."

"Well, I'm not doing much with the infants," added Julia. "Mine are too young to understand what it is all about and it may frighten them. We are just going to hollow out some pumpkins and make scary face masks. I am going to let them choose. Also, we are having good witches as well as the bad ones."

"I don't see the point," argued Emily. "All we are doing is following America's excessive commercial lead. Do you know that young Stuart gave me a Happy Halloween card yesterday? I really think it is going too far."

"I tend to agree with Emily on this one," began James. "By all means, let's use it to develop creativity through poetry, writing, music and painting, but please don't let us celebrate evil as a good thing. Also, we must take account of the guidelines from the diocese. We must cover the meaning of All Saints' Day as well, as part of our religious education lessons."

"Oh no, James. Are you saying we cannot do the witches play we have rehearsed?" questioned Anne, looking downcast.

"No, Anne. I have seen your children rehearsing their play and it is very good. As I remember you have good overcoming evil and it doesn't go too far. All I'm saying is let us enjoy Halloween, but don't let us go too far and do keep it within the context of All Saints and All Souls."

James and Doris were initially alarmed by what they had heard at the first training day for head teachers and school administrative officers, as Doris was now called. Initially, Doris was reluctant to attend the meeting.

"What's the point, James? If Prior's Hill closes there will be no room for me anywhere else. I'm too old now and I cannot see the point of training for all these changes. Maybe I should just go now."

James had never heard Doris speak in such a negative light before and was saddened and surprised to hear what she was saying.

"Doris Cole, I have never heard you speak such nonsense before and I don't wish to hear such nonsense ever again. We will fight this closure business and we will win. Until then we carry on as normal. Is that understood?" James spoke sharply to Doris, but felt that, given the circumstances that they were now in, it was necessary.

Doris was very quiet for the next few days, but gradually seemed to return to her usual cheerful self as the day of the course approached. James was heartened to see Doris in a new frame of mind as she was opening the post one morning. There were similar letters addressed to both James and Doris. Each letter contained course details as well as a very expensive looking name badge.

"Now that I have a new title, does that mean I get a pay rise," laughed Doris, pointing out her new name badge to James. "See this, James. 'Mrs D Cole, School Administrative Officer'. Sounds good, doesn't it?"

"Yes, it does, Doris," laughed James. "Great title, but sorry no more cash available."

"Thought so," replied Doris, pretending to look hard done by.

"Well I have a new title as well," added James, trying to look serious.

"Really, what is it?" asked Doris, anxious to know the latest news.

"Senior Ward Orderly."

The new Local Management of Schools initiative did sound exciting. From what James and Doris could work out, each school, regardless of size, would soon get control of part of their school's budget. The funding given to each school would be based upon the school's individual pupil numbers.

The new arrangement would allow for greater flexibility in ordering items for the school and would mean that funding could be diverted from one budget heading to another.

A computer, solely for administration, would be provided to allow these transactions, such as payments to suppliers to take place electronically. In addition, school governors, alongside their head teacher, would be responsible for making and administering budget decisions.

Although James and Doris had travelled together in James' sports car, they had to attend a number of separate meetings specific to their roles. James and Doris met up again during the lunchtime break.

"Looks exciting, Doris, doesn't it," began James enthusiastically. "At last small schools will have some control of how the money is spent. If we decide that staffing is a priority we can maybe increase expenditure in one area and save in another. The secondary schools have had this for ages and now it is our turn."

Doris looked glum. "That's as may be, James. It's this computer thing that worries me. I know nothing about computers. How am I expected to operate finances, pay bills and keep records when I don't know the first thing about them? My nephew has one and it looks very complicated to me."

"Don't worry, Doris. I'm in the same boat as you. We all are. There will be training and people to help us. Dr Skinner mentioned something about Area Finance Officers being appointed. They will help, particularly to begin with."

"Well, they won't be giving us extra hours, that's for sure, James. Oh dear, things are moving too fast. Maybe it really is time that I gave up. George and I have been talking about it for a while. He says that I spend too much time at school as it is, but I do enjoy it. Well, I have until now, that is."

"Don't you dare retire, Doris," exclaimed James, alarmed at Doris' comment.

Doris was not given to making idle threats and he could see that she was very worried about what she had heard. In view of all the closure threats, James needed Doris now more than ever.

"Look, I promise I will help you all I can, but please don't leave me to deal with this on my own."

"I know you will, James, but it is not easy for us older ones, you know. All I needed when I started this job was a typewriter and a spirit duplicator. Now look what's happening. That new photocopier you leased confuses me, the electric duplicator tries to cut off my fingers, and now we are talking about computers. It really is too much..."

"James, good to see you again, and you Doris too," interrupted Mike Collins, head teacher of Burbeck Primary. "Looks great doesn't it. Just what we need to get a bit of freedom with our spending?"

"Hello, Mike. Good to see you again too," beamed James, shaking hands with his colleague. "Yes, Doris and I were just going over some of the implications of what we have just heard."

Mike smiled wickedly. "Well, there are other advantages as well. My Gloria says she cannot cope with all this modern nonsense, as she puts it, and has resigned on the spot today. She's just walked out now. I've been trying to get rid of her for years and so I accepted her resignation willingly. You packing the job up as well, Doris?"

Doris glared, "I am most certainly not leaving Prior's Hill, Mr Collins," she replied frostily. "My brain is as active as the day when I started the job. I welcome anything new that will help our school to be even better. Good day to you."

Doris glared at Mike Collins, picked up her new pink manila folder and stormed out of the room.

"Sorry, I seem to have put my foot in it," began Mike. "I didn't mean to upset old Doris, but she is the same generation as my Gloria, so I thought it might be all too much for her as well. I hadn't realised that she was that sensitive."

"Don't worry, Mike, I know you didn't mean to upset her, but you may well have done me a favour. You see, the one thing that Doris hates being told is that she cannot do something because of her age. It brings out the worst in her. Yes, thank you, Mike. I don't know what I would do without Doris. She is truly wonderful."

"I just don't like that man," snapped Doris when she met up with James for the car journey home. "He is creepy. I like Gloria and she has been at the school for years. That Mike Collins gives her a right run around. She does her best, but it is never enough. You always help me out, James, but he just leaves her to it. I told her years ago to complain about him, but she never did and so now she is just walking away. I think it is disgraceful."

"Well, I don't know Gloria very well, but she is always helpful to me when I call the school. I think she may have just needed a bit of help," replied James. "Things are changing for all of us in education, Doris, and I suspect we have only just seen the beginning. We will do what we always do at Prior's Hill, we help each other and you make sure you tell me if it gets too hard for you. I will help you all I can, Doris."

"It won't beat me, James," replied Doris haughtily.

James was ready for the weekend. Two days away from school in one week on meetings and training sessions were always a heavy burden for a teaching head teacher such as James, and it seemed to him that he had tried to squeeze five days' normal school work into three. As well as his personal worries concerning Christian, and the possible school closure, James now had additional worries about Sue, as well as misgivings about Doreen Sparkle.

How he had wished that he could have been around to see what was happening in Class 2. He knew that Anne would give him a full appraisal, but he would have to wait until Monday for that. Meanwhile, he had the luxury of the whole weekend to himself and Prince. Maybe he would give Christian a call and talk a few things through with him? Sadly, it was not to be quite the relaxing weekend that James had planned.

Late on Friday evening, the telephone rang. James had just completed his marking for the week and Prince was snoring loudly after a long walk and a large dinner. James looked at Prince with some concern as he gazed at the young dog's rather large stomach. He really must start reducing the quantity of food that Prince had for his evening meal, but Prince did so enjoy his food. He is a big and growing dog, thought James, trying to justify himself.

"Hello?"

"Good evening, James. Rector here. Sorry to disturb you, but I really do need to discuss something rather serious with you."

"No problem, Rector, fire away," replied James, kicking himself for speaking to the pompous, yet well meaning, Rector quite so informally.

"Quite so. Well, I'll come straight to the point, James. Several governors and myself have received complaints this evening from some of the parents of pupils in Miss Barry's class."

James' heart sank. He felt he knew what was coming next.

"From the complaints that we have received it appears that the children have been engaged in some kind of devil worship today."

"Devil worship?" repeated James, not believing what he had just heard.

"Quite so. It appears that the children were engaged in some form of devil worship throughout the afternoon. I believe you have engaged a new supply teacher for Class 2 in Miss Barry's absence, a Mrs Doreen Sparkle?"

"Yes, that is correct. All of our regulars were taken and I had to find someone urgently."

"Well, according to the parents concerned, the teacher was anything but sparkling. She frightened the children and many left the school this afternoon in tears. James, we are a Church school and we really do need to be more careful as to whom we appoint to take charge of our children, even in emergencies."

"Well, this news shocks me, Rector. I really cannot comment until I have found out more. Leave it with me and I will call you back as soon as I have found out exactly what has been going on."

"Thank you, James. However, I should warn you that some of the governors are calling for an emergency meeting, and Sir Toby is arranging this for Monday evening. I should also warn you that the diocese has also been contacted. I have also received a call from the local newspaper this evening, and so I guess it will be covered in the newspaper by Tuesday evening's edition. This is serious, James."

When the Rector had finished his call, James decided to call Anne, his deputy.

"Hello, Anne. James here. I am so sorry to bother you so late this evening," he began.

"Hello, James. Did you have a good day at County Hall?" replied a weary voice. It was as James had feared. Anne was already asleep when he called and he had wakened her. He knew that she often went to bed early.

"It was very good, Anne. I will tell you all about it on Monday. Look, Anne, what has been going on in Class 2 this afternoon? Hubert has just called me and tells me that some parents are complaining about some kind of devil worship going on in Class 2."

"James, you are teasing me, I hope?"

"No, Anne, seriously. Apparently several governors have received complaints as well as the diocese, and even the local 'rag' is on the case."

There was silence at the end of the phone.

"Anne, are you still there?"

"Yes, James, but I'm shocked. It was quite a good day actually. Mrs Sparkle is a bit strange, but the children seemed to be quiet and working. I went in a couple of times to see what was going on and Jenny seemed happy enough as well. When I last saw them they were making witches' masks and they were…"

"Yes, Anne?"

"Apple bobbing."

Chapter 5

Laughter is the best medicine

"Apple bobbing?" repeated James, doing his best to stifle a giggle.

"Yes, Mr Young, apple bobbing."

"Let me get this quite clear, Mr Saunders. You wish to remove your children from Prior's Hill School, because Joshua was involved in apple bobbing?"

"Yes, that's right," replied the scruffy young man sitting opposite James.

James nodded and he, the scruffy young man and an equally scruffy, but attractive older woman, sat in silence in James' office. In his short time as head teacher, James had learned that the best way to deal with a potential conflict with parents was to listen carefully to all the facts, consider carefully and then count to at least ten before responding.

"Do you not think that you may be over-reacting a little?" suggested James calmly.

"Certainly not. Not when our children's spiritual and moral values are at stake," snapped the scruffy woman. "Mr Saunders agrees with me. Why are you teaching satanic rituals at this school? Surely there are many other things that you can teach the children? Presumably your curriculum does not include the celebration of evil forces?"

"Mrs Saunders…" began James.

"Miss Purdy," snapped the scruffy young woman. "Mr Saunders and I are not married."

"Well, I can assure you that we certainly do not celebrate evil," began James. "As a Church school, our curriculum is based upon Christian teaching and we always try to emphasise to the children how goodness overcomes evil."

"Then why did you allow Friday's orgy of evil?" snapped Miss Purdy.

"Come off it," replied James, feeling deep anger welling inside him.

"Yes, the supply teacher did let the children experience 'apple bobbing'. This is something that we don't usually do and I can assure you we will not be doing again, because of health and hygiene reasons, if nothing else. However, as for an 'orgy of evil' as you put it, you are exaggerating a minor issue, which I agree should not have happened, but it did and now I suggest that we move on to discussing rather more important issues."

"How dare you speak to my partner in this way," shouted Mr Saunders.

"Joshua and Samuel will be leaving this school immediately. We only came here because it was a Church school, and we thought they would get a more bible-based education than Abbotsford Primary."

"And another thing," began Miss Purdy. "My youngest was making evil looking masks and came home with a hollowed-out pumpkin with the most evil looking face carved on it."

James nodded. He now realised that there was no point in further discussion. He would just sit and listen to their continuing outburst.

"And do you know," continued Mr Saunders, "The children in Joshua's class were taking home the most horrendous pictures of old ladies being run over by heavy goods vehicles. Joshua even told me that the new teacher said that's what happens to grannies when they get old and are of no more use. His friend, George, said the same thing. We really are quite appalled, Mr Young."

"Oh dear," replied James, suddenly laughing heartily. When considering his responses during the early hours of the following morning, James still didn't know whether his outburst of laughter was as a result of nervous tension or because it really was so funny. He suddenly remembered the conversation that he had heard between Mrs Sparkle and Sarah Jayne as he had been leaving the classroom the previous day.

"Oh, I can explain that," began James, whose laughter ceased immediately when he saw the expression on Mr Saunders' face. For a second he thought that the scruffy young man in the blue anorak was going to hit him.

"That's it, come on, we're leaving," exploded Mr Saunders, grabbing his partner's hand and propelling the startled Miss Purdy through the office door.

Doris, who had been trying very hard to listen to the conversation outside the office door, looked startled as the couple swept past her. She had been confused by the sound of angry raised voices, as well as by James' laughter, and had wondered if she should intervene or get help.

"James, whatever did you say to them?"

At the end of the school day James called an emergency staff meeting.

"But I can only stay until four o'clock," protested Mrs Sparkle.

"If you wish to return to this school tomorrow, you will stay on a little longer this afternoon," snapped James. "I have a serious matter to discuss, and it involves you, Mrs Sparkle."

As soon as the children had left the school, all the staff including Jenny and Doris, gathered in the mobile classroom that had served as a makeshift staff room since the fire. From the look on their faces, James could see that they were well aware that something serious had happened.

They took the mugs of tea from the tray that Doris offered them in silence. There was a knock at the door and the Rector and Sir Toby Peatwhistle entered the room. They shook hands with James, and nodded to the assembled staff before sitting down.

"Sorry, I didn't make a cake. If I had known we were having a meeting, I would have made one," apologised Doris, as she offered mugs of tea to the two governors.

"Don't worry, Doris," began James. "Look everyone, I am so sorry to call an emergency meeting, but something rather serious has blown up, and I'm afraid I have just made it worse. I have asked the Rector, as well as Sir Toby, to be with us, as I feel that I should give a full explanation to you all."

"How do you mean, James?" said Emily, surprisingly kindly. "We knew that something had offended Mr Saunders and Miss Purdy about Friday's Halloween activities. It wasn't your fault. You were not even in school."

James retold Friday's telephone conversation with the Rector, his discussion with Sir Toby and the diocesan advisor, as well as his recent less than successful interview with Mr Saunders and Miss Purdy.

"The result of all this," finished James, "is that we shall be losing Joshua and Samuel, as well as gaining a reputation for organising an 'orgy of evil'."

When James had finished speaking, there were a few moments of thoughtful silence, which was only interrupted when the Rector began to chuckle.

"James, I really am so sorry, but I can rather see the amusing side of this. You all try so hard to do the right thing at Prior's Hill, and here you are accused of promoting evil. Does it not occur to you that you may well be dealing with people who are not, shall we say, well balanced?"

"Quite so, Hubert," added Sir Toby, laughing heartily. "Look, between these four walls, I am fully aware of young Dick Saunders. He worked for me a few years ago, but I had to let him go when he was caught stealing from my storeroom. I didn't pursue it with the police. He is not too bright and is easily led by others. I let him go and then I heard that he got linked up with an older woman from Sidmouth."

"Ah yes, she moved here with the two children a couple of years ago, didn't she? She met up with Dick Saunders and they have been together ever since," concluded the Rector.

"Her father was a Baptist minister, I believe," continued Sir Toby. "It seems that once she met Dick, they became fundamentalist in their beliefs. I believe Dick and the woman are rather heavily involved with a hard line Christian sect in the area."

"I had heard that as well," nodded the Rector. "Basically, James, you have nothing to worry about with this one. It just goes to prove that you cannot please everyone, all of the time. Yes, you must be well aware that you can easily offend parents, but as professionals it is your job to decide what should be taught and how, within the confines of diocesan and county guidelines, of course."

"Look, I am so sorry," began Mrs Sparkle, who had been sitting in subdued silence since the meeting began, and was now looking more and more uncomfortable. "All this is my fault. I shouldn't have done 'apple bobbing'. It's just that I have done it before and the children loved it. They got a bit wet of course, but I have never had this problem before."

"So what about grannies being ploughed down by articulated lorries?" began Sir Toby, his bright eyes twinkling wickedly.

By now the staff had descended into shrieks, giggles and guffaws of laughter. Even the Rector, who was not known for his humour, was wiping the tears from his eyes with a large bright red handkerchief.

Mrs Sparkle sat, red faced and in embarrassed silence. When the laughter had died down, she added, "But it is true, my grandmother was knocked down and killed by an articulated lorry. I told Sarah Jayne that yesterday and this comment seems to have started all this trouble. I am sorry." She began to cry. "I won't come back again after today. I am just so sorry for what I have done. I didn't mean to upset anyone."

Emily offered Doreen a paper tissue, and Doris went to make her another cup of coffee. The rest of the staff sat in embarrassed silence.

James broke the silence. "Doreen," he began gently. "I would welcome your return to this school tomorrow. The children like you, and from what I have heard they had a good time with you yesterday. Maybe we just need to talk in a little more detail about what you will be teaching the children each day?"

"My feelings exactly, James," said Sir Toby. He smiled. "This is not an issue to 'fall on one's sword', Mrs Sparkle. Thanks to you, I have had the best laugh that I have had in weeks! I just wish that Lotitia could have been here as well!"

As the staff left the room, laughing and chattering noisily as ever, James remained seated between Sir Toby and the Rector, who obviously had planned to speak with him alone.

"I handled the interview with the parents so badly. I shall never forgive myself for laughing at those parents. It was wrong of me to laugh at their concerns, which were obviously important to them. All this at a time when the school is likely to close, and we can ill afford to lose pupils now. It is unforgivable of me."

"Well, maybe you should have exerted a little more self control, James, but you know laughter is not a crime, and I am relieved to discover that you have finally discovered a sense of humour. May we be honest with you, James? Please treat this as a comment from friends who care about you, and not an instruction from your Chair of Governors and a crusty old parish priest. You really do need to 'lighten up', as they say, James. We all have huge respect for you and you have done so much good for our little school, but sometimes, you are a little too serious about the unimportant things in life. Laugh more, James, and don't feel guilty about it. It is a gift from God and you should never refuse a gift, you know."

The Rector smiled and patted James kindly on the shoulder.

"Hubert's right, of course," added Sir Toby. "You know, Lotitia and I were talking about you only the other day. We see you arrive at school early each morning and go home late in the evening. We see you here at weekends and most of the holidays. We never see you do anything socially nowadays and, I have to say, I haven't seen you laugh heartily since…"

James nodded, "Yes, you mean since Tristan died, don't you?"

Sir Toby nodded, "Yes, James. We know he was your soul mate and in the short time he was here, the villagers admired and, dare I say, loved that young man. Do you know why, James?"

James thought for a moment. "Well I guess it was because he did a lot for the school. He liked the children and they liked him."

"It was more than that, James," replied Sir Toby. "It was because he loved life. He laughed and saw the funny side of everything. The times when I saw Tristan, he was always laughing or making a joke. He spoke to everyone and made everyone feel good. That's why he was loved so much."

"You mean I should laugh more, and be more like Tristan?"

"James, you are missing the point, somewhat," interrupted the Rector. "You are a very different person from Tristan. You cannot be like him, because it is not within your nature. You have many other fine qualities. Yes, you do need to lighten up and laugh at yourself more, but more importantly you need to start to enjoy living life again. Now that would make our young Tristan smile with happiness, wouldn't it? There really is so much more to life than only this school, James."

By the time that he arrived home later that evening, Prince was waiting for him with his Christmas present – a blue rubber ball that Christian had given to him. James and Prince walked over to the woods that were close to James' home. He would have liked to take the young dog for a longer walk, but James was tired and reasoned that if the dog had a good run with his ball, he would not notice. James threw the ball for Prince, and waited while the young dog leapt off to retrieve it from the undergrowth.

James thought a great deal about what the Rector had said during his walk with Prince. He had still not spoken to Christian since their weekend crisis, he had heard nothing more about the possible closure of the school and James was feeling anything but cheerful. Yes, the Rector was right, he didn't have much fun nowadays, after all there was precious little to laugh about.

Maybe he needed a break away, but where would he go and with whom? He could no longer ask Christian after the way that he had treated him and there were few real friends with whom he was still in contact.

How James missed those evenings and weekends with Tristan. He smiled as he recalled the way that they had shared the highlights and sorrows of their day over the dinner that Tristan had cooked for him. The way they would laugh together – often ending in a cushion or pillow fight – whichever was closest to hand. How he missed being close to someone else and, above all, going to sleep in Tristan's strong and comforting arms and waking up beside him.

It was then that James felt that someone was watching him. It was a strange feeling, and for the briefest of moments James thought that he had caught a glimpse of Tristan, standing by one of the trees looking at him. James shivered as a strange sensation ran down his spine.

"Come on, Prince, fetch!" yelled James. "It's over there, don't tell me you need glasses." The young dog pounced on the blue rubber ball and brought it to James' side. The obedient dog dropped it at James' feet, and looked admiringly at James for the next part of the game. James knelt down and hugged the handsome dog.

"I'm not sure if you understand all that I'm saying, but you are the only one keeping me sane, Prince. When I am with you, I just feel that Tristan is close by." Prince looked at James with his big brown eyes as if he were listening to every word, and licked James enthusiastically on the cheek.

"My goodness, whatever are you doing here, James?" came a piercing voice that James recognised, but had tried hard for nearly two years to forget. It was Jasmine De Valle.

"Hello, Jasmine," replied a shocked James, who stood up and shook Jasmine's hand, but at a distance. "I might say the same to you. I live just over there and this is my dog's favourite walk."

James was careful not to get too close to the enthusiastic librarian, as he remembered the last time that they had met in her flat in town. How could he ever forget that night? He was right to keep Jasmine De Valle at a safe distance.

"Good to see you again, James," beamed Jasmine. "What a handsome dog you have here! Almost as handsome as his owner! I don't think we have met since my birthday party, have we?" Jasmine winked and laughed heartily in her loud voice. How James hated that laugh.

"Er, no, I don't believe that we have," replied James quietly, trying to think of an excuse to leave. Prince, always one to meet and greet new friends, was now busily having his tummy tickled by the enthusiastic Jasmine.

"Who's a beauty? You beautiful dog," purred Jasmine. "Who likes his tummy rubbed and who is a clever boy? I saw you catching all those balls that your master threw for you."

James watched, partly wishing that the ground would open up and make him disappear.

"We haven't seen you in the library for ages, James," continued Jasmine, looking sternly at James with her round, large cow-like eyes. "Did I really frighten you that evening? I am so sorry James, I felt awful about it and I didn't mean any harm. Did you think I was trying to seduce you?" Jasmine screeched with laughter and James cringed.

"Er, well it did feel a bit like that at the time," began James. "It's not just that Jasmine, I've had a few problems and it has taken me some time to come to terms with things, that's all."

"I heard about your boyfriend and I was so sorry," interrupted Jasmine, sounding sympathetic, her attention at last being drawn away from Prince. "It was dreadful for you and must have been a terrible shock. I wanted to come to the funeral to support you, but Doris said it wasn't a good idea – given the circumstances. I thought about you though and lit a candle for Tristan in my Church the following Sunday."

James nodded. He wasn't too sure what 'given the circumstances' actually meant, but nevertheless he felt exceedingly grateful to Doris for her timely intervention.

She had never told him about this conversation with Jasmine but made him realise, yet again, what wonderful friends Doris and George were.

"Look, James. I have an idea. Why don't you come over for a meal next weekend? It would be wonderful to catch up with the news after all this time. How is your dear little school? I do hope you are looking after my library?"

Jasmine paused as she saw the expression of horror on James' face, her cow-like eyes became even rounder and larger as she spoke.

"Don't worry," screeched Jasmine, "I'm a reformed character now. I don't drink and I don't make passes at all the handsome young men in town. I am a reformed woman," she added proudly.

"Reformed?" queried James, failing to notice any discernible difference in Jasmine's overall behaviour.

"Yes, I have seen the light," added Jasmine, proudly, still stroking Prince's head. "I am in a relationship. Indeed, I am in love, James. I am so happy, I could just burst! Do come to dinner, because I want you to meet Paul!"

James desperately hoped that she would not 'burst' any further in public. He well remembered the time when she had all but 'burst' out of her blouse, and the horror of that evening was still etched upon his being. He remembered Tristan's wicked comments after he had returned home and the hearty pillow fight that had followed.

James smiled. He was ashamed of his feelings and initial aggression towards this loud, outspoken woman. He knew that she meant well and also remembered how helpful she had been in setting up the new school library.

It was mainly thanks to her involvement that the school now had one of the best school libraries in the area. However, he was relieved to hear that she now had a partner. Jasmine was spoken for. Surely he was now safe?

"Of course I will come, Jasmine. That's very kind of you. I am so pleased to hear that you are in a relationship and I would love to meet Paul as well."

"Well, next Saturday at half past seven, it is then. I am still at the same place. Paul lives with me now and it is a quite a little love nest," Jasmine screeched with laughter. "Bring anyone you want with you – male or female, whatever you are into these days, James. I promise I won't seduce you this time!"

Once again Jasmine screeched with laugher, and pushed him heartily in the shoulder.

Before James could shake Jasmine's hand to say "good bye", a large pair of heavily made-up and very wet lips planted a lingering kiss on James' lips. Jasmine screeched with laughter and gave Prince a farewell hug and a hearty slap on his back.

"See you on Saturday, James. Remember, bring a friend and maybe a bottle – and not necessarily in that order!"

James watched as the librarian made her way down the path back to the road. As she had no dog with her, James did just wonder, if only for a fleeting moment, why she was walking alone in this part of the woods, and at this time of day?

Maybe, just maybe, she had been trying to find him? James dismissed the whole idea as unlikely nonsense, put Prince back on his lead and headed for the road, but in a different direction to Jasmine De Valle.

Since the death of Tristan, James had become a believer in fate and had tried to adopt a more flexible attitude to whatever life had in store for him. It seemed to him very strange that after the Rector and Sir Toby's words about laughter and 'lightening up' that Jasmine De Valle had appeared on the scene. He thought it very strange because although, to James, Jasmine could be a terrifying woman, there was never a dull moment when she was around.

After all, they shared similar interests in literature, music and education and now she had a partner, she was surely no longer a threat? No, he would no longer worry about an evening with Jasmine, but focus on the real problem. Who could he take with him to dinner at Jasmine's?

It was this dilemma that James was toying over when enjoying a few minutes on his own at the end of the lunchtime break. It was a precious few minutes when he could read his post, sign a few letters and reflect on the morning's activities. He had already eaten, and enjoyed, one of Mrs Hilary's special vegetarian lunches.

He had, as usual, called over to the kitchen to thank her, and she had replied in her usual blunt manner, "That's alright, Mr James," and shrugged. James knew that she was pleased with the praise that she received, but Mrs Hilary was one of those people who had difficulty in accepting and dealing with it.

Doris had told him a little about Mrs Hilary's life and it seemed that the poor woman had received very little praise and affection in her life.

"She's a good woman, James. I hope you know how highly she thinks of you," Doris had said a few days earlier.

James had given up telling her that his name was James Young and not Mr James, yet she would hear none of it. As far as Mrs Hillary was concerned he was, and always would be, Mr James.

James didn't mind – he was just grateful for the excellent meals that she cooked for the children and for him, and she even often prepared a 'little extra' for Prince. James was becoming seriously concerned about both his own, and Prince's, waistlines.

The door opened and Doris, accompanied by a panting Prince, burst into the office. James smiled as he saw the tiny woman fight with the strong automatic door closure on the office fire door.

It always gave her a great deal of trouble in opening it, and then keeping it open for both herself and Prince to enter the room. James always smiled when he saw the little woman push it open with her bottom and then twirl around before the heavy door snapped tightly shut.

"Good walk, Doris? Thanks for taking Prince as well. I really do appreciate it and I know he looks forward to it, don't you, boy?"

Doris sat on her chair, looking very pale and not saying a word.

"You OK, Doris? Look, I promise I'll get that door looked at. I know I've been promising you for ages and I hate to see you struggling with it…"

"That's all right, James, it's not that," Doris replied. James could see that she had been crying.

"What's the matter? Who has upset you?" James put his hand on Doris' shoulder and squeezed.

"It's nothing, James. No one. Just me being a silly old woman again." Doris sniffed and gave James a half-hearted smile. "This dog of yours gives me so much pleasure, James. I like taking him out at lunchtimes and George says it is helping me to lose weight. Prince is only a young dog, but seems to know so much already. The children love him as well. Did you have a good lunch, James? Mrs Hilary told me she cooked one of your favourites."

"She did indeed, but don't change the subject, Doris. Let me get you a cup of coffee and you can tell me all about it. No one upsets my Doris and gets away with it. Just tell me, what's been going on?"

Chapter 6

Christian's Story

To many observers, Christian Trill would seem to be a very fortunate young man. He came from a good home in a pleasant rural village near Derby. He lived in a modern detached bungalow with his parents, Alistair and Brenda and his younger sister, Patricia.

Christian attended a good school near to his home village and he had plenty of friends for company. Christian's father, Alistair, worked hard in Derby as a Post Office clerk and his mother, Brenda, topped up the family income as a part-time shop assistant in the village stores, as well as offering voluntary work to the local Catholic Church.

Alistair and Brenda Trill were pillars of the local community and particularly within Catholic Church circles. They attended and supported all the local charity and church functions, they would make generous financial donations to worthy causes; and Brenda was always ready to give a helping hand to those less fortunate than herself.

Christian achieved good results at his local grammar school, making his parents very proud of his achievement of ten GCE 'O' levels, all with good grades, with the exception of Latin, a subject that Christian hated, and only scraped a pass mark.

It was revealing and symptomatic of the relationship between father and son when Alistair, seeing these impressive results, commented only upon this less than fortunate result in Latin, and ignored the remaining considerably higher nine grades.

"You should have done better than this, son. Latin is a fine subject and will be essential if you wish to be a doctor or a vet," he frowned.

"I don't want to be a doctor or a vet, Dad, so what does it matter?" retorted Christian unwisely, before his mother gave him a hearty slap around the ear.

"Your father's right," grumbled Brenda. "You have been spending far too much time with young Peter and Shaun recently. Those two lads don't work hard. All they ever do is play football on the field and I don't want you to be like them." Brenda continued, "You need to be more like your sister, Christian. She works hard and you never see her playing around and neglecting her studies."

"Ma, she's only ten; she isn't doing much in the way of studying yet anyway."

"Well, she works hard with her piano practice. I never have to chase her to do it," retorted his mother, always one to have the last word.

In the weeks ahead it was mother and father, with little consideration of Christian's feelings, who decided that he should stay on for his 'A' levels in English Literature, History and maybe Economics.

"Such a useful subject, nowadays," stated Alistair emphatically, when Christian had declared his wish to study French to 'A' level. "Why on earth should you want to study and speak French? Very few people speak it nowadays as that country is going nowhere. It's alright for a holiday, I suppose, but German is the language of the future. Now, if you had said you wanted to study German, I could see the point. No, young man, you stick to Economics, that's the subject for modern times."

Apart from the occasional family disagreements such as this, Christian had a pleasant, if demanding, childhood. Alistair was firm, yet fair, with his pocket money. Christian had to earn it and, should he displease his father, it would be withheld for a week and "Given to the Church as your penance to the Good Lord," his mother would add in reverential tones, as she slipped his entire pocket money into the collection plate on Sunday morning.

Christian was expected to attend Mass each Sunday, to attend Sunday School as well as officiating as an altar boy as and when his turn came up on the 'roster'. How he hated that particular job, particularly as he became older.

He was now at an age when the other boys at school, particularly Peter and Shaun, would tease him relentlessly about his 'cissy outfit' and Christian was not too keen on the smell of Father Griffiths either: an elderly man who always smelled strongly of peppermint. It was a rich, sickly smell and made Christian feel ill during those interminable Church Masses and other services.

As Christian became older he would find excuses not to attend Mass on a Sunday morning, much to the annoyance of his devout mother and anger of his controlling father. Christian, an intelligent boy, quickly realised the benefits of saying that he had homework or a project to finish. His parents would look at each other and nod approvingly.

It was after one Sunday morning when Christian had been allowed to stay at home to finish his studies that his mother had suddenly burst into his bedroom. Christian quickly hid the magazine that he had been looking at and got up off the bed.

"What are you doing on your bed, reading magazines when you should be in Church?" said his mother, accusingly. "I came back early because Father Griffiths wants you to help him translate a letter urgently. It came from one of the Sisters in that French Convent we support."

"You see, I knew my French would come in useful one day," exclaimed Christian, getting up off the bed. "I'll go over to the Church now."

"Yes, my lad, and you make sure you tell Father that you have been working hard on your school work. Have you been to confession recently?"

Before Christian could reply he was out of the door and on his way to the Church. Whatever did the old man want with him? Surely there were other people in the congregation who could help with a bit of translation?

Reluctantly, Christian knocked on the door of the adjoining Presbytery and tried to block his nostrils as a strong smell of peppermint wafted out of the old building.

When Christian returned home, expecting the usual delicious smells of the Sunday roast to clear his peppermint filled lungs, he was instead greeted not by the smell of Sunday lunch, but by his angry parents sitting at the dining table waiting for him.

"Sit down," commanded his father.

"What's wrong?" asked Christian, sitting down between his parents.

"You sit there and ask what's wrong when you know full well that you have broken the Lord's rules in the most disgusting way imaginable!" shouted his father.

"And on the Lord's Day too," added his mother, boxing him on the ears.

"I don't understand…" began Christian.

"You lied to us Christian. You told us that you had homework to do and asked if you could be excused Mass. It was a lie."

"No, it wasn't. I finished it just as mother came in the room."

His father stood up. Alistair was a big, strong man and he grabbed Christian by the arm and flung him across the room with all his might.

"Ouch, that hurt, that bloody hurt!" cried Christian, shocked at what his father had done.

"Yes, and I'll do it again if you continue to lie to me," growled his father, who was by now bright red in colour and shaking uncontrollably. "How dare a son of mine come home with all this filth!"

Brenda, who was now visibly shaken by the violence that she had just witnessed, opened a plastic carrier bag that was on the table and flung a handful of glossy magazines at Christian.

"Call this decent reading, do you? It's filth, filth, filth!" she cried.

It was at that moment that Christian realised what the row was all about.

"You've been going through my things!" he shouted, gathering the adult magazines from the floor.

"Yes, we have and a good thing too. The filth that we found in your room! It's evil, Christian, don't you know that?"

Christian, who was now standing by the door in tears, shaking, found himself screaming, "Yes, I am gay. I am a queer, I am a homosexual. It's my life and what are you going to do about it? I'm pleased you found out and I don't care!"

With this devastating announcement, Christian fled through the front door, slammed it behind him and left Alistair with his mouth open and Brenda collapsed on the floor in tears.

You all right, Christian?" enquired Peter Flanagan as he opened the front door to greet his friend. He was surprised to see him on a Sunday, because Christian usually had 'Church things to do'.

Peter Flanagan was a tall, slim and handsome boy, nearly a year older than Christian. He and Christian had always got on well together, and particularly since Peter had intervened to stop a fight between Christian and some older boys who were bullying him.

He and his friend Shaun often met up with Christian for a kick around the park with a football, although, if the truth be told, neither Christian nor Peter were that keen on football. They just enjoyed each other's company.

"Not really, Pete," replied Christian. "Just had a bust up with my parents. I've left home."

"Oh shit!" exclaimed Peter, looking concerned, "You've been crying as well. What's that on your arm," he asked spotting the red bruise that was appearing on Christian's arm. "Your dad been throwing his weight around again?"

Peter knew that this was not the first time that Alistair Trill's temper had got the better of him. He had hurt Christian several times before as well as Brenda, his wife.

Christian's sister, Patricia, so far, appeared to be the only one in the family who had escaped her father's wrath.

"Look, come in and stay here. Ma won't mind. She likes you anyway. You stay here until things calm down a bit."

Peter led Christian into the untidy home. Kath Flanagan, a well meaning yet disorganised woman, greeted Christian with a kiss. She was a heavy smoker and Christian, who had an aversion to cigarette smoke as well as peppermint, shuddered.

"You want a Coke?" she asked, wandering to and opening the fridge door before Christian could answer. She still had the cigarette in her mouth and gave the ash a casual flick on the linoleum floor before she poured out a glass for Christian.

"Christian's dad hit him again. Can he stay here until things calm down?"

"Of course he can, my love," Kath Flanagan answered without hesitation. "That man's a bully. I feel sorry for your mum, Christian. I'd have got rid of him years ago, if it had been me. Yes, of course you can stay, but make sure your mum knows you are here, OK?"

Kath lit another cigarette and shuffled off. "Programme's starting. Make yourself at home, Christian. Pete, bring out that camp bed and sleeping bag that we used for Graham at Christmas. Christian can sleep on that. It's quite comfortable," she added.

"Well Graham didn't complain," grinned Peter, quietly to Christian. "He spent the night in my bed."

Graham was Peter's older cousin, and he and Peter were the best of friends. It was only the previous Christmas that Peter had discovered that Graham had a secret of his own.

"They know, Pete. What am I going to do?"

"They know what?"

"They found those magazines you let me borrow. They went through my things. They know I'm gay. I've left home. I'm never going back."

"Oh shit!" replied Peter.

A small part of Christian's first night away from home was spent on the floor on a small and uncomfortable camp bed, inside a well-worn and rather smelly sleeping bag.

However, a much larger part of the night was to be spent in the arms of someone he knew well and trusted. This was not to be the first time that Christian found himself in the arms of someone of the same sex.

"Christian Trill, you are needed in the headmaster's office. Right away, please!" came the stern voice of Maggie, the school secretary, as she poked her head around the door during double maths. "Come with me now, please," she ordered.

Christian's mathematics teacher, Mr Roberts, gave the determined school secretary a withering look and wandered over to Christian. The grey hairs that sprouted from the old schoolmaster's nose seemed to take on a life of their own. Over the years many pupils had watched the determined sprouting of Mr Roberts' nasal hairs with fascination.

"Got you out of that problem, eh Trill? Well, never mind, I will save the answer to that particular question until you return. Go on, be quick!"

Although Christian was relieved to leave the mathematics lesson that he hated, he also knew what was going to happen next. He knocked hesitantly on the door of Dr Tapper's study. The set of indicator lights at the side of the door flashed green – this was the signal for Christian to enter the hallowed turf of Dr Tapper's inner sanctum. He had been in Dr Tapper's study several times before and none had been particularly pleasant occasions, as Christian recalled.

"Ah, young Trill, come in," boomed Dr Tapper. "I have your parents with me, as you can see. They tell me that you left home under, shall we say, difficult circumstances yesterday."

"Are you all right, my love?" oozed Brenda. "We have been so worried about you."

Alistair said nothing.

"We want you to come home with us now, to talk things through, don't we Alistair?"

Alistair would not look at his son and said nothing.

"Well, young Trill," boomed Dr Tapper. "You pop along home now and sort out those problems and we'll say no more about it, eh?"

Christian said nothing.

"Come along, young Trill. Go with your parents please. I have other parents to see now."

Christian said nothing.

"It seems to me that you are an extremely defiant young man, Trill. Do as I say at once."

"Christian, wherever are your manners? Come along with us now," ordered his mother.

"I'm not going anywhere. I am staying with Pete."

"Oh no you're not," exploded Alistair who, until then, had been biting his tongue as he was about to explode at his young son's attitude and defiant behaviour. "You are coming home with us right now!"

"Is that so you can beat me again?" exclaimed Christian, revealing his bruised arm to the alarmed headmaster. "No way, you bully!" he shouted.

"Oh really. I do think we should all sit down and calm down," replied Dr Tapper with a sigh. "Did you do this to your son, Mr Trill?"

Alistair said nothing.

"Well, young Trill. I think you had better wait outside the office whilst I have another little chat with your parents," he said kindly and added, "Let me try and sort this out for you."

After what seemed like several hours, Christian saw his parents leave by the side entrance, his mother in tears. Both parents left without even looking at their son.

"Young Trill, come back into my office, please," said a kindly voice.

Christian sat down in front of the serious-looking headmaster.

"Christian, I have had a long chat with your parents. A very long chat indeed," he sighed. "I understand that you have had a few problems recently. I think there may be a few issues concerning your sexuality that are troubling you?"

"Yes, I think I'm gay," replied Christian.

"Quite so," replied the headmaster, hastily. "Don't be too alarmed, young Trill. In my experience some boys do tend to go through this phase in their lives. It will soon pass and you will become quite normal again."

"Normal?"

"Yes, as I said, it is only a phase. It is a bit like… It is much like bed wetting, young Trill. It is a phase that most boys get over very quickly and then you will become normal again. Until then you must just curb your desires."

Christian nodded. The only thing that he desired right then was Peter Flanagan's bed.

"Now, until we can get some sort of reconciliation with your father, you have a choice of either going to stay with your aunt whom, I understand, lives close by."

Christian shuddered at the thought of staying with Aunt Emily. She always smelled of boiled fish and he hated that almost as much as peppermint.

"Or with the Flanagans. I am sure Mrs Flanagan won't mind you staying there a little longer, and you know Peter well, don't you?"

Christian grinned, yes he could honesty agree that he knew Pete very well indeed.

The next few days that Christian spent with Kath Flanagan and Pete were some of the happiest that he had known for some time. Kath was a good natured, if chaotic woman, who did the best she could for her large family.

There seemed to be an endless stream of older brothers and sisters coming and going to and from the house, and although Pete was the youngest of the family, he seemed to bear more than his fair share of household chores. Her husband, Michael, was away at sea, but from all accounts he was a good man who adored his family, and Mrs Flanagan missed him dreadfully.

It was a home that was full of laughter. Peter's older brothers and sisters seemed to come and go as they pleased, and Christian was never quite sure who lived there or not.

Often they would arrive with boyfriends and girlfriends, and it became all too confusing for Christian to follow. He did remember Eddie though. Eddie was "a stunning good looker" as Christian put it one night when whispering to Peter about their day together.

"Ugh, don't say that, Christian. I have never thought of my brother like that. Don't you dare make a pass at him either. He would smash your face in. He hates poofs!"

"Yes, but he knows you're gay, surely?"

"Yeah, they all do. No one minds. Ma thought it was cute although Dad didn't seem too pleased when he found out. Ruined his macho image, I guess!"

"How did they find out?"

"Ma just knew. She came in my room one Saturday morning just as I was wanking off and she threw this packet of condoms on the bed. Told me that she loved me and to always be careful. That was it. They all knew after that."

It was nearly a week before Christian returned home to his parents. Kath Flanagan walked him around to his home and he was greeted at the door by his mother.

"Hello Christian. Thank you for looking after him, Mrs Flanagan. Please let us know how much we owe you for his keep."

"I shall be most offended if you try to pay me for a Christian act of kindness," snapped Kath. "You should know as well as I, the command of Suffer Little Children."

Although the significance of this statement was lost upon Christian, Brenda ushered him inside the living room where he was greeted coolly by his father. A small suitcase was laid on the table.

"Christian, your mother and I have had a long talk. We have taken the advice of your headmaster, Dr Tapper and our doctor. We think you should go away for a few months."

Christian was taken aback. "Where to?"

"To a special place where they can give you help. You need help to get out of this phase you are going through."

"It's not a phase. It is just me. I can't help it."

"Don't raise your voice to me," shouted his father.

"Look, dear. Dr Tapper knows a special place where they treat people like you. It is called The Step Back Project. They help young people like you who are confused," began Brenda.

"I'm not going!" shouted Christian.

"Yes, you are!" retorted Alistair.

"It's only for a few months. It's like a summer camp, but with counsellors, psychologists and psychiatrists to help you," continued his mother.

"Yes, with special help and medication you will be normal again," added his father, almost cheerily.

"Medication!" exclaimed Christian. "Forget it. I'm not bloody going to stay with a bunch of shrinks and have my brains blown out with medication! No way!"

The months ahead were bleak for Christian. Although now barely seventeen, he had left home and headed for London with no job, no prospects, nowhere to stay and very little money. He had some savings to start himself off and Peter was able to help him with a little money as well.

"Look, you are welcome to it," his friend had told him at the station, handing him a wad of notes. "If I get my 'A' levels I am coming to London as well. It is my first university choice. Maybe we could share a flat together or something?"

Although Peter and Christian did stay in contact for a few weeks, Christian soon found that he had other problems to contend with.

Christian had left his parents' home intending to get a job in the big city. However, he quickly realised that the sort of clerical job he was looking for was impossible to get without qualifications. He looked older than his seventeen years and eventually found his way into bar work as a pot washer. This was at a pub called the 'Horn and Crumpet' in the poorer part of the city, and he soon became sick of the stench of stale beer and endless glasses to wash. It was a thankless task and it went nowhere to paying the rent of his cheap room, let alone living expenses.

It was not long before Bill, the landlord, decided that Christian could do with promotion. He had been impressed by Christian's good timekeeping and reliability and reasoned that he could trust him to work at the bar as he was short staffed.

Christian jumped at the chance to leave 'pot washing' and was relieved as soon his replacement, a spotty youth called Toby, was taken on to replace him. Christian was given a new uniform and the landlord spent a whole thirty minutes showing him what to do, how to operate the till as well as how to change the barrel and refresh the optics. Christian could now consider himself fully trained.

Christian's good looks and muscular build did not go unnoticed for long. Each evening at around ten o'clock a pleasant, and well educated man in his late forties would appear at the bar. He would always wait for Christian to serve him and it was not long before the two started chatting.

Christian, a friendly boy by nature, was flattered by Edwin's attention and generous tips, and it was not long before Christian started to pour out his troubles to him. Edwin Smiley was a good listener and Christian realised that he was the only person to really listen to him since he had last seen Peter in Derby.

"So your parents had trouble with you being gay. You're not the only one, Christian. There are many like you and me. When I was your age, it was even more difficult. My parents threw me out as well. I know what you are going through."

It was this understanding of shared experiences that drew Christian and the older man together and it was not long before Edwin was asking Christian out on a date.

"Just as friends, you understand?" said Edwin. "I would never take advantage of someone so much younger than myself. I like you and maybe we can have a good evening together?"

Christian and Edwin enjoyed a good meal at the local Indian restaurant. They had a few drinks together and it was not long before Christian found himself not only in Edwin's beautiful apartment, but in his bed.

To begin with, Edwin Smiley was kind, thoughtful and generous to Christian. He made few demands and for once in Christian's life, he began to feel that he had at last found someone like himself whom he could trust.

One of the first things that his new friend demanded was that he give up the bar job and look after Edwin and the home that they would share together. It was, as Edwin explained, a way that "Christian could put a bit back" for his kindness in giving him a home.

Christian readily agreed and was happy to look after Edwin, that is until Christian discovered that in order to keep a roof over his head, his friend was expecting him to 'do favours' for a number of his other close friends. Christian quickly realised that he was being pimped and one morning, when Edwin was at work, he quickly packed his rucksack and prepared to leave.

Edwin had already prepared for such an eventuality, after all, it hadn't been the first time that one of his 'young guests' had left in such a hurry. After discovering that the metal external security doors had been locked, the window security grills bolted, and telephone hidden, Christian realised that the situation was serious and he was being held as a prisoner against his will.

Later that evening, when Edwin returned home from work, Christian greeted him with a kiss and a glass of his favourite sherry as usual, and quickly bolted out of the door as soon as the older man had put down his briefcase. Edwin made a feeble attempt to chase Christian down the street, but the athletic Christian was too fast for the older man. It was a breathless Christian who called his friend, Peter, once again asking for help.

"I haven't heard from you in ages," said Peter. He had been upset and disappointed that his good friend had not remained in contact with him, but understood when Christian explained what had happened and the situation that he had found himself in.

"The bastard," he exploded. "Have you reported him to the police?" Christian lied and told Peter that he had, although, in reality, he hadn't as Christian still liked and felt sorry for Edwin Smiley.

Later that evening, Peter Flanagan arrived by train from Derby and once again rescued Christian from his current troubles. Peter arranged for them both to stay together with his aunt and uncle for a couple of nights in Harrow. Christian had every reason to be grateful to his friend and wondered if they had a chance of being together once again.

They were walking together in a nearby park and it was as if Peter was reading his thoughts. "You know, Christian, we really are best friends and I will always do what I can to help you. You know that. I am starting university here shortly, as you know."

"Great," replied Christian. "Maybe we can see much more of each other then? We could find somewhere to stay together, just as we said last year."

"Well, yes, maybe," replied Peter, and Christian sensed that something was wrong.

"You've found someone else, haven't you?" he questioned.

"Yes, I have Christian. I'm sorry, but I hadn't heard from you for ages and I thought you had fallen for someone else. I didn't plan it; it just happened. I was so lonely and I went to a party and I met this guy and…"

Christian kissed Peter gently. "Please, you don't have to explain anything to me. I understand and, if I'm honest, it's all my fault. Let's just be friends."

Peter's aunt and uncle took an immediate liking to Christian and it was not long before Peter's Uncle Frank and Aunt Eleanor suggested that Christian stay with them for a few days.

The generous couple were very fond of their nephew. "He's the only one of the Flanagan's who has any sense," was how Aunt Eleanor put it one day after speaking to her sister. "Don't get me wrong, I love my sister dearly, but Kath is such a muddler. That husband of hers and all those children. No, Peter is the only one who speaks any sense. You are very welcome to stay with us until you get back on your feet, Christian. We have plenty of room in this big house, and at least it will bring Peter to see us now and again. We are hoping he will live with us when he goes to university."

Christian smiled and nodded, but said nothing because he didn't want to disappoint the couple and knew that his friend already had other ideas, and another love.

Frank O'Leary was a good Catholic boy from Dublin who had found his way to London many years earlier. He had done well in the city, worked hard and had become a popular employee with the estate agents, Whitney and Walker. As time went on, Frank's 'gift of the gab' – a real Irish asset, had been noticed by the partners and, in due course, Frank was asked to join the partners in helping to extend their growing chain of estate agencies throughout the city and beyond.

Frank worked hard and, together with his beautiful wife, Eleanor, found themselves following, if not leading, a busy social life in the city. Frank made many contacts and it was not long before his easy-going and friendly disposition had won him many friends as well as favours owed to him. He was a generous man and was well-liked by his employees and it was clear to all who knew him that he really did care for his workers.

It was the morning when Christian was due to leave with Peter by train for Derby. Peter had already asked his parents if they would mind Christian staying in his old room until he found a job and somewhere to live. Kath Flanagan had readily agreed. She was very fond of Christian and, as far as she was concerned, he was always welcome to stay with her and the Flanagan family.

Privately, she was disappointed that he and Peter had not become a couple. She had rather hoped that they might and was not too keen on Peter's new 'toff' boyfriend, as she put it.

"Have you heard from my parents?" enquired Christian. "It's ages since I spoke to them. Mind you, they have probably wiped me out of their memories by now. I tried calling a couple of times from Edwin's, but there was no answer."

"Christian, hadn't you heard?"

"Heard what?"

"I am so sorry. This is very bad news, Christian," began Peter. "Your father died shortly after you left home. Heart attack, I think. I know you had your problems, but I really am sorry."

Christian remained silent for a few moments.
"My mum?"

"Not good either, Christian. She had some kind of breakdown and couldn't cope. She went to hospital for treatment and I think she is now living with your Aunt Emily. Patricia is staying there as well. She called Ma once to ask about you. We hadn't heard from you so Ma lied and said you were well and happy. She seemed content with that. Christian, I am so sorry that you had to find out like this. I thought you would have known. I am so sorry. Do you want to stay here for another few days? I am sure Aunt and Uncle won't mind."

"I don't really know, Pete. Maybe I could just be alone for a while."

There was no question of it, Aunt Eleanor and Uncle Frank made it quite clear to Christian that he was very welcome to stay with them for as long as he wished. There was plenty of room in their large house and they enjoyed his company. Christian kept himself to himself for a few days, appearing only for the occasional meal and helping with chores around the house. After a few days, there was a knock at the door of the bedroom.

"Christian, it's Frank. May I come in?"

"Of course, Frank. It's your house, after all. Thank you so much for letting me stay here. I really do appreciate it."

"No trouble at all, my boy. Look, I wonder if you would do me a favour? Trevor, one of the office staff in the Harrow branch has been taken ill and we are short-staffed at a very busy time. I wonder if you would like to help out in the office? At least until Trevor returns. Maybe you fancy being a trainee estate agent for a while?"

This was how Christian Trill became a popular and successful young estate agent in the Harrow office of Whitney and Walker. Supported and encouraged by Peter's Uncle Frank, who would often call into the office to see how he was getting on, Christian quickly became a popular, reliable and effective member of the sales team.

Frank gave Christian a great deal of advice and support, for which Christian would always be very grateful.

"Remember this, young man. We are here to sell houses, but we are also here to sell a dream. Be friendly, be honest and be professional and you will not go far wrong."

These words were to stand Christian in good stead for his professional as well as his personal life, and he often recalled these softly spoken words of advice from the kindly Irishman.

For the next three years, Christian continued to live with Aunt Eleanor and Uncle Frank, whom he now regarded as his own family. Eleanor and Frank were a childless couple and it pleased them to have a considerate and well-mannered 'adopted son' to fuss over. It was one of the happiest periods of Christian's life, and he was touched that Peter still telephoned him regularly and often came to see him at his aunt and uncle's welcoming home.

It was one evening when Christian, Aunt Eleanor and Uncle Frank were seated together for dinner when Frank suddenly announced, "I have a promotion for you my boy. As you know, Whitney and Walker are growing rapidly and we have just bought a chain of small estate agents in the Bridgehampton area. There is a branch near the town of Abbotsford that desperately needs a shot in the arm. Nearly all of the staff resigned as soon as they heard that we were taking them over. I have a proposition for you, young man."

"Goodness, this sounds, serious, Frank. You know I will help, if I can."

"I would like you to take over the position of Deputy Manager of that office, Christian. You have been with us for nearly three years now. You are a quick learner and you have done really well here. Everyone likes you and you would be doing me, and Whitney and Walker, a great favour if you would take it on. I have come, not only to look upon you as the son we never had, but I am also very proud of you. We both are, aren't we, Eleanor?"

"I, I don't really know what to say," stammered Christian. "You really think I can do it?"

"Yes, of course. I have asked several people about you and we are all confident that you can. Also, Mr Pound, the manager, is likely to retire in a few years' time and maybe, just maybe if you do well, you could even become manager of that agency. How about it?" the friendly Irishman beamed with pleasure.

Christian could see that Aunt Eleanor looked saddened. He knew what she was thinking.

"Well, thank you. I will accept, but I am really going to miss you both. You have been so very kind to me. You have become like parents to me."

"And you, a son to us," added Aunt Eleanor, wiping away a tear. "As long as you keep in touch and come and see us from time-to-time. That's my one and only condition. Your room will always be ready for you. Come and go just as you please, with or without a boyfriend."

Although Eleanor had always known that Christian was gay, Christian had always been very careful not to bring anyone home. Eleanor was sometimes a little saddened by this, because all she now really wanted for Christian was someone with whom he could share his life and love.

Two months later, Christian Trill was sporting a new suit and a new briefcase and was heading off to see one of his first clients, a young man by the name of Tristan Peters and his partner, James Young, a local primary school head teacher.

Chapter 7

Old Friends and New Enemies

So much was spinning around in James' head. He and the staff had agreed that it was in the children's best interests to set aside their worries about the future, and for it to be business as usual at Prior's Hill School. They decided to avoid talking and worrying about what may or may not be. James had readily agreed and, for his part, had promised that he would immediately call another staff meeting as soon as he had any news to share. James had been both touched and surprised by the support and encouragement that Emily had brought to the meeting.

"We'll fight like hell, James, but will still do our best for the children. That is why we are here," said Emily firmly, her steely grey eyes flashing dangerously.

James was very worried, because even though governors, staff and parents had all agreed to write letters, attend a protest march and write to their MPs as well as the Department of Education, he sensed that it would not change anything.

The school was in a mess and although he was doing his best to ensure that things ran more or less as normal, he knew that it would not be long before parents would soon forget the heady fighting talk of the recent public meeting, and would start to move their children to other local schools.

James no longer had confidence in the ability of the Local Education Authority to change their planned course of action, and he felt badly let down. His hopes were now pinned upon Sir Toby Peatwhistle and the Diocesan Education Office, and he had heard precious little from either in recent days.

James was also in a state of confusion about Christian. He had not heard from him over the last two weeks or so. It had been Christian's turn to stay at James' flat, but he had failed to arrive on Saturday morning. James knew that he could hardly blame him, and wondered if he should call and apologise for his abrupt behaviour during their last weekend together.

However, James did not want to give Christian any false hopes about the future, but although he found it hard to admit this to himself, he missed Christian very much. Somehow he felt that any warmth of feeling shown towards Christian was a betrayal of Tristan, his life and the love that they had shared.

Prince too seemed to sense that something was wrong. He would sit with his head on James' lap in the evenings watching him with his big, brown and doleful eyes. The young dog often sat in his basket, and seemed disinterested in going for the walks that he had previously thoroughly enjoyed. At home, both he and James seemed to have little interest in doing anything, and James was now beginning to wonder if he had done the right thing in declining Christian's offer.

It was Friday evening, and the dinner party with Jasmine and Paul the following day was fast approaching. James didn't really want to attend and he shuddered at the thought of the last evening that he had spent with Jasmine some two years earlier. Although he was tempted to telephone and say that he had a sudden illness and would not be able to go after all, the decent streak inside this confused young man made him realise that this was not the right thing to do, and that he had to face her.

It was true that he was curious to meet the new love of her life, yet he didn't want to go alone. He had thought about asking Anne to accompany him, but Anne was a delicate flower at the best of times and James knew that Jasmine was everything that Anne disliked. Anne always did her best to avoid conflict and confrontation and, above all, disliked loud people. James knew that dinner with Anne and Jasmine would not be a great success.

He wondered about asking Doris and George to accompany him, but he knew that taking two guests instead of one was not the done thing. He also knew that Doris was not too keen on Jasmine either. The ideal guest to accompany him to Jasmine's dinner party would be Christian, of course, but would he agree to come? There was simply no other choice. James put off the telephone call for as long as he could. Prince put his paw on James' lap and he reached for the telephone.

"Hi, Christian. Look, sorry I have not been in touch for a while. It has been crazy at school this week and I just haven't had a moment."

James listened to Christian's surprised, yet warm, comments with his free hand rubbing Prince's head. Christian sounded relieved that he had called.

James continued, "Yes, and I've missed you too, Christian. Look, I'm really sorry about my rotten behaviour last week. We need to talk again very soon. Yes, Prince misses you too. How about coffee tomorrow morning? I also have something special to ask you."

Saturday morning was not easy for either James or Christian. Initially there was an awkward silence between them, but James threw his arms around Christian and gave him a big hug and a lingering kiss on the lips.

"Look, Christian. I've been a bastard, I know. I'm sorry for last weekend. I have missed you so much this week and, look, Prince has too."

Christian fell to the ground and hugged the big dog who happily responded with endless big, wet licks. Eventually, Christian stood up, grinned and brushed Prince's hairs from his newly dry-cleaned trousers.

"Do you ever brush this dog, James? He's covered in loose fur. He needs a good brush every day. I usually do it when he stays with me!"

James laughed as he pulled Christian close to him once again. "Look at the state we both get into when you are not around. I need you, we both need you, but I just need more time."

"You told me that last week, James," replied Christian, somewhat sharply. "Look, I know I can never be a replacement for Tristan and I don't expect to be. I do have other qualities though, James. Just look for those in me and maybe you will come to like me as well eventually. Give me a chance and let me into your life."

"Don't be daft, Christian. I do like you. You are my best friend and I cannot be without you. You asked me about love. I just don't know at the moment. I'm not even sure I know what it means any more."

James' eyes were beginning to fill with tears and Christian pulled him close to him once again and stroked his head.

"Look, stupid, let's just see how it goes. No commitment, no plans and, yes, you can have all the time that you need. Do you know, James, how envious I felt of Tristan when the three of us first met? I adored you from the start, both of you, but it was you I couldn't keep my eyes off. Do you know that?"

James didn't say anything for a moment, but looked closely at the stocky, handsome man holding him so tightly and so protectively in his strong arms.

"But Tristan was gorgeous, everyone said so. I couldn't even begin to compare with him."

"Mr Headmaster..." began Christian. James pushed Christian away and sat on the sofa.

"Please don't ever call me that, Christian," James spoke quietly and with determination, just as if he were speaking to a naughty child.

"Now, what have I done?" exclaimed Christian, sitting beside James. "I just don't understand you sometimes."

"I'm sorry, Christian, but Tristan often called me that, particularly if he was annoyed or irritated with me. He never really showed his anger, but just called me that. I always knew that I had done or said the wrong thing."

"OK, OK, I'm sorry. My, you are a touchy old thing today aren't you? I promise I won't call you that ever again."

It was at that moment that Christian realised, looking at his friend sitting so miserably on the sofa beside him, that James was still grieving and hurting badly, and needed a close friend to support and look after him. He now knew what he had to do.

Over a brief sandwich lunch, James had touched upon the delicate subject of his dinner date with Jasmine and her friend Paul. Tentatively, James suggested that Christian might like to accompany him. Christian readily agreed. He would do anything to help James, but he was also curious to know more about Jasmine De Valle. He had met her before, briefly, when he had to do some research in Abbotsford Library for a local property developer.

She had been courteous and helpful, yet a little cool towards him too. Abbotsford is a small community where everyone seems to know everyone else, and Christian had made it his business to find out a little more about the mysterious librarian when he got back to his office.

"She's quite a one, I hear, James. Can't wait to spend an evening with her. I gather she's been chasing anything in pants for the last few years. Susie, in the office tells me that no man is safe in Abbotsford. Is that true?"

James giggled, "Hmm, well, yes it is I'm afraid. She even fell for me. My being gay didn't put her off at all – in fact, I think she was rather turned on by it and saw it as her greatest challenge. Tristan thought it was highly amusing!"

"Yes, he told me," laughed Christian.

"What? Tristan told you about that?"

"Yes, he thought it was very funny," sniggered Christian. "Don't look so surprised, James. Tristan told me a lot about you. He just adored you, but he also thought you were very funny. I now know what he meant. He often told me about the odd things you did and got up to."

It was half past seven when James and Christian opened the wooden gate leading to Jasmine's ground floor flat in the centre of Abbotsford.

Before the pair could get to the front door, it burst open and Jasmine was excitedly screaming, "So good to see you! Come in! You must be Christian! I am so pleased to meet you! My goodness, you are a cutie too. Now, do take your clothes off and make yourselves at home!" Jasmine shrieked as she heard herself being so risqué.

Jasmine planted two wet kisses on the mouths of both speechless guests, as they were dragged inside and propelled, almost by force, into Jasmine's small, yet tidy, living room.

"I am so pleased that you could come. Lovely to meet you, Christian," Jasmine gushed. "Now, I would like you to meet my dear friend, Paul."

James thrust forward a bottle of red wine and Christian presented a box of After Eight chocolate mints to the delighted Jasmine, who looked radiant in an elegant lavender evening dress. James thought that she looked more feminine than he had ever seen her before, and he was pleased to see her looking so happy.

A well built, yet older looking man came into the room. Paul peered through a pair of round, black rimmed spectacles, and smiled broadly as he greeted both James and Christian with a warm handshake and beckoned them to the sofa. Paul wore a smart black waistcoat and trousers and a crisp, white shirt. As James commented afterwards, the couple made James and Christian feel totally under-dressed for the occasion.

"Lovely to meet you both, I have heard a lot about you, James, but it is also a pleasure to meet your friend." Paul watched as they sat down. "Now let me get you both a drink. Wine or beer?"

After he had carefully served the drinks and finally sat down beside Jasmine, Paul continued, "James, I gather you and my Jasmine were really good friends, or should I say, very close friends at one time."

James spluttered on the red wine that he was starting to sip, "Er, yes, Jasmine was really kind when I moved to Prior's Hill, and helped us to set up the school library. She did a magnificent job."

"Yes, I heard about that," guffawed Paul. "She told me quite a few other things as well."

"Oh, really," enquired James, feeling his cheeks glowing red.

"Oh, don't embarrass the poor love, Paul," gushed Jasmine. "It's all water under the bridge now, isn't it, James? I think I have now got over being rejected," she teased. "You know, James," she whispered, "it really doesn't do much for a lady's self-confidence to be rejected by a gay man."

"Er, no, I am so sorry about that," agreed James, who was by now highly embarrassed. He looked towards Christian for support.

Christian appeared to be thoroughly enjoying himself, and was listening with great amusement to the conversation between Jasmine and James, when he suddenly caught James' eye and the 'look' that seemed to plead, "Please help me."

"Well, I guess it was better to find out sooner rather than later, Jasmine," interjected Christian, trying to lighten the conversation. "Anyway, it really is very kind of you to ask us both over for dinner. We have been looking forward to it all week, haven't we, James?"

"Don't get me wrong," laughed Paul, returning to his original theme. "It's just that I think it is so hilarious that my Jasmine picks up a gay man as a lover!"

"Well, I can tell you, we were not lovers, Paul," began James, sharply, his hackles rising. "We just shared several interests, that's all."

Christian, who by now was feeling quite awkward about the way the conversation was heading, intervened once again.

"I think it was more of a literary and musical interest, James, wasn't it?"

James nodded heartily, taking several large sips of red wine, whilst deciding, wisely, to leave further explanations to the more diplomatic Christian.

After an awkward start, James and Christian found that they were thoroughly enjoying the evening with Jasmine and Paul. The couple were generous and thoughtful hosts and, soon, copious amounts of wine were flowing. Jasmine's flat was only a short walk from where James lived and, for once, they felt uninhibited by the need to watch alcohol consumption because of a lengthy car drive home afterwards.

James had forgotten to remind Jasmine that he was vegetarian but, thankfully, she had remembered and produced a delicious looking cheese and spinach quiche especially for him. She placed it proudly at the side of James' plate.

"Now, this isn't one of your supermarket efforts, James. Paul made this especially for you this morning. Pastry is Paul's speciality," she added proudly. "They say that hands have to be at a special temperature to make pastry properly."

"This looks and smells delicious, Paul. Thank you so much."

"Think nothing of it, James," replied Paul. "Jasmine and I tend to share the cooking, but my pastry is always better than hers. I am good with my hands, you see!"

A peal of laughter burst from Jasmine's lips as she brought in a huge plate of beef, roast potatoes and an assortment of roast vegetables from the kitchen. James and Christian sat in astonishment looking at all the food that was now surrounding them.

"This is wonderful, Jasmine. You really shouldn't have gone to so much trouble. This is so kind of you both."

"Well, I felt I owed you an apology, James, for the way I behaved. No, we won't get back to that subject again, but I just wanted to say, sorry. As I told you in the park, I am now reformed." Jasmine placed a large jug of gravy beside Christian whose eyes, by now, seemed to be popping out of his head.

"Now just tuck in boys. There's plenty more in the kitchen. Drink up now please, because I want to serve this rather better wine with the meal," added Paul, opening yet another cork with an antique looking silver corkscrew. "We've been saving it for a special occasion, and I think this is it. I guess we can manage with the same glasses. What do you think, Jasmine?"

"As long as it's wet, I doubt the boys will mind very much, I know I don't!" shrieked Jasmine.

Over dinner, hosts and guests chatted continuously. Despite Jasmine's tendency to dominate any conversation, Paul had a very pleasant way of intervening and toning down Jasmine's more outrageous behaviour. The more James and Christian talked to Paul, the more they liked him. He seemed very kind and gentle and above all, obviously adored Jasmine.

"So how did you two meet?" began James. "In the library?"

Jasmine put down her glass, looked at Paul and they both burst out laughing.

"Go on, guess! You'll never guess," roared Paul.

"Well, maybe it was at the Music Society? I know Jasmine is a member," began James, puzzled at this new game that they seemed to be playing.

"Wrong, wrong," sniggered Jasmine, between large slurps of wine.

"Well, let me try," interjected Christian. "From what James tells me, how about the local drama group?"

"Wrong, wrong," screeched Jasmine, slipping her hand in Paul's. "They'll never guess. Never. Let's tell them."

"Well, I wish you would," replied James, now beginning to feel irritated by what he regarded as a senseless conversation, and the inane laughter was fast beginning to annoy him. "Just tell us how you met."

"It was at Brown and Co.," giggled Jasmine, "You know, the undertakers in the High Street."

There was a pause and Christian could see that James was uncomfortable with what he was hearing.

"Yes, I know Brown and Co. very well. They buried my Tristan," James said quietly.

Jasmine, now realising that she had entered sensitive territory, put down her glass and resumed a calmer demeanour.

"Well, my mother had just died. I went to the undertakers to see the body just before the funeral and that's where I met my Paul."

"Oh, I see," said Christian, anxious to help James move on with this particular conversation. "I am sorry to hear about your mother. So, Paul lost someone special as well at the same time? An amazing meeting for you both, I guess?"

This time it was Paul who roared with laughter, his ample frame moving up and down as he laughed heartily. "No, you still don't see, do you? I work there. I am a mortician, with a speciality in embalming."

"He's very good at it too," beamed Jasmine proudly. "My mother looked lovely. More quiche, James?"

It had been a very good evening and James could not remember the last time that he had laughed so much. When they had said their good-byes to Jasmine and Paul, they walked down the road laughing together about the unexpected events of the evening.

Christian knew how James felt about being seen together in public, and he had avoided slipping his hand into James' until they had moved out of the well-lit parts of the town and into the darker and silent road leading to James' apartment.

"Well, that was a surreal evening, Christian. I really enjoyed it though, didn't you? Aren't those two a scream?"

"I sure did. Jasmine and Paul can certainly cook. They were really generous with all that wine as well; I think we polished off about six bottles between us this evening."

"I'm not surprised. Mind you, I think Jasmine managed to sink most of them," laughed James. "Jasmine's not a bad old thing, is she? A bit outspoken maybe, but her heart's in the right place. That Paul is nice too, but there's something just a little strange about him. His cooking is wonderful too – that pastry really was melt-in-the-mouth stuff. I'm surprised that he is a mortician and not a baker."

"That was so funny, James. I thought you were going to have a fit when Paul told us about the job. It certainly was a conversation stopper. I noticed that you didn't have any more quiche or touched the dessert afterwards though?"

"Well, embalming bodies is a bit of a turn off, Christian. I kept wondering where the hands that had made my wonderful pastry had been earlier during the day! Did you also notice that smell of formaldehyde about the house? I couldn't get it out of my mind or nose!"

By now Christian was choking with laughter and pulled James closer to him. "It has been a wonderful evening, hasn't it? I loved meeting your friends. They are both such interesting women."

James stopped and looked at Christian. "What did you just say?"

"I said it has been a wonderful evening."

"No, the other part."

"I said they are both interesting women," laughed Christian. He paused, looking at James, with his eyes glinting in the moonlight. "You haven't got it yet, James, have you?"

"What do you mean? Got what?"

"James, for an intelligent man you can be so thick sometimes."

James recalled that Tristan had sometimes said exactly the same thing about him.

"James, let me put you out of your misery," roared Christian looking at the bemused James. "It isn't Paul, you idiot. It's Paula. Paula is a woman and not a man. Jasmine and Paula are lesbians."

James had enjoyed his weekend after all, and he and Christian seemed to have moved on positively in their relationship. James hadn't mentioned the thorny subject of Derby, and Christian hadn't raised the issue either. Both were happy to live for the moment and to enjoy their time together.

"You look happy today, sir," observed Stuart, as he was struggling with a hard set of fractions that James had set for him.

"I am Stuart, but then I am always happy when I teach Class 4."

There were giggles in the class, "Not always, sir," observed Debbie. "Not since the school burnt down anyway. You've looked worried."

James smiled. This was one of the things that he liked about teaching this age group. The children were by now very observant, and most recognised the subtleties of moods, joy, sadness, pressure of work and other feelings.

"Well, I have been a bit worried, Debbie, but things are looking a bit better now. You are all working well in this barn classroom of ours, and Mrs Cook tells me that she is pleased with your progress so far this term."

Debbie nodded, "My dad says the school will be closed soon and we will have to go somewhere else. What will happen to you and the other teachers then?"

"Oh no, Debbie, whatever gave your dad that idea? No, the school will be rebuilt again very soon, you just wait and see," lied James.

"My mum said the same thing," joined in Stuart. "She says that County Hall will close Prior's Hill as it is too expensive, and we will have to go to Coombe. I like it here and I don't want to go to Coombe. Their football team is rubbish and Mr Treader is very strict."

James smiled. "Look, Stuart Bell, is this just a clever ploy to avoid finishing those fractions? It will soon be break time so please get on with them. Remember, if they are not finished soon, you will have them for homework tonight."

Stuart and the rest of the class groaned. They liked James, but they knew when he meant business.

It was lunchtime and James was pleased to have a few minutes on his own to catch up with some telephone calls and to read his post. He looked at the handful of messages that Doris had left on the desk for him and one, circled in red felt tip pen, caught his eye. 'Urgent – Call Sir Toby after school', it read 'Or, better still, call in for a drink with the Peatwhistles after four o'clock'. James smiled as he read Doris' neat handwriting, comparing it to his own hasty scribble. He wondered if Sir Toby had at last received news from County Hall and the diocese?

The office door opened with a thump and Prince leaped inside and bounded happily to James for a cuddle. James was, as usual, delighted to see Prince and ruffled his fur. He smiled as he saw Doris battling with the door once again and gave her a cheery greeting as she took off her coat and headed towards her desk and chair.

"Hello, Doris, how are you today? Sorry I missed you at break-time, but I wanted to talk a few things over with Emily. Did you enjoy your walk?"

"Yes, thanks, James. I always do enjoy my stroll with Prince. It is good exercise for me as well as him."

"Well, we both appreciate it, don't we, boy? You know you only have to say if you would rather not walk him each lunchtime. I know you are busy. Can I get you a coffee, Doris? I also have news to tell you about our evening with Jasmine De Valle!"

"No, no coffee now thank you, James." Doris turned away on the new swivel chair that James had recently bought for her and started typing.

"Doris?"

"Yes, James?"

"You seem to have been a bit down recently. Is everything all right? I've not done anything to upset you, have I? I know I can often put my foot in it without realising."

"No, James everything is just fine. I would tell you if you had, wouldn't I?" Doris stared at James.

"Well, it's just that last week you seemed very upset when you got back and you have seemed much quieter than normal. I know I am not always the most sensitive bloke in the world, but you sometimes forget that I too know you very well, Doris."
Doris fell silent for a few minutes.

"I think I will have that cup of coffee. James?"

"Yes, Doris?"

"There is something bothering me. I am sorry that I did not tell you, but I didn't know how."

"My God, don't tell me you are pregnant! Good old George!" laughed James, who was promptly hit by a flying paper clip.

"Those days are long gone, thank goodness, as well you know, cheeky," chuckled Doris.

James looked serious. "Go on, tell me. What is it?"

Doris rolled her chair over to James' desk and sat with her owl-like eyes facing him sadly.

"I didn't know how to tell you this. I don't want to hurt you. I know how much you have been hurting."

The little woman began to cry. James was alarmed and got out of his chair, knelt beside the chair and put his arm around the distraught Doris.

"Look, you are really worrying me now. What the hell is wrong? Tell me, just tell me, Doris."

"It's... it's Tristan. I've seen Tristan in the village!"

Chapter 8

The Visitor

Doris' comments had, understandably, shaken James to the core. He knew his reliable secretary well enough to know what a straightforward and astute person she was. She would never make up anything as bizarre as this. The incident in the playground had clearly shaken Doris too and, at first, she had been reluctant to tell James the whole story.

According to Doris, this was not the first time that the slim, blond-haired young man had leaned over the school wall staring at her and then, as she approached, suddenly disappeared. Each time she had seen him had been at the end of lunchtime play, when the children were just returning inside the school building and the playground was empty.

Doris always returned to school with Prince by the small gate at the bottom of the school field and spotted the young man leaning over the school wall, staring silently at her, no facial expression, no hint of recognition, just a blank stare. Each time this had happened, Prince growled and had pulled the little woman towards the young man, but by the time they had reached the school wall he had disappeared.

"I know this sounds ridiculous, James," sniffed Doris. "I am sure it was Tristan! I know it's impossible, but all I can tell you is what I saw. Prince seemed to recognise him too, except he growled, which is unusual for him."

167

"All right, Doris. Calm down. I believe you, but it is very strange. Obviously it's just someone who looks like Tristan, but it's strange that he appears each day, and just stares at you like that. What was he wearing?"

"That's just it, James," continued Doris with a whisper, "You know how Tristan always wore those pale blue denims and tight fitting white shirts? He always liked that combination, didn't he? Well, this young man wore exactly the same!"

"OK, but that's hardly unusual clothing, Doris. Many of us wear pale denim jeans and white shirts nowadays. If you have a good body, we try and fit into tight shirts as well, Doris!"

"Hmm, I guess so," murmured Doris.

"Look Doris, I'm going to make you another coffee and then I'm going outside to look for myself."

"Thanks, James. I'm all right now. It was just such a shock."

It was nearly four o'clock when James made his way down the long winding driveway to Prior's Hill Manor House where Sir Toby and Lady Lotitia Peatwhistle lived. James always liked to be punctual and he knew that the Peatwhistles appreciated this positive side of his character.

He walked up the stone steps to the main entrance and, just as he was about to ring the door-bell, the door opened and Peggy Skinner, Lady Lotitia's reliable and long-serving maid, greeted him warmly. She had clearly been waiting for him to arrive.

James shook Peggy's hand warmly. "Lovely to see you again, Peggy. Everything alright with you?"

"Yes, thank you, Mr Young. I was so sorry to hear of all your problems at the school. Even so, my Carol is really happy in your class this term. The barn classroom seems to be working very well and I think the children like it."

James smiled, as he followed Peggy into the impressive hallway, with dozens of dark, oil portraits of the Peatwhistle family ancestors adorning its high walls.

"Well, yes, it does seem to be working and, I have to say Peggy, young Carol is really pulling out the stops this year. She is a pleasure to have in the class and I am very pleased with her. I shall miss her when she leaves us at the end of the year."

Peggy beamed with delight at these comments. "Yes, she is a good girl and does try hard. Thank you, Mr Young. Now you just come this way, young sir. Sir Toby and the Rector are ready and waiting for you in the study."

James had never been in Sir Toby's study before, and he was intrigued to see where the old man spent much of his time. Peggy led the way down a narrow corridor and knocked on the old oak door.

"Do come in," James heard Sir Toby say, in his quiet, cultured voice. Peggy curtsied, and left James to enter the magnificent room.

"Ah, James. You got my message. Jolly good. Now, as you can see, the Rector has already beaten you to it."

"Good afternoon, Sir Toby," said James, warmly shaking the hand of the old man. "Good afternoon, Rector. Yes, I received your message. I hope I'm not late?" he added anxiously.

"No, not at all, James. The Rector came a little earlier to go over a few other important things with me. You are on time as usual."

"You look exhausted, James. Everything alright, I hope?" enquired the Rector.

James sat down in the comfortable brown leather armchair that Sir Toby had beckoned him to sit in. "Yes, thank you, Hubert. It's just been another very busy day. The usual joys and sorrows of a village school, I guess. Very tiring, though."

"A bit like life, well lived," beamed the Rector and, for one moment, James had the sinking feeling that the Rector was about to launch into one of his interminable sermons. James' mind was still on Doris' concerns, and the issue of the mystery visitor was troubling him greatly. The last thing that he needed then was a lengthy sermon about life from the well-meaning Rector.

It was clear that Sir Toby was also thinking the same thing and he quickly intervened. "I will ask Peggy to bring us some refreshments," he interjected quickly. "That will help to refresh you, James. Is tea alright for you?"

"Lovely, Sir Toby, thank you. I always enjoy my cups of tea here. I am not sure which blend Peggy uses, but they are possibly the best cups of tea that I have ever tasted."

"It is a very special blend that Lotitia orders from 'Fortnums', James. I am not sure exactly what she orders, but I do know that I have to post them a rather large cheque each quarter for the privilege," he chuckled.

"How is Lady Lotitia?" enquired James. "I was rather hoping to see her today. I have not seen her since the beginning of term. Is she well?"

There was a pause as the old man gathered his thoughts, and James could sense that he was considering his reply carefully.

"Well, I guess it is just the years getting to us all," he sighed. "Lotitia had a little bad news recently and has taken it rather badly. She has remained in bed for a few days' rest."

"Nothing too serious, I hope?" asked James, concerned, but not wishing to pry too closely when his genuine interest in Lady Lotitia's health may offend.

"Well, perhaps not. We shall have to see what develops," replied Sir Toby, shaking his head. "We will just have to see what develops."

There was a tap at the door and Peggy Skinner entered the study with a trolley laden with cups and saucers, a pot of tea and a large plate of jam and cream scones. She cast an eye towards James and winked.

"Peggy, you know how much I love cook's scones, don't you? This really is a treat."

"Well, it's me Lady's instructions. Lady Lotitia says she hopes that you enjoy them and that you will come again and see her soon, Mr Young," replied Peggy with a broad smile. "I hope you all enjoy them. Thank you, sir." Peggy curtsied and scurried out of the room.

"Bless the Good Lord for all his bounty," began the Rector, delving for one of the plates and placing on it a very large scone, filled with lashings of rich strawberry jam and cream.

"Quite so," added Sir Toby, pouring the tea and passing a cup to James. "As I recall, milk but no sugar."

"Praise be!" said James, although he didn't quite know why he had said that, and felt embarrassed afterwards that he had.

Maybe it was the influence of young Ryan, a new pupil from Ireland to the school, who had given him the idea. Ryan was always coming out with this kind of expression, much to James and Emily's great amusement.

"Now to business," began Sir Toby, putting on his reading glasses and leafing through several pages of neat handwritten notes.

Despite several weeks passing since the devastating news from County Hall that Prior's Hill School would close at the end of the school year, it was clear that Sir Toby had been anything but dilatory in his duties as the school's Chair of Governors.

James knew that he had instructed his London lawyer to work on his behalf and that he personally would be exerting his influence as a previous and well-respected leader of the County Council, to dissuade members from making the final decision to close the school, until he had more information.

As a considerable benefactor to the diocese, Sir Toby had also decided that now was the time to call in a few favours and to enlist the support of the bishop to their cause. As good fortune would have it, Bishop Colin was an old school friend of Sir Toby's and, in their student days, had both rowed for Cambridge. James later discovered that this early relationship between these two students was to be pivotal for the future of the school.

"The long and the short of all my recent endeavours is that my ancestor, Sir George Peatwhistle, back in eighteen something or other, had the wisdom and foresight to draft a rather clever document before his death. He was a lawyer of some repute himself and it was certainly thanks to him that the Peatwhistle estate was passed on to his successor in such good financial shape. I knew there was a Trust Deed relating to the school in the hands of the county authorities, together with a copy safely deposited with the diocese in Bridgehampton. Strangely enough, the County Hall copy has disappeared and there is no longer any trace of it. Even more shocking was that the Trust Deed for the school has also gone missing from the Diocesan Office and this was explained as possibly happening during the fire that they had in their offices some fifty years ago. The disappearance of these important documents has consequently placed the school in a very precarious position."

"This is sounding serious, Sir Toby," commented the Rector, frowning deeply, his face smeared with a mixture of crumbs, jam and cream.

"Well, it could have been very serious," continued Sir Toby, "but I think the Good Lord is on our side. When I went to London to discuss this problem with Charles Warner, my lawyer, he too could find nothing relating to the deed in any public or Church repository that he has access to. Now, gentlemen, this is the interesting part. James, do you remember that ferret-looking little man, the parent lawyer chap who was at the meeting in the school? He had rather a lot to say for himself, as I recall."

"Yes, you mean Ray Parsons. His boy is in my class," replied James, intrigued as to where this conversation was heading.

"Well, as I said, your Mr Parsons looks like a ferret and appears to be a ferret by nature," smiled Sir Toby. "Thank goodness, it was his persistence and his endless offers of help that I finally became quite irritated with him and suggested that he speak directly to my lawyer, Charles, and that the two of them should sort it out together." The old man smiled to himself as he recalled trying to dissuade the persistent Ray Parsons from troubling him further.

He continued, "I think Mr Parsons has a little inferiority complex and he was irritated to have been asked to stand aside in favour of my well known and expensive London lawyer. I didn't mean to hurt his feelings. However, I understand that he offered his assistance to Charles who, surprisingly, agreed to accept Mr Parsons' offer of help."

James found it remarkably easy to imagine the conversations between Ray Parsons and Sir Toby. Ray had the reputation of being a very effective local lawyer: effective because of his cunning and lack of charm. James recalled several meetings with this pedantic parent, who would delight in quoting education law and precedence to him at every opportunity.

Fortunately, James was perceived as no threat to Ray Parsons or to his ambitions, and so the clever lawyer was happy to support the school whenever he could. Indeed, maybe this was another way in which he could enhance his reputation locally, by making a name for himself as someone who helped to save the school?

Sir Toby chuckled, "Is it not strange in life that the most amazing of coincidences can occur when they are least expected? According to Charles, Parsons got on a train to London the very next morning and insisted upon a meeting with Charles when he arrived, unexpected and unannounced. Parsons said that I had sent him and so Charles, who was by now very busy with a Royal divorce or some other trivia, agreed to have a chat with him and, over coffee, happened to stumble upon the fact that Parsons had been mentored by a Mr Bridges of Plumbridge and Brookes of Chatham during his years as a trainee lawyer. There is a correct name for the apprenticeship of lawyers that I cannot quite remember."

Sir Toby paused for another sip of tea and a nibble from the jam and cream scone that was still sitting untouched on his plate. The well-built Rector leaned forward to take another jam and cream filled scone. He offered a second one to James, who declined the offer, but was still puzzled by where Sir Toby's story was heading.

"Look, Sir Toby, my head is spinning, but I am enjoying the story," spluttered the Rector, with yet more crumbs getting the better of him. "You do tell it so well, Toby. Do please continue."

It was true that Sir Toby now seemed to be enjoying himself as a storyteller.

"It turns out that Messrs. Plumbridge and Brookes happened to be the very same firm of lawyers that Charles Peatwhistle instructed to draw up the deeds relating to Prior's Hill School all those years ago. It is amazing that they are still in business and, needless to say, the staff who were there at that time have long since passed on, but Mr Bridges, Parsons' mentor, is still alive and kicking to this day. Although long since retired, he kindly agreed to take up the matter with the present day team. Yesterday, Charles called me to say that a current partner from Plumbridge and Brookes had telephoned him to say that they had found a third copy of the original Trust Deed pertaining to the school in their vaults and were sending him a photocopy by courier right away."

"Good old Ray!" shouted James, immediately regretting his outburst.

"Yes, indeed, James," replied Sir Toby, amused at James' enthusiastic outburst, and looking very pleased with himself. "I had a very cocky and self-congratulating Ray Parsons visit me this morning with wonderful news that will shake County Hall to the core. It seems that, despite their best efforts to close us down in favour of financial gain, we have triumphed!"

"I think you may have missed a part out, Sir Toby. I still don't understand how this changes anything, do you, James?" enquired the Rector, looking puzzled. He had finally put his plate to one side, yet was still hungrily eyeing the remaining two scones.

"I'm just coming to that part, Hubert. It seems that Sir George bequeathed what was originally arable land as a gift for the perpetual benefit of the village, but placed it in the trust and care of the diocese of Bridgehampton, to build and maintain a school for the 'education and delivery of the young in perpetuity', added Sir Toby reading carefully from his notes. It required the county authorities to 'provide and pay for all staffing and all such necessities to enhance and encourage the education of the young until their fourteenth year, or at a later age deemed appropriate by the Church authorities'. You see!"

"Yes, but surely they can still close the school and sell off the land?"

"It is not possible, Hubert. Both Ray Parsons and Charles tell me that there is a further clause in the deed that states that, 'If the school be closed or ceases to be maintained in any way, the school building and land reverts to the Peatwhistle Estate without reparation or compensation by future heirs of the Peatwhistle Estate'. In short, County Hall would get nothing if they stopped maintaining the school," he added, triumphantly.

"I think I now see," repeated James, slowly. "It means that if the County refuse to repair and rebuild the building, the land cannot be claimed and sold off by them, but it will revert to you, Sir Toby! That is brilliant news!"

"Precisely," agreed Sir Toby, putting down his notes and removing his glasses. "Charles has spoken to the County's lawyers and made it clear that if they cease to maintain the school, I shall have the school knocked down and build a large housing estate and make lots of money from it! I won't do that, of course," he added hastily, seeing the look of fury already creeping over James' face.

"This is excellent news, Sir Toby," boomed the Rector, "but do you think County Hall will rebuild the school? They say they have no money to do so."

"Well, this is where my old friend Bishop Colin comes in. He is still feeling very embarrassed by the situation of the 'lost' Trust Deed and feels that the diocese has let the school down very badly. Indeed, I did remind him of this fact when I spoke to him. As a Church school, they are liable for some of the rebuilding costs and he now feels sure that they can come to some agreement with County Hall to fund it jointly. I shall not be letting him off that particular hook easily either, James. I know that you need two additional classrooms so that your growing numbers can be accommodated more comfortably and to replace the outside classroom. I have asked the bishop and County Hall for that as well as a new school hall!" he added triumphantly.

James could control himself no longer and, thankfully avoiding the urge to hug Sir Toby, grabbed the old man by the hand instead and pumped it up and down vigorously. Sir Toby was visibly touched and laughed at the young head teacher's enthusiasm.

"I am pleased to be of some help, James. Too often, we crusty old governors can do very little to make a real difference. If I can, in some small way, play a part in repairing and extending our beloved school then Lotitia and I will be more than satisfied."

"So what happens next?" enquired James, excitedly.

"Well, more meetings, I'm afraid. More discussions between Charles and County Hall and the bishop. I suggest we put Parsons in charge of day to day operations, James. He is a cunning little man. Good to have on your side, but a bad enemy. Let him take charge, as well as take the credit for this, James," Sir Toby added, wisely. "Yes, it will mean waiting James and, forgive me, but I know how impatient you can be," he smiled at the young head teacher. "I also have some other news that may help our cause."

"It gets better than this?" laughed James.

"Well, it seems that Ray Parsons was reading the Trust Deed very carefully, once he had received his own copy. In the small print, you know all the conditions and legal 'speak', there is a clause that puts a time frame upon any urgent work that needs doing; for example, any circumstance that prevents the school's pupils from continuing their education. Circumstances may include such disasters as..."

"A fire," interrupted James, who was now beside himself with excitement and could not wait to tell the staff, and Christian too, of course.

"Precisely," nodded Sir Toby, smiling broadly, amused by the boundless enthusiasm of youth. "I think you will find that they are only allowed a short breathing space to begin and complete the necessary work. Failure to do so will mean that the building and land will revert immediately to the Peatwhistle Estate. As you can see, gentlemen, Sir Charles Peatwhistle was a very clever, indeed, cunning old man. Maybe not dissimilar to our Mr Parsons!"

"Good for him!" exclaimed James. "If he is looking on, and I am sure he is, he will be thrilled by all the plans that we have for his school. I shall buy a bottle of wine and toast your wonderful ancestor over dinner!"

"Hear, hear," beamed the Rector, raising his empty teacup.

"James, you should also know how highly Ray Parsons regards both you and the school. He is desperate for it to remain open. After all, he does have seven children, I believe, and should keep you in business for many years to come."

James felt as if he were walking on air as he strode from the Manor house back to the school. Suddenly he heard a whisper, "Mr Young, can you spare a moment?" It was Peggy Skinner. James smiled as he watched the little woman scurry from the corner of the house to the side entrance and wait by the old privet hedge. It always amused him to watch Peggy walk, because she moved so fast: almost as if she were on wheels. He walked over towards her.

"Peggy, thank you so much for tea and the scones were delicious. Please tell Cook how much we enjoyed them. The Rector thought so too," he added, realising that the Rector had polished off three scones as against his one.

"You are welcome, Mr Young. Lady Lotitia always says that I must look after you well. You have made quite an impression upon Her Ladyship."

"I like her, Peggy. She and Sir Toby have been very kind to me. By the way, I do wish you would call me James, Peggy."

"It's not my place to do so, young sir. I knows my place around here. Now, I don't want to speak out of turn, Mr Young, but there's few I can talk to. There's trouble a-brewing. I knows I can trust you though."

"Yes, you can Peggy, but what can I do to help?"

"There will come a time when you must," whispered Peggy mysteriously. "There will come a time, young sir."

James was becoming alarmed. "What do you mean, Peggy? What trouble is brewing? What can I do to help?"

"There's trouble a-brewing, young sir," repeated the mysterious maid. "I sense it. Speak to Her Ladyship. Let her tell you. She trusts you. There'll come a time when all will be clear, young sir. You are not here by accident, you know. You never have been," Peggy whispered mysteriously, before she scurried off behind the hedge and into the side door of the grand old building.

James' previously happy jaunt back to the school was now replaced by more thoughtful steps as he pondered upon Peggy's words. Peggy was a strange woman, there was no doubt, but her words could not be easily dismissed.

James' mind went back to the day of his interview when, against all the odds, he was appointed as head teacher. Peggy had predicted that before the interview. There had been several other occasions when Peggy had told him things that had become clear much later on. Although, in the past, James would have dismissed her comments as 'those of a simple mind', he was no longer so arrogant and he was rapidly learning about the ways of village life and its people. He knew only too well that Peggy and other villagers knew the ways of the world, and had both an understanding and a clarity of vision that he would never have or fully understand.

James would often make a point of wandering out of the school building when he had a few minutes to spare or at the end of the school day. He would stand and watch by the old horse chestnut tree that graced the front of the beautiful old stone building. James loved that particular part of the school and he would often sit on the wooden bench seat that Bert and Eddie had made in memory of Tristan, surveying the picturesque scene before him.

James would lovingly rub the brass inscription plate with his fingers to keep it polished and, in a way, it made him feel close to Tristan once again. 'In loving memory of Mr Tristan. A great friend of Prior's Hill School', it read. The inscription always made James feel very proud, and now, in a way that he could not explain, almost happy.

It hurt James to see the scars of the fire that had caused such havoc to the school and to the community that it had served for so many years. Part of the building had been roped off and James could see the blackened windows and walls. Part of the roof on one wing had collapsed and was now covered with a huge, grey tarpaulin to keep out the worst of the wet weather. It was a sad sight, but looking at it made James even more determined to do his best to make Prior's Hill even better than it was before the fire.

After the revelations that Sir Toby had shared with both himself and the Rector that afternoon, James found himself once again sitting on the bench seat beneath the oak tree. The old tree had been a source of comfort and refuge. It was a place that James regarded as special, somewhere to think and reflect during times of both joy and sadness.

It was the end of the day and the children and staff, with the exception of Cedric, the caretaker, had by now all gone home. The playground was silent and all that James could hear was the occasional loud click as Cedric closed and locked the tall Victorian windows, as well as the occasional dog barking in the distance.

The conversation that James had with Doris earlier in the day came back into James' mind. She must have been mistaken. He knew that her eyesight was not as good as it used to be, and she wore very thick lenses in her glasses as a result. Maybe it had been a trick of the sunlight against the old tree.

He suddenly remembered the glimpse of the man that he had seen in the park a few days earlier, when he had been walking with Prince. No, surely that had been Jasmine? Whatever he reasoned disturbed him greatly and he made up his mind to get to the bottom of the mystery as soon as he could.

"Good afternoon, Jay," came a soft voice from behind.

James swung around and gasped at the young man standing by the wall.

"You've been thinking about me, haven't you?"

The handsome, tanned young man with straw-coloured blond hair was now seated astride the old stone wall. He was smiling broadly, his brilliant white teeth gleaming in the last of the afternoon sunshine.

"You miss me very much, don't you?"

"Tris… It can't be. You're dead…!" shouted James, his heart thumping as if it would burst. His mouth was dry and he felt breathless. He felt he was going to pass out.

"Am I? Maybe you are just dreaming. Jay, why are you sitting on my seat?" asked the blond-haired young man, quietly. James noticed that he was wearing the all too-familiar pale blue denim jeans and tight fitting, brilliant white, open necked shirt.

"You think about me a lot, don't you?"

James nodded. He could not speak.

"Do you still love me, Jay? Do you want me to come and sit with you on my seat? Close your eyes, just close your eyes and if you wish hard enough maybe I will," he said quietly. "Come on Jay, you can do better than that. Close your eyes and try harder."

James pulled himself together, and turned around suddenly.

The blond-haired young man had gone.

Chapter 9

The Secret

It had been a very busy morning. Emily had an urgent dental appointment and James had offered to take Class 4 for the morning's lessons.

"That's very kind of you, James," Emily had said, and for once appeared touched by James' concern. "I would go tomorrow afternoon, but Mr Late says he has a free appointment later this morning and it really is troubling me. I think I have an abscess."

"Not a problem, Emily. You have helped me out often enough. I really don't mind."

"Aren't you supposed to be going to County Hall this morning, James?"

"Well, it is yet another meeting about local management. To be honest, Emily, I would rather be in school. I'm meeting with Colin Treader later in the week, so he will fill me in with what is happening."

It was true that, after James and Emily's initially stormy relationship, they now appeared to have come to 'an understanding' about many things. To be realistic, James would never approve of some of Emily's methods, which he considered to be antiquated and, for her part, Emily would never feel easy with some of James' 'more progressive ideas'.

However, both accepted that the needs of the children came first, they now respected each other and, often, they seemed to get on rather well together.

"I'm not sure if it is our James who is calming down at last or whether Emily is just giving up the fight," commented Anne to Doris one morning over coffee, when James was safely outside on playground duty.

"I reckon it's a bit of both," smiled Doris. "Thank goodness! Do you remember the awful rows they had when James first came?"

"Yes," laughed Anne. " I shall never forget them! I have to say, I used to make private bets with myself as to who would win the battle. I never won, they always seemed to find a way for both to win!"

"Yes, I know what you mean," nodded Doris. "Apart from all the problems with the fire, it has been quite a good term so far, hasn't it? Reasonably calm, anyway."

"Where's Julia and Doreen?" asked Anne. "Do you think I should take their coffee out for them?"

"I think Doreen wanted to catch James in the playground and I guess Julia has been held up with her parents. Remember it is 'Book Morning'. She had quite a large group in there when I called in earlier."

"Oh, yes, I had forgotten. This 'Parents in Partnership' thing is going rather well, isn't it? Good for James for introducing it. Julia seems to really have taken it on board. I think he did it at his last school, didn't he, Doris?"

Doris nodded, "Yes, by all accounts it really worked well there. By the way, have you heard how Sue is? Will she be back with us soon?"

"I had a chat with her last weekend. She's still with her parents in Wales, you know. The doctors are pleased with her and I think she should be back with us in January. Meanwhile, we have the lovely Mrs Sparkle still spreading fairy dust in Class 2," laughed Anne.

"She is a bit strange, isn't she?" whispered Julia, who had just come into the room and was now joining in the conversation. "I caught her skipping on the field yesterday with the older girls. Mind you, she seemed to be enjoying it!"

"Why was that strange?" enquired Anne.

"Well, she kept falling over! She is not really built for it. I tell you, it was very embarrassing to watch," giggled Julia.

The three women shrieked with laughter, imagining the spectacle of Mrs Sparkle rolling on the field.

"Oh dear, we really mustn't talk about her like this," laughed Anne. "She will be in at any moment. Julia, we were just saying how James seems to be calming down," Anne continued, changing the subject.

"Oh, isn't he a doll?" whispered Julia. "I would fancy him myself if he wasn't gay. He really is so good looking!"

"Julia, that's no way to speak about your headmaster," laughed Doris.

"Oooh, this headmaster can smack me whenever he wants to," whispered Julia, in a seductive voice.

"I was so pleased that James took us all into his confidence about the rebuilding yesterday," added Anne, noticing Doris glaring angrily at Julia. "I thought Emily was going to hug James when he told us all about the meeting with Sir Toby and the Rector. It's such good news, isn't it?"

"It certainly is," agreed Doris. "I shall just be pleased to have the school back to normal, but James seems to think that this idea of two extra classrooms and a new hall is done and dusted! I keep telling him, it won't be like that. Where's the money coming from for a start?"

"Well, as we both know. If James wants it, he will find a way of making it happen. I have never known such a determined young man. Does he ever stop, Doris?"

"I doubt it, Anne. If he does then there will be something very wrong with him. It's just his nature, I guess, but I just wish he would slow down a bit sometimes and let the rest of us catch up with him!" laughed Doris. "In many ways, I think he is now much worse at 'switching off'. Tristan used to make him relax. He would tease him relentlessly and force him to laugh. He had a wonderful way of calming him down. Now all James ever seems to do is to work and think about school."

"That can happen only too easily," mused Anne. "I find myself in the same boat sometimes. Hasn't he got someone else now, though? I thought he was very keen on that young man who came to Tristan's funeral, the estate agent. He seemed nice, I liked him."

"He is lovely, Anne," nodded Doris. "But you know James. Nothing is ever quite good enough and I'm very much afraid that no one will ever match up to Tristan."

"I think you're right. Tristan was unique, I agree, but I would hate to think of James going through life alone, particularly as he is still so young."

"Well, we will just have to make sure he doesn't," whispered Doris conspiratorially. "I think Christian is perfect for him and I am going to make sure that James realises it sooner rather than later."

"Good luck, Doris. Just make sure James doesn't catch you meddling in his love life!"

"Oh, he's used to it, by now," said Doris, as she gathered up the used coffee cups and started to wash them. "I've always found with James that what he doesn't know, he won't worry about."

"You've seen him, James, haven't you?" asked Doris, quietly.

"Who do you mean?"

"That young man who looks like Tristan. Don't avoid the question, James."

"Oh, him?" replied James casually. "Yes, I saw him the other evening actually, Doris. It's not Tristan."

"You sure, James?"

James put down his pen and sat back in his chair.

"How can it be, Doris? Think about it: We buried Tristan two years ago. You were there. This man is obviously an impostor."

"Or a ghost... Do you believe in ghosts, James?"

James laughed. "I don't think I do, Doris. I try to keep an open mind and not dismiss any possibility, but what would Tristan's ghost want with us? One thing I do know for sure is that Tristan would never harm, hurt or worry either of us. No, this guy isn't a ghost, he is flesh and blood just like the rest of us, I am sure of it."

"Well, why is he watching us. Why does he keep appearing like that?"

"Oh, he wants something."

"What do you mean, James?"

"Oh yes, he's after something. I don't know what just yet, but I promise you one thing, Doris. I am going to find out."

It was late afternoon when James rang the doorbell of the Manor House. He had not asked for an appointment or had been invited. At first, no one appeared to answer the door and so he rang the bell again.

Eventually, the heavy old door slowly opened and Peggy Skinner appeared in the doorway.

"Oh, Mr Young. 'Tis you. I'm so sorry to have kept you waiting. I was upstairs with me Lady. Do please come in."

"Is Lady Lotitia still unwell, Peggy?"

Peggy nodded. "I'm afraid so. Please don't tell anyone, but I am very concerned about her. Sir Toby is too."

James also was concerned. He was very fond of Lady Lotitia and it had been many weeks since he had last seen her.

"I am very sorry to hear this Peggy. May I ask? What is wrong with her? Is she seeing a doctor?"

"That she is, young sir. It's not that easy. You see it's not a cold or flu. 'Tis all up here," said Peggy sadly, pointing to her head.

"I understand," replied James. "Maybe it is depression. Some people are like this from time-to-time."

"No, 'tis not that, young sir. 'Tis more than that, I knows. In all the years I have worked for me Lady, I have never seen her like this before. Well, maybe just once…" Peggy, now realising that she had said too much, shook herself and quickly changed the subject.

"Now what can we do for you, Mr Young?"

"Well, I really came to see Lady Lotitia. I am worried about her and thought I should see her. Remember you asked me to call and see her, Peggy?"

"Indeed I did, young sir," whispered Peggy. "Please wait here and I will see if she is awake. She asked to see you the other day, which is why I mentioned it. She is very weak, but I am sure she would like to see you."

After what seemed to James to be some considerable time, Peggy reappeared. She scurried towards him, looking serious.

"Me Lady is delighted that you have come to see her. Now, she has just got up especially to see you and is sitting in her bedroom. She is worried that you will not recognise her as she hasn't been to the hairdresser for quite a while. I told her she looked fine and that I am sure you would understand."

"Of course I will, Peggy," said a relieved James, fearing that Lady Lotitia would not agree to see him. Peggy led the way up the grand staircase to a magnificent corridor on the first floor. It was crammed with beautiful furniture, oil paintings and many items reflecting the lives of its present as well as previous occupants.

"It's this door here," said Peggy, knocking softly on the door at the far end of the corridor.

"Do come in, James," came a voice that James recognised so well.

Lady Lotitia, looking weak and very pale, smiled as James entered the large bedroom. She was sitting in a comfortable armchair in the well-lit bay window overlooking her beloved rose garden. She beckoned James to the chair at her side. James hardly recognised her as the strident and eccentric woman who had questioned him so vigorously at his interview, the first time that he had met her.

"I have asked Peggy to bring you some tea, but I don't think there will be any scones as Cook is off duty today," she smiled at James who shook her hand and sat beside her. "I am pleased you have come, James. How are you, what?"

"I'm alright, thank you, Lady Lotitia, but more to the point, how are you? I have been very worried about you."

The old lady sighed, and for the first time James saw a frightened and vulnerable old lady, instead of the tyrannical and eccentric image that Lady Lotitia liked to cultivate for the benefit of those who didn't really know her.

"Not too good, James. Not too good at all, what?" Lady Lotitia seemed to drift away into a kind of sleep. Her eyes closed. She was conscious, but not really awake.

"She goes like this sometimes, Mr Young, don't worry," whispered Peggy who had re-entered the room silently with a pot of tea and some biscuits.

"She's like this for a few minutes and then she wakes up and is almost back to normal again. Just pour your tea and wait for a few minutes. It's the drugs that Dr Jackson gave her to calm her down, I think. Sorry, Mr Young, I could only find some shortbread biscuits today. If we had known you were coming, I would have asked Cook to bake you something special."

"You are very kind to me, Peggy, but I must watch my waistline!" said James, patting his stomach. Peggy smiled and scurried out of the room.

After a few minutes, Lady Lotitia's eyes re-opened. "Hello, James. Where did you come from? Is it the governors' meeting? My, how time flies. I don't think I have read the minutes of the last one yet. How is the fire? What?"

"No, it's not a governors' meeting, Lady Lotitia. I just came to see you."

"Thank God!" exclaimed the sick woman, "I don't think I could cope with Hubert's ramblings tonight. He means well, but I find him so tiresome sometimes. Now, how about a gin, what?"

"Well, I'm very happy with tea," replied James.

"May I pour a cup for you? It's still nice and hot."

"Oh very well," snapped Lady Lotitia. "I expect Toby has told you that foolish Dr Jackson said that I have to take endless pills and no alcohol, what? I tell you, James, it's the alcohol I need, not the damned pills!" Lady Lotitia rested her head back on the comfortable armchair and James thought she was about to drift into sleep once again.

He took his chance and said quietly, "You've seen him, haven't you?"

Lady Lotitia raised her head and stared at James. "Yes, I've seen him. That boy will put me in my grave. Make no mistake, James, he will put me in my grave."

James spotted the young man again the following afternoon as he and Prince were going for their usual walk in the nearby woods. James had just thrown the blue ball that Christian had given the playful dog and Prince had gone hurtling into the undergrowth trying to find it. The young man appeared suddenly, once again dressed in pale blue denim trousers and a tight fighting white shirt, sitting upon an old tree stump in the distance. Prince had growled furiously when he spotted him, but upon James' command, had returned obediently to his side. James, determined to receive answers to his many questions, chased towards the young man, with Prince bounding at his side. However, by the time that they had reached the tree stump, the young man had once again disappeared.

"Hi, James. Where have you been? I've been calling you all week. Are you trying to avoid me?" came the angry voice at the end of the telephone.

"I'm sorry, Christian. It's been one hell of a week. I have so much to tell you. I'm sorry for not returning your calls."

"Hmm, well that's nothing new, is it?" continued an angry Christian. "Either you want to see me or you don't." In a calmer voice Christian said quietly, "I miss you very much, James, and Prince."

"I'm not making excuses, Christian, I promise," pleaded James, now realising how hurt his friend was. "I will tell you everything when I see you. You will understand, I know."

"Hmm, well I better had, Jay. I love you, you know."

"You mean a lot to me as well, Christian, you know that."

"OK, I get it. Well, I will just have to try harder to 'woo' you, I guess. It's your birthday next week, James, and knowing how you hate surprises, I have arranged a little surprise for you," Christian laughed wickedly.

James smiled to himself. One thing that Tristan and Christian had in common was that they both loved surprises and took great delight in tormenting James, who hated anything that was not planned well in advance.

"Oh yes? Hmm, well, I guess it depends on what it is, I suppose."

"Well, I am collecting you and Prince in the car next Friday evening. Pack a small suitcase and tell Prince to pack his best toys as well."

"What? Is Prince coming as well? So we are not going to the theatre then?" said James, trying to sound disappointed. "I am sure Doris and George would have him for the weekend."

"Oh no, not our Prince. He is coming as well. After all, he is part of the family now!"

"Where are we going?"

"As I said, it's a surprise Jay. You will just have to wait and see, won't you?"

It was the end of the school day. The last of the afternoon sun was shining through the branches of the old horse chestnut tree, and James sat on Tristan's bench seat with a pile of exercise books at his side. It was now getting windy and James placed a heavy stone on top of the red exercise books to stop them from being blown away. He was marking Stuart's essay and chuckled to himself as he read the boy's response to some writing that James had set the class about 'Ambitions'. It was not one of the usual trite, "When I grow up I want to be a footballer" pieces of writing that James had expected, but a thoughtful and very moving account of how his young pupil wanted to work for one of the charities working in Africa. The boy went on to discuss the immense poverty, war and corruption in some of the countries in that continent. James felt a lump in his throat and immense pride in Stuart's words. They were some of the most powerful and thought provoking words that he had read from one of his pupils for some long time. He must share this essay with Emily the following day, and give this usually very quiet boy plenty of praise and encouragement.
James heard a rustle in the wind and became aware of a presence behind him.

"I know it's you, Sam. Stop playing games and come out from wherever you are. Talk to me properly."

There was a pause, a rustle of wind and suddenly the young man in pale blue jeans and a tight fitting white shirt stood in front of him grinning broadly.

"Hmm, I thought so," said James, glancing up at the young man, whilst pretending to continue correcting Stuart's work.

"My, you're a cool one, Mr Headmaster," came a voice, which James recognised as having a slight American accent.

James gave the young man a brief glance. "Well, it is Sam Rivers, if I'm not very much mistaken. I think you had better come and sit by me, on Tristan's seat," said James, in his best head teacher's voice, placing the pile of exercise books on his lap and beckoning that the young man should sit beside him.

"You're a bossy one, aren't you, Mr Headmaster?" said Sam, sitting beside James, a little hurt that James was not as surprised, nor giving him as much attention as he had expected and had hoped for.

"I know all about you, Sam Rivers," said James, dismissively. "So you thought you would play a few tricks on us, did you? I have often been told how much you look like Tristan." James looked at the blond-haired man at his side. "Yes, I guess you do a bit," he continued, with a shrug, and carried on with his marking.

"I do, don't I? Anyway, I think I am rather more handsome than Tristan," protested Sam.

James now looked carefully at the impostor. "Tristan had whiter teeth, more generous lips and was considerably younger. Also, I might add, he had a naturally tanned skin. He didn't use fake tan!"

"Ouch, you do have a sharp tongue!" exclaimed Sam Rivers, pretending to be shocked, and hitting James gently on the shoulder. "No need to be so harsh, Jay. I did my best. I just wanted to surprise you and old Doris. And I did, didn't I?"

"Well, maybe a little," nodded James, calmly. "I saw through it the second time, though. "You forget that I knew Tristan very well. You could never copy that. So, what is it you want?"

"Ooh, you are 'Mr Cool', aren't you?" replied Sam, putting his arm around James and began to stoke his hair gently. "I just thought that you and I could carry on where Tristan left off. I thought you would like that."

James stood up, shaking with anger. "How dare you! There was only one love in my life and you are trying to make a joke of that. How dare you! Why don't you go back to the hole you came from?"

"You mean back to the rose garden, I suppose?"

James suddenly remembered the significance of what he had said and continued, "Anyway, you are supposed to be dead. Yes, in the rose garden."

"I'm sorry, 'Mr Touchy'," laughed the impostor. "I didn't mean to upset you. Far from it. As you can see, I'm far from dead and I have no intention of returning to feed the roses, which I have to tell you, are nothing more than a packet of dried-up old tea leaves." Sam's teeth gleamed as he said this.

Despite James' earlier comments, he could see that Sam Rivers was indeed a very handsome man. "Well, you still haven't told me what you want? Tell me!" he demanded fiercely.

"I'm here to see my mother. She will be so pleased to see me after all these years," replied Sam defensively. By now, James had calmed down and sat once again at the side of Sam Rivers. "I see," he nodded.

"If you will only give me some of your time, I will tell you everything and why I am here, Jay."

"That's another thing. Why do you call me 'Jay' and 'Mr Headmaster'?" exploded James. "Only Tristan called me that."

"I know a lot about you, Jay. I have been watching you for a very long time. You would be surprised at what I know about you." This time, Sam's tone of voice was almost threatening and James began to feel very uneasy.

"Well, why don't you just go and see her, and then clear off. We don't need you here!" he shouted.

"Oh, I think you do, James. Just think how wonderful it would be to be back in Tristan's arms, and he in your bed. You know you want to, Jay. Just give me a chance. One tiny chance. You won't regret it."

"How dare you!" exploded James once again. "I could never feel anything for you. You, you impostor!"

"Maybe not now, but you will in time," came Sam's persuasive soft voice.

"Never! So why are you here?"

"For an intelligent man, you can be so 'thick' sometimes, Jay," came a voice that sounded so much like Tristan's reprimanding tone of voice.

"Just clear off and leave me alone!" yelled James.

"Now, that's not a very nice thing to say, is it? You asked, and I told you. I am here to see my mother," repeated Sam, in his soft voice.

"If you didn't know already, she's in an old people's home now. She lost her mind. I cannot remember where she is exactly, but I could soon find out. Anything to get rid of you!"

"Oh dear, not that 'old bat'," replied Sam, calmly. "I thought she was long dead anyway."

"But she's your mother?" began James.

"To hell she is!" exclaimed Sam Rivers, his brilliant blue eyes flashing dangerously. "That old woman is not my mother!"

"OK, OK, calm down," said James, taken aback by Sam's sudden outburst. "Well, so who is your mother then?"

"Lady Lotitia Peatwhistle, of course! Don't you recognise the family resemblance, Mr Headmaster?" announced Sam Rivers, proudly.

Chapter 10

Birthday Celebrations

James walked into the small and welcoming restaurant in Abbotsford. He looked nervously inside the near-empty dining room. There was no one else to be seen other than a young couple at the far end of the room, huddled together giggling and whispering excitedly.

"Table for two wasn't it?" said the welcoming young waitress. "You can either wait in the lounge until your guest arrives, or sit at your table right away. I can get you a drink whilst you are waiting. What can I get you, sir?"

"I think I'll sit at the table to wait, thank you. Just a glass of red wine, please," said James, looking anxiously at his watch.

"Right you are, sir. Now you just let me know when you want to order something and I'll be right over. You've been here before, haven't you? It was some time back wasn't it? I think I remember you and a young gentleman coming in and asking for a vegetarian dish."

James lied, "No, I don't recall having been here before. Maybe it was someone else?"

James walked to the table that had been reserved for him at the opposite side of the room – well away from the young couple. He hadn't wanted to come here anyway, but Sam had insisted that they meet for dinner. James, not wishing to be seen in public with Sam, had suggested going for a drink at a pub far away from Prior's Hill.

However, Sam had insisted that the 'The Pantry' in Abbotsford would be an ideal place to meet and talk, and James had reluctantly agreed. It was a weekday evening and James was confident that he wouldn't meet anyone who knew him. After all, Abbotsford was usually lifeless on weekday evenings. James had been to the restaurant once or twice before with Tristan, and he had been hoping that he would not be recognised or remembered.

"They do several vegetarian meals there too, Jay," Sam had told him thoughtfully at their last meeting. That was another thing that James didn't understand. How did Sam Rivers know so much about him?
Despite having serious misgivings about the stranger that had suddenly burst into his life, James was curious to find out much more about the circumstances that had brought Sam back to Prior's Hill, and the link that he claimed to have with the Peatwhistle family.

Whilst sipping his glass of red wine, James' mind went back to some two years earlier when, during a tearful conversation with Lady Lotitia, she had told him that Sir Toby had sent their only child, Giles, away from Prior's Hill in disgrace to America after discovering that he was gay. Giles' childhood friend, Sam Rivers, then an estate worker for Sir Toby, had followed him to America.

Lady Lotitia had later told James that her beloved son, Giles had died from AIDS and it was his lover, Sam Rivers, who had brought Giles' ashes home. Sam too had later died from the same disease, and the remains of the two boys had been buried together, secretly, in Lady Lotitia's rose garden.

The villagers had not been told the truth and were still under the impression that Giles Peatwhistle, who would one day have inherited the Peatwhistle Estate, was alive and well and was a successful businessman in New York. Sam Rivers, it was said, had been stabbed and killed by a drugs gang in New York. Now, it would seem, much of this story was in doubt.

"Good evening, Mr Headmaster," came a 'chirpy' voice.

James looked across the small dining table and saw a grinning Sam Rivers sitting in front of him.

"My God, how did you get there? I didn't see you come in!" exclaimed James.

"I'm just light on my feet, Jay. Anyway, you seemed to be in another world. What were you thinking about?"

"Oh, just this and that," smiled James, shaking Sam's outstretched hand. Sam looked as handsome as ever and was no longer wearing his trademark jeans and white shirt, but a pair of smart trousers and a dark blue, crushed velvet jacket.

"Don't I get a kiss? Aren't you pleased to see me?" said Sam softly, as the waitress placed a glass of beer in front of him.

"Not here and no, not particularly," snapped James. "The waitress already recognises me," he hissed. "Just keep your voice down, will you?"

Sam laughed, "Oh well, you didn't say never then, so I guess I am still in with a chance. Yes, I had forgotten. You came here for your twenty-ninth birthday, didn't you? I remember now. As I recall, you had pasta. Anyway, why are you ashamed to be seen with me?"

"Well, that's just the point. Of course I bloody am!" retorted James. "You are supposed to be dead, remember? Whatever will people think?"

James regretted speaking those words as soon as they had left his lips. Sam roared with laughter: his white teeth gleaming in the candlelight.

"Oh, Jay. Sometimes you can be so pompous, but we wouldn't have you any different, would we?" Sam stretched across the table in an attempt to hold James' hand.

"I, I didn't mean it like that, and you know it. It's just that you are supposed to be dead. I just don't know what to think about all this."

"Well, that's why I'm here. Just chill out, Jay. Let's enjoy ourselves and maybe, if you are a good boy, I will tell you more of my story. You will be fascinated, I know."

"Maybe!" exclaimed James. "It had better be a good story, after all this nonsense."

"Well, I must say," began Sam, trying to look badly disappointed, "I had rather hoped that you would have asked me to enjoy a cosy meal in your flat this evening. I would love to see Prince again, and maybe I could have stayed over?"

For once, James sat speechless, looking at this impostor in his life.

"Hmm, well maybe not," continued Sam, looking at James' horrified reaction to his teasing. "We shall just have to make the best of it here. Never mind, there's always another time. We should have asked the lovely Christian to join us as well, don't you think? He is such a sweetie." Sam picked up the menu and started studying it closely. "Great, I see they do garlic mushrooms, I love those, don't you?"

"You leave Christian out of it! I am here to listen to you as you asked. There's nothing between us and there never will be. You may look a bit like Tristan, but you are nothing like him."

"Well, maybe and then again, maybe not," replied Sam mysteriously. "You could have said no to my invitation this evening, but you came, didn't you? Go on, admit it. You are not only intrigued, but you like me as well, don't you? Just a little bit, maybe?"

"You talk nonsense, Sam. I came here out of good manners, nothing more, and, yes, I am curious to find out what you are up to. After all, you seem to have been trailing me. Why?"

"Mmm, I see you have a choice of vegetable risotto or pizza, Jay. I'm sorry, it doesn't seem to be quite as good as the last time we were here."

"There you go again! We have never been here. I came here with Tristan, not you!"

"OK, OK, if that's what you want to think..."

James and Sam said little more until after Sam's garlic mushrooms had been served. James had decided to have vegetable soup, but regretted it immediately he tasted it. He put his spoon on the plate and pushed it to one side.

"Don't you like it, Jay? Look, I'll get the waitress to get you something else."

"No, it's alright, Sam. I thought I could taste some meat stock, that's all. Anyway, I'm not really in the mood for soup. I'll wait for the pizza instead." James had ordered a vegetarian pizza and was surprised to see that Sam had ordered the same.

"Are you a vegetarian then, Sam?"

"I guess. When you've lived with one, it just becomes a habit."

"There you go again," snapped James, "You are pretending to be Tristan again. I wish you would stop your play-acting!"

"What have I said, this time!" exclaimed Sam, looking genuinely surprised at James' outburst. "Giles became vegetarian for health reasons and, in the end, it became too much of a bother to cook something different for myself. Why did that upset you?"

"I'm sorry," said James, now feeling contrite. "I just thought... Never mind, so tell me about Giles, Sam."

"Well, I think you know it all, really," began Sam.

"No, I want to hear it from you, Sam. I have heard about you from other people, but there are so many different stories. I want the truth."

"Another drink? How about a bottle of wine?"

"No, I'm working tomorrow," replied James.

Sam beckoned the waitress across. "A bottle of what my friend has just had and two fresh glasses, please."

"I said, no I didn't want another," protested James.

"You will. Trust me," replied Sam, breezily.

"You told me that Lady Lotitia is your mother," began James, once again trying to steer Sam back on course.

"And so she is, Jay," Sam paused, and poured himself a glass of wine from the newly arrived bottle of wine and, without asking, poured a fresh glass for James too.

"A toast is called for," began Sam. "I would like to wish you a Very Happy Birthday, Mr Headmaster," he began, standing up as he made his toast.

"Shhh, sit down. You're embarrassing me," whispered James, shocked. "Anyway, it's not until the end of the week."

"I know," said Sam, " But I thought that as you would be away for the big day, and I had you here to myself tonight, I would make it special."

"Well, it certainly is different," agreed James, now reluctantly beginning to enjoy the evening. "This is a meal that I won't forget in a long time. Anyway, how do you know I'm going away for my birthday?"

Sam ignored the question.

"I am the product of a love tryst between my beloved mother, Lotitia Peatwhistle and some bit of 'rough' from the North," he began. "My stepfather, as that's what I call Toby, was abroad for nearly a year and Lotitia got bored, very bored. She was a lively young woman in her youth and after years of a loveless and childless marriage to a man older than herself, yearned for much more." Sam laughed, "It sounds like the beginning of one of those romantic novels, doesn't it?"

James smiled and nodded, and began to sip the wine that Sam had poured for him.

"It's the old, old story," continued Sam, who James now recognised as a good storyteller. "Husband away for too long, wife gets bored and starts getting involved in a bit of 'hanky panky' that she shouldn't have. In Lotitia's case, she began an affair with a lorry driver, and I was the product of a night of alcohol-induced sex without protection. Not much to be proud of, is it?"

Sam paused, as he took another sip of wine. "I guess it could have been worse. At least it wasn't rape and, from what I know about my real father, he was certainly quite a stunner by all accounts and she was up for it."

Sam Rivers beamed at James from across the table and held out his hand, which James ignored.

"Well, Lotitia was frightened at what Toby would say when she found out that she was pregnant. She couldn't pass it off as Toby's because he had been away and, in view of the family honour thing, knew that Toby would immediately divorce her. Toby desperately wanted a son and heir, but a love-child was certainly not the answer. Lotitia feigned illness and went to stay with friends in London until I was born. No one knew, other than Aunt Peggy."

"You mean, Peggy Skinner, Lady Lotitia's maid?" interrupted James.

"The very same 'potty' woman," nodded Sam. "That bloody woman nearly ruined my life. It was her who suggested that Lotitia give me up to her sister, Rita Rivers."

"I see," nodded James, beginning to fit the pieces of the jigsaw into place.

"Rita was a childless woman, who was happy not to have been lumbered with one. She lived in one of Toby's 'tied' cottages and it was soon made clear to her that she would only be able to continue living there, if she agreed to take me on as her son."

"Was there a Mr Rivers?"

"Yeah there was, for a time. A bully and a drunkard. John Rivers used to beat me. Rita went away for a bit when Lotitia was pregnant, and then returned with me. She told John that I was his. He never asked any more questions, but he knew I wasn't. He used to beat me to get his own back on his unfaithful wife, or so he thought."

"That's dreadful, Sam. I am so sorry."

"No need to be," grinned Sam. "I got my own back when I was about seven or eight years old. One day he was working on the chimney above my room. He had been drinking heavily that morning." Sam stopped, looked at James and then suddenly burst out laughing. "Should we say he had a hangover that he never got over!"

"What happened?"

"Well, the ladder he was standing on went up past my bedroom window. When he was at the top, I pushed the ladder away from the wall and he impaled himself on some iron railings below. You know, those tall ones with the narrow pointed spikes. I could hear him screaming for ages. Dreadful gurgling screams, but it pleased me to hear them. I can still hear them sometimes. Yes, I got my own back alright."

"Did you get help for him?" asked James, now shocked by what he was hearing.

"No, I just closed the window and put on my headphones. Lotitia had given me a new cassette player the day before. I listened to that instead. After a while, the screams stopped. It took weeks to get all the blood off the path and railings, though."

James was silent as he realised that the man he was having dinner with was a cold-blooded killer.

"You killed him?"

"Yes, what's wrong?"

"That's an appalling thing to do. Not even to get help for him either. It's wicked, Sam. Surely someone found out!"

"Do you want to hear this bloody story or not? No, of course not. Sure, folk had their suspicions about what happened, but how could dear little Sam do such a thing? No, I am never caught! You see, James, I am rather clever as, one day, you will no doubt discover."

James sensed that Sam was now becoming agitated, and wondered what he meant by 'I am never caught'. He let Sam continue his story.

"Mother, or should I say Rita, went a bit loopy after that. I can't really remember too much about it. Aunt Peggy used to come to the cottage to see us and sometimes take me up to the big house. I liked it there, it felt right. Lotitia always made a fuss of me and bought me things; new things, not all the old second-hand rubbish Rita used to give me from the charity shop. She made me feel special and I felt at home there. I was more at home there than in the grubby little cottage where I lived with Rita," Sam added, bitterly. "I now know why."

"What about, Giles?" asked James, now desperate to know more of Sam's story.

"Giles was born about a year after me. I think I had triggered some kind of maternal feelings in Lotitia, and Giles arrived soon after. Toby knew about me then, but always refused to see me. He would disappear whenever I was around. So, as you can see, it became natural for Giles and I to be, and play, together. We became like brothers. They were good times."

The waitress arrived carrying two large pizzas. Her eyes fell upon Sam Rivers and she looked startled.

"These look and smell delicious," said James, trying to divert the waitress' attention from Sam.

"Well, you just let me know if you want anything else," said the waitress, not taking her eyes off Sam.

"We both went to your school. It was a good little school and I was happy there. The headmaster was a bit strict, but I have happy memories of playing cricket on the school field. I was always playing cricket. I was very good at it, too," said, Sam, proudly.

"I know you were," replied James, now moving on from being quite so horrified that he was dining with a murderer. After all, he reasoned, maybe Sam did have a good reason, however wrong, that made him do what he did.

"How the hell do you know that?" said Sam, sounding astonished.

"You see, it's different when the tables are turned, isn't it? You say you know everything about me, but I also know a fair amount about you," laughed James. "I am only teasing, we have some old silver cups in school with your name engraved on them."

"Oh, I see," laughed Sam, now looking more relaxed. "More wine, Jay?"

"Yes, please," nodded James. Sam was right; wine did help.

"Where was I? Yes, Giles Peatwhistle was there as well. We were inseparable from the start. We did everything together and went everywhere together. I was at the Manor House far more than my own home. Rita didn't care, I don't think she even noticed whether I was there or not. They were good days. Maybe my best days," he added sadly.

"It was good that you found such a good friend."

"I guess. It ended soon enough, though. Giles was sent away to prep school when he was about nine or ten and I stayed behind at Prior's Hill. It was never the same after that. Lotitia rarely asked me over then, unless it was holiday time and Giles was around. I used to look forward to the holidays when he came home."

James nodded, "When did you realise that you were in love with him?"

Sam laughed, "Whoever said I was in love with him?! He was a good 'shag', I suppose. Picked up all sorts of tricks from that posh school of his. He tried them on me, and I liked it."

"So, you're not gay?"

"Depends what you mean, I suppose. I like both. I guess you would call it bisexual, nowadays. Giles had a good body, liked cricket and I guess I was just happy to play ball," he grinned.

James nodded.

"As we got older and during those long summer days," Sam continued, "Giles used to ask me up to the big house. There was so much space and we would get up to all sorts of things. Lotitia never seemed to mind as long as we kept out of her way. Once I went into her bedroom and started looking in cupboards, drawers and boxes. I don't know why, but I guess I was curious or maybe I was looking for some money. I never had much at Rita's. Anyway, I found some letters that changed my life and my view of the Peatwhistles."

Sam paused and looked across at the far side of the room to the couple who were just leaving. "Nice blouse, great boobs," he said loudly and beamed as the young woman passed by, now pink with embarrassment. Her young man glared at him and put his hand around her protectively.

"Stuck up bugger," yelled Sam after the young man, who turned as if to thump him. "You lost your sense of humour?" The young woman pushed the young man out of the restaurant. "I was only being friendly. She wasn't much to look at, was she?"

"You've already had too much to drink, Sam," said James, concerned at the outburst. "How about some coffee?"

"No, I want another bottle of wine," demanded Sam.

James ordered two coffees. Sam didn't appear to notice and carried on with his story.

"What were in the letters?"

"Oh, this and that. The ramblings of a near middle-aged woman mostly, but I soon realised that in one of the letters from her friend that she was referring to a baby who was being looked after by Rita Rivers. I was the baby they were talking about, Jay, and it proved that Lotitia is my mother. I still have the letter, and a few others," he added proudly, tapping the side pocket of his jacket.

"You kept them?"

"Oh yes. A kind of protection, Jay. I'm not stupid. I knew they would come in useful one day. I was always being given treats you see. Maybe a new toy, a cassette recorder, new cricket pads, sweets and things. I felt like I was a pet dog being given 'tit bits' from the master's table. I tell you this James, it was after I found those letters that things began to change."

"How do you mean?"

"I mean from that point I was no longer content to be a lap dog getting treats from the top table. I wanted to be at the top table and not beneath it!" Sam's eyes flashed dangerously once again. The brilliant blue of his eyes flashing in the candlelight.

James knew that Sam had to calm down. The waitress was already looking at him and pointing him out to the barman.

"I knew then that I had to stick to Giles through thick and thin. Yes, Jay, we were friends and, yes, we became lovers. Then Toby mucked it all up. He discovered that Giles was gay and sent him away. I followed Giles and soon we were having a pretty good life together in San Francisco. Giles was livid with his father and refused to speak to him. He used to write to his mother now and again, but in the end, Toby got a private detective to find Giles. He was furious when he found out that I was still with him. He cut off Giles' allowance and so we both had to get jobs, or rather, I did."

James nodded.

"Giles got into all sorts. He still had plenty of money and so he took drugs, had numerous 'one-night stands' and in the end he was ill, very ill. People were catching this disease all around us in San Francisco, Jay. It was terrible. It was like some terrible curse was taking hold of the city. Friends, work mates, everyone around us were dropping like flies. The money was gone and the doctors' bills were horrendous. I couldn't keep working and care for Giles at the same time. I didn't know what to do."

Sam started crying and James was alarmed. He put his hand across the table to comfort him.

"That must have been an awful time in your life," James said softly. "What did you do?"

"I wrote to Lotitia asking for help. I told her it was serious and that Giles was dying. She didn't reply to my letters. I telephoned and begged, but she wouldn't take my calls. In the end, one day Toby answered and said he would get the police on to me if I carried on calling for money. He told me never to call him again."

James shook his head, finding it hard to believe what he was hearing. "I don't understand. Giles was her son, and Toby's too."

"Giles had these awful lesions all over his body. They were so painful and would appear overnight. He became very weak, lost a huge amount of weight and just gave up the will to fight. Yes, James, you asked if I loved him. Of course, I bloody loved him! Why else would I have nursed him into his grave," Sam sobbed.

"You and Giles went through a very bad time," said James, quietly, now feeling very sorry for the unhappy young man in front of him. "I know a little about AIDS, but I had no idea how it was destroying whole communities in the States. I just cannot believe the way in which you and Giles were treated by the Peatwhistles. It sounds so unlike them. What I still don't understand, is why you are here, following me around like this. What is it you want from me?"

"It's easy, James. I want you to help me get what is rightfully mine. Mine and Giles. Giles is now gone, but I am still here. I looked after him and it is me who should inherit the Peatwhistle estate." Sam's blue eyes started flashing dangerously once again.

"You're not in the Peatwhistle blood line, Sam. The Peatwhistle line stopped with Giles. He was Sir Toby's son, and not you. You have no possible claim on the estate!"

"Have I not? Lotitia is my mother and she is a very wealthy woman in her own right. Surely what she has should be mine, after all, I am her only living son. If anything should happen to Sir Toby, some of his estate would be claimed by Lotitia as well. How dare you say I have no claim on the estate, James!"

"Well, I can tell you now, Sam Rivers, I am sorry to hear what you have been through, but I have no intention in helping you to upset the Peatwhistles. They are my friends and I like them. I will play no part in your plans."

"You already are doing, James. Who said anything about upsetting them anyway? I don't want to upset them. I just want them to realise that I am their only, dear son and they can, like all loving parents, in time, reward me accordingly," continued Sam coldly.

"Well, you don't need me," snapped James.

"Of course, I do. They trust you and they don't trust me. Toby hates the ground I walk on and Lotitia wishes that I hadn't been born. Now, if you and I should become lovers, things would be very different. I know you wouldn't find it too hard, Jay. You already like me. I know I can make you love me. It would be like being with Tristan all over again. See!"

James had initially given Sam Rivers the benefit of the doubt, but now James realised that he was talking to a very confused, unstable and maybe dangerous young man. He knew that he would have to handle the situation very carefully.

"Look, Sam. Go and see Lotitia and talk to her. I am sure she loves you. I have heard her talk about you both very lovingly. She is a good person. Sir Toby too would accept you in time, I am confident. After all, you are their only link with Giles and you are Lotitia's son. Go and talk to them."

"You certainly are naive, James. I always thought you were. Surely you can see that some things never change? With the Peatwhistles it is all about blood, honour, 'stiff upper lip' and keeping the locals in their place. How do you think they would feel about Lotitia's bastard son, who is supposed to be dead, taking over the Peatwhistle Estate?"

"Who said anything about taking over the Estate? Surely what you want is acceptance into the family and some help to start again?"

"Oh no, James!" exclaimed Sam, angrily. "You have missed the point yet again. I intend to claim the Peatwhistle Estate and what is rightfully mine and, one way or another, you are going to help me to do it! Giles would want that as well," he added.

"How do you work that one out?" snapped James, appalled at the implications of what he had heard.

Sam didn't seem to hear his reply, but continued speaking, as if in a trance.

"Some of our friends and a local charity helped us with drugs and medical bills, but in the end, he went. I tell you, James, it was not a good end. Giles died in agony. I know he would still have died, but they could have helped him to die in comfort and in peace. I shall never forgive the Peatwhistles for making him suffer like that, and it is now time for them to pay!" Sam started sobbing again.

A concerned waitress suddenly appeared. "Is everything alright?" she asked James. "Is your friend ill? Is there anything that we can do to help?"

"It's your bloody pizzas," groaned Sam. "They're off. They made me ill. Oh, my stomach," he groaned, dramatically. "You've poisoned me!"

The concerned waitress beckoned to Adrian, the chef, who had appeared at the door of the kitchen. He ran across, looking very concerned.

"I need a doctor," groaned Sam, turning a strange colour, as he started twitching and gurgling loudly.

"I'll phone for a doctor," shouted the waitress.

"Let's get him some air," cried Adrian.

"I need a bucket, I'm going to throw up," groaned Sam. "I wanna shit as well!"

"Oh God, let's move him quick," yelled Adrian.

James helped Adrian to carry Sam out of the door. They sat him on the steps and propped his head on a cushion that the chef had thoughtfully brought with him.

"The ambulance is on its way," yelled the waitress. "I'll get you a glass of water!"

"I'll get the bucket," added Adrian, helpfully.
James turned to speak to the young chef.

"Run for it, Jay. Run for it now!" came gleeful laughter from the doorway.

James turned around suddenly. Sam had vanished.

"You all right, James?" said Christian the following evening. "I hope you are looking forward to your birthday surprise. I am really excited! Where were you last night, by the way? I phoned several times, but there was no answer."

"Oh, I had a meeting," lied James. "Yes, I can't wait, Christian. Remind me, where are we going?"

"Oh, crafty? Don't try that one again. I'm not telling you!"

James laughed. "Well, you must admit it was a good try. I am looking forward to spending some time with you, Christian. It seems ages since we had a meal together. How many nights do we pack for?"
"Two nights, James, you know that already!"

"Christian? Look, Christian, please don't take this the wrong way, but have you ever told anyone the pet names you have for me?"

"You mean, the name 'Jay'? Well, I guess a few people may have heard me call you that already, but no, why?"

"No, I mean the other. The one I don't like you using. The one that Tristan used to call me, you know 'Mr Headmaster'. I hate you calling me that."

"I know you do, Jay and that's why I don't call you it anymore. Tristan told me he called you that when you were being pompous, but I have never told anyone else about the name, nor will I ever call you it again if you don't like it. You know that. Why do you ask?"

"Thanks, Christian. Yes, I do know that. No, it's just something someone said... Have you told anyone about my birthday next weekend?"

"Why are you asking me these things? Are you OK, James? I may have mentioned it to Doris, but that's all. You have been behaving a bit strangely recently, Jay. Do you want me to come over for a chat and maybe a cuddle?"

James laughed, "Well, of course I would, and particularly the cuddle bit, but no, not tonight. I still have some marking to finish and I want an early night. Let's catch up properly at the weekend."

"OK, Jay, if that's what you want. I will see you on Friday then, say about five? You make sure that you leave school on time for once."

"I'll try. What's the news about the job, Christian? I meant to ask you the other day."

"I thought you would never ask, Jay. I turned it down."

"You did what? Why did you do that? It was such a great opportunity for you!"

"Yes, it was, but there will be other chances. Above all, it is you that is important to me, Jay. I love you and I want to be with you. The job can wait."

James was silent. He felt terrible. Christian had rejected a job offer because of him and, for his part, James didn't know if he felt the same way about his friend.

"Thank you, Christian. Look, let's talk about it properly at the weekend."

"James, there's a private call for you. She wouldn't give her name, but she sounded like 'that woman', Jasmine De Valle."

"Oh, shit!"

"Pardon, James," Doris, giggled. "She still has that effect upon you, then?"

James grinned. "Well, if I'm still on the phone after ten minutes, please intercept the line and say I am needed urgently to rescue a cat or maybe a football from a tree. Anything please, Doris."

"Hello, Jasmine. Good to hear from you. We did enjoy dinner with Paula and yourself last week. Thank you so much."

"You are more than welcome, James," came the strident voice at the end of the line. "I am so pleased you enjoyed it. We did too. Paul is such a scream, isn't he?"

"Yes, he, I mean she, certainly is. Good cook as well. We are very happy for you both."

"We must do it again very soon. We also liked Christian very much. Isn't he handsome? A lovely boy. James, you have a real treasure there," Jasmine purred.

"Thank you, Jasmine. It is very kind of you to say so. Now, what can I do for you?" James was anxious to get on. He had promised Julia that he would read a story to Class 1.

"James, there is just something that you ought to know. There's talk going around about you."

"Go on," said James, his breathing now heavy. He had a feeling what was about to come next.

"It's just that, young Debbie Ploughwright came into the library this morning to get a book for her mother. She knows that I know you. She said that you and a friend went to the restaurant where she works the other evening and that your friend was taken very ill. Is Christian alright? I was very concerned," probed Jasmine, in a voice of disbelief.

James' heart sank. He knew that once Jasmine was on the case, he would never hear the end of it. He decided that he would have to 'blag it' as best he could.

"No, it wasn't Christian. It was an old school friend, actually. He didn't feel well after the meal, but I'm sure it wasn't the food. I had the same and I was fine," added James hastily.

"Well, I am pleased Christian is alright," said Jasmine sounding relieved. "Young Debbie was very concerned because her boss said if it was food poisoning they would be closed down, and she and the chef, Adrian, would get the sack. She is really worried."

"No, no, do please reassure them both, Jasmine. I am sorry we caused so much trouble. I did settle the bill because my friend left very suddenly."

"Well, that's what I didn't understand," persisted Jasmine. "Debbie said that your friend seemed to be very upset and gave the impression that he wanted to avoid paying, but I said that you were too honourable for that sort of thing."

James laughed, "Of course, Jasmine, why should she think that, I wonder? No, my friend had just a little too much to drink and he felt unwell. Maybe he was a little delirious, that's all."

Jasmine De Valle continued, knowing full well when she was being put off the scent. "Debbie says it was very strange because she remembers you eating there a while ago with Tristan. She says she is sure it was the same young man, but I told her it couldn't have been. After all, Tristan died over two years ago, didn't he?" questioned Jasmine with increasing incredulity.

"Look, Jasmine. I have to go now. I have a class waiting for me. Do please give Debbie my apologies and please tell her that she must have been mistaken about Tristan. It was just an old school friend visiting who had far too much to drink, that's all."

"Well, it does happen if one drinks too much, doesn't it James?" giggled Jasmine. "Well, anyway, I just wanted to make sure that you were both alright. Do please give my love to Tristan."

"You mean, Christian, Jasmine."

"Yes, of course I do. James, do you mind me asking? Are you 'two timing' Christian? I hope you don't mind me asking, but as you are a good friend, I care about you and what people are saying."

"It's none of your business and no I'm not," snapped James.

"I'm sorry James, but…"

"Good-bye, Jasmine," said James, coldly, replacing the receiver.

Doris came back into the room and looked at James, who sat silently, deep in thought.

"What did 'that woman' want?" she asked ungraciously. James remembered that Doris was not too keen on Jasmine De Valle and usually referred to her as 'that woman'.

James smiled. "Well, just a chat really. She caught me having dinner with Sam Rivers the other evening, that's all. She thinks I'm 'two timing' Christian."

"You did what?" Doris could not contain her curiosity. "You're not, are you?"

James ignored the latter question. "You know that guy who is pretending to be Tristan. Well, I found out it's Sam Rivers."

"You didn't tell me before?" said Doris accusingly. "I have been worried sick about that. I was sure it was a ghost."

"I wanted to be sure before I said anything, Doris. I was going to tell you earlier, but you were on that course and I have been teaching all day. No, it's Sam Rivers. He does look like Tristan though, doesn't he?"

"The resemblance is uncanny, James. If I'm not very much mistaken that's poor old Rita's boy. Yes, Rita Rivers. She lost her mind and is in a home somewhere. I thought young Sam was dead. I think he was somewhere in America. He was a good friend of Giles Peatwhistle, as I remember. I am sure Emily would know more than I do."

James knew that once Emily and Doris were on the case, Sam's secret would be out. He needed to find out more, much more about what was going on.

"Doris," he said urgently. "Well it seems he isn't dead and there are some strange things going on that I need to get to the bottom of. Please don't mention any of this to anyone for the moment, until I say. Is that alright with you?"

"Of course it is, James. You have only to say. You know I can keep a secret."

James put his arm around his reliable secretary. "I know the secret is safe with you, Doris. I know I can always rely on you."

"James? Is Sam Rivers trying to blackmail you or get money from you? What does he want?"

James shook his head, but he knew that Doris' comments were not far from the truth. "No, of course not. What have I to hide and I haven't got any money anyway! No, he's just a bit strange, that's all. He wants to surprise his mum, I guess."

"Funny way of showing it," grumbled Doris. "Anything else you want me to do? How about I look up all his details in the records and in the log book? That might shed a bit of light."

"Brilliant!" laughed James, suddenly spinning the little woman around on her new swivel chair. "Just brilliant! Yes, please you do that as soon as you can and let me know what you find."

Doris shrieked with laughter. "Stop that, James. My head's spinning enough already!"

Chapter 11

The Surprise

"Happy Birthday, James," chorused the staff as he walked into the staff room at break time.

James blushed. He hated these occasions, but knew only too well, that school staff always enjoyed celebrating these significant events with their colleagues. He did too, but not when he was on the receiving end.

"Thank you everyone. Today, I am older, but I'm not sure if I'm any wiser."

"Well, we were all hoping for some improvement, James," giggled Doreen Sparkle.

"Thanks Doreen, and I love you too! By the way, I've brought some jam doughnuts in for you all, to help me celebrate."

James handed around a large plateful of sticky jam doughnuts and had thoughtfully remembered to provide some paper napkins as well. The staff gratefully took one each.

"I'll take one for Emily as well, and leave it for when she gets in from playground duty, James," said Doris thoughtfully. "Cedric and the dinner ladies can have theirs when they come in. I see you provided some for the kitchen staff as well, James."

James nodded, "Yes, I took those over earlier." He could never understand why it was that it was always the celebrant of the birthday who, traditionally brought in the staff room treats. Surely it should be the other way around? He took the last doughnut for himself and sat down, sipping his coffee.

"Any nice treats planned for tomorrow, James?" asked Julia, delicately peeling her doughnut apart, revealing its jammy core.

"Well, yes I have, as it happens," grinned James. "Christian is collecting me this evening and taking me away for a couple of days. Prince too! I am really looking forward to it."

"Where to?" asked Doreen, biting so vigorously into her doughnut that a dollop of red jam spurted out onto the side of her well-rounded cheeks. "Oops," she giggled, mopping her cheek with the paper napkin and licking her lips furiously.

James joined in with the hoots of laugher that came when the others had spotted Doreen's predicament. He looked happily at the supportive and friendly staff around him, now mostly covered with sugar around their mouths.

"Well, that's just it. I don't know. He says it's a surprise. I'm not that keen on surprises, but I shall just have to be patient and see."

"Our James, patient?" giggled Doris. "Look, James, George and I would be very happy to take Prince for the weekend if you prefer. He knows us well enough and we have had him to stay for a few times already. He is no trouble."

"Thanks, Doris. That's very kind and I know Prince would be happy with you, but, no, Christian was insistent that Prince must come as well."

The school bell rang; it was the end of playtime. Doreen groaned, "That was quick. I swear that as I get older, playtime gets shorter."

"I shouldn't worry too much, Doreen," smiled Anne. "Remember who is on duty this morning? Emily! Have you noticed that as it gets colder we tend to get a shorter break?"

James laughed, "I thought it was just me, Doreen. That explains it!"

"Oh, James, don't forget that you have Dr and Mrs Morgan coming in to see you this morning with their young daughter, Emily."

"Thanks for reminding me, Doris. It had slipped my mind. Yes, I'll show them around. Are they moving into the village?"

"Yes, they bought that old cottage up on The Green. It's been empty for ages. Dr Morgan is taking over from Dr Jackson, you know."

"Oh really? I liked Neil Jackson, he's been very good to the school with his first aid courses and letting us borrow all that equipment for our training day. When is he leaving? I must try and call in to thank him, and say good bye."

"He left months ago, James. I think he got a job in Ireland somewhere. Apparently there's less pressure on the Health Service over there and I think he has family living close by."

"Oh, that's a pity, I liked him."

It was just five o'clock when James and Prince arrived back at James' flat. James had already packed a suitcase and a bag for Prince, which he had left ready by the front door, and was relieved to see that there was no sign of Christian just yet.

He smiled to himself. Despite Christian's insistence that James be on time, it was invariably Christian who would be late. He just had time to take Prince for a run in the woods before they left.

"Hello, gorgeous," came a voice from behind a tree. "You pleased to see me?"

"Hello, Sam. I wondered when you would turn up again," said James, sighing. Sam's sudden appearances and disappearing acts no longer surprised him.

"No, I'm not, as it happens. You left me with a lot of explaining to do the other evening. First you feigned food poisoning that nearly got the chef and the waitress the sack, you made a frightful scene that my friends got to hear about and then you disappeared without paying. No, I am not pleased to see you, and I never want to have dinner with you again!" snapped James, concerned that Prince was glaring at and snarling very unpleasantly at Sam.

"Vicious dog you've got there, James. I wouldn't keep a dog like that!"

"Enough, Prince," commanded James, throwing the rubber ball for him. "Go, fetch!"

The young dog remained by James' side, still snarling at Sam. "What's the matter with you, Prince? Stop that right now!" Prince stopped snarling and James put him back on his lead and held him close and well away from Sam.

"I'd get rid of him, if he were mine."

"Well, that's your answer to everything, Sam Rivers, isn't it? Always the easy way out!" snapped James.

"Look, I can see that you're angry with me. I'm sorry about the other night. It was going to be my treat, honest, to celebrate your birthday. It's just that I forgot my wallet and I had no money on me. I didn't want you to pay. After all, it was your birthday treat."

"All you had to do was tell me the truth and I would have happily paid. Anyway, I don't expect anything from you. All that nonsense with the food poisoning? I really thought you were very ill at one point."

Sam grinned. "You must admit that I'm good, I'm very good! It started off as a bit of a joke and then I just got carried away with the part, that's all! I enjoyed it!"

"Well, I didn't," replied James, still angry. "Look, I'm short of time and I want to take Prince for a run. I must go."

"When are you going to help me, James?" asked Sam, blocking James' way on the path, with his outstretched arms.

"I thought I made it perfectly clear the other evening. Whatever quarrel you have with Peatwhistles, is of no concern of mine. Just leave me out of it and please stay out of my life. Get out of my way please."

Sam looked despondent and looked down at his shoes.

"You promised you would help, Jay. I need you to plead my case. They will listen to you."

"I did nothing of the kind, how dare you! I like the Peatwhistles. They have been good to me and I am not about to hurt them."

"Oh yes, I heard how thoughtful they were with you and your beloved Tristan. All that business with the cottage that they were going to let you live in, until they found about you, that is."

"That's all 'water under the bridge', now. Anyway, how do you know about all that?"

"As I said before, I know everything about you, Jay. I made it my business to."

"Look, I will spell it out once more. I cannot and, even if I could, I would not help you. You are a self-centred pretender and, however charming you can be, you don't fool me for one minute."

"Now, is that so, Mr Headmaster," replied Sam, slowly and carefully walking around James, his blue eyes flashing dangerously. "I believe you will have to help me eventually. You will have no choice, but to help me. I have spent a lot of time studying you, James, and I can destroy you in an instant, if you get in my way!"

"Are you threatening me?"

Prince growled and snarled at Sam, straining at his leash.

"No, not yet, but I will if needs be," grinned Sam. "Have a good weekend in London, won't you, Jay? I shall be thinking about you and, who knows, maybe I will be watching you as well," he laughed.

James walked on thoughtfully with Prince at his side. Sam disappeared.

"Where the hell have you been?"

Christian was standing outside James' gate, looking angry. Prince bounded up to the young man, who knelt down to make a fuss of the young dog. Soon he was covered with dog hairs, leaves and mud, and above all, many big licks. Christian started giggling; he was not one to stay angry for long.

"I'm sorry, I'm sorry. I was on time, I promise, but you weren't here and so I took Prince for a run. Then I met someone I knew and I got chatting. That's all," began James, holding Christian's hand.

"That's OK, James," said Christian, giving him a quick peck on the cheek, knowing full well that James hated such demonstrative behaviour in public places. However, Christian reasoned that as he was inside James' front gate it didn't count as a public place.

"Why didn't you let yourself into the flat? You could have made yourself some tea while you were waiting?"

"I don't have a key, James, do I?"

"No, sorry, I forgot."

"Who was it?"

"What?"

"Who did you meet in the woods?"

"Oh, er, just Jasmine. She sends her love to you," lied James.

At last James, Christian and a very happy dog piled in to Christian's battered old Ford Escort. Christian was not in the slightest bit interested in cars and James shuddered each time he rode in the once proud-looking car.

"You could try washing it sometimes," he began. "Maybe even a body re-spray. The engine seems OK, and it would give it a few more years. At least it wouldn't look such a heap of junk."

Christian laughed, "No, it's alright as it is. I've had it for years and I will use it until it finally dies on me."

"Hmm, that could well be sooner rather than later. You reckon it will get us to London?" muttered James, as the red Escort swept noisily out of the town.

"How do you know we're going to London? It was meant to be a surprise. Who told you, Doris?"

"You told Doris?" questioned James. "Anyone else?"

"What do you mean? No, of course not, James. Doris called to ask if we wanted her to look after Prince for the weekend. I said no because I wanted Prince to be with us. This is a family outing, see?" Christian smiled happily at his friend beside him. He did, in many ways, feel it was a family outing. James and Prince had been the closest that he had to having a family, with the exception of Aunt Eleanor and Uncle Frank that is.

The old car finally slowed down outside a smart looking large, detached house in Harrow, on the outskirts of the city. Christian drove through the impressive open gates and onto the sweeping driveway leading to the front door of the large house. The face that was watching at the window suddenly disappeared and Aunt Eleanor appeared beaming at the front door.

"Christian, Christian, thank goodness you have made it. I always worry about you in that old thing." She looked disapprovingly at the Escort. "Now, you must be James." Aunt Eleanor shook James' hand and then kissed him. "Welcome, James. I know you are a close friend of Christian and you are very welcome here. Is that your lovely dog?"

James opened the side door of the car and Prince bounded out relieved to be free at last, and sat looking at Aunt Eleanor.

"My goodness, what a handsome dog!" she exclaimed, patting Prince, "and so well behaved too. He is also very welcome. I like dogs, but we have never had one ourselves." Prince reciprocated with a large lick on the cheek. Aunt Eleanor chuckled, "I can see that we are going to be good friends, Prince. Do please come in."

Aunt Eleanor led James and Christian upstairs, Prince was told to stay downstairs because James thought that letting the large dog upstairs might be frowned upon.

"Oh, don't worry, James. I really don't mind Prince upstairs or in your bedroom. He is very welcome too."

She opened the door of a large bedroom and, because it was now dark, drew the heavy curtains across the large bay window overlooking the garden below. It was a pretty room, with large flowery wallpaper, a large double bed and beautiful antique furniture.

"It has a bathroom and shower over there, so you are quite self-contained," said Aunt Eleanor. "There's plenty of towels in the bathroom, but just ask if you need more."

"This is lovely," exclaimed James. "Thank you for letting Prince and I come to see you as well."

"Well, my dear, we have been wanting to meet you for ages. Christian is always talking about you and Prince. We feel we know you well already. Now come down and meet Frank when you are both ready. I thought I heard him just come in. He has had a late meeting tonight."

"Yes, I feel the same," lied James. Christian had told him very little about Aunt Eleanor and Uncle Frank, or indeed very little of his life before he had met James.

James' birthday weekend was memorable and it was clear that Christian had worked very hard to give James a birthday to remember. James had awoken on a sunny Saturday morning in Christian's arms, feeling relaxed and very happy. Prince was still snoring loudly from his bed at the side of the room. James rubbed Christian's tousled hair and kissed him.

"Good morning," he whispered gently in Christian's ear.

"Morning, Jay," grinned Christian. "Happy Birthday!" Prince heard that the boys were now awake and leapt over to the bed to join in the fun. He put his large paws on the side of the bed and looked at Christian and James with his loving, big brown eyes.

"I guess we had better not let him do that," laughed James. "He will get paw prints all over these lovely sheets."

"Relax, Jay. Today is your day and we are all going to enjoy it, including Prince." Christian jumped out of bed, rummaged in his holdall and came back with a small, neat parcel, which he gave to James with a large envelope.

James laughed, and opened the birthday card. He was touched by the loving words written inside and kissed Christian gratefully. He shook and felt the package, wondering what was inside. He ripped the wrapping open to find a beautiful presentation box that contained a gold fountain pen, together with a matching ball-point pen. Both had his name inscribed on their barrels.

"I know it's boring, but I asked Doris and she told me of all the fuss you made when your old fountain pen went missing. Tristan gave it to you, I know. I cannot replace Tristan's pen, but I can give you one of my own, with all my love," Christian kissed James lovingly.

"This is perfect, Christian, thank you. You are so thoughtful. Yes, I was upset when I lost the other pen, but this is just perfect."

"There's one from Prince too," said Christian passing James a large flat package, tied with a large red ribbon. "Go on, open it!" commanded Christian.

Inside the well-wrapped package was a gilt picture frame containing an oil portrait of Prince. It was beautifully done and had captured Prince's boundless enthusiasm for life perfectly.

"My goodness! Whoever did this is incredibly gifted," exclaimed James, admiringly. "This is a wonderful gift, Christian, I mean, Prince. Who painted it?"

"Believe it or not, that dinner lady of yours, Anna," laughed Christian. "Doris said that she was a gifted artist and so one day when I was looking after Prince I took a photo and gave it to Doris, who asked Anna to paint the portrait. It is such a lifelike resemblance isn't it?"

"I shall treasure this always, and the pens too," replied James, touched by the thought and care that had gone into the selection of his gifts.

"You boys up yet?" came Aunt Eleanor's voice from the landing.

"Just coming!" shouted James. "Hurry up, Christian. I need a shower before breakfast as well!"

"Well, there's plenty of room for two," came a voice from inside the shower.

Over one of the best breakfasts that James had ever had, he got to know Uncle Frank and Aunt Eleanor. He liked them both immediately and he could see how much they thought of Christian. Indeed, it was mutual.

"So are they really family?" he had said earlier to Christian, when they were dressing.

"No, James, but they are the closest to it and closer than any real family that I have had. I adore them both. They have been so good to me over the years."

James could now see what Christian had meant. He watched the way that Aunt Eleanor would fuss over him, smooth down his hair and put her arm around him when she was talking to him. Uncle Frank, too, was a charming man. The friendly Irishman always had a tale to tell and would often take the opportunity to pass on words of advice to Christian, who always listened carefully, and clearly valued his wise counsel.

"Now, my boy, I have been very impressed with what you are achieving in Abbotsford. I hear that your sales are impressive and they all like you. Well done!" Uncle Frank had exclaimed over breakfast.

"I enjoy it, Uncle Frank, it really is my kind of job."

"Well, to be honest, my boy, I was a little disappointed that you turned down the partners' invitation to launch and manage the new Derby branch. I thought you wanted to go back to your roots and so I put your name forward."

"I'm sorry to have let you down, Uncle, but I have other priorities now," smiled Christian, looking at James beside him.

"Yes, I can see that now, my boy. I have to say, Christian, I have never seen you look quite so happy as this. I guess this is James' doing?"

Aunt Eleanor giggled, "Well, Frank, I can see why Christian would not want to leave this young man! More coffee, James?"

"No thank you, Aunt Eleanor," replied James. "I am full to bursting," he beamed, looking very satisfied. "What a breakfast! I'm sorry, I shouldn't have said that, should I? My mother always corrected me when I said that as a child. She said I should say that, 'I've had sufficient, thank you'."

"That's quite alright, James," laughed Aunt Eleanor. "I know what mothers say to us when we are young, stays with us always. Do you see your parents often, James?"

"No, they are both dead," replied James.

"I am so sorry," said Aunt Eleanor quietly. "I guess you have other family?"

"I did have a brother, but he died some time ago. No, it's just me and Prince now. I have some very good friends as well, though," he added, looking at Christian and smiling.

"Well, please regard us as your honorary aunt and uncle as well," continued Aunt Eleanor, "but please, neither of you have to call us aunt and uncle, you know. Eleanor and Frank would be fine."

"I wouldn't dream of it," replied Christian hastily.

"Neither would I," added James.

"Well, James certainly has many good friends," continued Christian. "Doris, for one, his secretary, would kill anyone who upset James. I have never known anyone so fiercely loyal to their boss," he laughed.

"She is much more than a school secretary to me," laughed James. "You asked me if I had any family. Well, I guess I would include Doris and George and..."

"Most of Prior's Hill," added Christian. "This guy may not have any real family alive, but he is loved by everyone who meets him. That's family enough, I think."

"Not exactly," responded James, horrified yet pleased that Christian thought so highly of him. "Have you met Emily?"

"That's my point," roared Christian. "Even she, one of your avowed enemies, gave you a jar of home-made strawberry jam yesterday, and don't you deny it, James!"

"How did you know that?" exclaimed James.

"Doris, of course!"

It had been a wonderful day. A long, leisurely breakfast, with an equally large one for Prince, followed by a walk in a nearby park. A hearty lunch, cooked lovingly by Aunt Eleanor, followed by a nap and, later, another long walk in the park for Prince.

"I have had a wonderful day," said James as he stood in a park throwing a large stick for the delighted dog.

"It's not over yet, Jay. We are going out for dinner in Soho tonight. I've booked a table."

"Oh no, not more food!" groaned James. "Your Aunt Eleanor has really gone to town with her cooking. That vegetarian roast was just superb! Does she always cook such huge quantities?"

"She did when I lived here," grinned Christian.

James was getting ready for dinner. He thought that they might be going to the cinema or theatre and had thoughtfully brought a smart pair of trousers and jacket with him. He had a leisurely shower and took out the trousers that were still carefully packed in his suitcase. As he unfolded the trousers, a large white envelope fell on the floor. James recognised it as another birthday card and opened it.

"You ready yet, Jay?" yelled Christian, as he re-appeared from the bathroom looking very handsome in a dark blue suit and striking purple tie. He walked over to James who was sitting on the bed, still not dressed, looking at the large birthday card in his hand. His eyes were damp; he had been crying.

"Whatever's the matter?" said Christian, now very concerned, and putting his arm around his friend. "You had some bad news?"

James passed the card to Christian. On the front of the card it said, 'Just for You' in large gold letters, intertwined with an assortment of large balloons and champagne bottles. Inside were the words, written in neat handwriting.

'To my Jay, with all my love and best wishes. Remember, that wherever I am, I shall always love you. From your Tristan. XX'.

James, Christian and Prince drove home in silence after breakfast the following morning. After the incident with the birthday card, James had not really wanted to go into the city. Christian had understood this, and, after James had calmed down, had decided to take him on a tour of his old 'haunts'. James had said very little after receiving the card and Christian tried to explain it away as being a birthday card that maybe Tristan had sent in the past and that it had somehow got stuck in the suitcase. James knew otherwise, and shuddered as he realised that the birthday greeting had been written in Tristan's own scrawled handwriting: the very same handwriting that James had teased him about so often.

"Well, this is it," Christian had announced proudly as they walked in the door of 'The Horn and Crumpet'.

"What a stupid name," James had said. "I am sure that has no historical significance."

"Well, I think you may be wrong," Christian had replied. "Originally it was called 'The Horn and Strumpet'. You see, it was once a brothel!"

"Never!" James had exclaimed, sounding shocked.

Christian had gone on to explain that, some ten years earlier he was first a pot-washer and later a barman at this very pub. James listened carefully; it was good to hear Christian talking about himself and his past. James had often wondered, but had never liked to probe too much into Christian's past for fear of upsetting him.

"My God, I think that's young Toby!" Christian exclaimed.

"Ex-boyfriend?" grinned James.

"No way! He was just a spotty kid when I worked here. He took my job as a pot-washer when I was promoted. Look, we must go and speak to him." Christian went to the bar to order a drink.

"Hello, Toby. How's the pot-washing and old Bill?" The barman looked at Christian for a moment and looked puzzled. "Do I know you? You look familiar?"

"I'm Christian. We used to work here together quite a few years ago."

"Christian! Yes, I do remember you. You've changed a bit. Put on a bit of weight, I think. Great to see you after all this time. Yes, I am still here, but not pot-washing any longer."

"Well, that's good," beamed Christian, shaking hands with his old work-mate. "All those dirty glasses I had to send back! Bloody disgusting it was!"

"Well, that's because you forgot to tell me about putting the rinse aid in that stupid machine," protested the now good-looking young man, acne spots now long gone.

"What about old Bill?"

"Bill has long since retired, Christian. Still owns the joint and pops in from time to time, but I am managing it for him now."

"My goodness, well done!" said Christian, pleased at his young friend's promotion. "No chance of a lock-in nowadays then?"

"Never, not like in the old days anyway. We would lose our licence. No, I'm very careful about that sort of thing."

"Good for you. This is my friend, James, by the way."

"Pleased to meet you," replied Toby. "Now let me get you a drink. This one's on the house. By the way, you may like to know that the strange old guy who used to chat you up, has been locked up. The newspaper said he was pimping young guys. I always thought there was something creepy about him."

Over several rounds of drinks, Christian explained to a bemused James about life for a young teenager in London. He told about the alcohol, booze, rent boys - a life that he had been part of for a time, yet this was now all a distant memory. He told him about Edwin Smiley and the time that he had been held as a prisoner by him. James sat listening to his friend in the busy, noisy pub. It was not the kind of place that James would have chosen to spend an evening in, but he realised that he was now feeling much happier and, at last he was discovering much more about his friend.

"I cannot believe all that you are telling me, Christian. You had a dreadful time here."

"It happens, Jay. It wasn't all bad though. I met young Toby and Bill, who were kind to me. I don't even feel bad about Edwin now. He was good to me and I liked him at the beginning. It's just that he wanted favours in return."

"That's just taking advantage of someone with nothing," commented James. "I hope he was locked up and they threw away the key."

"As I said, it happens, Jay. There's lots of youngsters in the city who have been disowned by their families because of their sexuality. I know it's not right, but what can we do?"

"We fight it, we bloody fight it!" exclaimed James, angrily. "I had this conversation years ago with Tristan. We be ourselves; we do not hide or apologise. We live our lives as best we can and by doing so we fight prejudice, inequality and bigotry. I will not apologise for who I am and neither will I hide or run away."

"My goodness," laughed Christian. "I have rattled your cage, haven't I? I didn't mean to upset you, I just wanted to tell you as it was. You're a right 'fireball' when ignited, aren't you?"

"Things have to change Christian. They will change. Not in our lifetimes probably, but when I hear this kind of thing, the prejudice, people dying from AIDs with no care or support, it just makes my blood boil. James' mind went back to Sam and his story and he said no more.

Chapter 12

A Shocking Discovery

The weekend away had done James a lot of good. He had returned to school refreshed and ready to take on the world once more. The incident with Tristan's birthday card had shaken James badly and he had no real explanation for it, other than Christian's theory that the card had somehow been left in the suitcase from a previous year. This didn't ring true as James knew that he hadn't been away with Tristan since their last camping holiday in the Lake District, and that didn't involve a suitcase. Still, it had been a good weekend and he had got to know Christian's aunt and uncle well, and liked them. Even more importantly, James had now learned much more about Christian. Until that Saturday evening in the 'Horn and Crumpet', he had no idea what Christian had been through. He now saw his friend in a new light.

"My, someone's happy this morning?" smiled Doris, swinging around on her swivel chair. "I can't remember the last time that I heard you humming, James. I guess the weekend was a success then?"

James laughed, "It's a song that Christian kept playing over and over again on a new cassette tape he has in his car. He loves it and I cannot get it out of my head. I tell you, Doris, that new car cassette player is worth much more than his car. Yes, it was a great weekend, thanks. Aunt Eleanor saw it as her mission to feed me up. She's a brilliant cook."

Doris nodded, "Yes, it is a battered old thing, isn't it? You'll have to talk him into changing it. I am pleased it went well for you." She swung her chair around and carried on typing.

After a few minutes she turned around again. "James?"

"Yes, Doris?"

"I hope you don't mind me asking, but have you two thought about moving in together? You seem to get on so well and two can live as cheaply as one, you know," she added, her eyes twinkling through her large, round owl-like spectacles.

James smiled. Doris was always making hints in this direction. Earlier in the year, she had introduced him to a young man from County Hall who had called to install the new computer system.

"I'm sure he's gay!" she had whispered loudly from the stock cupboard. "Go and chat him up. Ask him out. What have you got to lose?"

"My self-respect?" James had snapped. Later, during the fitting of some cables, he had noticed the young technician in a different light, and had offered to make him a cup of coffee.

"Thanks, mate," he had replied with a charming smile. "That would be good, but I won't be long. I've got to be home early tonight. We're having her folks over for dinner tonight, and she says I've got to be there on time."

James assumed "she" must be his wife and gave the young man his mug of coffee, and returned to his office. James, for his part, had made sure that Doris was teased mercilessly about this for some time to come.

"Well, no, Doris. I have been waiting for you to find some nice technician for me…" he began, only to be interrupted by an eraser flying in his direction from the other side of the room.

"Stop it, James," Doris giggled. "You know I'm only trying to help."

"I know," laughed James. "Seriously, I do like Christian very much, but after Tristan, I am not sure I am ready for another relationship just yet. It would seem… kind of disloyal."

"Well, don't you wait too long. Christian is an attractive young man and will soon be snapped up by someone else if you are not careful. Do you really think Tristan would mind that you found some happiness? I know he would be pleased for you. He was that kind of person."

"I know, Doris. I know what you are saying."

"You're not still seeing that Sam Rivers are you? James, please tell me you're not?"

"It's not that I am seeing him, Doris. He just keeps appearing, uninvited, that's all. There's something very strange about him."

"Well, I don't like him," said Doris firmly.

That was that, thought James, smiling to himself. Once Doris had made up her mind about something or someone, there was no changing it, as her long-suffering husband, George, knew to his cost.

"Did you find out any more about him?"

"No, nothing that you don't know already, James. The records are very sketchy. He was an average pupil by all accounts, talked a lot and was very good at cricket. Indeed, he seems to have been quite an athlete. He won lots of cups and certificates. His name keeps appearing in the records for sports."

James nodded, "Well, it was a long time ago."

James continued looking at the budget print-out that he had just received from County Hall.

"Doris, they seem to have charged us twice for this invoice. Have a look at this."

"James, there was something else that I should tell you."

"What's that?"

"Young Sam Rivers was a very good actor."

"How do you mean? School plays, nativities and things? Good for him."

"Well yes, by all accounts he was good at that, but there was something else written in the log book."

"Go on."

Doris slipped off her chair and retrieved one of the old, leather-bound, school log books from the locked cupboard. She had stuck sticky yellow notes on several pages.

"It seems that he was quite a troublemaker. Have a look at these."

"What do you mean?"

"Well it says here that he was punished for putting the blame onto another pupil for his own misdeed, and here is a similar entry when another pupil was blamed for breaking into the school at night. It turned out it was Sam Rivers, who was spotted by a neighbour because of his bright blond hair, but he refused to take the blame. This one here is the strangest, James, because it seems that young Sam Rivers was punished for impersonating a member of staff on the telephone."

"James, there was a call for you from Sir Toby. He wonders if you would call in at the Manor on your way home. I said it would probably be all right, but that you would telephone if it wasn't. I don't think you have any meetings tonight."

"Thanks, Doris. No meetings tonight, so I will call in. I hope he has some good news about the rebuilding."

Doris looked at the reluctant young head teacher getting ready for football practice and smiled. She knew how much he hated the game, but knew that he would put up with it for the sake of his pupils.

"I was hoping for a response weeks ago," he continued, grabbing his metal whistle from the desk drawer.

James' impatience never ceased to amaze Doris.

"Come off it, James. It's only been a couple of months since the fire. What do you expect, miracles?"

"Of course," laughed James, rushing out of the office door. "After all, we are a Church school!"

It was nearly five o'clock when James rang the doorbell of the Manor House. He was surprised when Sir Toby answered the door himself as, more often than not, it was Peggy's duty. James realised that it was Peggy's day off.

"Good afternoon, James," said Sir Toby, giving him a friendly handshake and a slap on the back. "Thank you for coming over. I know I should come over to you for our meetings, but I wanted to be here in case Lotitia needed me."

"Of course. How is she?" asked James, as Sir Toby led him to his study.

"Not good, James. I really think she should be in hospital, but Dr Jackson will hear none of it. He says that she is exhausted and just needs plenty of bed rest."

James nodded, feeling uneasy, but he didn't know why.

"Do sit down, James. I'm afraid I cannot offer you tea as it is Peggy's day off and Sylvia had to leave early today. I do have a very good malt here though. Would you care to join me for a glass or two?"

The old man opened a very well-stocked cocktail cabinet in the corner of the room and took out two fine-looking whisky glasses from inside.

"No, not for me, thank you, Sir Toby. I'm driving, and I also have quite a lot of marking to do when I get home."

"Ah, I wish all young men were as sensible as you, James. How about a small beer? Now that won't be a problem, I am sure."

James disliked beer, but to keep Sir Toby company he accepted. "Thank you, Sir Toby, but only a small one, please."

Sir Toby busied himself preparing the drinks and James smiled as he placed two silver coasters on the highly polished table in front of their two chairs. Someone had trained Sir Toby very well.

"Now, James, to business. I am pleased to tell you that I heard from the diocesan architect this morning. They say that re-building the damaged part of the school and re-roofing all the building will start in January. Not a good month for roofing work, I know, but at least it will be started and hopefully the weather will be kind to us."

"That is excellent news," beamed James. "Have all the funding issues been sorted out with County Hall?"

"Oh yes," smiled Sir Toby, looking very satisfied. "They wouldn't dare do anything else. I understand that Charles had to threaten them, but in the end they agreed."

"And the extra classrooms and hall?"

"Ah, well that may pose more of a problem, my boy. The diocesan architect suggests two phases. The first is the repair and re-roofing of the original building and the second phase will be building the two new classrooms and a new hall, possibly starting the following year."

James looked disappointed. He had so longed for this moment, but his plans included the new building as well.

"The school is growing so fast, Sir Toby. We badly need additional space."

"I know, James, and that is what I told them. However, all is not lost, indeed to the contrary. County Hall are looking at closing another small school in the area which, I believe has only six pupils at present."

James nodded. He knew the school in question. Spotten Primary was a village school where Stephen Sage and his wife Eileen had reigned supreme for many years. Stephen was the head teacher and taught the older children, and Eileen taught the infants. The village had become popular with city dwellers as a place to buy good value second homes.

As a consequence, the child population in the village had fallen to an all time low, resulting in only six pupils, four juniors and two infants, in the current academic year. Despite village protests, even the most determined advocate of village schools could see that Spotten Primary School was no longer a viable proposition. Indeed, if the truth be known, it had not been viable for the last twenty years or so.

James had visited the school as part of the area's new 'clustering of schools' initiative and had been amazed to see that such a school still existed. Quaint, it certainly was, but efficient or financially viable, it was not. The Sage couple lived in the adjoining school house, which over the years, had been absorbed into the main school.

The few remaining pupils ate in the Sage's dining room for their cooked school lunches, which were brought in by taxi from Ledgers Comprehensive School each morning. James had been amused, and surprised, to discover that the pupils watched BBC School's Television Broadcasts in the Sage's living room on their brand new, and very large, colour television.

The school had a large hall and a dining room that was rarely used. The playground was huge and James watched in amazement as the eight children, who were there when he visited, trying to fill the space now long since vacated by past generations of happy, shouting village children.

There was a deep sadness hanging over the school, but, as is often the case in rural villages, the villagers saw the school and the small parish church as the centre of their community and were determined to keep the school open, whether there were any pupils attending or not. Now, with just six pupils and at a time of financial constraint it looked as if the axe was finally about to fall.

"Yes, I think you mean Spotten Primary. I know it."

"Well, as good fortune would have it, the headmaster and his wife are retiring, which is an ideal opportunity for County Hall to close the school, with much reduced opposition. It surprises me that such an uneconomic school has been kept open for so long. The good news, James, is that the school is a voluntary aided Church school, and its eventual sale will release much needed funds that we can use to extend Prior's Hill. Now I think it is intended that the Spotten children should come here, but there will, no doubt, be the usual protests and time-consuming public meetings before all this is settled. However, I think we can safely say that the outcome is a forgone conclusion. I have had a word with Bishop Colin and he is determined to push this one through, as are County Hall. For once, we are all in full agreement, except the good people of Spotten, of course."

"Excellent news, Sir Toby!"

"Now are you sure that you can wait that long, James?" laughed Sir Toby. "I know that you like things done yesterday, but these things take time, James. However, I am sure it will happen."

"Yes, I can wait, Sir Toby. Thank you! Meanwhile, it will be good to get the school back to normal again."

The old man nodded and smiled and took a sip from his glass of malt whisky.

"Sir Toby? There is another matter that I would like to discuss with you. Forgive me, but it is personal. I don't mean to pry into your affairs, but I don't know what else to do."

Sir Toby sighed. "Yes, I knew you would raise it sooner or later. You have met Sam Rivers haven't you?"

James nodded.

"It was a huge shock to us, I can tell you James. We thought he was dead, as you know, and his re-appearance had a devastating effect upon Lotitia. That is her problem now, I am sure."

"I can imagine. How long has she known that he is alive?"

"Since the beginning of the summer. We have always slept in separate rooms, James. However, for several evenings I heard Lotitia crying, sobbing and sometimes screaming. When she awoke me, I would go to her room to calm her down and comfort her as I thought she was having nightmares again. Later, I discovered that Sam Rivers had been appearing to her – in the rose garden, in her study and once in her bedroom."

"In her bedroom?" exclaimed James.

Sir Toby shook his head. "I don't know if that is really what happened, James. Lotitia swears that it was, but you know as well as I that Lotitia is not a well woman. She drinks far too much and sometimes... well, she tends to imagine things."

Sir Toby continued, "For several weeks, I tried to humour her. Sam Rivers was dead, we knew that. His ashes were buried in the Rose Garden and then, I began to wonder, what proof did we have that he and indeed our Giles were actually dead? I made enquiries though a private detective and we finally received all the proof and documentation that we needed. Giles was confirmed as having died of that dreadful disease, AIDS, but there was no trace of Sam Rivers."

James nodded, finally taking a sip of the beer that he hated so much.

"It was then a question of waiting. I knew that he would turn up sooner or later, and he did. He appeared in here, unannounced, suddenly one evening. I don't know where he came from. One minute he was here, and then he was gone." Sir Toby shook his head sadly.

"What did he want?"

"Oh, the usual, money. Yet more money. That's what he always wants. However, this time he wanted me to sign over the estate to him. I told him, I would never sign over the estate that my ancestors and myself have worked so hard for over the years to a crazy homosexual! I'm sorry, I'm sorry, I shouldn't have said that, James."

"That's alright," replied James, coldly. "We are often called far worse."

"I'm sorry James. I meant no harm to you or people like you. You see Sam Rivers is not like you, Tristan or anyone of your kind."

"My kind?"

"You are sincere, intelligent and kind, James, but Sam is a manipulator, harsh, cold and cruel. If you have not seen him in that light yet, you will, I can guarantee it. You mark my words!"

James nodded. "I do know what you mean. I had dinner with him one evening. Yes, I do know what you mean."

"You had dinner with him?" Sir Toby's bushy eyebrows shot upwards in surprise.

"Yes, I wanted to find out more about him. He was friendly and wanted to talk and so I agreed, but I wished I hadn't. You see, Sir Toby, somehow he wants to involve me in his plans to get you and Lady Lotitia to sign over the estate to him. I thought you should know."

"Even if I wanted to, I couldn't. My lawyer ancestor, Sir George Peatwhistle, saw to it that the estate would always be held in trust to pass on to the eldest male Peatwhistle heir. I have no heir and so, in the event of my death, the estate will pass to the eldest male cousin, and certainly not to my bastard stepson, if indeed, that is what he is. As you have already heard, James, Sir George certainly had a fine brain. He thought everything through exceedingly carefully and, in a way, it looks as if he foresaw this kind of circumstance. So why do you think Sam has involved you, James?"

"I don't really know, other than that he looks like Tristan and maybe he thought he could form some kind of relationship with me, perhaps to give him a degree of respectability."

"Yes, he does look very much like Tristan, doesn't he? However, it is interesting that this amazing similarity has developed since Tristan appeared in the village. Before he and Giles went to America, I think you would have said that although he did look a little like Tristan, it was not as close a resemblance as it is now. It seems that he has now modelled himself upon your dear friend."

"Yes, I had wondered about that," replied James. "He seems to be mimicking his hair style, clothes and mannerisms. He is very good at it too."

"There's something else you should know, James," continued Sir Toby. "My detective's enquiries revealed that Sam Rivers is also being investigated by the New York Police Department. We don't have all the details yet, but Sam Rivers, under a number of different names and identities, is being investigated for fraud, as well as a number of other misdemeanours."

"What was Sam like as a child?"

"Devious, spiteful, cruel, yet thoroughly charming," responded Sir Toby. "Lotitia didn't tell me about him at first. I gather you may know the circumstances of his arrival?"

James nodded, not wishing to put the old man through further embarrassment.

"It nearly led to the destruction of our marriage, James. At first I was happy to bring him up as my own son, but Lotitia would hear none of it, and arranged to place him with Peggy's sister, Rita, as her own. I agreed, and knowing that Lotitia is always so very fragile, I felt it would be best for her and the child. That way we could keep an eye on the boy, support the family financially and it would cause the least embarrassment for everyone. A year later, our own son, Giles, was born. We hadn't anticipated that he and Giles would become such close friends and…" Sir Toby paused and poured himself another malt whisky.

"Lovers," added James.

"Quite so. Neither had we anticipated what a cruel child Sam Rivers would grow into. It is believed that he killed his father, John, the man who brought him up as his own. John Rivers worked for me, you know. He was a good worker and didn't deserve what happened to him. Nothing was ever proven, but we knew that Sam was involved in his death. It was then that we sent Giles away to school. He was due to attend public school anyway, but we brought it forward a year to get him away from Sam Rivers. We thought it for the best."

"But the two of them continued their friendship, even then?"

"Yes, they did. They became inseparable. On a good day, Lotitia and I would watch them playing cricket, cycling and laughing. They looked so happy together. Sometimes Sam would be charming, a delightful boy, who was a pleasure to have in the house. Other times, he could be devious and cruel. He stole from Lotitia many times. He always denied it, of course, even when he was caught red-handed. In the end, we gave up on him."

"Then you sent Giles away to America?"

"Yes, we did when we found out that he wasn't like other boys. We hoped he would find a nice girl. We thought that would be the end of it, but Sam Rivers followed. We didn't hear from him after that."

"Sam told me he asked you for money to help pay for Giles' medical bills, but you refused?"

"Oh no, that was afterwards when Giles had passed away. Of course, we would have helped our son if we had known how seriously ill he was. The last thing we knew was when Sam Rivers arrived here with Giles' casket. You can imagine what that would do to a mother… and his father."

There was a pause and James could see in the darkened room that Sir Toby was wiping away tears in his eyes. James felt that it was now time to leave. Too much had already been said, but a very clear picture of Sam Rivers had now formed in his mind.

"I really ought to be going now, Sir Toby. Thank you for the drink and thank you for sharing this with me. I know it is painful, but I feel uneasy about what is happening and I wanted to talk to you about it."

"Thank you James, it is good to talk to you. I know it will remain in confidence. You have become so much a part of our lives here, James. We are both grateful to you… for your friendship."

As James was retracing his steps down the corridor to the front door, he stopped suddenly and turned to Sir Toby.

"Do you mind me asking? Who is Lady Lotitia's doctor?"

"Why do you ask? It's Dr Jackson, of course. He has been our doctor for quite a few years. Is there a problem?"

"It's just that Dr Jackson left Prior's Hill nearly a year ago and moved to Ireland. I know because his replacement, Dr Morgan, has only recently been appointed and his little girl has just started at Prior's Hill."

"So? What are you saying, James?"

"Well, I'm saying he cannot be treating Lady Lotitia. Maybe another doctor from the clinic is attending?"

"No, Lotitia and Sylvia have both said it is Dr Jackson. Indeed, he very kindly delivers Lotitia's pills himself each week. He came only this morning, as it happens. I was at County Hall, but Sylvia spoke to him."

"Don't you think that is strange, Sir Toby?"

"Well, no, why?"

"Our surgery is not a dispensing one. If we need any medicines, the doctors write a prescription and then we have to get the medicine from the chemist in Abbotsford. Why is this Dr Jackson, who is supposedly in Ireland, delivering tablets to Lady Lotitia personally? My advice is to stop Lady Lotitia taking the tablets immediately and get them analysed. Maybe it's time to get the police involved."

Chapter 13

Lunch at Coombe

"James, we really do need to talk about Christmas," announced Doris swinging around urgently on her swivel chair. "I know we have the usual things planned ages ago, but what are we going to do about the children's presents this year? There's only about a month to go, you know. We need to get on with it."

James stopped pumping up the new football that he had in his hand and returned to his desk. "I don't know if there is a special knack to blowing these things up, but these pump adaptors never seem to work for me?"

"Oh, let me do it," laughed Doris, taking the still flat ball from him. "You really don't get on with this sort of thing, do you? I give you credit for trying though, James, I don't think the boys have any idea about what you go through in encouraging them with their football."

"Well, if I don't help them, who will? Certainly, Emily won't and there is no one else around here but me to do it. We've tried parents, but they never stay for long. A couple of sessions and then they always have something else to do. Yes, Christmas. I think it's more or less sorted, isn't it?"

"Well, you organised the entertainment months ago, I have spoken to the PTA and they have the party planned. I am sure Anna's husband, Ted, would be Father Christmas again, if asked."

"Oh, he's good," laughed James. "He even took me in last year with all those stories about Rudolph! He's a natural."

Doris nodded. "He's been doing it for years. I do remember one year though that one little girl was so overcome that she wet herself – on Santa's knee!" Doris giggled as she took it upon herself to pump the football like an expert. It was increasing in size very rapidly and James was impressed.

"That really was convincing," laughed James. "Maybe we should supply Father Christmas with a plastic sheet or something, just in case we have any more over-excited infants. You are putting me to shame with that ball, Doris."

"Well, I did it often enough for my lad when George was away," replied Doris, now puffing. "What about the presents? I know your predecessor used to buy a job lot of cheap sweets from Woolworths and get them wrapped up for Santa to give out."

"No, we're not giving them sweets," said James firmly. "We should be setting an example, particularly in view of our dental health policy. No, not sweets."

"Well, they will eat them anyway..." began Doris, taking a look at James' glare, and deciding that it wasn't worth finishing the sentence. "How's that? One pumped-up football!"

"Thanks, Doris. That's great! What about we give each class teacher a certain amount to spend for each child and they can buy whatever they think is appropriate? They know their children well enough and the PTA say they will pay for them," added James.

"You think Emily will go Christmas shopping for her class?"

"Well, if she won't, I will. Let's ask them and see what they come up with."

The phone rang. Doris answered it. "Yes, of course, Sir Toby. Yes, he's free now, but is teaching after lunch today." The diminutive secretary looked at James, who nodded. "In about ten minutes? Yes, that will be fine."

A few minutes later there was a knock on the door. James answered it. "Come in, Sir Toby. Good to see you. How is Lady Lotitia this morning?"

"Much better today, thanks to you, James. Look, I won't hold you up for long, but we do need to talk."

James offered his Chair of Governors a cup of coffee that Doris had just made and the old man accepted gratefully.

"Thanks to you, James, we have avoided poisoning Lotitia by the skin of our teeth. After you told me about those tablets, I telephoned the surgery and they confirmed that no doctor from the surgery has been to see her, nor do they have any record of prescribed tablets. Indeed, they knew nothing of her recent illness. I called the police and they sent someone immediately to take a statement. They also took the tablets away for analysis. I knew myself what the answer would be, because by yesterday morning Lotitia was already improving and was looking much brighter. She ate a little breakfast for the first time for well over a week. She is so much better today, James. I am so relieved."

"I'm pleased as well," sighed James, thankfully. "Please do give her my best wishes. Have the tablets been analysed yet?"

"Yes, PC Wright called this morning and confirmed that the tablets had not been dispensed by Abbotsford Chemists after all. The label was a crude forgery produced on a photocopier. The tablets were, indeed, a poisonous substance with the main ingredient, I am told, being rat poison. In a short time those tablets would have killed her. Of that, there is no doubt." Sir Toby shook his head sadly.

"I am appalled, Sir Toby," said James quietly. "Do you think, as I do, that Sam Rivers was behind this?"

"I most certainly do," replied Sir Toby, angrily. "That boy is dangerous. Who knows what else he will try to do? However, Lotitia is adamant that, apart from once when he appeared in her bedroom and begged her to change her will in his favour, only Dr Jackson has been to see her."

"Dr Jackson?"

"Yes, and the surgery here have spoken to him in Ireland. He is adamant that he has not seen Lotitia for well over a year. He is as puzzled as we are. It is also interesting that the so-called doctor has only ever called on Peggy's day off. Peggy has never seen him. Maybe that is because she would recognise her own nephew."

A chill ran down James' spine. "Her nephew? You think Sam Rivers called to see Lady Lotitia disguised as Dr Jackson?"

"I think it is perfectly feasible, James. Even more suspicious is that Sylvia told me today that Lotitia's solicitor called a few days ago as well. Apparently, when I was in London sorting out this school issue, Lotitia wanted to change her will. Ray Parson's senior partner, old Court Russell, arrived with the document and, apparently, Sylvia was asked to witness it."

"It wasn't Court Russell...?"

"No, not at all. I asked Ray Parsons to check and he tells me that Court has been in hospital for a prostate operation. He has not been working for several weeks."

"You think that was Sam as well, don't you?"

"I do, particularly as, again, it was on Peggy's day off. The police have taken statements from Lotitia and myself, Peggy and Sylvia, as well as Cook. They will also be coming to interview you as well, James."

"Not a problem, Sir Toby. You know that I will help in any way that I can. I am still confused though. Surely Lotitia would recognise her doctor and her lawyer, as well as her own son? They cannot both be Sam Rivers."

"It sounds strange, I know James. The only thing I can say that may shed some light was that when the police put that question to Peggy, she didn't seem surprised, but said that Sam was always good at dressing-up."

"What did she mean by that? I know he was good in school plays. It says that in the records here... Sir Toby, Doris also found an entry in the old log book saying that Sam was reprimanded by one of my predecessors for impersonating a member of staff. This seems to link."

"Please make sure you give the police that piece of information, James. Maybe you could give them a photocopy of the entry in the log book? I have already told you that the Sam Rivers I knew could be devious and spiteful, as well as charming. Remember too that he can also be very cruel as well as... dangerous."

James sat at his desk, thinking. Little of what Sir Toby had said, made that much sense. How could Sam Rivers be such a good actor as to take in Lady Lotitia and Sylvia? To try and kill the old lady in order to gain some money would surely be easily traced and would not give Sam access to the Peatwhistle Estate anyway. It was true that James did find Sam both attractive and charming, but he was also well aware of the devious and spiteful side to his nature as well.

"James, sorry to trouble you, but when you were talking to Sir Toby, Colin Treader called. He asked if you could go over to Coombe School tomorrow mid-morning and maybe stay for lunch? He wants to talk to you about the London trip next year. He has some ideas that he would like to share with you."

"Oh, I could do with a chat with Colin, but I'm teaching tomorrow, aren't I?"

"Well, you were," smiled Doris, "but I happened to mention it to Emily and she says she owes you half a day for her emergency visit to the dentist. Do you remember that you covered for her? She says that, if you like, she will take Class 4 for English and History tomorrow and you can go to see Colin."

James laughed "You see, Doris. She is coming around. Yes please, I will go and thank her now. I could do with a change of scene for a few hours."

The following morning, James' little blue sports car drove down the winding lane into the attractive village of Coombe. This was the village where Tristan and he had planned to buy their first home together, a pretty little cottage called Lavender Cottage that he could just see in the distance. It brought back to him so many memories of their plans, that were all torn away so cruelly after that fateful car accident.

Coombe Primary School was a very well-managed village school run by Colin Treader and his team of five dedicated teachers. This six class school was larger than Prior's Hill, but its pupil numbers had spiralled downwards in the last year or so as parents moved their children from Coombe to Prior's Hill once again.

At first, James had thought that Colin would be resentful, but this hard-working head teacher had told James that, to the contrary, he was very relieved, because the rapid increase in 'refugees' from Prior's Hill a few years earlier had put a considerable strain upon both his accommodation as well as staffing resources. Parents and governors had been vociferous in their complaints about growing pupil numbers.

James had smiled to himself about the usual elitist dichotomy facing many village schools. As soon as a school became too popular, parents would complain. If the school became too small, they would complain because of the strong likelihood of closure. If anyone upset them or their child, parents would vote with their feet, placing the school under threat if too many took the same course of action at the same time. Indeed, it seemed that it was all right for the privileged few to receive the benefits of education in a small school, but it was not to be made available to many others.

Colin Treader liked James. In this enthusiastic and earnest young man he could see himself some thirty years earlier. As a well respected local head teacher, Colin was coming to the end of a highly successful career, whilst James was at the beginning of his. Colin was pleased for James and did what he could to help and advise him, without appearing to be interfering.

Colin also knew that James had been under considerable personal, as well as professional, pressure for some time and made a point of calling him occasionally, involving him in local developments, as well as providing a willing 'ear' for James to share some of his problems. James, in turn, respected his peer and knew that Colin would be discreet, and all that he said to him would remain in confidence.

For many years, Colin had taken his eldest pupils on a school visit to London. This was a four-day, three-night visit where the children and staff would stay in a very cheap London hotel, see the sights and the event usually culminated in a visit to the theatre to see a musical or popular play. For most village children, this was the first time that they had ever been to the capital city and, indeed, for many, it was their first time outside the county border. Colin believed firmly that this school visit provided his pupils with their first taste of independence, away from their often smothering families, and to become aware of the world beyond the narrow confines of Coombe.

For two years, Colin had also included the eldest pupils from Prior's Hill School, but had abandoned this less-than-successful joint venture as Colin, a highly organised man by nature, realised that he could no longer cope with the poorly behaved pupils from Prior's Hill, their previous head teacher or Emily. In James, Colin recognised a kindred spirit, one with whom he could work with and, as a result, had asked Prior's Hill to join with Coombe in the following year's London visit.

James was delighted to have been asked, although Emily had resolutely made her views perfectly clear at a recent staff meeting. "I am not spending another four days of hell with that rude, controlling man ever again! If you agree to it, James, it will be without me!" she had said firmly, her firm jaw locking into the position that James knew only too well.

"If Emily won't help, I'll come instead," Doris had whispered to James after the stormy staff meeting. "I did go one year and Colin and I get on well. He is organised, just like you James, and he will not tolerate poor behaviour. I can easily cope with it."

James walked into the attractive main school entrance and waited patiently for Colin's secretary to appear.

"Good morning, Mr Young. Lovely to see you again," smiled Sally, appearing from behind the reception desk. "Mr Treader is teaching at the moment. Is he expecting you?"

James nodded, "Hello Sally. Yes, Colin called Doris yesterday and asked me to join him for a meeting after break and to stay for lunch. It's the London visit, I believe."

Sally looked puzzled, yet nodded politely and disappeared. She reappeared a few minutes later.

"Mr Treader is teaching at the moment, but he asked if I would take you to his classroom and he will have a word with you there."

James walked down the well-decorated and brightly-lit corridor with its many notice-boards proudly displaying fine examples of pupils' work. It looked impressive and James could see why Coombe School was usually so popular with parents, many of whom had moved specifically into the village so that their child could attend their local school. Sally led the young head teacher into a large, bright Victorian classroom where some thirty pupils sat, in smart maroon uniforms, busily writing in their exercise books.

"Good morning, James. Good to see you again," said Colin, greeting his colleague with a friendly smile and shaking his hand. "As you can see, my lot are busy now and so we have a few minutes to talk. How can I help you?"

"Er, you asked me to call for a meeting about London today, and to stay for lunch, Colin."

Colin looked puzzled and led James to the corridor where they would not be heard.

"James, I didn't call you," he said quietly. "I'm still waiting for more details from the tour company I use, so I have no more news just yet. I am trying to get a better price. Maybe Sally got mixed up and called you about something else?"

James shook his head. "You didn't call? I don't think it was Sally. Doris told me that it was you asking to see me today about the London visit. I don't understand."

"Don't worry, James. Just a mix up, I expect. Look, I finish in an hour or so. As you are here now maybe we could still have a natter? It's always good to see you. How about a pub lunch?"

James found himself enjoying lunch at 'The Coombe', a very homely pub right in the heart of the village. James remembered that he had been there before with Tristan when they were looking at Lavender Cottage and he remembered that he had enjoyed it then. He began to tuck into the large Stilton Ploughman's whilst Colin was enjoying a Ham Ploughman's.

"These look good," commented James, now feeling very hungry. "The bread they use is terrific."

"Made in the village, James. It really is a great pity that you never moved here. It is a smashing little place. We love it here. You would have liked it here too. Did you know that Lavender Cottage is still up for sale?"

"Really?" said James, looking surprised. "After Tristan died I pulled out of the sale, as you know. I thought the other young couple that were so interested when we were looking, bought it?"

"They did," nodded Colin. "Sadly, their marriage didn't last long. They split up. Great pity, as I understand that there is a baby on the way. Yes, they broke up and it's back on the market again."

"For a lot more money, I guess?"

"A bit, but I don't think they are asking the true value, because they want to get rid of it quickly and move on. They have done a fair bit to it too, by all accounts. A new bathroom and kitchen, that sort of thing. Why don't you think about it again, James?"

James shook his head. "No, I couldn't possibly move there now. It was going to be our home, mine and Tristan's. It would bring back too many painful memories for me."

Colin paused. "Look James, I hope I'm not speaking out of turn but, I like you and, as you know, I always speak my mind, but this is not intended to hurt you." James nodded.

"I think that maybe you are worrying too much about the past and what you see as bad memories. From what I hear about you, and your relationship with Tristan, you have many good memories to enjoy. I find that as I get older my memories comfort and inspire me. They don't depress me. I find that memories are even more important now than they were when I was younger."

"What do you mean?"

"I think you would be foolish to turn away from the past. You chose Lavender Cottage together because you liked it and you were both inspired by it. Nothing has changed, except that Tristan is not physically here to share it with you. What I am trying to say is that maybe Lavender Cottage is just what you need to help you remember Tristan in a good and positive way. Remember this in life, James, always try to turn a bad thing into something positive. It helps. Turn yours and Tristan's dream into a reality."

James nodded. Yes, what his wise colleague was saying did make a great deal of sense, but how would Christian feel about such a move? As James relaxed, he began to talk about recent events at Prior's Hill and some of the things that were troubling him. Without going into detail about the Peatwhistles, he mentioned the appearance of a young man who looked remarkably like Tristan and was now troubling him greatly.

"He must have been at the school some fifteen years ago, Colin, maybe more. No one at Prior's Hill has been there long enough to remember him. How long have you been here, Colin?"

Colin laughed. "That's a bit like asking a woman her age, James! I have been at Coombe for nearly thirty years. I am due to retire soon, but I wanted to get a few things sorted out before I go. What did the boy look like? I have a good memory for faces, but not names, unless they have either been very, very good or very, very bad."

James gave a description of Sam Rivers and as soon as he said, "Brilliant blond hair," Colin put his glass down.

"Yes, I do remember that little bugger," he said slowly. "He was called Sam, something."

"Sam Rivers, yes, that's him!" exclaimed James.

Colin replied slowly and deliberately. "Great mimic, as I recall. Caused havoc on one of my early London visits. We worked with Prior's Hill in those days as well. He took great delight in winding up my boys and mimicking them. I remember he would call out rude names and say bad things from the back of the bus, pretending that he was one of my children. I remember reprimanding a couple of boys for something that they had not done. My boys said it was Sam Rivers, but I didn't believe them at first."

"What made you change your mind?"

"It was one night in the hotel. We had a good day and the children were very tired. We had been on the Tube, visited the Houses of Parliament and Madame Tussauds – all the usual sights. The children were tired and we all went to bed quite early. I was awoken just after midnight by the night porter who said that he had seen one of my boys in the hotel office. The boy had managed to open the safe and had taken some money. The night porter managed to catch a glimpse of the boy who was wearing a maroon uniform."

"And brilliant blond hair?" added James.

"No, the night porter described him as being in a maroon uniform, so it must have been one of my lads, but with dark brown hair."

Colin paused, continuing to eat his lunch.

"I went back upstairs, woke up all the boys, read the riot act, searched their rooms, but we found nothing. All the boys claimed to have been asleep, but one of my boys said that his maroon sweatshirt had disappeared."

"Did you find it?"

"Yes, we did, later. It was under his bed and he said he had folded it up on the chair. We left London under a cloud that year. That was why I stopped the London visits for a year or two. I was so embarrassed and angry."

"Did you ever find out who it was?"

Colin put down his knife and fork. "Not conclusively, but I am sure that I knew who did it. A few days later, I received a phone call from the hotel saying that they had found a cheap brown wig stuffed in the top of one of the wardrobes – the room where Sam Rivers was sleeping."

"Right, but I guess that didn't prove it was him," replied James.

"Well, not in itself it didn't, I agree. It was later during that summer when Prior's Hill came to play football here. Sam Rivers was in the team and I recognised him at once, he was always so self-assured and cocky. He was a brilliant footballer though, a good all-rounder. He was so athletic and won everything in the area. Sometimes it looked as if his body was made of rubber and, I believe, he was also double-jointed and could bend so easily. He would always land perfectly, say when taking part in the high jump, and bounce off again like a rubber doll. He was amazing to watch."

James nodded, "Yes, he has remained very fit. I had dinner with him a few weeks ago and I noticed how smoothly and quietly he moves. Like a cat. He also has this amazing skill of appearing and disappearing, as if from nowhere."

"At the end of the match, Sam Rivers came up to me and just stared with those piecing blue eyes of his. I was taken aback. It was not the sort of thing I expect from a boy. He was so cold and... calculating. All he said was, 'You never did find out who did it, did you sir?' He then laughed and walked off! I knew then that it was him and he was playing a game with me. I shall never forget Sam Rivers, James! He is the only boy who has ever got the better of me!"

"Good lunch?" asked Doris, as he walked back into the office.

James nodded, and then told Doris what had happened and that Colin had not asked to see him after all. Doris looked puzzled as James told her a little of what Colin had said.

"Well, that is strange, James. It certainly was Colin who called. I swear to you it was."

Doris handed James a letter and looked concerned.

"James, this came for you just after you left for Coombe. A young woman delivered it. She said it was urgent and that you should see it immediately upon your return. The only thing is..."

"What's the matter, Doris?"

"Just look at the handwriting!"

James looked closely at the large white envelope in his hand. He looked at the name and address on the envelope. He recognised it as being written in Tristan's scrawled handwriting. He carefully opened the letter, sat down at his desk and read it slowly. Doris sat in silence, looking concerned.

Inside the large white envelope was one sheet of paper in Tristan's familiar handwriting. It read:

'Dear Jay,
You have betrayed me. Warning Sir Toby about the tablets was not a good idea, because the police are now involved. It is all your fault. Remember that when I play a game, I always win. Watch your back now, because nothing is as it seems.

I do hope you enjoyed your lunch with Colin Treader. I am sure that he remembers me very well. People tend to.

Remember, when it gets worse, that I have always loved you, Jay.

Tris XX'

James took a deep breath, gritted his teeth and handed the sheet of paper to Doris. She read it in silence and handed it back.

"You must call the police, James. This is serious," she said quietly.

James didn't answer.

"What did she look like? This woman?"

"Medium height, slim build. I think she had blonde hair, but she was wearing a headscarf, so I couldn't really be too sure. Why do you ask?"

"Anything else?"

"She was very attractive, but wearing a lot of make-up. I remember thinking that she looked a bit too glamorous for this time of day. Maybe it was fine for going out for an evening event, but she certainly wasn't working, dressed like that! Do you know her?"

"I think we both do, Doris. If I am not very much mistaken, I think we will discover that our mysterious lady visitor is none other than Sam Rivers."

Chapter 14

Deja Vu

James was troubled. Sam Rivers had not appeared in person for several days, yet James knew that he was still around. He just sensed it. Whenever he was in the school playground alone, in the barn-classroom after school or walking in the woods with Prince, he expected Sam Rivers to appear, but he did not.

James had already been interviewed twice by the police, the first time by PC Wright, the community police officer and parent of a pupil in the school, and then the following day by Detective Sergeant Russell, a grey haired, serious-looking man who, although appearing to be a thorough interrogator, seemed to lack much in the way of personality, James thought.

Doris had agreed. "His eyes are too close together for my liking," she had stated firmly. James smiled; the poor man was already damned.

It was a cold, wet, wintery evening and James had taken Prince for the briefest of walks in order to escape the cold. Man and dog hurried back to the warmth and comfort of James' flat. They both ate and the contented dog settled down to an evening in front of the fire.

How James longed for a real open fire, instead of the dry electric radiant heater glaring so brightly in front of him. His mind went back to Colin Treader's words about Lavender Cottage. Yes, that would have been his and Tristan's real home.

He had really looked forward to living there. It had a real open fireplace, was situated in a friendly village and yet not too far from Prior's Hill. Before he had discussed this with Colin, he would have shuddered at the very possibility of living there, but now, somehow it did seem more appealing. However, he doubted that Christian would feel the same.

James wondered about Christian and the likely future for their relationship together. It was true that he had not given Christian the kind of attention that James knew he deserved. James really liked and missed him whenever he was not around. He was witty, kind and thoughtful, yet James could not understand why he could not feel the same with him as he had felt with Tristan. He thought of Doris' words.

Christian was certainly an attractive young man and James knew that he would not wait for him for ever. He had already turned down a generous job offer just to be with him and for this, James was deeply touched. Neither had James shared with Christian the problems that he was facing with Sam Rivers. Deep inside, James knew that this was deliberate, because he did not really know how to deal with the issue and the questions that would undoubtedly follow.

The doorbell rang. Prince, now fully awake after his after-dinner slumbers, leapt barking angrily at the door.

"It'll be another salesman, Prince," grumbled James, walking barefoot to the door. He opened it and immediately a gust of icy cold wind blew inside. James glanced outside and could see trees swaying and bending in the violent stormy wind. Black clouds were in the sky and James knew that they were in for a very heavy rain storm. Prince ran to the gate barking, growling and snarling furiously.

"That's enough, Prince! Come here!" The angry dog turned and obediently ran back inside the hall and to the warmth of the electric fire.

Something pricked the side of one of James' bare feet. He looked down and realised that his foot was touching something sharp. He switched on the outside light and picked up what looked like a large funeral wreath full of flowers that lay propped against the steps.

Puzzled, he picked it up, took the wreath inside and closed the front door. Clipped to the centre of the wreath was a small envelope. James opened the envelope and pulled out a small, black edged card upon which was typewritten:

'To a good friend whose life was so tragically cut short. May you rest in peace'.

The following morning James left his flat early and called to see the local florist, whose name was printed on the envelope. The young florist looked startled when James opened the large bag and revealed the wreath that was inside.

"Ah yes, Mr Young. I do remember this one. I made it up myself yesterday afternoon. I thought it was strange, because we are usually asked to deliver tributes to the undertaker or possibly to the church or crematorium," said the helpful young woman. James recognised her as the parent of one of the new infant pupils in Class 1.

"The person who ordered it – what did he look like?" asked James.

"No, it wasn't a 'he', Mr Young. It was a young woman. She came in during the afternoon to order it. She paid cash and then said she would come back later for it. She was late coming back and I waited for her for about fifteen minutes and then, just as I was locking the shop, she arrived to collect it. Is there something wrong with it? I can always remake it for you, if you like. Maybe you didn't like the choice of flowers?"

"No, it's fine, thank you. This woman, did she say anything to you?"

"No, not really. She seemed very upset, so I didn't like to pry too much. She said it was for a friend who died in a car crash. That's all. Is there a problem, Mr Young?" repeated the anxious florist.

"This woman? What did she look like?" asked James, already knowing the answer.

"Well, she was a very attractive young woman with beautiful blonde hair. She was of slim build, medium height, I guess. It was so strange…"

"Why's that?"

"Well, even though she looked so sad and was crying, she was heavily made up, and very well dressed. She looked as if she was going to a party and not a funeral."

It was morning playtime and James stood in the school playground watching the children excitedly run out of the school building to play. The heavy rain had stopped and, even though there was a cold wind, it was fine enough to let the children outside for their morning break. James knew that as long as the children wore their coats they would not notice the cold weather. It was the endless wet days that James, along with the rest of the nation's primary teachers, dreaded.

He stood watching the children play a similar variety of games that had been played in the Prior's Hill playground for generations. Conkers, marbles, skipping and all manner of chase games were still played as enthusiastically as when the school had first opened. Standing in the playground, and beneath the old horse chestnut tree, always reminded James that he was merely the temporary custodian of the village school and that it was up to him to maintain it in good order, and ready to pass on to his successor when the time came.

"Mr Young, Peter Parsons says that we are all going to London next year. Is it true?" asked Stuart excitedly.

"Well, Stuart, since you ask so nicely, yes, it is. I am trying to arrange a visit jointly with Coombe School. There's a lot of work to do, but yes, I hope it will happen. I remember saying that we would try last year, but it was too expensive for us to go on our own."

There were whoops of joy from the other children standing around James.

"I have never been to London," said Stuart.

"Oh I have, loads of times," interrupted Peter Parsons. "But it will be more fun going with the school rather than parents, don't you think?"

"Will the girls come as well?" asked Stuart.

"Of course," laughed James. "You don't think we are going to leave the best pupils behind, do you?"

The boys groaned and the girls pretended to look angry. James was often amused by the pretend 'hatred game' that both boys and girls in Class 4 seemed to play. How things would change when they became a little older, he thought.

"Mr Treader is very strict though, don't you think?" added Peter, thoughtfully. "Somehow, I don't think I will get on with him very well. However, I must get to know him rather better before I pass my judgement upon him."

James smiled. He had often thought that Ray Parsons' son already had the makings of a good lawyer, if not a judge. For a ten-year-old, Peter had an impressive way with words and always made his views very clear.

"Of course you will, Peter," replied James, briskly. "He is a very kind man, but he does expect good behaviour. I am sure you won't let us down, Peter."

"Oh no, I won't," replied Peter. "I was thinking more about Charles. He does tend to let the side down somewhat, don't you think?"

"I'm sure Charles will be fine," smiled James, recognising where Peter was coming from. If there was any trouble, Charles would surely be at the centre of it.

James looked around, he had not seen Charles for a while and Peter's comments had made James wonder what he was up to. He didn't have to look for long because Charles, an impish looking ten-year-old, was busily chasing Polly with, what to James looked like, a used-condom.

"Charles Gordon, come here at once!" commanded James, in his most serious and commanding voice. Charles immediately stopped chasing the screaming Polly and, now more subdued, was walking over to James and the other pupils, still holding the offending item, which he was still waving from side-to-side, almost gleefully.

"What do you think you are doing with that, Charles?" James asked angrily.

"Just playing kiss chase with my balloon," replied Charles defensively. "I didn't steal it from anyone. I found it over there," he said pointing to a large shrub by the corner of the building.

"That's not a balloon, that's a Rubber Johnny," yelled a delighted Stuart Bell. "My dad uses them to stop Ma having more babies."

"Put it in the bin now please, Charles," said James, briskly. "Go inside, wash your hands and then come back and apologise to Polly. Polly, you stay with me and we will make sure he does."

Polly, who by now was crying with a combination of both horror at being chased by a condom as well as being the centre of such uninvited attention, slipped her hand into James' and together they walked around the playground.

Doris burst out of the side door and came hurtling to James as fast as her short legs could carry her. "Mr Young, Mr Young, come quickly please!" she shouted, waving her arms furiously.

James walked briskly towards her. "Whatever is the matter, Doris?"

"James, come quickly. There's been a car accident. It's Christian. He's been taken to hospital!"

It was like a nightmare continually repeating itself. James could still remember only too clearly the first time that Doris had appeared on the football field bringing him the shattering news that Tristan had been involved in a serious car accident. Later that evening he had died. Now it seemed to be happening all over again. James fought back the tears as he ran to his office to collect the car keys, whilst Doris arranged for Anne to take charge of the pupils.

After what seemed like hours later, although it was, in fact, only minutes, James and Doris arrived breathlessly at the entrance to Abbotsford Hospital. James headed for the reception counter. He remembered only too well the way in which he had been dismissed so abruptly the previous time he was there, and he was ready to be far more assertive this time around.

"I've come to see Christian Trill. He has been involved in an accident," he announced sharply.

The young woman at the desk looked at James and Doris and asked, "What is your name? Are you relatives?"

"I'm James Young. I'm a friend of Christian Trill. A good friend."

The young woman nodded and started looking through pages in a register. James watched impatiently and the young woman looked puzzled.

"There's no one of that name been admitted to this hospital so far today, Mr Young."

"There must be. Can you check again, please?" James demanded. "Maybe one of your colleagues dealt with his admission when you were away from the desk."

"I have checked it again, Mr Young. I have been here all morning and no one of that name has been admitted," the receptionist replied, kindly.

"Maybe my friend has been taken to another hospital?"

"Well, it is possible, but you say that the accident happened locally this morning. He would have been brought here. Were the police involved?"

James looked at Doris, who was standing at the side of him, looking as if she too was about to faint. "James, the call came from the local police station. I didn't get to ask who I was speaking to, but I'm sure it was PC Wright."

"Would you like me to telephone them for you?" asked the young woman, kindly. "Let me help you to get to the bottom of this. Look, neither of you look too well. Please take a seat and I will get someone to bring you a drink. Is tea alright for you?"

James nodded and he and Doris sat in the near-empty waiting area. He could see the young receptionist making several phone calls and, before long, a porter arrived with two cups of tea.

"Mr Young? I was asked to bring you this."

James and Doris took the tea gratefully. Doris sat in silence, gently sipping from her cup.

"I cannot believe that this is happening all over again, Doris. Why is it happening again? Is it me? First Tristan and now Christian." Tears were running down James' face and Doris put her arm on James' shoulder to comfort him.

"I don't understand either, James. This is just so very cruel..."

Doris paused, bit her lip and sat in silence, wondering whether to say what had just sprung into her mind.

The receptionist came over to them and sat beside James. "Mr Young. I've called the police station and they say that there have been no serious car accidents in the area this morning. They put a call through to PC Wright who says he hasn't had any reason to call the school since yesterday, and that was about a matter with which he says you, Mr Young, will already be familiar. However, he did say that you should try to call Mr Trill yourself. Do you know what he means by that?"

"Just what I was thinking..." began Doris.

James leapt to his feet. "May I use your telephone please? It is really very important!"

Later that evening James and Christian sat together on the large sofa in James' flat. James had his arm held tightly around Christian. Prince sat contentedly by their feet and for the first time in many months, James felt content as well as relieved. James told Christian of the phone call that Doris had received, supposedly from the police station, how they had rushed to the hospital to see him and were shocked that he had not been admitted there.

Christian sat in silence and James repeated once again the message that he had received from PC Wright and how they had called Christian at the estate agency where he worked, together with the immense relief that he had felt when Christian's cheeky voice had answered the phone.

"It wasn't really my day to be in the office, James, and you were lucky to catch me. I had a couple of surveys to do in the morning. Anyway, I had a call first thing to say that a client wanted to meet me in the office to talk about a property that she was very interested in and that it was urgent. Thinking it might be a good sale, I cancelled one of my appointments so that I could meet her, but she didn't turn up. Just as I had given her up as a time-waster and was about to leave for the second survey you called me. You seemed in such a panic. I'm pleased I was there though."

"Hmm, well I can guess who that woman was," began James.

"James, as you can see, I'm fine. I really don't know what all the fuss is about. You said something about a wreath being delivered here yesterday. What was that all about?"

It was at that point that James felt obliged, indeed he wanted, to tell Christian everything that had happened in the previous few weeks. He told of the continuous appearance of Sam Rivers, how they had a meal together, the poisoning of Lady Lotitia as well as the appearances of the blonde-haired young woman. He had also revealed the incident about the delivery of the wreath the previous evening and his suspicions that the whole unpleasant incident had been set up by Sam Rivers.

Christian sat open mouthed, looked alarmed. "James, why didn't you tell me this before? Why have you kept all this to yourself? This is very serious. Are the police involved? Anyway, why is he trying to involve me as well?"

"To hurt me, Christian. In a nasty warped way, I think Sam Rivers wanted me to fall in love with him and for me to help him to get his hands on the Peatwhistle Estate. Instead, when I discovered what he was doing with Lady Lotitia's pills, he knew that his plan hadn't worked and that I was working against him. This is a warning for me, Christian. He knows how to hurt me." James sat in silence as his mind ran over possible future scenarios and the consequences for them both. "You're right. I should have told you. I guess I was just trying to protect the Peatwhistles and I thought I could handle it myself."

"But surely you sensed that something was wrong, very wrong. I mean, for this guy to go around pretending he is Tristan. He must have a screw loose somewhere! No, this guy sounds crazy. He needs medical help."

"Yes, I know you are right, but somehow I, I just kept hoping..."

"That it was Tristan, back from the dead?" said Christian, jumping in to complete the sentence that James had begun.

"I guess so."

"James, look, you are an intelligent man. Couldn't you see that this wasn't possible? Surely you knew that this character was just messing with your head. Not just yours, but the poor old Peatwhistles and Doris!"

"I know," James nodded sadly.

"James, are you in love with Sam Rivers? Maybe just a bit?"

James sat in silence once again, looking at the floor.
"I think you are, maybe just a little bit. I wondered because Jasmine said something to me the other day that made me wonder if you had found someone else. After all, you have not been the same since our weekend away, James. You don't seem interested in me any more. I sensed it and I have done for a while now."

James nodded and held Christian's hand tightly. "Maybe you're right. In the early days anyway. In Sam I saw Tristan, and I wanted to be with him. I cannot deny it, Christian. It was only later when I saw the real Sam Rivers. He is devious, manipulative and cruel. He will go to any lengths to hurt people. I know that now and he is nothing like Tristan. I am not in love with Sam, but I am still in love with Tristan, and always will be."

Christian smiled. "I wouldn't expect that to ever change, James. All I ask is that maybe you will, in time, find room for me as well."

"That doesn't bother you, Christian?"

"Look, how many times do I have to tell you? I liked Tristan as well and I miss him. I'm in love with you, James, but I think we can always find a place in our hearts for Tristan as well, don't you?"

James kissed his friend on the lips. "This incident today, although horrible and wicked, has done me a big favour. The one thing that I have learned, Christian, is that I love you very much. In the hospital when Doris and I were waiting to find out about you, I realised how much you mean to me and that I really do love you. I felt that you were going to be torn away from me and I felt so helpless. I never want to be apart from you again."

Prince, who was now sitting beside the couple, looked at them both and licked both their hands lovingly.

Chapter 15

A Different Form of Flattery

It was the weekend, and at last James and Christian had decided to move in together. Christian had already moved most of his things into James' flat and had given his landlord one month's notice of his intention to vacate the property.

James too was the happiest that he had been for some time, now realising that, thanks to the disturbing issues of previous weeks, it was Christian with whom he wanted to share his life. He was excited at the prospect of all the things that they could now do and plan together and, James being the impatient character that he was, wanted to get on with it right away.

"I made coffee and toast for you, Christian, but not sure if you wanted anything else this morning."

"That will be fine, Jay," came a sleepy voice from inside the bathroom. A few minutes later a very tired Christian appeared in the kitchen, still wearing only boxer shorts and a white vest. James looked up from his newspaper and went to pour the coffee that was brewing in the percolator. Prince scampered over to greet the sleepy young man.

"Ouch, Prince, that hurt!" exclaimed Christian, as the heavy dog rested his paws on Christian's knee. "Your nails need clipping, boy."

"Yes, he needs longer walks on paths to keep those claws down. I think he only ever has walks on grass nowadays. I'll make a point of taking him for brisk walks on paths instead. What are we doing today, Christian?"

Christian took a sip of coffee. "Well, I wanted to talk to you about something that you may not be too keen on at first, Jay. Bear with me and I will explain."

Christian put his coffee down on the table and James, who was busying himself washing up the previous evening's dishes, put his arm around him.

"Hey, you're covering me in soap suds again," yelled Christian, flicking suds back at James.

"Well, this must be the first time that I have ever gone to bed with a sink full of dirty plates. You are already having a bad effect upon me, Christian Trill. Go on, what is it?"

"Well, I've been thinking. We've agreed that my place isn't really suitable for Prince, yours is in a far better position, but is maybe a bit small for the three of us."

"You want us to move? That's fine by me. I was thinking exactly the same thing," began James, now sitting beside Christian. "We will save on your rent so we can easily afford a bigger place and maybe with a proper garden?"

"Or we could buy something?" began Christian. "Look, we are paying out a lot of money in rent. I am an estate agent, for goodness' sake, and there are some amazing places on the market now. It's a good time for us to buy something for ourselves before the prices go crazy again."

"I'd love to buy a place of our own. I've been thinking the same thing," James responded excitedly. "Have you anywhere in mind?"

"Well, yes, I do as a matter of fact," began Christian. "It came on the market a few days ago. I didn't mention it because I didn't know how you would feel. It's a little cottage…"

"You going to say Lavender Cottage in Coombe, aren't you?" laughed James.

"Well, yes, but I didn't know how you'd feel about it now. How did you guess?"

"If you'd asked me before last week, then maybe not. You remember that I had a chat with the head teacher of Coombe, you know, Colin Treader? He mentioned it to me when we had lunch together. Actually, he gave me a good talking to and shook me up a bit. I then realised that, yes, I would still like to live there, but only if you would be happy there too."

"Does it bother you that you and Tristan were going to live there together?"

"No, not now. In a funny sort of way I think that Tristan is leading us both there. I always loved it. It is perfect for us. How about you?"

"No, I have always liked it and it was the first property that I sold down here. When you cancelled the sale after Tristan's death, I thought about it for myself. I didn't want to hurt your feelings and so I let it go. Anyway, I couldn't have afforded it on my own."

"Do you think we can afford it now?"

"Well, the young couple who bought it have split up. They want a quick sale, so I guess if we offer them a bit more than they paid for it they will be happy enough. They've already made quite a few improvements as it was a bit of a mess when you last saw it. I can easily get a mortgage for us both through my contacts with the building societies that we use."

"Can we go and have a look at it soon?"

Christian laughed, "Of course. I'm thrilled you are so keen. When do you want to go?"

"Now!" said James, suddenly banging his hand on the table. Prince leapt out of his basket and made for the door, barking, knowing that a walk or at least a ride in the car was about to happen.

"OK. Funnily enough, I just happen to have the keys in my briefcase!"

Christian drew his battered old Ford Escort to an abrupt halt at the side of the narrow road and together the happy couple, with an equally happy dog, walked to the broken iron fencing that lay between the road and the fields in the distance. James could see Colin's school and the small village church at the side from the top of the hill where they stood. Between the church and the school, there was a small playing field at the side of which was a cluster of pretty whitewashed cottages.

Coombe was certainly a picturesque village, as it nestled in a lush green valley dotted with cows and horses grazing in the fields. Although Prior's Hill could be described as looking a 'chocolate box picture', Coombe village looked much more natural, more normal – a working village where ordinary people lived. It was not lost upon James that he and Tristan had stood in this very same spot, looking at the village below, some two years earlier. He was surprised that instead of the pain that he had expected, he now felt happy and fulfilled. He sighed and slipped his hand into Christian's and watched Prince sniffing the iron fencing.

"See, Lavender Cottage is one of those," announced James, proudly. "It's that one on the left. The one with the green railings."

Christian laughed, "I know! I sold it once before, remember? I think I've nearly sold it for a second time as well. You do really like it don't you?"

James squinted his eyes looking at the pretty little cottage in the valley below. "Yes, I do. I really do. It's beautiful. It's an incredible setting. We'll all be happy there, I'm sure."

The pretty white cottage glowed in the morning sunshine, its profile set against a perfect blue and almost cloudless sky.

Christian's old, red car pulled up at the side of the green railings.

"I think you'll agree that it looks much smarter than it did the last time that you were here," said Christian, unlocking the front door leading to the small inner porch.

James remembered it all as soon as he walked inside and immediately the memories came flooding back. He wandered into the small living room and noticed that the cracked, worn linoleum had now been replaced by a comfortable looking shag pile carpet. It had been very well decorated. James liked the new wallpaper and the pretty curtains in the window.

No longer were there any signs of the peeling, yellowed-white paint that he remembered so vividly. Instead, the skirting boards and cupboard doors and been stripped and sanded down to reveal a golden natural pine that had been sensitively varnished with a matt protective finish.

James walked into the dining room. The hideous utility furniture had now gone. The room was empty, yet had been recently well decorated and, again, cheerful looking curtains hung at the small, paned windows. Similar to the living room, the timber had also been stripped and sanded to reveal old pine timber. It too had been carefully varnished to reveal the natural grain and knots in the wood.

"Christian, this is such an improvement. Look, they've even left those wonderful open fires in both rooms! We could get a wood burner for one of them."

"Yes, they have really improved it and for an extra three thousand pounds, I think it's a pretty good deal. We can always negotiate it down a bit, of course."

"Well, from what I can see, Christian, I say pay them what they are asking. It's worth it. Maybe negotiate for the curtains and carpets. I am very happy to keep them. They are lovely and will save us buying new!"

"Right you are, squire!" teased Christian. He led James into the newly-tiled kitchen and on to the bathroom and separate toilet. There were now smart, new kitchen units fitted, a new fridge freezer and what looked to be a new bottled-gas cooker, as well as a new gas water heater.

"I think this is a good idea, Jay. Look, bottled gas, this is ideal for living in such a remote spot with all the power cuts we are sure to get if the weather is bad again this year."

James nodded, "I feel that I could move in here tomorrow. There's not really anything to do. A few changes in the future maybe, when we can afford it, but it's perfect as it is!"

"Yes, I think so too. We still have the survey from the last sale and it reads very well. There's only a small garden, but it will be enough for Prince. Anyway, we have plenty of space outside. Look!"

Christian pointed out of the dining room window to a large, open green field outside.

"Look, that's common land, and anyone can use it. It's ideal for a quick 'chase the ball' game with Prince, morning and evening."

"If you think you are going to get away with a quick 'chase the ball' game twice a day, then you're very much mistaken," laughed James. "He expects a long walk and your undivided attention! Don't you, boy?" Prince sat waiting in the hallway. James was very proud of how well this intelligent and sensitive dog behaved and knew that he could take him almost anywhere.

"OK, OK, I'll do my best. That dog has you wrapped around his paw, Jay, and you know it."

"Indeed, I do," said James, "but just you wait, I'll give you two weeks of living full time with him and he will be controlling you as well! Talking of dogs," continued James, "have you noticed that awful 'doggy' smell has gone? I was dreading that."

"Yes, I had noticed, Jay. Brenda was a very house-proud girl, and I think that would have been one of her first challenges when they moved in."

James and Christian walked up the narrow staircase to the two bedrooms. The old iron beds, that James had remembered in each room, had now disappeared. Both rooms had been redecorated and new carpets had been fitted. There were now new curtains and good quality ceiling and wall-light fittings installed. James wandered over to the window of the main bedroom. The views were breathtaking, and just as he had remembered from his first visit. He could clearly see the church and school set amongst the hillside.

"I remember you telling us that there was no upstairs bathroom, and suggested an extension with an en-suite bathroom," began James.

"You do have a good memory. Yes, I remember saying that as well. This room would be ideal for a conversion, but it would cost quite a bit. As you can see, Tim and Brenda didn't get around to that. Maybe we could do it sometime in the future?"

"It doesn't really bother me, Christian," replied James. "Let's keep it as it is and maybe when we get some more money, we can think about it later."

James and Christian took their time looking around the small cottage and eventually walked out of the back door into the small garden.

"This is perfect. Yes, it's small, but we could easily have a small shed over there and maybe some shrubs, instead of just lavender?"

"Well, in time, maybe we could even buy a bit of land from our neighbour," said Christian, nodding towards the small bungalow at the side of the cottage. "They have masses of land and it's all down to grass. Tim told me that an elderly couple live there. Maybe, when they get to know us, they might sell off a piece to us so that we can have a bigger garden. It must take them ages to cut all that grass."

"Well, it's certainly worth thinking about," agreed James. "Christian, it's perfect as it is. I love it. If you're happy as well, then let's go for it! The sooner the better!"

"You really sure about this?" Doris had enquired anxiously as soon as James had told her about Lavender Cottage. "Do you think it really is a good idea dragging up the past and living somewhere where you were going to be with Tristan? Surely it would be better to look at something completely different?"

"I know what you mean, Doris, and I have thought about it very carefully. Actually, I already feel very much at home there. Christian and I have talked about it a lot and he loves it too. It will be just perfect!"

Doris smiled. She knew only too well that once the impetuous young head teacher had made up his mind there was no stopping him.

"James, the Rector is here to see you," announced Doris.

The Reverend Doctor Hubert Langdon-Hobbs and his portly frame breathlessly greeted James as he reached the top of the flight of narrow stairs leading to James' office. He sat down with a sigh on one of the comfortable chairs in the corner of the room.

"Tea, Vicar?" began James, immediately recognising that he had slipped into a television comedy routine that he had seen recently, and promptly 'bit his lip' and asked again, now very seriously, "Tea or coffee, Rector?"

"You needn't try to cover up the joke, James," guffawed the Rector. "I have had that one thrown at me nearly every day of my working life as a priest. My parishioners seem to think it is amusing, but I must say that after thirty odd years, it is now wearing a little thin. You look happy today, James, I must say."

"I am," replied James, beaming broadly as he offered the Rector a mug of tea, as well as a plate of chocolate digestive biscuits that Doris thoughtfully kept in her bottom drawer for such occasions.

"Might I ask? Is this good humour something to do with a certain young man by the name of Christian Trill?" queried the Rector.

"My goodness, news travels fast around here, Rector."

"Indeed, it does," smiled the portly priest. "Nothing escapes our attention in this village for long, James. I have to say that June and I are delighted. From what we have seen and heard he is a good living young man. He is well known and liked by the partners and staff in his office, I hear. He sounds eminently suitable for you, James."

"My goodness, you have done your homework!" James exclaimed.

"Well, I guess people are my business and, I have to say, that when it comes to you, James, I, and indeed most of the villagers, are very protective of you. You are a remarkable young man and we have learned to respect, no, we have come to love you."

James was silent for a moment. "I am very touched, Rector. I love this village, its people and its children. It is my life."

"I know it is, James," nodded the Rector, taking two chocolate digestives from the plate that James had placed in front of him. "I think we have all learned from you and your love of Tristan. We have all learned and admired the way in which you have dealt with your own personal loss and the way in which you still found the energy to fight for our school. You are well liked and, I have to say, admired, James."

James smiled. "Now, what are you after, Hubert? You are up to something, I know!"

"No, I mean every word, James," replied the Rector, dipping one biscuit into his mug of tea and watching the chocolate melt to just the right consistency before taking a large bite. "I admit to having some misgivings about you at first. Your declared sexuality troubled me deeply, I confess. However, I have learned a great deal from you and Tristan about love and commitment and I am sorry for any misgivings that I had. I am also sorry for all that trouble about removing the school stage, James. I now know that I was wrong."

"Well, thank you, I appreciate you saying that, Hubert. Anyway, isn't it I who should be confessing to you?"

The Rector smiled and licked the remaining chocolate from his biscuit. He sighed and put down his mug of tea.

"James, I have called in to see you about another matter. I will be leaving the Parish shortly. I have already told Sir Toby and I would like you to know as well, in confidence for the moment, of course."

James was silent and nodded. "Yes, of course, but, I'm shocked. I appreciate you telling me, but surely you are not of retirement age yet, Hubert?"

"I am very close to it, James. You see, priests never really retire but, my health has not been so good recently, and so we are going to move closer to June's sister. I will still carry out some duties, but it will be less onerous than here. You see, James, I have five parishes to look after here. It is hard work."

"Yes, I see, Hubert. I'm really sorry. Whatever you say, you and June have been very kind to me and I shall miss you."

The Rector took James' hand. "I have seen you develop from an impatient, heady youth to a kind and sensitive young man in the last two years, James. June and I will miss you and the village. I will be leaving after Christmas and I hope that my successor will be in place by Easter. The bishop tells me that there will have to be a brief interregnum, but in a way, I think that will be good for the village. Therapeutic, in fact. Be yourself, James, and stick to your fine principles. May God Bless you, my boy."

James watched the portly priest walk unsteadily down the narrow staircase from his office and outside to the school playground. He could see pupils of all ages, taking his hand and chatting to him and leading him to the school gate. James smiled to himself. Yes he had found the Rector to be a real challenge during his first year at the school, but now he knew that he truly liked and respected him. James also knew that he would miss him.

"Christian, do you remember the other evening?" asked James, vaguely.

"Hmm, was that the one when you stripped off all my clothes after our egg and chips and then you sexually attacked me, or maybe the one when you seduced me in the shower when I got in from work?" began Christian with a smile playing on his lips.

"You know what I mean! No, I mean when you told me that Jasmine had been speaking to you and told you that she had heard that I had dinner with Sam Rivers?"

"Go on."

"Well, why did she want to see you? I was just wondering, that's all," said James quietly, realising that he sounded very controlling.

"I wondered when you would get around to asking me about that? I forgot to tell you what happened. We were so involved in other things, Jay."

"Go on, tell me! You know I hate secrets, and particularly where Jasmine De Valle is concerned," laughed James. "I hope she didn't call in to see you, just to tell tales on me?"

"Of course not, James. Don't be so paranoid. She's not a bad woman, at all. Just a bit loud, maybe. I rather like her and Paula too," he added.

"There's a side to Jasmine that you don't know, Christian. I know her pretty well, I think. Remember that she tried to seduce me once!"

"Yes, both she and you have told me. Funny, her story is a little different from yours, Jay," he grinned.

"You're winding me up, aren't you?" demanded James.

"Well, yes, a little, I guess. No, she just wanted to see me. Apparently, Paula and she are thinking about buying a larger flat and thought I could help. They have plans, you see."

"Hmm, well, I guess the flat is a bit small, but it's close to Jasmine's job, so maybe they just fancy a change."

"It's more than that, Jay. They want to start a family."

"Right, has Paula been married before? Jasmine hasn't got any kids, I know."

"No, Jay, I said that they wanted to start a family," said Christian slowly and deliberately.

James thought for a moment.

"I see, adoption, you mean? Gay couples aren't allowed. It makes my blood boil when I see the circumstances in which some kids live. Gay or straight, what does it matter as long as the children are loved and cared for?"

"No, James. Come off your 'hobby horse', please. Just listen and think."

James was silent again.

"You mean? Oh God, no! You don't mean artificial insemination from a donor bank or something, do you? That's a bit weird, don't you think?"

"Well, we got there in the end, Jay," grinned Christian. "No, they don't want to use a donor bank or someone they don't know. What they would really like is for you to donate something very special to them, Jay. Let's call it a gift. They like and admire you a lot and they both think that with your good looks and intelligence, your genes would be ideal! I said I would ask you."

It was Monday morning and James had just taken school assembly. He returned to his office for a few moments to collect the pile of exercise books from his desk. The telephone rang and Doris answered it.

"Prior's Hill School. Good morning, how can I help you?" began Doris, pleasantly. James smiled to himself. Doris' telephone manner had improved so much since he had arrived at the school. He recalled how blunt she used to sound when answering the telephone when they first met. He had to use all his charm and tact to help her to adapt to a more friendly tone of voice.

"Good morning, PC Wright. I'm very well, thank you. Yes, George is too. James is right here. I'll put him on for you," continued Doris. Doris handed the receiver to James and then left the room.

"Good morning, PC Wright. It's James Young here, what can I do for you?"

"Good morning, Mr Headmaster. My, you do have a commanding-sounding telephone voice, don't you," replied a voice that James recognised only too well. It was not PC Wright's voice at all.

"Sam, what the hell are you doing pretending to be PC Wright?" shouted James, angrily. "You're still playing your silly games?"

"Calm down, calm down, Jay. I must say that I much prefer your telephone voice. You really sound so masterful when you use it," responded Sam, mockingly.

"What do you want? I'm busy. Anyway, talking of PC Wright, I should think that the police will have a lot of questions to ask you, if they haven't already."

"Oh, James. You know me much better than that. They are still looking for me, you know. I am so easy to find if you look. As you know, Jay, I am everywhere. I see that you are just off to the barn with your stack of exercise books? I do hope the children don't give you too much trouble today."

"How the hell do you know that?"

Sam ignored the question and continued, "I do hope you liked my little game the other day. So funny don't you think? You really believed that Christian had been in a car crash, didn't you? It was so, so fitting, don't you think? I thought it was very funny. You looked really ill in the hospital waiting-room, and Doris too. That was a good one."

"How dare you! Why are you being so cruel? I've not done anything to deserve it!"

"You really don't think so, Mr Headmaster? Firstly, you shun my love for you. I thought I was doing you a favour and yet you try to shut me out of your life and won't help me. Secondly, you are trying to destroy my chance to get my own back on the Peatwhistles. I deserve to inherit the Peatwhistle Estate. I'm owed it! Then you betray me to the police and they are making my life very uncomfortable at the moment. You still don't think you deserve it?"

"The sooner they catch up with you, Sam Rivers, the better. You're crazy; you need psychiatric help and a long jail sentence. Take my advice; give yourself up."

"Oh, you think so, Mr Headmaster? Well, remember this and remember it well. I always win. I always get my own way, but if I fall then you will fall with me," came the cold response.

James thought for a moment. "Another thing. What kind of person leaves a funeral wreath as part of a game? It was sick, pretending that Christian was dead. You know I love Christian. It shows a very warped and cruel mind."

There was a chilling pause and for a moment, James thought that Sam had replaced the receiver.

"Oh, Mr Headmaster, you are so mistaken. As, I told you, I always win and, if not, I will take you with me. Those lovely flowers were not for Christian. Oh no, they were for you. I just thought you should see them before you die."

Chapter 16

A Winter's Tale

Storm clouds were gathering over Prior's Hill. James had been listening to the local weather forecast and was very concerned. It sounded as if the area was due for a heavy snowfall, the first of the season. James was grateful that he now lived in Abbotsford and no longer had the long drive over the treacherous hills to Prior's Hill.

Over the last few days there had been a biting wind and James, for once, had agreed with Emily that it was far too cold to allow the children to play outside. Instead, all but the youngest pupils had been frog-marched by Emily for a brisk walk around the playground, well wrapped up in their coats and scarves, and immediately back indoors again.

The old boiler that had been suspected as being the cause of the fire that had devastated part of the school building had now been replaced, temporarily, by a number of fixed bottled gas radiant heaters, and supplemented by a number of free-standing gas heaters and electric fan heaters and convectors.

James was not only concerned about the safety of using such appliances, but shuddered to think what the heating bill would be for the winter season. He had been assured that this emergency heating system was a temporary measure, and that a brand new central heating system would be installed when the repairs and rebuilding started in January. Meanwhile, James and his staff continually reminded pupils not to run around indoors, to keep well away from the heaters and ensured that heaters were turned off once classrooms were vacated.

Julia, in Class 1, was much more fortunate. She was in the mobile classroom that was untouched by the fire in the main school building and had the benefit of her own oil-based system which, when working correctly, maintained the classroom at a pleasant temperature. However, even this ancient system began to fail occasionally during the cold weather and, on more than one occasion, James had arrived in school to find out that the Class 1 heater had failed.

Fortunately, Toby Chapman, a new pupil in Class 1, had a father who worked as a plumber and heating engineer. He knew all about heating systems and, as most good head teachers know, it is usually far better to ask parents for help than an outside contractor. In this case, Pauline and Ralph Chapman worked long hours and it was in their best interests to ensure that the infant classroom was fully operational and that young Toby could attend school without it being closed for lack of heating.

Fortunately too, Class 4 pupils in Sir Toby's barn were generally well catered for. Bert and Eddie would ensure that the heating was switched on well before the children arrived for their lessons, and Emily had already commented that it "was very cosy to work in."

The weather forecast had alarmed James. He had occasionally implemented the school closure procedure in the past; for example, when the school fire had given him no alternative. However, he knew only too well that this was always highly unpopular with parents who could not get to work or had to make emergency arrangements for child care. He also knew that in the case of heavy rain or snow, parents would be quick to criticise any decision that he made and would ask why he had not closed the school earlier, to avoid their children being 'put at risk'.

In common with most of the nation's head teachers, James always felt under huge pressure when he heard such a weather forecast early in the morning. Either way, he knew that he could not win.
James made a decision to keep the school open, but he would consult with Sir Toby about closing early if weather conditions deteriorated further. He took a cup of coffee into the bedroom for Christian, who was still fast asleep, and kissed him.

"I'm just off now, Christian. The weather is going to be bad today and I don't know when I'll be home. You be careful and don't take any risks on the roads."

"Morning, James," yawned Christian. "Thanks for the coffee. No chance of a cuddle then? Yes, I heard what you said. I think I'm office based today, so I'll try to avoid any car journeys to remote villages. You taking Prince with you today?"

"I was going to ask you about that, Christian. He'll hate staying behind, but I won't be able to walk him at lunchtime and I don't want to ask Doris to go out in this dreadful weather. Any chance of you coming home at lunchtime to give him a run?"

"No problem, Jay. Tell you what. I'll have a late lunch and then come home to work. I have some paperwork to catch up with and I can look after Prince at the same time."

"That's brilliant. Now you be a good boy," he said, giving Prince a big hug.

"I will, Jay, don't worry," came a cheeky voice from beneath the duvet.

By lunchtime the first of the snowflakes appeared. As usual, it drew the children to the windows to look outside at this magical event that had occurred too rarely during their short lifetimes. James smiled to himself, a heavy snow covering was always a source of great fascination to children and it was to him too.

Often, and to the despair of some parents, James would allow the children outside to play in the snow, but only when it was fresh and had not turned into slush. As with all the most sensitive of teachers, James remembered how much he had enjoyed the snow as a child, and wanted his pupils to experience the same joy and excitement as he had done.

"Mr Young, look! It's covering everything so quickly," shouted Tilly Thomas, excitedly.

"Are we going back to the barn for lessons after lunch, Mr Young," asked Polly. "I haven't got any boots with me."

"Well, Polly, you are supposed to keep a pair in school, you know that. No, I don't think so, not if the snow keeps falling so heavily. We'll ask Mrs Armstrong if we can stay in the hall this afternoon. As long as we work quietly, I'm sure she won't mind."

"I don't like the look of this, James," announced Emily peering through the staff room window onto the carpet of white on the field below. It's already settling on the lanes and you know that if it gets very deep, the school bus cannot get through."

"Yes, I've just been out to check, Emily. I see what you mean."

"Do you remember some years ago, Emily, when we couldn't get all the children home? We had to stay here all night with some of them," began Doris.

"Yes, I do," laughed Emily. "I don't want to go through that again. Didn't Lady Lotitia and Sir Toby come over with flasks of soup and cakes for us all?"

"Yes, they did. Bert and Eddie brought over blankets, cushions and sleeping bags too. I think the children rather enjoyed it," recalled Emily. "We didn't get a wink of sleep, though. I was so tired the next day!"

"Well, I don't want to go through that, thank you," replied James. "Look, let's make a decision. I think we need to start closing now. Let's call the parents on the emergency list and get them to start contacting who they can get hold of. Let's see if the bus company can come earlier as well."

By two o'clock, most of the youngest pupils and those who lived within the immediate vicinity of the school had been collected by their parents. James stood in the playground, checking classroom lists and noting which child had been collected and by whom.

"It's looking really bad up there now," said Mrs Flanagan nodding towards the main road, linking Prior's Hill to Abbotsford.

"I just heard the top road's been closed," added Mrs Day, holding her small child by the hand. "Look it's nearly reached the top of my boots! Home's the best place to be. You try and make sure you get off home early as well, Mr Young."

Doris suddenly appeared at his side. "James, the bus company has just called back. They say that the road is impassable. They cannot get through. We will have to get the children home another way."

A few minutes later a convoy of large four-wheeled vehicles drew up outside the school gate and James recognised the parents driving them. Simon Tucker, the enthusiastic, young chairman of the PTA got out of one of them and trudged over to the gate.

"It's alright, James. This has happened before. I called a few parents to get the rest of the children home. I think we can get most of them where they should be."

"Thanks, Simon, let me just check the lists and then maybe you could help to see them across the lane and into the cars."

James winced, he realised that Simon was allowing far too many pupils in each vehicle and there certainly would not be enough seat belts for all. Normally, he wouldn't have allowed it, but James deemed this was an emergency and he would need to make a decision.

"That's nearly all I can get in, James," shouted Simon. "Look, we had better go, it's coming down more heavily now. I can't do much about those kiddies from the other side of The Green though. That's blocked off, we can't get through."

"Alright, you go now. I'll think of something. Thanks, Simon. Give me a call when you get them home please. I'm staying here."

"A bit like the Captain going down with his ship, eh!" laughed Simon, clambering into his vehicle.

"I really hope it doesn't come to that!" replied James.

By now, village and school appeared to be mostly deserted. Only a handful of pupils remained behind, huddled together in the entrance hall. The dinner ladies had left earlier and Cedric had called to say that he couldn't get in to clean the school.

James had already sent Anne, Julia and Doreen home, whilst Emily and Doris remained with James in the playground.

"Look, you go now, please? There's no point in us all being trapped here for the night."

"A bit late for that now, James," laughed Emily. "I'll never get my car out now. Looks as if we will all be here for the night, after all!"

James was surprised to see Emily in such good humour. Usually, if there was a problem, Emily would find a way to blame him for it and then spend all her time grumbling.

"Doris, would you mind calling the parents of the children that we have left, please? Tell them not to worry and that I will get something sorted for them. They will be safe here. Maybe the pub will help with some food and I will have a word with Sir Toby as well."

"Look, James. I think we have the answer," shouted Emily, pointing to a large tractor, complete with a large trailer, heading towards the school gate. Look, it's Mr and Mrs Freeman!"

Mr Freeman gave James a cheery wave and Harold, who had been watching from the door, shot outside.

"It's Dad and Mum," he shouted, "they've come to rescue us. I knew they would!"

"Well, we are pleased to see you, Mr Freeman," smiled James, shaking the farm worker's hand. Despite an earlier battle with the Freemans, he had come to like and respect them. They were good, honest and hardworking folk and he admired the care that they took of their large family.

"Well, I thought we could get the rest back on the trailer. They'll be all right if they sit down together real tight. It's not that far to go and the tractor's ideal."

"Hmm, well I'm a bit concerned. Is it safe?" questioned James.

"Yeah, of course it is, 'eadmaster. Them kids are on and off it all the time when we's harvesting. It's the same, but only a bit of snow! They might gets a bit wet, but I tells you, they won't half write some good stuff when you gets 'em to write their news."

James trusted the Freeman's judgement, knowing only too well that these good people were the last to put their children, or any other children for that matter, at risk.

James nodded. "Well thank you. I'll go and tell the children now."

"I'll takes 'em as well, if yer likes. Doris is only down a bit from our place and the other old girl is just a bit further on. No trouble dropping her off."

James smothered a smile as 'the other old girl' glared at John Freeman, her steely grey eyes flashing dangerously. He could hardly bare to think of her 'being dropped off' somehow.

"No, I'm not leaving you, James. I can stay here tonight or you can come and stay with us," Doris began protesting.

"Thank you, but no, you are not staying here, Doris," James replied kindly, yet firmly. "You are going home now. George will be really worried about you." Doris' mouth opened to protest further, but as she caught a look of James' determined glance, thought better of it and closed it again. "I'll be fine. Anyway, I shall stay at the pub tonight. I need to be here in case I have any phone calls from parents."

One of the lasting memories that would stay with James well into the future was a picture of six pupils, Doris and Emily, together with Mrs Freeman, huddled in the back of a trailer with a tarpaulin thrown over them for good measure, and being driven not so regally out of the village by John Freeman and his tractor. How he wished he had a camera!

It was early evening and James had long returned to the relative comfort of his office. The snow was by now the deepest that James had ever known and he even found it difficult to recognise the outline of the school swimming pool. He was amazed to see that the sports shed had all but disappeared beneath a huge mound of snow.

It was still snowing heavily and James was hoping that the electricity supply would not fail. Meanwhile, he had heating from the office fan heater, there was plenty of coffee, chocolate digestive biscuits in Doris' drawer and even a bottle of sweet sherry in the filing cabinet. James remembered that he had eaten no lunch and he was now very hungry.

The telephone rang and James answered it. He half expected that it would be Sam Rivers again, but was relieved to hear Christian's cheerful voice.

"Hello Jay. It's me, Christian. Are you all right? I'm worried about you."

"Christian, let me call you back. I'll call you right away." James was still not sure that it really was Christian calling. After the threats that Sam Rivers had made the previous evening he felt very uneasy. He dialled his home number and was relieved when Christian answered.

"It's me again. Did you call a moment ago?"

"Of course, I did, silly. Don't you even remember a call from me ten seconds ago?"

"No, it's not that. I'll explain when I see you. Is everything alright with you and Prince?"

"Yes, no problem at all. Prince is a star as usual. I did go into work very briefly and then saw the heavy snow and came home again. We closed the office to let everyone go early. It has given me plenty of time to catch up with some work, and Prince didn't complain."

"I'm sure he didn't, Christian. He would love you paying him endless attention all day. Did you manage to give him a walk?"

"Yes, but only a brief one. He didn't seem to mind too much. He did what was essential and then spent all the time rolling in the snow!"

"Just like the kids," laughed James. "I hope you dried him off well. Did you feed him as well?"

"Of course. Now what about you? Are you coming home tonight, Jay?"

"No luck, I'm afraid. I can't even drive out onto the main road. We managed to get the children home, but only just. No, I'll stay here tonight and hope to be home tomorrow."

"What are you going to do for food?"

"Well, I've got biscuits, but that's about it. If it gets desperate I may even break into the school kitchen, but then I would have to face the wrath of Mrs Hilary. It may not be worth it!"

"Look, why don't you go to the pub? You told me that you stayed there from time-to-time. They will feed you and give you a bed, I'm sure."

"Well, I'll see," replied James. "I have got some marking to do. I'm warm, have plenty of drinks and I can sleep in the chairs here. It's not too bad. What are you doing?"

"Just been watching the news, Jay. All the roads are closed and it looks really bad. There was also some other news that you will be interested in. It's about Sam Rivers."

James' heart seemed to miss a beat. "Oh?" he asked knowing that, although he had reported it to PC Wright, he had still not shared the conversation and Sam's subsequent threats to kill him with Christian. He had not wanted to worry him.

"Well, it seems they want him for attempted murder!"

A chill ran down James' spine. "What do you mean?"

"Well, you know that mother of his?"

James nearly gave away the Peatwhistle's secret, but remembered just in time, "Yes, Rita Rivers? She's in an old folks' home somewhere. I think she's being looked after by nuns."

"Yes, that's her. Well, apparently, her doctor called in to see her yesterday afternoon. After he had left, one of the nuns found her dead. It sounds suspicious; apparently it was a drugs overdose."

"Are they certain it was Sam Rivers?"

Christian was clearly bursting to tell James all the news. He continued, "Well, apparently one of the nuns thought the doctor's visit strange, because she didn't recognise him as Rita's doctor. They called the surgery to check and the surgery confirmed that no one from the surgery had been to the convent that day. They found Rita dead and the police were called. The TV news said that the police were regarding Rita's death as suspicious and that they wanted to interview Sam Rivers in connection with a similar case of impersonating a doctor in the area recently. They also warned the public to be vigilant and not to allow anyone purporting to be a medical professional into their homes without checking their identification first. It sounds as if the net is closing in on the bastard, Jay!"

James sat silent in his chair. He suddenly felt that staying in the empty school during the dark winter's evening alone was not such a good idea after all.

"James, are you still there? James?"

"Yes, I was just thinking about that poor old woman, Rita. What sort of person would kill their own mother?"

"Maybe she wasn't, James. Who knows?"

"Who wasn't, Christian?"

"I said, maybe Rita Rivers wasn't Sam's mother after all. Anyway, he's a dangerous lunatic."

A few minutes later saw James negotiating a very difficult path across the school field in the direction of the 'The Prior's Arms', the village pub. After Christian's telephone call, he felt that he didn't really want to be in the school alone all night after all. He had telephoned Les, the landlord, to ask if they had a room available and maybe they could feed him. Les had sounded surprised to hear him and had made the point of saying that they had not seen him for nearly two years.

"We quite understand, James," he had said kindly. "Jill and I know that you have had a bad time. I doubt that you felt like socialising. Yes, as we've always said, there's a room for you here if you need to stay over and we can rustle up a meal for you. It won't be our usual full menu tonight though, because I doubt if anyone else will turn out, but we will cook you something."

James was grateful. He liked Les, but he didn't care for Jill at all. She was an abrasive, outspoken and sharp-tongued woman who really had no business running a pub. Unlike her softly spoken, Irish husband, Jill tended to put off more customers than Les attracted. Neither was James too keen on staying in one of the pub's bedrooms either. The pub always smelled of stale beer and cigarette smoke and James hated both. Still, it was better than going through the evening without food and a decent bed for the night.

The snow nearly reached the top of James' boots. It was hard work trudging through the deep, soft snow and he was grateful for the light of the nearly full moon glistening upon its shiny surface. He had no torch with him, but had thoughtfully left the school's outside lights on and Les and Jill had also done the same at the pub. As James walked across the field, he was sure that he was being watched and expected Sam Rivers to appear from nowhere to taunt him. It was for that reason that James carried an old cricket bat into the 'Prior's Arms'.

"My goodness, Mr Young!" exclaimed the friendly Irishman as James stumbled through the door and into the cosy lounge bar. "You want a game of cricket in this weather? You must be joking!"

James lied, "Good evening, Les. No, I thought it might help to flatten some of the snow."

"Pretty bad out there, isn't it? I hear that you are quite the hero this evening, Mr Young. Got all the children home safe and sound, I hear."

Jill and Les were always a reliable source of village gossip and James nodded gratefully at the confirmation that he had done the right thing.

"Well, Jill is just preparing your room now. She'll come over and see what you'd like to order in a few minutes. What would you like to drink? Something to warm you up maybe?"

"Coffee would be great. Thanks, Les."

"What, coffee? You are not working now, Mr Young. What you need is a glass of 'Irish'. On me, maybe?" James smiled. "Yes, that would be nice. Thank you."

"Oh, I nearly forgot. Your dinner guest is already here. Just over there in the corner."

James walked over to the far table in the corner of the small lounge bar, carrying his glass of Irish whiskey, which he placed carefully on the table. The other occupant of the table was reading a newspaper and, in the darkness, James couldn't see the face.

"Good evening, Mr Headmaster. I wondered when you would show up. You've kept me waiting, you know."

"Sam Rivers, what the hell do you think you are doing here?"

The glamorous young woman put down her newspaper and glared at James and spoke softly, "I don't know who you think you are, but how dare you speak to me like that?"

James sat down, speechless, looking at the attractive, blonde haired young woman who was now smiling at him.

"Now tell me, sweetie, who is this Sam Rivers? Has be been upsetting you? Now do tell Jennifer about the nasty man," she purred. "Is he an ex-lover?"

"Jennifer? You must be joking. You are Sam Rivers. I know you are!"

"Oh, my dear, do stop making such a fuss. My name is Jennifer, Jennifer Miranda, and, I have to say, it is such a pleasure to have your company for dinner this evening. I was beginning to think that you had stood me up."

"How could I have stood you up when I didn't even know you would be here," hissed James.

"Well darling, you are here now, that's the main thing. Now, let us enjoy the evening, I am sure we have so much to talk about."

Jill suddenly appeared with two dinner menus, "Good evening, Mr Young," she said coldly. "It is kind of you to grace us with your presence once again after all this time. Your room is ready when you want it, but will you be needing a double or a single tonight?"

"Well, that rather depends upon how the evening goes doesn't it, my sweet," purred Jennifer Miranda, looking deeply into James' eyes.

Jill's eyes were, by now, on stalks, and it was clear that she was now feeling a little embarrassed at the situation unfolding in front of her.

"Er, yes, well, I suppose it does," spluttered Jill. James had never seen the abrupt landlady quite so startled before. "Well, just as you like. Come to the bar to order when you are ready. Mr Young, I remember that you are a vegetarian. There's a really tasty cauliflower cheese on the menu tonight."

"Oh darling," purred Jennifer Miranda, "please don't worry about James. We'll both be getting quite enough 'meat' later. More than enough."

"What did you say that for, Jennifer?" exploded James. "Goodness knows what she'll be thinking now. She's one of the biggest gossips in the village. My reputation will be ruined."

"Oh sweetie, please don't worry. She'll just think that you've picked up a pretty young woman to keep you warm in bed on this cold winter's night. Maybe she'll think that you 'bat for the other side' after all, James. Your reputation will be enhanced and so, you see, I've done you a favour, big boy."

Jennifer Miranda's gloved hands reached out to hold James' hand. She gave him a devastating smile and her beautiful blue eyes flashed dangerously. Suddenly, despite the heady sensation that James had been feeling, the truth came flooding back from the evening that James had spent with Sam Rivers at The Pantry. He leaped to his feet in anger.

"You impostor! I know it's you, Sam Rivers. Don't try to trick me any more. I know your game."

"Just sit down," came a deeper voice, "and you won't get hurt. I have a gun under the table and if you move any further I'll blow your balls off. Just you try me."

James sat down and noticed that the gloved hands of Jennifer Miranda had now disappeared under the table. He could not take any chances.

"That's better. Now be a good boy, try to look relaxed and enjoy my company. You are indeed privileged this evening," purred Jennifer Miranda.
James took a deep breath and a large mouthful of Irish whiskey.

"Now Mr Headmaster, just you listen to me. Yes, I am Sam Rivers, but as you can see Jennifer Miranda is my dear sister. We are very close. If you hurt Sam, you hurt Jennifer. Get the picture, Buddy?" said Sam in a low voice.

"You're crazy – off your head! You need help, Sam."

"Yes, I know. That's what they have been telling me for years. Indeed, that nasty psychiatric institution in New York kept telling me exactly the same thing. It was supposed to be a hospital, but it was really a penitentiary for the criminally insane. Get the picture now, James? After all, what is wrong with loving your sister and being her sometimes, James. I have always loved her…"

Sam's voice seemed to trail off into the distance as if he were thinking of something far away and of another time.

James noticed that the gloved hands remained under the table.

"All my sister wants is a nice young man to look after her and a beautiful estate in the country. Why don't you give her those things, James? They are both in your power to give. She is such a lovely girl and she would make you very happy. If you won't, I will just have to help my little sister, won't I?" Jennifer's voice had now completely disappeared and it was Sam speaking very firmly and coldly once again.

By now, despite the cold of the evening, James was sweating heavily. He realised that as well as being very foolish and cruel, Sam Rivers was insane and very dangerous.

"OK, OK. What is it you want from me?"

"Oh, just your love and respect to begin with, Jay. I also need your help in getting my hands on the Peatwhistle Estate."

"I've already told you. I can do no such thing. Surely you know that? I have no power over the Peatwhistles."

"Maybe not immediately, but you will. I had a plan, but you blew that one when you started telling tales out of school, didn't you? I have many other ideas, James. I am actually a very clever boy," Sam began talking excitedly. "As you have seen this evening, I am an amazingly good female impersonator. I can impersonate anyone, man or woman, young or old. You see, James, I call it a gift from God. I was denied my birthright, but God has given me a way to get it back!" Sam beamed excitedly.

"Yes, I have to say you are good, very good indeed," nodded James.

"When you have finished speaking to me this evening, you will spend the next few days wondering if that doctor, lawyer, teacher, parent or County Hall adviser are really who you thought they were, or were they really me, in disguise? I tell you, James, I have had such fun following you and tricking you over the last two years. Tristan's death was just so, so very convenient. I could not have planned it better myself. You will never know the answers and you will always wonder." Sam started to laugh cruelly.

James saw that Jill was staring at them both from across the bar, looking puzzled.

"Sam, I think we should order. Jill and Les are looking at us oddly. What do you want to eat?"

"Ah, so you haven't completely forgotten your manners when dining with a lady?" replied Jennifer Miranda, giving James another alarmingly charming smile. "I'll have whatever you are having, my dear. Whilst you are there could you order another dry Martini for me please, Sweetie? I'll settle up with you later and, James, don't try any funny business at the bar. I'm watching you."

James headed for the bar. Now was his chance.

"What can I do you for, Mr Young," asked Les. "She's an attractive young woman, isn't she? She's been in her a lot recently. She's thinking of moving into the village. A very quiet sort, but really charming. Known her long?"

"Les, keep nodding and taking the order, but please listen carefully. I am being held at gunpoint. Please call the police and tell them to get here quickly. Ask for PC Wright. That woman is not who you think she is. It's Sam Rivers and they want him for murder. Tell them it is an emergency."

"Right you are, sir," said Les, biting his lip and then disappearing behind the bar. There was a pause and then James heard Les and Jill laughing heartily. He turned to go back to his place, but Jennifer Miranda had disappeared. He heard the click of the outside door catch.

"You didn't believe me, did you?" hissed James angrily when Les and Jill re-appeared from behind the bar, still giggling at what they thought was a joke.

"You been drinking already, or has that Irish gone right to your head or what? She's a fine young woman. She's been in here a lot recently. Always sits at that table and drinks dry Martinis. That's no man, I can guarantee it!"

"Well, you're wrong, Les, and if you don't believe me, you would have one hell of a shock at bedtime," snapped James. "It is a long story, but you will just have to believe me. Sam Rivers is an impostor, and an impersonator and that was her, I mean, him, just now. The police are looking for him. He killed his own mother earlier today. Now get me the police urgently, please!"

"Yes, but Sam Rivers died in America some years ago..." began Jill.

"Phone!" demanded James.

James was now safely inside in the dingy and uninviting guest bedroom at the 'Prior's Arms'. He had carefully checked the adjoining bathroom, wardrobe and looked beneath the bed. He had locked and propped a chair against the door and was now standing by the window of the bedroom. Les had eventually called the police, but he had been told that the road from Abbotsford was impassable and that they probably wouldn't be able to get anyone from the police station out to see him until the following day. "Unless you are pregnant or having a heart attack, there is very little we can do at the moment," Les was told by an unsympathetic emergency operator. James would have to wait.

***

357

James looked out of his bedroom window, across the peaceful moonlit-filled playing field that was covered in thick, sparkling white snow and to the rear of the school. He noticed that the outside lights that he had switched on before he had left had now gone out. The only light still on at the school was from his office window. James could see, silhouetted against the light, the figure of a young woman staring from his office window.

Chapter 17

The Christmas Party

Prior's Hill school was closed for the rest of the week. The heavy snowfall had been one of those significant and memorable events that happen maybe only once or twice in a generation and in villages, such as Prior's Hill, this disruptive event would be much talked about for years to come. The day before the school was due to re-open, James had managed to drive into the village to check that all was in order at the school and found that the caretaker, Cedric, had also struggled to drive into the village, on his old moped, surprisingly.

The main road was now open once again and the lane to the village was passable, albeit with care. Milk lorries and tractors had already ensured that the lane connecting the village with the main road had re-opened the day after the heavy snowfall, but the main problem now was sheet-ice with many roads freezing during the severe drop in night-time temperatures. Several of the hamlets outside Prior's Hill were still cut off from the outside world and James knew that it would be several days before children from the more remote areas would once again appear in school.

The end of the autumn term was rapidly approaching and the following week was busy with the Christmas Party, complete with a visit from Father Christmas and party entertainment, as well as the traditional Carol Service, which nearly all of the villagers would attend.

After the Carol Service, it was usual for pupils, staff, parents and villagers to walk to the Manor House where coffee, orange squash and mince pies would be served in the old ballroom and where children from the school would sing a number of well-known carols and festive songs.

It was an afternoon of much merriment and enjoyment for all, yet James recalled with horror the first of such events that he had attended as head teacher of the school. He had been appalled by the children's poor quality singing and, although not a proficient pianist himself, had done his best this year to cope with a cassette tape recording with Jasmine De Valle playing the piano. He and the older children had practised regularly and James was confident that their singing would now be much easier upon the ear.

James was grateful that Jasmine, although declining to play the church organ, had kindly agreed to accompany the children on the piano, both during the Carol Service in Church, as well as for the Manor House entertainment. This was an invitation that neither Emily or Doris had approved of, when they had heard the news of the librarian's involvement, and James had smiled to himself when he heard Doris 'tut-tutting' as she furiously typed a letter.

"That woman..." Doris had begun complaining over her coffee.

"What do you want her at the concert for? She's neither a parent, nor a villager," Emily had grumbled.

"Well, if either of you can learn to play the piano by next week to accompany Class 4, you will be very welcome, and then I will cancel Jasmine's invitation. Until then – she is coming," James had snapped.

Cedric had been detailed to clear as much snow away from the pathways as possible and to grit them ready for the following day. He had arrived early to complete the cleaning that should have been carried out during the afternoon of the heavy snowfall. Also, because James now knew that Sam Rivers had been into the school office, he asked Cedric to replace the locks to the main and side doors of the school, as well as the lock to the school office.

"What do you want to do that for, sir?" grumbled the confused caretaker. "I only replaced them in September?"

"I think we have had uninvited guests recently," replied James. "Let's do it again to be on the safe side."

"Whatzat?" questioned Cedric. James remembered that Cedric rarely switched on his hearing aids when he was in school nowadays. James, by nature, usually spoke quietly and often detailed Doris to pass instructions to Cedric for him, as he seemed to understood her rather better, and without Doris having to repeat herself too often.

Maybe it was the pitch of her voice. James shouted his reply once again to the bemused caretaker. Cedric, now understanding what he had to do, nodded amiably and wandered off to continue gritting the path.

There was a knock at the door and James left his office to open the rear school door. It was Les from the pub.

"Mr Young, can you spare a moment? I need to talk to you about something important," said the publican, smelling strongly of beer and cigarettes, one of which he still had in his hand. He caught James frowning at the smouldering cigarette and he immediately stubbed it out on the stone wall and trod on it.

"Good to see you, Les. Look, do please call me James. We have known each other long enough. You were the first person that I met in the village, remember? Come into my office. It's a bit cold in there I'm afraid, as the heating has been off for a few days."

Les followed James into his tidy office and sat down on one of the comfortable chairs that James had provided for visitors.

"Now, what can I do for you? Thank you for putting me up at the pub the other night. I hope it wasn't too much trouble at such short notice?"

"No, not at all, James," said the friendly Irishman, "Jill and I are always pleased to help the school when we can. Our two used to come here, you know, and Jill used to be a school governor."

"Yes, I do remember," nodded James. "I've never met your children, of course. They left a long time before I came here. I think Jill was on the interviewing panel when I was appointed."

"That she was," agreed Les. "My Jill is a funny old stick, I know. She's a bit awkward sometimes. She doesn't mean any harm. She has a heart of gold, really."

James wasn't so sure about this last statement, but nodded in agreement.

"Look, James, I have to apologise about our behaviour the other evening," Les began. "It's been troubling us both since PC Wright called in the other day to take our statements. We thought you were just 'fooling around' and we hadn't realised it was so serious."

James' eyebrows shot upwards. Those who really knew James also knew that, since taking on his onerous duties as head teacher, this serious young man very rarely fooled around, and certainly not in public.

James nodded, "Yes, I was a bit annoyed that you didn't call the police when I asked, but I can understand why you didn't. It's not a problem, Les. Don't let it concern you anymore."

———

363

"Well, that's just it," continued Les. "My Jill can't sleep for worrying about it. She wakes up sweating and I don't feel too happy either. What if that crazy woman, I mean Sam Rivers, had shot you? You could have been killed and it would have been all our fault! No, it really does bother us, James. That Sam Rivers needs locking up after that stunt he pulled the other night. Have you spoken to PC Wright yet?"

"Yes, several police officers came to see me the following day. I gave them a statement and they say that they are taking it very seriously."

"Are they giving you any kind of protection?"

James smiled. "I don't think so. I am just being careful. Locking doors, making sure I am not out at night on my own and that kind of thing. They'll soon catch up with him and give him the help that he needs, I hope."

"Help? You are being too soft on him, James. He needs locking up and the key throwing away. The pervert."

"Why do you say that, Les?"

"Well, he's always been a bit odd. We used to know Sam Rivers really well. To tell the truth, we felt a bit sorry for him when he was a kid. The Rivers never had much and Sam often used to play with the Peatwhistle's lad, Giles. They were inseparable. He seemed normal then – real happy. Then Sir Toby sent Giles away to this posh boarding school and Sam went around the village like a lost soul until the holidays when Giles came home. Sam went to the local secondary school and never made any real friends there. They all said he was a bit strange. He used to wander around the village and we often used to chat to him, give him a glass of cola, that sort of thing. Anyway, he got friendly with our Julie. She was about the same age as him, but in a different class. She was a sensible girl and we didn't mind them playing their records and tapes together. It seemed to keep them out of mischief. Maybe, looking back, we should have been more careful," Les paused.

"I'm forgetting my manners, Les. Can I get you a coffee?" asked James.

Les shook his head. "No thanks, James, I've got to be getting back soon."

"So why were you uneasy about the relationship?" asked James, anxious to get to the bottom of the story.

"Well, we weren't really worried about there being a relationship, if you see what I mean. There were already rumours about Sam being a 'poof' because of his close friendship with Giles, but he seemed a nice enough lad, well mannered and that sort of thing. Julie seemed to like him, but just as a friend and nothing more than that. No, it was just that one afternoon when we had closed after the lunchtime trade, we heard loud pop music coming from Julie's room. I thought nothing of it at first, but after a while Jill asked me who was playing the music. I said it was Julie, of course. Jill said it couldn't be as she had gone to see her grandmother in Abbotsford that morning. I remembered after she said it, because I had asked Julie to pick up a motoring magazine in town for me," Les paused as someone knocked on the door.

It was Cedric, who put his head around the door. "All done, sir. Just off now for me lunch. Back later on and I'll pick up those new locks as well."

"Right you are. Thank you, Cedric," smiled James.

"I'm sorry Les, please go on."

"Well, we went up to Julie's bedroom and opened the door and Julie was sitting on the bed looking at record album sleeves."

"Right, so she had come home from her grandmother's early?"

"No, you don't understand. It wasn't Julie, it was someone wearing her clothes! I went over and grabbed her and it turned out to be Sam Rivers wearing a wig that looked just like Julie's hair and he sat there, as 'bold as brass' if you like, wearing some of Julie's clothes and some of her make-up as well! The resemblance with our Julie was uncanny."

"No!" exclaimed James. "What did you do?"

"Well, I remember that Jill gave him a right mouthful and pulled the wig off and 'boxed his ear' for him. I think it hurt because he shouted. He said that Julie had said he could come round and wait for her to get back from her grandmother's. Apparently, he fancied trying on some of her clothes and could see nothing wrong with what he had done. He sat there as 'cool as a cucumber'. I can see him now. I also remember him saying that he and Julie were the same size. We were livid and I thought Jill was going to have a fit. I remember her screaming at him! He just sat looking at her. No emotion, no apology. Nothing."

"I can imagine," smiled James, having witnessed Jill's wrath once or twice before at governors' meetings. He remembered that was the main reason why her re-nomination to remain a school governor had been unsuccessful. "What happened?"

"Well, Julie got home a few minutes later, and although she admitted that she had agreed that he could come over and wait for her, she certainly hadn't agreed to let him try on her clothes and make-up. She called him a pervert and screamed at him as well. I threw him out and that was the last time he came over to see Julie. I don't remember seeing him around the village much at all after that."

"Well, that is an amazing story. Thank you for telling me, Les. Seems that you witnessed the birth of Jennifer Miranda first-hand, doesn't it?"

"Well, that's just it, James. When that woman first came into the pub some time ago, I remember saying to Jill that I had seen her before somewhere. Jill agreed. Since then, she came in regularly, but not every day, you understand. She wouldn't be in for several weeks sometimes and then she would appear and be in each evening. She always drank dry Martinis and sometimes had a meal. Once she told us that she was thinking about moving into the village. She seemed very nice and we liked her. The other evening was the first time that I have ever seen her with anyone and that was with you. I am sorry, James, but we really thought that you and she had a date. Jill was surprised because she said she knew that you were…" Les paused.

"Gay, homosexual or indeed, a poof, are maybe the words that you are looking for," replied James, coldly. "Don't worry, Les. I am used to being called all sorts of names by now. So, you didn't recognise her as being Sam, then?"

"No, James, of course not. As I said, we both thought we recognised her, but in our business we get so many visitors, it's hard to say. Jennifer Miranda had blonde hair as did Sam Rivers, but when Sam dressed up in our Julie's clothes, he wore a short brown wig that Julie had. It was her aunt's and she loved trying it on when she was little, but Sam must have found it in her things. Maybe it was the hair that threw us. I just don't know. Look, I must go now. Jill is on her own and she will kill me if I don't get back soon."

James nodded and understood the publican's anxiety to keep Jill happy. "Thank you for telling me about this, Les. I do appreciate it. Have you told the police all this yet? I am sure they need to know all this."

"Yes, we gave them a statement after they saw you, James. Yes, they did seem very interested in what we told them."

"I am sure they were, Les. It does form a very clear picture and it helps to understand Sam Rivers, doesn't it?"

Les walked downstairs and opened the door to leave. "Look James. I am so sorry for doubting you the other evening. Come over soon and the drinks and a meal are 'on us'. Despite what I know you're thinking, I'm not homophobic, really. Come over for a meal and let's prove it to you. Bring your friend as well. Christian, isn't it? Anyway, I tell you, I'll not sleep easy until Sam Rivers is safely locked up and out of the way."

James decided to tell Christian about the meeting with Jennifer Miranda. He knew that if he didn't tell him, he would find out from others in the close-knit community anyway. He hadn't wanted to worry him, because Christian's protective nature and reaction to anything that would hurt or upset James was already predictable. James collected a meal from the Chinese takeaway on his way home from school, knowing that it was one of Christian's favourite meals, bought a bottle of wine and prepared the table for dinner. He decided that he would tell Christian the rest of the story when he had settled down to a good meal, and they had both begun to relax.

The door burst open and James knew that Christian had arrived. Prince, who had already been waiting at the front door for well over an hour, yelped with delight as his lively friend walked through the door. James watched Christian and the happy dog play together with Christian sitting on the carpet trying to take off his shoes.

"My goodness, what a welcome!" giggled Christian, as Prince covered him with big licks. "Now it's your turn, Jay. Come over here!"

James looked forward to this time of day, and was now beginning to forget those lonely evenings when he and Prince had only each other for company. The flat seemed so alive when Christian came home from work. His often outrageous, spontaneous and demonstrative personality contrasted so much with that of James', who had learned to hide his true feelings.

"Now, bed and a cuddle or dinner? Which is going to be first tonight, Jay," grinned Christian, brushing dog hairs off his smart suit.

"Dinner, of course," laughed James. "I have a treat for you in the oven and I don't want it to spoil. Anyway, I have a pile of marking to do after dinner so you can forget about anything else until later." James gave Christian a big hug and kiss, rushed over to the oven that was keeping the take-away meal warm and poured Christian a large glass of wine.

Towards the end of the meal, James poured Christian the rest of the wine from the near empty bottle and went over to switch on the coffee-percolator. He sat down and began to tell his story. Christian listened in silence, nodding from time-to-time, and occasionally biting his bottom lip, something that he always did when he was either angry or anxious. James finished the story, poured the coffee and walked over to Christian.

"Bloody hell, James! He could have killed you! This has all gone too far. You get the police over right now and tell them everything," he exploded, pulling James protectively towards him.

"Calm down, Christian. This is why I haven't told you everything until now. I've already told the police all that I know and they are looking into it. I don't want you to worry. I really don't believe that Sam Rivers would do anything to harm me."

"That's as may be, James, but there is a maniac loose out there. I don't want you walking in those woods at night with Prince any more. I'll do it or we'll go together. Please be careful. Lock the doors behind you and try not to be on your own until this idiot is safely behind bars," continued Christian quietly, holding James tightly in his strong arms.

"The problem is that we just don't know where he is, no one does. Sam Rivers is very clever. I don't know how he does it. I'm OK; I've always got people around me in school."

The one thing that James had not revealed to the now-worried Christian was that he had seen Jennifer Miranda staring out of his office window during that moonlit winter's night. James shivered as he recalled the scene in his mind.

"James, those entertainers you've booked. How much do you think their fee will be?" queried Doris peering at the school cheque book and the latest bank statement.

"I think it's about a hundred pounds, Doris. That's what I remember Marion saying, anyway. We used to have them at my previous school and I was so impressed with them that I thought it would be good to have them here. The children will love it!"

"Hmm, yes, I thought you said that. We don't have enough in petty cash, James, so we'll have to give them a cheque. What are they called?"

"Coffee and Cream," laughed James. "Yes, I know it is a silly name. Better not make out the cheque just yet in case they want it made out to a different name. I'll sign the cheque now anyway and maybe you would find out and fill in the name of the payee before they leave."

It was the day of the Christmas party, a day that James always anticipated with mixed feelings. He always enjoyed planning the Christmas party and giving the children an afternoon to remember, but it was always a day when things could potentially get very difficult and James hated events that might get out of control. Emily had echoed his feelings earlier in the staff room during morning coffee break.

"I know we have to have these parties and I know how much the children enjoy them, but I shall be so pleased when it is over. I can feel 'one of my heads' coming on already."

The other staff nodded in sympathy knowing full well that Emily with 'one of her heads' was bad news for all who came into contact with her.

"Did you remember to bring some music for the party games, James?" asked Anne. "I brought some tapes of what I thought was really modern music last year, but young Alison made it very clear to me that it was old-fashioned."

Doreen groaned, "Oh I know. They just seem to grow up so fast nowadays. It wasn't that long ago that I was in the dance halls myself, boogying the night away."

James smiled, recognising that the terms 'dance halls' and 'boogying' immediately categorised Doreen as being in the 'stone age' in the minds of her young pupils.

"Well, I've done my best. Christian's taste is more modern than mine, so I delegated the job to him. He's put together a couple of tapes. He seemed to enjoy doing it and it kept him quiet for ages."

"When are we going to see Christian again, James?" asked Emily. "I've only seen him briefly. He seems a nice young man and it would be good for him to meet us all. I'm sure you've told him all about us."

"Oh yes, he knows you all very well, already," James replied, looking very serious. "I've told him about how you torment me endlessly, Emily. No, seriously, I have asked him to join us for the Carol Service and then over to the Peatwhistle's afterwards. He hopes to get some time off to join us. I think he's looking forward to meeting you all properly."

"Well, the party is all ready, James," said Doris, sitting down with her mug of coffee. "The entertainers have just arrived and are setting up their stage in the hall. Cedric is helping to carry some of the things. I've just been over to the kitchen and Mrs Hilary has made a huge pile of sandwiches and sausage rolls and we've all brought in some cakes. Have you seen all the food that the parents have sent in, as well? It's amazing! The children are never going to get through it all – not after school lunch. It's going to be such a waste of good food, James."

"Look, Doris, let's put out just what we think the children will eat and save the food that will keep for their break-times after the holidays. Biscuits and crisps will easily keep for a long time. Maybe we could take any cakes and sandwiches that are left over to Maudley House. The old folk may enjoy them as long as we make it clear that the children haven't touched any of it!" replied James.

"Yes, that's a very good idea, James. I used to hate seeing all the left-over food thrown into bin liners afterwards. It just seemed so wrong," nodded Emily, approvingly.

James sat with his staff at the side of the hall watching the performers, 'Coffee and Cream'. How the children laughed at the Clumsy Clown, sat spellbound as they watched the amazing string puppets and screamed with delight at the antics of 'Mr Rubber Man' who twisted and turned and contorted his body so effortlessly. It was a breathtaking, fast-moving show and James sat enjoying watching the children's response, as much as the show itself. These were enchanting memories that his pupils were storing up for the future and James was proud to have had a part in arranging it. Staff too were roaring with laughter at the antics, and in one sketch when the Clumsy Clown pretended to trip over Emily's feet, James thought that she would fall off her chair as she was laughing so much. Doreen Sparkle had been asked to play a small part as an assistant to Mr Rubber Man and Doris and Anne had tears running down their cheeks as they watched Doreen throwing herself wholeheartedly into the role.

After the entertainment, James took all the children outside to run off some energy, whilst the staff and parent helpers moved desks and covered them with Christmas paper and put out the food for the party. James watched as the children hurtled around the playground, shouting and shrieking with joy. He was so grateful that the snow had now melted away and that the weather was kind for this special day.

"I really do think that this is possibly the best party that we have ever had at Prior's Hill, Mr Young," announced Peter Parsons, breathlessly appearing at James' side.

"I am pleased you are enjoying it, Peter. You seemed to be laughing a lot at the Clumsy Clown. I was watching you."

"Yes, he was rather good, I thought. Anyway, the final verdict will be made after the food and Father Christmas," announced the lawyer's son.

"Right you are, Peter," laughed James. "What about you, Polly. What was your favourite part?"

"I liked those puppets. They looked so lifelike. I thought they were string puppets, but their faces looked so lifelike. They looked real. It was spooky," shouted Polly, trying to be heard above the noise from the children in the playground.

"Look, there's Santa!" cried a voice.

James watched as Father Christmas, complete with a huge sack thrown over his back, walked by the stone wall and into the school playground.

"Ho, Ho Ho," boomed Santa, stopping by the gate. The pupils ran over to him and stood cheering loudly.

"Yes, it's me again. I come here every year to see all you good children. You have been good, haven't you?" Santa demanded.

"Yes, we have!" chorused the pupils.

"Well, in that case, I will be giving you a present when you go back indoors. I have something for each of you."

"Where's Rudolph?" asked Tilley, looking down the lane. "You can bring him in as well. Mr Young's dog, Prince, won't mind."

"That's very kind of you, but Rudolph is resting. He has a very busy time ahead of him and so he needs a lot of sleep. He will be out and about on Christmas Eve though, so don't you worry."

Father Christmas turned to go inside the school building. "I'll see you children later and you too Mr Young."

"Alright, Father Christmas. We'll be inside in just a few minutes. I am sure Mrs Cole will give you something to warm you up while you are waiting."

"Thank you, young man. Ho, Ho, Ho," replied Father Christmas, trying to adjust the beard that was slipping to one side.

"That isn't Father Christmas. I know who that is," began Peter Parsons.

"Don't you dare say anything, Peter Parsons. Don't you do anything to spoil it," warned James.

The children returned into the main school building and sat at their desks, which had now been transformed into banqueting tables, they put on the party hats that they had made a few days earlier and began to hungrily tuck into platefuls of sandwiches, sausage rolls, cakes and biscuits that had been put out for them. James and the staff walked around the hall pouring mugs of orange squash and topping up rapidly emptying plates. The PTA had provided crackers, balloons, whistles and streamers and James, for a brief moment, wished that he had declined the offer of crackers and whistles because the noise was horrendous.

When the children had finished eating, and James had insisted upon silence, Anne put on the 'Jingle Bells' music and Father Christmas appeared once again, giving each pupil a small parcel with their name written neatly upon it. Pens, pencil cases, colouring pencils, books and small toys soon adorned the party tables and James and the staff were pleased to see that their pupils seemed to appreciate their small gifts. James noticed that even Peter Parsons sat happily looking at his new pen and James thought for a moment that he winked at him.

It was half past four and some of the staff had already collapsed into the tiny chairs in the corner of the infant classroom, which sometimes doubled up as a staff room, looking exhausted, but chatting together happily.

James handed out glasses of 'Lambrusco' wine, which he knew that most of the staff enjoyed, but had also thoughtfully provided fruit juice for those who did not want to drink alcohol at that time of the day.

Teachers, caretaker, secretary, dinner ladies and kitchen staff were, for once, all together. James made a very brief announcement, thanked everyone for making the party such a success and the staff raised their glasses and drank a Christmas toast.

"This is such a good idea, James. I don't think we've ever had a get-together like this before, as a staff, have we?" asked Anne. "The children really enjoyed the party. I think it's one of the best."

"Did you see all that food? I am so pleased that we kept a lot of it back," said Emily. "I'll take the perishables to the old folks on my way home."

"Thanks, Emily," replied James. "Like you, I hate seeing food go to waste. Mrs Hilary, you did us proud once again. You even made Carol and I some vegetarian sausage rolls! You made us both feel very special! That was very kind of you."

"Jean and I does what we can for the kiddies," beamed Mrs Hilary, and James thought how good it was that these warm-hearted women now fully accepted that they were such an intrinsic and important part of the life of the school.

"I have never seen such entertainment as that," laughed Doreen. "I thought it was so funny. Aren't they a clever act? Tell me, Doris, how many performers were there?"

"I think it was just two, that's why they are called 'Coffee and Cream', but I have to say I only actually saw one, the young woman who collected the cheque," replied Doris thoughtfully.

"You really surprise me," began Julia. "I thought there were four of them. I don't see how two people could do all that. The lighting and music as well. It was spectacular!"

"Cedric, you helped them bring in their boxes from the van, didn't you?" shouted Doris to Cedric, who was standing at the side of her eating a ham sandwich.

"Well, I only seen one. 'Twas a young woman. My, she was a fit young thing. Those boxes were 'bloomin' heavy."

James, who was listening to the conversation between Doris and Cedric, thought for a moment and then felt the colour draining from his cheeks. He put down his glass of wine and headed towards the door of the classroom.

"I'll be back in a moment," he said. "There's just something I need to check."

"Are you OK, James?" asked Doris, anxiously. "Do you want me to come as well?"

"No, it's fine. I'll be back in a moment."

James left the classroom, headed down the wooden steps and dashed across to the main school building. He ran into the now-empty silent school and into the office. He pulled open the drawer of the filing cabinet and retrieved the school cheque book that Doris had used to pay for the afternoon's entertainment. He found the cheque stub relating to the last payment made. In Doris' neat, clear handwriting James read the last entry. It was for a payment of £105 for 'Pupils' Christmas Entertainment' and the payee was none other than Jennifer Miranda.

Chapter 18

The Confrontation

"Great news, Jay!" shouted Christian as soon as he got home from work. Christian was home early for once and James and Prince had not expected him home for some time. Even Prince had been thrown off-guard and was still happily sleeping in his basket after his brisk walk and substantial evening meal.

James too had arrived home much earlier than usual. Clearing up after the party had not taken as long as he had expected, because there had been so many willing helpers. He had even been able to take Prince for a decent walk in Abbotsford before he came home. James had kept his promise to Christian and was careful to avoid his usual route in the woods until Sam Rivers had been apprehended by the police. Due to the Christmas activities, little in the way of written work had to be marked in Class 4 and, for once, there was little in the way of preparation necessary for the following day's activities either.

Prince gave Christian his usual lavish welcome and Christian stood in the doorway as James hugged and kissed him.

"Great news!" Christian repeated. "We've got the cottage! Our offer has been accepted and the vendors are giving us all the curtains and carpets!"

James beamed and hugged Christian again. "That is brilliant news! Some good news for us at last! I'm really pleased. Did you have to raise the offer?"

"No, I did as you said and offered the asking price they wanted. They were delighted and that's why they gave us the rest as a gift! Now all I have to do is to get us that mortgage, Jay."

"Is that going to be a problem for us? I know some banks don't like lending to gay couples."

Christian frowned. "Well, we are both in good jobs, but they are tightening up on loans again. I had a chat today with the guy at the building society I normally use. To be honest, I was a bit disappointed, because we may need a larger deposit than I originally had thought. Also, we are first-time buyers and, as you say, not the usual husband and wife arrangement either. My problem is that I don't have much in the way of savings, only what I have put by for a replacement car when mine finally dies. You see, Jay, I owed Peter quite a lot of money after all my London problems. He helped get me started again. It's all paid back now, but it has left me a bit short for other things."

James nodded. "I have a bit saved, but I have been spending too much on this flat really. It would have been alright for two people to share, but I've been paying it on my own. Don't worry, Christian, you've done really well to get this moving. Just find out the minimum deposit that we will need and maybe we can try for one of those larger percentage mortgages? I'll apply for a personal loan from the bank if we have to. There's always a way around it. As you say, we're both in good jobs, after all."

"Hmm, maybe. Well the good thing is that we don't need to do much to the cottage when we move in. From what we saw the other day, all we need is a bit of furniture and we can get what we need urgently second-hand."

"That suits me fine, Christian. I have you, Prince and the cottage. The rest of it will come later. You wait and see."

Over dinner, the couple chatted excitedly about their plans for their new home together. Christian cleared away the dishes and started running the hot water to begin the washing-up. "Jay, there's something else that I wanted to ask you."

"Go on?"

"Well, you remember Uncle Frank and Aunt Eleanor? Well, they will be on their own at Christmas. They have no children of their own and they have 'sort of' adopted me."

"I noticed that, Christian. They adore you; anyone can see that. They are lovely people and I like them as well."

"Well, I wondered if we could either go there for Christmas or maybe they could come down here and stay with us? I know we are a bit short of space, but I am sure we could manage. Would you mind?"

James thought for a moment and put away the plate that he was drying. "No, of course not, but it is very short notice, you know. Look, I know they mean a lot to you and I would like them here too, but I really would love our first Christmas together to be just the three of us here. Christmas is nearly here and I am already planning what to cook. It's what I have dreamt of... since losing Tristan. Maybe it's just selfish of me?"

"Don't worry, James, I would like it to be just us too. They'll understand, I'm sure. Anyway, they haven't said anything, so they may already have something planned."

"I have a better idea, Christian," continued James. "Why don't you ask them to see the New Year in with us? They can come down for a few days. We've both got time off work and we can really enjoy having them with us, and maybe show them a bit of the area. They can sleep in our room and we can sleep in the living room. Prince will love it!"

Christian beamed, "That's a brilliant idea! I think that's even better than them coming over for Christmas, because we'll have more time with them. Anyway, Uncle Frank will be working on Christmas Eve morning, so it would be a dreadful rush for them to get down here. I'll phone them now."

It was the last day of term. By lunchtime, nearly all of the Christmas decorations had been taken down and the children had each been given a plastic carrier bag in which to put the Christmas decorations, hats and Christmas nativity figures that they had made, as well as the cards and presents that they had received. James looked at the now stark, blank walls of the hall and classrooms.

It had always been the same and, as Doris had pointed out, most primary teachers celebrate Christmas twice. Firstly, they celebrate it in their schools with cards, parties, Christmas trees and Christmas dinners and then on the last day of term they take down all the decorations of Christmas, go home and start all over again with their families.

It was an exhausting time of the year and, as much as James loved his job, he couldn't wait to lock the school gate for the last time and begin his own Christmas celebrations with Christian and Prince.

He dragged out the still fresh Christmas tree onto the playground ready for the rubbish collection after Christmas. It seemed so wrong that this fine tree would never actually see Christmas. He made a mental note to ask Doris to phone local hospitals and residential homes to see if anyone wanted a large Christmas tree. He spotted Jack Sparrow pottering in his garden and waved to him. Jack walked over to the wall to speak to James.

"Thank you for your kind gift, young sir," he began. "There was no need, but much appreciated nevertheless."

"Well, thank you for all the milk deliveries and all the other things that you have done for us this year, Jack," replied James, shaking hands with the toothless old man. "You are such a good friend and neighbour of the school. I don't know what we would do without you."

"Well, I does what I can, young sir. Jean tells me that them kiddies had a lot of fun with that entertainer yesterday. I could hear them laughin' and shoutin'. They really enjoyed it, didn't they?"

"Yes, they certainly did, Jack," laughed James. "I do hope we didn't disturb you too much."

"No, I likes to hear kiddies enjoying themsells. If I didn't like kiddies then I wouldn't live next door to school, would I?"

"That's true, I guess. You said entertainer, Jack. Did you see how many there were? From their performance, it looked like there were three or four of them, but Doris thinks there were only two."

Jack scratched his nearly bald head. "Now, that's a puzzle, young sir. I was out here tidying up a bit and I sees just one young woman heaving boxes out of that van likes she's a farm worker. My, she must have some muscles on her. Your Cedric came out to give her a hand, but she didn't really need him. She put old Cedric to shame, I can tell you. Muscles like a man, that one." Jack guffawed with laughter as he revisited the scene in his mind.

"So there was just the one woman."

"From what I could see, young sir. Never seen anything like it. Strong as an 'orse, that one and there's no mistake."

James and the pupils from school silently filed into the village church. It was already partly full of parents and villagers, and James was pleased that he had the foresight to ask Doris to put reserved notices on the pews that would be used by pupils and staff. The Rector was busying himself with lighting candles and asked James if two of the youngest pupils would like to light a candle on the Advent wreath. James nodded, "Good idea, Rector. I'll ask Julia to arrange it."

"I'll also be making my own little announcement at the end of the service, James. I really will have to tell everyone that I am leaving. You see, I have been putting it off."

"I quite understand, Rector," nodded James. "This village has become your life. I can see that."

"The same as it has for you, James," smiled the Rector.

James heaved a sigh of relief as he spotted Jasmine De Valle waving to him from behind the piano. She had arrived quietly and unannounced for once and James saw that Paula was also sitting with her, looking as if they were about to play a duet together. James smiled and then remembered that he hadn't replied to the couple about their earlier request. Well, this was certainly neither the time nor the place to discuss it, he thought.

James noticed that the Rector was signalling to him that he was ready to begin and James returned to his pew. He could see Christian sitting by the side of Cedric at the back of the church and beckoned to him to sit by him. Christian grinned and shook his head and pointed towards the door. James understood that he couldn't stay for long.

James had planned a very traditional service that parents and villagers expected each year, even though he would have preferred something much more relevant and modern.

Although he didn't mind some of the traditional carols and readings, James would have liked to have used some of the modern hymns, a little drama and maybe a modern version of the Christmas story. Anne had warned him not to change the well-established pattern and, for once, he was grateful to have taken her advice. James was at last learning that there are some battles that are worth fighting, but there are other issues that are best left as they are. The church was full and James was pleased to see that both Sir Toby, as well as Lady Lotitia, were in one of the rear pews. Lady Lotitia smiled and gave him a little wave. James waved back just as the Rector stood to welcome the congregation and Peter Parsons stood to announce the first carol.

"What a wonderful service," beamed Lady Lotitia, standing outside the church porch as the pupils walked out of the church and along the path towards the Manor House. "Such wonderful singing and the clarity of their reading was just superb, what?"

"Thank you, Lady Lotitia. Yes, the children have worked hard and I was pleased with their singing this year. You'll hear them again later, of course. Are you feeling better now?"

"Yes, James, thanks to you, I am now fully recovered, what?" smiled Her Ladyship. "Look, after the get-together, I wondered if you and your friend would like to stay for something a little stronger and Toby and I can say a proper thank you to you. You saved my life, you know, James."

"I would be delighted, thank you. I am not sure about Christian though. He was here for the Carol Service, but I think he had to go back to his office and I'm not sure how long he will be. I'll mention it to him and see, but I will come over once the children have all gone home."

"Splendid," beamed Lady Lotitia. "We have so much to thank you for."

Later in the afternoon, James' pupils once again sang to the assembled parents and villagers in the huge music room at the Manor House. The spacious room had once been a ballroom, but Lady Lotitia had insisted that 'ballroom' was too grand a title for 'a small country house' and had insisted that it be renamed the 'Music Room'. James noticed that the room was as large as his classroom and the hall put together plus a sizeable piece more. All the pupils, together with their parents and many villagers comfortably fitted into the room. Peggy and a group of villagers busily handed out tea, coffee and hot mince pies to the assembled gathering, whilst pupils enjoyed cola and mince pies at the far end of the room and were gathered around a huge grand piano over which Jasmine De Valle presided.

"James, darling, how good to see you!" gushed Jasmine De Valle. "Such a treat to be able to accompany your divine children this afternoon. Aren't they singing well?"

"They certainly are, Jasmine, thanks to you. I really appreciate you helping us like this and it is good to see Paula too."

"We're delighted to help, James. We were hoping to catch you. Did Christian mention that other little matter we spoke about?" she whispered and very embarrassingly, James thought, pointed to his crotch.

"Er, no, no yet. I'm sorry, Jasmine. I really don't think... Maybe we could discuss it another time."

"Of course!" beamed Jasmine, "but it would be good to know soon. A girl's eggs are not as fresh as they once were once she's turned forty, you know," she guffawed loudly, smacking him gently on the shoulder.

James smiled and turned to return to his class.

"What was that all about," hissed Doris loudly.

"You really don't want to know," replied James, now pink with embarrassment.

The concert went well and parents and villagers were full of praise for the children's singing. James was pleased and, for once, he too was delighted with their achievement. After the concert, most parents collected their talkative offspring from the school playground and before long the playground was empty with only James and the old horse-chestnut tree for company.

"I've put your presents and a Christmas cake in your car," smiled Doris, once again looking like a well-laden packhorse. "Thank you for your gift, James. I promise I won't open it until Christmas Day. I hope Prince likes his."

"Thank you, Doris. It really is very kind of you. It has all gone really well. Thank you so much for all that you have done. Are you going now?"

"Not yet, I have a few letters to finish before I go. I thought I would also take Prince for a walk. He's been such a good dog and he has spent most of the afternoon asleep under your desk. You are going over to the Peatwhistle's now, aren't you? Is it alright to take him for a walk? I always enjoy walking him."

"You bet, Doris. Christian was going to take him home, but he had to go back to his office, so I guess by the time you're back, Christian will be here to take him home and give him his dinner. If not, I'll call back to school after I've seen Sir Toby and Lady Lotitia. Have a wonderful Christmas and remember to come over to us on Boxing Day evening. Don't forget! I am cooking something special for you both, but you had better warn George that it is vegetarian!"

"I won't! Have a wonderful Christmas, the three of you." The little woman gave James a big hug and James swung her off the ground.

"Now off you go. Don't be too long finishing and going home!"

At last it was the end of term and it was now time for James to begin to relax. As he walked once again down the stone-filled driveway to the Manor House, he reflected upon the term that had now almost finished and admitted to himself that, despite many problems, it had all gone rather well.

He had been very pleased and proud of his pupils at the Church service and Christmas Concert, and he knew that the children too were very pleased with themselves.

As James got closer to the front entrance he could hear voices; loud, angry voices and he could also hear crying. He didn't want to disturb the Peatwhistles if they already had visitors, but he knew that Lady Lotitia would be expecting him. Maybe they were watching the television? James walked to the side of the house and heard the voices coming from the breakfast room. He stopped at the side of the patio doors that led to the Rose Garden and listened to the heated conversation. There was a woman sobbing and it sounded like Lady Lotitia.

"You devious old bag! You almost destroyed my life and you won't even do this for me? Your lives are over, but mine is just beginning. For years I've been nobody, the one who got the left-overs and never the real thing. I'm the one who was treated like dirt, whilst you Peatwhistles got the 'touched forelocks', the bowing and the scraping. Now, it's my turn. Your precious Giles is dead, yet I'm still alive! For God's sake, I am your son just as much as he ever was!"

It was Sam Rivers arguing with his mother. James knew that he shouldn't listen to the conversation, and that he should call the police who were looking for Sam. James' heart was beating wildly; he knew there was something badly wrong. He couldn't leave whilst this was going on.

"Yes, it was me who looked after your precious son for all those months, and don't you ever forget it! It was me who treated all those hideous sores on his body and mopped his brow when he had a fever. It was me who worked all hours and stole to get enough money to pay the medical bills, feed us and pay the rent. It was me who was with him when he died. Yes, I loved your son! Where were you, his mother and father?!" Sam was now screaming at Lady Lotitia and Sir Toby with uncontrolled rage.

"We did what we could at the time. You didn't tell us everything. You asked and we sent you money from time-to-time. You didn't tell us how sick he really was." James could hear Sir Toby's quiet, distinguished voice speaking from the far end of the room.

"How could I?!" yelled Sam. "Giles was dying from AIDS! You didn't even want to know him when you found out he was gay. You would have turned away from him then, just as you did before. He begged me not to tell you!"

"Toby's right. How could we have done more, if we didn't know?" Lady Lotitia had stopped crying and was now speaking in a much calmer voice.

"You owe me a big debt! Giles is dead, but I'm still your son. The Peatwhistle Estate is mine by birthright!" exclaimed Sam.

"You foolish boy!" replied Sir Toby, calmly. "That is just the point. It is not yours by birthright. There is not a drop of Peatwhistle blood in your veins. This estate will never be yours."

"Yes, you are my son, Sam and I am truly sorry for what I did, but all I can do is to leave you a little money when I have gone," said Lady Lotitia, sadly.

"I truly have no love for you, Sam. Rita was your mother, and by all accounts you killed her."

"So who was my real father? Do you even know who he was, you old slut?"

"I am not at liberty to say. I promised long ago that I would never reveal the secret, Sam. Yes, it was a mistake and I am so sorry that you have been so hurt!" Lady Lotitia sobbed. "All you need to know is that Rita was your mother. I may have given birth to you, but she was a proper mother to you."

"That is not good enough! Rita was not my mother, you are! It was by an accident of birth that I was not your eldest son. You deny me my rightful inheritance, you deny me a real father and you deny me the right to be your son! You bloody woman, may you rot in hell!" screamed Sam, pulling out a small gun from his pocket. "You will do as I say!" he added, placing the small pistol on Lady Lotitia's forehead.

"Put down that gun now, Sam!" yelled James. "This will get you nowhere!"

Without being in full control of his actions, James found himself flying though the patio doors and leaping onto Sam Rivers' back. There was the sound of a single gunshot, a scream from Lady Lotitia and a groan from James as he fell to the floor in a small pool of blood.

A split second later a large mound of golden fur threw itself through the open patio doors. A snarling, growling angry dog leapt onto Sam Rivers, pushing him to the ground. There was another gunshot and a yelp as Prince fell on the carpet next to James' body, and a groan from Sam Rivers as he found his head coming into contact with a heavy croquet mallet wielded furiously by Doris.

"My God, Doris! What are you doing here?" exclaimed Sir Toby who had quickly retrieved the gun from the floor and was now pointing it at Sam Rivers. "Doris, call the police and get an ambulance! Quickly now, James is in a bad way!"

Just as Doris was dialling for the emergency services, PC Wright and two other policemen appeared through the patio doors.

"No need for that, Doris. We're here now. An ambulance is already on its way! We've been watching and heard the gun shots."

The police officer who was kneeling beside James spoke. "He's alive. He's bleeding quite a bit, but we'll see what the medics say when they get here."

James groaned and saw his beloved Prince lying by his side in a pool of blood. "My dog, that's my dog," he whispered weakly. "Get a vet, get him to the vet please!" James looked at Doris with pleading eyes and passed once again into unconsciousness.

Two ambulances and three police cars, with their sirens blaring and lights flashing, sped into Prior's Hill and down the driveway to the Manor House, just as Christian was parking his red Ford Escort outside the school building. When Christian heard the sirens he restarted the engine of the old car and followed the vehicles into the Manor House. He sensed that something was very wrong. He saw a stretcher being taken from the side of the house and carried into one of the ambulances. Christian jammed on his brakes, stopped the car and ran over to one of the police officers. "What's happened?"

"Now then, sir. This area is out of bounds. There's been an accident, that's all. Please leave the grounds right away."

Christian saw Doris standing and crying by the doorway. Doris immediately spotted him and ran over and hugged him.

"Christian! Thank God you're here! It's James! He's been shot! They've shot Prince as well!" she cried. "You go with him, I'll stay here with Prince." Doris ran back inside the building.

Christian had so many questions, but could say nothing. Instead, he ran over to the ambulance and demanded to be with James.

"I'm his partner and I'm going with him," he demanded firmly.

The medic looked at PC Wright, who nodded, and continued treating James. Once again James became conscious. "Where's Prince? Please help Prince!"

"Doris is looking after your dog, Mr Young," said PC Wright, kindly. "We'll take good care of him and get him to the vet."

"I'm here, James," sobbed Christian, holding his hand. "I'm coming with you, Jay. I love you very much. You just keep thinking about Lavender Cottage and the three of us. We are going to be so happy, James. Remember how much I love you. I won't ever leave you."

A second stretcher carrying Sam Rivers, accompanied by two police officers, was lifted into the second ambulance. Both police officers got into the ambulance and the doors were firmly closed.

Two ambulances with lights flashing and sirens blazing sped their way out of the driveway. As they left the village, Bert and Eddie were to be seen speeding down the driveway from the nearby farm. The old van stopped outside the breakfast room and the two farm workers ran inside the building. Within seconds a large bloodstained golden retriever had been placed upon one of Lady Lotitia's best Chinese rugs and covered with a blanket and placed into Bert's van. Two men, a small lady and a badly injured and bleeding dog were soon speeding out of the village.

Chapter 19

A Perfect Nightmare

James was in a state of half-sleep: that often delicious time when we feel totally relaxed and at peace with the world, but still not fully awake. His chest felt uncomfortable and he felt a sharp pain in one arm. These discomforts were swept to one side when he saw Tristan walking towards him. Tristan was wearing a white gown and his long blond hair was swept back from his face as he walked. He was holding something for James to see. James felt excited yet tearful; it was his beloved Tristan coming to see him, but why was he wearing a white gown? Then James remembered that Tristan was dead. Did this mean that he was he dead too?

Tristan walked closer towards him and now James could see his happy, smiling face. He had something important to tell him, he was sure. His white teeth gleamed in the bright light that filled the room and his bright blond hair glowed. He looked so handsome. Tristan got closer; he was only a short distance away now. James felt his heart beating rapidly; he would soon be able to touch him and to hold him. Oh, how he wanted to feel his warm body close to his once again. What was Tristan carrying in his hands?

James watched the beautiful face getting closer to his and then became disappointed and horrified to see that it appeared to be changing, dissolving and then reforming in front of him, rather like a ball of clay. What was happening? No longer was it Tristan's happy, friendly face, but that of Sam Rivers. It was true that the face, the jaw line, the brilliant white teeth and colour of hair were similar, but the overall appearance of the face now looked mean and cruel. Thin lips and a turn of the mouth no longer made for a happy, generous and loving disposition, but now there was a face that was going to harm him. James groaned as he realised that it was no longer his loving Tristan coming closer towards him, but it was someone far crueller. Sam Rivers started stroking James' hair gently, but James could now see that he had a large hypodermic syringe in his hand. James groaned and began to shout as the long, sharp needle pierced his skin.

"No! No! Go away, Sam! I don't want to die!"

"James, James, wake up! It's me, Christian. You're having a bad dream. I'm here, not Sam. Nothing will hurt you. Look feel my hands," said Christian gently.

"Get him away from me, Christian! He's trying to kill me and Prince. Christian, get him away!" shouted James.

"Jay, you're safe. Sam Rivers has gone. He's not here. Feel my hands protecting you," Christian kissed James gently on the lips.

James opened his eyes, stared and then, seeing Christian, gave a faint smile. "What's happened? My chest hurts and there's something attached to my arm. What's happened? Am I dying, Christian?"

"You had an accident, Jay. You're in hospital. You've had an operation, but you are going to be fine."

A nurse walked into the room and smiled when she saw that James was awake and talking. She walked over to him and put her hand on his brow. She looked at the dials on the equipment at the side of James and smiled.

"You've had a good sleep, Mr Young. You're doing well. Your friend will let me know if you need anything."

"What accident? Yes, I do remember now. My God, Sam Rivers... Prince! What happened? Christian, is Prince dead?"

Christian smiled and gripped James' hand. "No, Prince isn't dead, but he has been poorly just like you. He had an operation as well this evening, but I called Doris earlier as she went with him to the vets. She says he's doing fine now. He's staying at the vets overnight, but he is awake and doing well, James. You'll both soon be home with me again."

James sighed with relief. "Thank God, I don't know what I'd do without that dog. I love him so much."

"Yes, I do too, James, and Doris adores him as well. Do you know that you're both heroes? You're the toast of Prior's Hill?"

"What do you mean?"

"You and Prince saved Sir Toby and Lady Lotitia's lives!"

"We did?"

"You did! You're my hero as well, Jay. I'm so very proud of you!"

"What time is it?" James murmured.

"About three in the morning, Jay. Now, you get some more sleep. You'll feel better when you wake up."

"You go home and get some sleep as well, Christian. You can't sleep here."

"Not likely. I am staying in this chair right by your side until you get out of hospital and I get you back home."

The next few days were anxious ones for Christian. As promised, he stayed by James' bed-side, helping to look after him and paying very little attention to his own needs. He helped to wash and shave James, and it was not until Doris suggested that he too might like to go home and "freshen himself up" that he realised that he needed to pay a little attention to his own personal hygiene.

"Christian Trill, you are beginning to smell," Doris had stated, less than tactfully. "Why don't you go home and shower, shave and get a change of clothes? I can stay here with James for a few hours."

Christian grinned. "OK, Doris. James warned me what a tyrant you can be."

"You've seen nothing yet," laughed James, "Anyway, Doris, I rather like seeing Christian unshaven. I think he looks even more sexy like that!"

"Oh you boys!" laughed Doris. "It's so good to see you laughing again, James. Does it still hurt?"

"No, not really. It just feels as if something is too tight for my body, that's all."

"Having a bullet removed is no joke, Jay, but the doctors say that there will be no lasting damage. You were very lucky. Strange, it was almost the same as the operation that Prince had," said Christian.

"Tell us again what the vet said today, Doris. I couldn't take it all in earlier?"

"The vet says that, like you, Prince is very lucky. The bullet has been removed. He lost a lot of blood, but he's recovering nicely. Apparently, he's eating really well now, which is a good sign. He can come home tomorrow and, as you will still be in here for a day or two, George and I are going to look after him at our place."

"You sure, Doris? That really is so kind," asked Christian anxiously. "I need to be here so that would be a weight off my mind."

"Well, I think it's time you went home for a good sleep as well Christian. You've been here for three days now. I can take it in turns with George to keep an eye on James, as well as Prince."

"Thank you, Doris, but I do need to be here. I'll go home now for an hour or so to shower and change, but I'll be back very shortly."

Christian took James' hand and kissed him. "I won't be long," he promised.

"My goodness, that boy is devoted to you, James. I hope you know how lucky you are," began Doris after Christian had left the room. "I've never known anyone give so much care and love, James. He really loves you."

"I know Doris. I realise now how wonderful he is. To be honest, I've not been too good to him. I know I have taken him for granted. You see, I found it hard to let go of Tristan and with all this Sam Rivers business as well…"

"I know, James. You don't need to explain. Christian understands as well, I'm sure. I think you'll find later that this whole incident has brought you even closer together. It'll work out fine, you mark my words."

"I still don't really know what happened, Doris. The police say that you walloped Sam with a croquet mallet. I bet that didn't do him any good!"

James' diminutive secretary grinned, her bright eyes sparkling beneath her large owl-like glasses.

"Yes, apparently he had concussion and was 'out for the count' for a while," she said proudly. "You see, I took Prince for a walk as I promised after you had gone over to the Manor House. Usually, he's a good dog and walks beautifully, but he suddenly started pulling and I couldn't control him. He started to snarl and growl and I thought he had seen a cat. Anyway, he eventually pulled me right over and ran off over to the Manor House. I followed Prince over there and, as soon as I saw what was going on, I grabbed the nearest thing to hand."

"The croquet mallet!"

"And walloped Sam Rivers hard on the head with it. I don't know what came over me. Then I saw you and Prince and all the blood... It looked terrible. You were very brave, James, and Prince too. He is such a remarkable dog."

"He is, isn't he?" smiled James. "Goodness knows how he knew I was in trouble. He hated Sam, I know. He always snarled whenever he saw him. He has never done anything like that to anyone else before."

"I tell you, James, that dog has been sent by Tristan to protect you."

"Yes, I have always thought that as well, Doris," replied James quietly. After a few moments, James tried to sit up in bed. "What happened to Sam?" he asked suddenly.

"Well they brought him into this hospital for treatment. They kept him in overnight. There were police officers outside his door. The following day, he was well enough to be transferred to a prison with a hospital wing on-remand until his case comes up. I don't know which one he is in though."
James thought for a moment.

"Doris, please be honest with me. Was there any trouble when he was here?"

"What do you mean?"

"Did he try to escape? I asked Christian, but he didn't answer. I think he did."

Doris paused and thought for a moment. She knew James too well to know that she couldn't avoid the truth and get away with it.

"Well, yes, he did. Only for a few minutes though."

Doris paused and wondered if she was doing the right thing in telling James the truth of what had happened.

"Go on."

"Well it was just before you came around, apparently. He'd given the police the slip and managed to get out of his room without anyone noticing. They found him standing by your bedside in a surgeon's white coat. Christian had nodded off for a few seconds in the chair. Apparently when the police came in, Sam Rivers was standing by your bed stroking your head. He didn't cause any more problems and left quietly with the police officers. Maybe I shouldn't have told you all this just yet."

That night James slept well. It was the first night for a while that he had undisturbed sleep and one without unpleasant dreams or nightmares. Maybe it was because just after he fell asleep, Christian had crept into bed beside him and held him close. James went to sleep as Christian was murmuring into his ear, "I love you, Jay. We'll be going home soon."

"I'm so pleased you had that shower, Christian," murmured James, happily.

The following morning the doctor had pronounced that James was making good progress and that he hoped he would be going home on Christmas Eve.

"We've got to run a couple more tests, James, but I am confident that we will have you home for Christmas. Mind you, I hear that the hospital does a very good Christmas lunch," he smiled.

"No, thank you, Doctor, I'll take my chances with Christian's cooking," laughed James. "That is great news. I was hoping that I'd be home for Christmas. You see, I want to go home as soon as I can, because I can't wait to see my dog."

"Ah, is that the magnificent Prince?" asked Dr Blythe. "He's the talk of the town, I hear. I really want to meet him as well. I believe that he helped you to save the Peatwhistles' lives? You must be very proud of him."

"I am," replied James. "I just want to see him again. The vet let him go home yesterday. They tell me he's fine, but I just want to see him for myself. I have been so worried about him."

Dr Blythe thought for a moment or two and then said to Christian, "Well, bring him over to see James. It will do both man and dog the power of good to see each other. Indeed, I shall make a note of that on your records, James. It's the best medicine you both could have."

"Are we allowed to bring dogs into the hospital?" asked Christian, surprised at Dr Blythe's suggestion.

"Well, strictly speaking, no. However, we do sometimes allow Guide Dogs and the like into the car park. I think Prince falls well within that category. Besides, you're in a private room and so I don't see why you can't bring him to the window at least. You must get some benefit from paying all that money. Yes, bring him to the window and I will have a word with Matron. I'll see what we can do for you, James."

When Dr Blythe had left the room James asked anxiously, "Christian, how the hell are we paying for this? I didn't know I'd gone private."

"Calm down, Jay," smiled Christian, holding his hand. "It's the Peatwhistles. Sir Toby is on the board or is a trustee or something. Anyway, he called the hospital when you were brought in and said that you had to have the best treatment. Anyway, he's paying for it."

"I thought the nurse was joking when she asked if I would like a glass of wine last night," laughed James.

"I wish I'd accepted now. That's very kind of them though, isn't it?"

"Yes, it is, Jay, but you did save their lives."

Later that afternoon when Doris called to see James, Christian left the room for a moment and met George in the car park. Christian could see Prince in the back of the car and the happy dog seemed to be laughing at him.

Slowly, Prince got out of the car and Christian knelt down to hug him. Prince looked lovingly at Christian and licked him.

"He's still a bit weak, Christian," said George. "He's got stitches and, as you can see, he's wearing that plastic funnel-thing to stop him trying to pull them out. He's still on painkillers and antibiotics, but he seems fine. The vet said not to take him on proper walks until he's stronger. We're just letting him do what he wants. He's sleeping a lot at the moment."

"I have a surprise for you, boy," said Christian and the happy dog slowly followed Christian to the window of James' hospital room. Christian knocked on the window and Doris opened it. "Just as I thought. Come over here, James. You have a visitor!"

James slowly and carefully got out of bed and went to the window. He cried when he saw Prince looking up at him. "I just want to cuddle him," he said.

"Well, why don't you then?" came a voice from the doorway. It was Sally, one of his nurses. "Dr Blythe had a word with Matron and said it was essential for your speedy recovery to see your dog. Besides, we want to see you two heroes together as well. I've brought a wheelchair and if Mr Trill would like to bring Prince into the waiting room, we'll meet him there. How about it?"

"Brilliant," shouted James, clambering slowly into the wheelchair that Sally had brought for him. "Let's go."

Minutes later, the two heroes were reunited in the hospital waiting room. James, in his dressing gown and sling and Prince with his bandage and plastic collar looked like the war-wounded being reunited again after a major battle.

Doctors, nurses, office staff, patients and even a stern-looking Matron appeared as from nowhere and looked delighted to join in with the celebratory atmosphere. Christian took several photographs whilst Matron hissed, "If the hospital board finds out I've allowed this, there'll be trouble!"

"I really don't think so, Matron," came a voice from the entrance door. It was Sir Toby with Lady Lotitia. "What you have displayed today, Matron, is both common sense and a true sensitivity to your patients' needs and welfare. I think you should be congratulated too."

Lady Lotitia could be seen wiping away tears from her eyes. "Without you both we would be dead. I thank you from the bottom of my heart." She bent down and hugged the happy dog.

Suddenly, there was spontaneous clapping and cheering from the assembled gathering and it was quite some time before Matron could restore order to her hospital once again. There were many tears of joy shed in the waiting room of Abbotsford General Hospital that afternoon.

James awoke the following morning feeling refreshed and happy. He was excited to be going home and was concerned that Christian had spent yet another cramped, uncomfortable night in the hospital bed. He knew that Christian was exhausted and he wanted the three of them to be home together as soon as they could.

"Wake up, Christian," James said gently. "The nurses will be on their rounds shortly. They mustn't catch us like this."

Christian, who was still half-asleep, stumbled out of the small hospital bed and fell back into the armchair and resumed his sleep there. A few minutes later one of the nurses came into the room.

"Good Morning, James. Good Morning, Christian. I hope you both slept well," smiled Nurse Sally Walters breezily. She had, in fact, called into the room an hour or so earlier and caught James in a deep sleep in Christian's arms. She understood what needed to be done, had quietly closed the door and left them to continue their blissful sleep.

Whilst James was waiting for the final agreement from Dr Blythe that he could go home later that day, there was a knock on the door.

"Come in," shouted James and was very surprised to see Patsy Peters walk into the room.

"Hello, stranger," smiled James, as Patsy walked over to his bed and kissed him.

———

413

"James, I am so sorry I've not been in touch since the funeral. I've only just heard how ill you've been and what happened. How are you now?"

James introduced Christian to Patsy.

"Yes, I do remember you, Patsy. We met at Tristan's funeral. You're his sister, aren't you?"

Patsy nodded. "Yes, and I still miss him dreadfully. I know you do too, James. Anyway, nice to see you again, Christian."

"How is Puneet and little Carl?"

"Puneet is well and working very hard in the new business and little Carl is not so little any more. I would have brought him to see you, but Puneet thought that we should have a chat together this time without him. Thank you for all the birthday and Christmas presents you've been sending Carl. It's very kind of you to remember, James."

"Well, I'm just continuing what Tristan would have wanted. Carl is the closest that I am going to get to a nephew and so I'm happy to do it. I'd like to see him again sometime. Are you still living in Neston? Wasn't there some talk about you moving?"

"We thought about it, but in the end we decided that we were better off where we are. Carl is so happy at the school and so we decided to build an extension instead. You really must come over and stay with us one weekend. Christian is welcome too. Carl would love to see his Uncle James again."

"We'd love to. It's lovely to see you again, Patsy, but why are you really here?"

Christian smiled to himself. Yes, he remembered that James hated small talk and wanted to get on with the real purpose of Patsy's visit. "Look, you two, I'm just off to get some coffee. You can catch up for a few minutes. Would you like some coffee, Patsy?"

"No thanks, Christian, I won't be long. I've got to pick up Carl on my way back."

Christian tactfully decided to leave James and Patsy to talk on their own. He guessed that Patsy had something important on her mind that she wished to share with James.

"James, I know some of what's been going on. I saw it on the news. It's dreadful that you have been hurt like this."

"Yes, it has been a difficult few weeks," admitted James, "I'm getting over it now. I'm hoping to go home later today or tomorrow."

"I saw the photo of this Sam Rivers person on the television. The police were looking for him. I couldn't believe how much he looked liked like Tristan, James!" exclaimed Patsy.

"Yes, I know. It was very scary at first, Patsy. He's almost identical until you get very close. I had dinner with him once. To begin with, it was just like being with Tristan."

"When I saw what was going on I wondered, I wondered…" began Patsy, not knowing quite how to end the question.

James looked at her closely. Yes, she was certainly Tristan's sister. Long blonde hair, similar nose and brilliant blue eyes. Indeed, she didn't look unlike Jennifer Miranda. "You're going to ask if I fell in love with him, aren't you? Christian asked me the same thing. The truth is, maybe, just a little. It was wonderful to feel so close to Tristan again, to hear him laugh, look into his beautiful, blue eyes. Then, I noticed how cruel he was. He wasn't really at all like Tristan. He just wanted me to think he was. It was such a cruel trick to play on me."

"Did he remind you of anyone else?"

"No, Patsy, why should he?"

"My father maybe, Grant Peters? Forget about the blond hair, but picture the bright blue eyes, the handsome features, the brilliant white teeth, the same physique. Surely you can see some similarities, James? Think about when we were young and all played together. Remember Dad taking all of us to the swings and to the fairground? Remember that smile, James, the laugh and those twinkling, sparkling blue eyes? He was a very handsome man in his younger days. Do you also remember when he lost his temper and those violent mood swings? Do you remember the way he shouted and often hit Tristan if he had too much to drink? Do you also remember those cold, steely eyes and his thin pursed lips…?"

James sat up as a shiver ran down his spine. "My God. Yes, I do remember! It's all come flooding back. That's why I thought I knew Sam Rivers so well. Maybe it was the similarity with Grant Peters, and not just Tristan that I was remembering?"

Patsy had thought carefully about what she was going to say to James, because she did not know what his reaction would be.

She continued speaking quietly. "Look James, I don't want to alarm you as you have been so poorly, but you need to know the truth. I believe that Sam Rivers is mine and Tristan's half-brother and that Grant Peters, our father, was his father too."

"How's that possible?" demanded James. "You lived so far away from Abbotsford. How on earth did your father sire a child down here? It's too much of a coincidence."

"Well, you remember that Dad was a long distance lorry driver? When Mum died it was Tristan who looked after me when Dad was away. He was a wonderful brother and always did his best by me. Well, sometimes Dad would take me with him. Occasionally, I believe he would feel guilty and felt that he should do something to help the family. I went with him on some of his long journeys. Sometimes we stayed in the lorry, sometimes a cheap boarding house and a few times, if someone else was paying, in nice hotels. I had lots of aunties and some were very nice. Others were just girls, only a bit older than me, that smelled of cheap perfume. I can still smell it sometimes when I'm depressed. Sometimes we stayed in their homes and often different aunties would meet us in the hotels or boarding houses. A few times, Dad took me along to meet them, but mostly I was left in the lorry alone all night. I now know that most of them were prostitutes, James. Dad was over-sexed and could never get enough. I know that now."

Patsy looked as if she was about to burst into tears and James poured her a glass of lemonade and put his hand on her shoulder.

"James, I always felt that you were my big brother as well as Tristan. Later, as I got older, I used to have schoolgirl fantasies and thought that one day you and I would get married," she laughed. "You fell for my brother instead though, didn't you? You're still a handsome boy, James, and I can see why Tristan fell for you."

Patsy wiped the tears from her eyes and she continued. "Well, we started coming to Abbotsford a lot. We stayed in a large hotel a few miles away from the town. We used to go to our room and then a very posh-speaking woman would visit us and stay the night. It happened a lot and I had to call her Auntie, and Dad made me wear one of my best dresses whenever she came. I never did know her other name, but when they were doing it, I sometimes used to hear Dad calling her, "Lolly, Lolly." I thought it was a funny name for a woman at the time. If the hotel had a spare room, Aunt Lolly would pay for me to have a room of my own. That was nice because I couldn't hear what they were doing. We used to have breakfast together: a big breakfast with lots of different things to eat. It happened many times. I liked Aunt Lolly and she used to buy me things like books, comics, sweets and sometimes even pretty clothes."

Christian crept back into the room with a coffee for himself and one for James. He sat quietly in the corner of the room whilst Patsy continued her story.

"Well, one day Aunt Lolly came to the hotel and they had a big row. Dad shouted at her and he hit her across the face. He called her a slut and that he never wanted to see her again. She cried. She cried a lot and I remember she went into the bathroom to wash her face. It was bleeding, you see. I remember her saying that he was an animal and that he had no right to be bringing up a child. She said 'good bye' to me and left."

James nodded and Patsy wiped away more tears from her face with a paper tissue. She seemed so relieved to be able, at last, to tell someone her sad story. She spoke quickly and breathlessly.

"Dad was in a violent mood after that and kept shouting at me. I remember that he hit Tristan really hard when he got home, and he drank heavily for days. You and Tristan were so kind to me. You took me to the cinema, we had bike rides and I really enjoyed the time we had together. I nearly forget about Aunt Lolly until one day, when he was sober, Dad asked if I wanted to go to Abbotsford again. I asked if it was to see Aunt Lolly and he just shrugged and said, 'Maybe'. We met Aunt Lolly in the hotel and when they were having a drink together, Dad sent me off to watch television in the lounge. I didn't understand because Aunt Lolly looked much fatter and then I heard them mention the word 'baby'. Dad got very angry and started shouting and said she should have got rid of it, but Aunt Lolly didn't answer. He started banging his glass on the bar and the waiter came over and told him to stop it. That's when Dad punched the waiter and then hit Aunt Lolly on the face again. She fell to the floor and Dad was thrown out of the hotel. I remember Aunt Lolly coming over to me and saying that she didn't want any fuss, that she was alright and didn't want the police called. I think she gave the barman some money. Before she left, she gave me five pounds and told me to buy something nice."

"That's certainly an amazing story, Patsy. I'm so pleased you told me," replied James, realising that yet more pieces of this complicated jigsaw were gradually fitting into place. Yes, Patsy's story began to make a great deal of sense.

"James, I'm not very clever, I know that, but I have been thinking about this for days now. What if the baby was Sam Rivers? It would explain why he looked so much like Dad and Tristan. It would explain why we kept coming down here as well. You see, I think Sam Rivers is my half-brother and Tristan's too. James, I'm frightened. Do you think we need to tell the police?"

"Hmm, that figures," said James slowly. "One thing that I've always meant to ask you, is why you and Puneet moved down here. It is so far from where you were brought up. Why choose Neston?"

"James, I've never told anyone this before, but Puneet is Muslim, as you know. Well, in our area there's a lot of racial hatred, James. Puneet and I could never have got married and brought up children safely there. The name-calling, teasing and tormenting would have been awful for us, let alone a place for a child to grow up in. I thought about it a lot and Puneet said he would go anywhere with me, just as long as we were safe and could be happy together. I was already pregnant with Carl and so I chose the only other place I really knew. I liked the Abbotsford area, it seemed a friendly enough place and I had spent many hours alone in the lorries at night. There was no trouble and it seemed a very safe place for our child to grow up. That's why we came down here. I thought that we'd be happy here."

"This is all so very strange," replied James thoughtfully. "Tristan and I came down here partly because of you. We'd heard you talk about it I guess, and it seemed like a place that we already knew. This is uncanny, don't you think, Christian?"

"Spooky, I'd say, but I still don't understand why Sam Rivers had such a fixation on you, James?"

James shook his head. "Neither do I. Tell me, Patsy, have you spoken to your father about any of this? You know that he and I are not exactly friends."

"Well, after Tristan's death he did very well financially. As he was Tristan's next-of-kin he got everything from the sale of Tristan's flat and all his things. I felt dreadful about that, because some of those things were yours, James. Tristan also had a little money saved, but Dad spent the lot within a few months. He went on fancy cruises and holidays with some of his women and was 'stoned' most of the time. I think he had more or less spent the lot by the time he died."

"Grant's dead?"

"Yes, he came back from his last holiday looking the best I've seen him for a long time. He'd met quite a nice woman, Janet, and he'd smartened himself up. He had even been going to a health farm to detox and get fit again. We went to see Puneet's family one weekend and I called in to see him. Anyway, Dad suddenly took ill and died. It was only a few months ago. I didn't bother to tell you, James, as I knew you had problems with him over the way he had treated Tristan."

"I certainly did, Patsy. What did he die of? Was it booze and cigarettes? Something like that?"

"No one really knows, James. I spoke to Janet at the funeral. She's a nice enough woman and I wish that Dad had met her years ago. She told me that he came home from the pub one evening, felt really ill and went to bed. The doctor came a couple of times, but Dad never really recovered consciousness for long. Janet told the doctor that she thought he should go to hospital, but the doctor said he would get over it in a couple of days. She thought it was strange, because apparently, the doctor arrived without Janet even calling the surgery or the emergency services. She thought that the pub had called and sent the doctor to the house, but they said they hadn't called anyone. You see, Dad was often drunk and a good night's sleep usually did the trick. Anyway, this doctor came to see Dad a couple of times and brought tablets and stuff with him, and said they didn't have room to treat him in hospital and that he could be looked after better at home. Dad died a couple of days later."

James looked at Christian, who was now sitting with his mouth open. He knew that he had to call the police right away.

Chapter 20

All is Not What is Seems

It was Christmas Eve and James was now back at home and once again reunited with Christian and Prince. It was a happy homecoming and James was touched by all the flowers, gifts, cards and 'get well' messages that he had received. There was even another pot of home-made strawberry jam, delivered personally by Emily. James gasped in amazement when he saw the large Christmas tree dominating the corner of the living room, together with streamers, balloons, tinsel and coloured balls that now decorated every corner of his small flat.

"How on earth did you manage all this, Christian?" James gasped. "I had planned to do something for us, but nowhere near as grand as all this!"

"Guess who?"

"Doris?"

"Yes, she insisted. I came back briefly to collect a few things when you were in hospital and it was all done. I think George helped a bit as well, though," he laughed.

Prince too was delighted to see James again and the happy dog would not let him out of his sight and sat on James' feet for much of the time.

425

James was concerned that Prince might still be in some pain as he still found it difficult to walk, and the plastic collar seemed to be irritating him. He also seemed to be sleeping a lot, yet he was eating well and, when awake, seemed attentive and alert.

"Look, if you're worried I'll take him to the vet this morning for a check-up before Christmas, James. Will you be alright on your own for an hour or so? I could get Doris to come and look after you if you like?"

"Don't you dare," grinned James. "I love Doris dearly, but I've had all the fussing over that I can take for a while. Yes, do please take Prince for a check-up. I just want to make sure he really is alright."

"Talk about fussing," laughed Christian, "That's all you've done with Prince since you got home. I think the poor dog needs a break away from us both, Jay! Anyway, what will you do when I'm out?"

"I'm going to sit here and read that book you gave me last Christmas. You remember giving it to me? I've never had time to even open it. I'm really going to enjoy it and I've promised myself that I will finish it before I go back to school as well!"

"Good for you! Anyway, we're off. Give Doris a call if you need anything and I'll be back as soon as I can."

James had just settled down with the book and another mug of coffee, when the doorbell rang. James still found it uncomfortable to walk, but slowly managed to get to the door and open it. It was Detective Sergeant Russell and another man whom James did not recognise.

"Good afternoon, sir," began Detective Sergeant Russell. "It's good to see you out of hospital, Mr Young. We would like to have another word with you, if that's convenient for you, sir? This is my colleague, Detective Sergeant Wilson." James shook hands with the younger and much friendlier looking man.

"Yes, of course," replied James, indicating that they should go into the living room. They sat down and James offered them both a cup of coffee, which the older man politely declined.

"In my job, I have to say 'no thank you' if I'm offered too many coffees, otherwise I am wanting to pee all day," he replied, unnecessarily to James' thinking.

"Thank you, Mr Young. If you are having one, I'll join you," nodded the younger detective.

"Forgive me for still being in my dressing gown. I am finding it easier than getting dressed at the moment."

"We quite understand, sir. You had a nasty ordeal and it's good to see you up and around again. Thank you for all the information you gave us yesterday. We thought we would drop by and ask you a few more questions, and to reassure you that we are on the case," said Detective Sergeant Russell.

James nodded.

"First of all I wanted to explain that we have taken all of your reports very seriously and apologise for not intervening earlier in that skirmish at the Manor House."

"Skirmish," snapped James. "My dog and I, let alone the Peatwhistles, were very nearly killed."

"Yes, although we did arrive on the scene promptly, it was nowhere near quick enough to prevent what could have been a tragedy, I agree. However, I hope that our explanations will reassure you. You see, we had been following your movements and that of Sam Rivers very closely for some weeks now. As you already know, Sam Rivers is now safely in custody, but refuses to tell us anything."

James frowned.

"Since you first contacted us some weeks ago, we've been in touch with our colleagues in America. Indeed, in no less than three States, Mr Rivers has created considerable interest, as well as over here, of course. We know that Sam Rivers has perpetrated a number of crimes, and all have to be taken into account."

"Yes, I guessed that," nodded James.

"You see, he's a very slippery customer indeed. He's wanted under a variety of names in the States, as well as over here. As you have already seen, he's a master of disguise and intrigue and seems to have the amazing ability to be in two places at the same time. You're aware of that, I believe?"

"Yes, I am. I find it hard to understand how he can come and go so easily. It amazes me. Do you know how he does it?"

The younger detective put down his coffee and took over the conversation from his colleague. "Well, from our enquiries, it would seem that Sam has always had a desire to dress-up and pretend to be someone who he is not. He's very good at it as well. You may not know this, but when he left England to be with Giles Peatwhistle in the States, he got a job in the cosmetics department of a large city store. We understand that from there he went to work in a pharmacy; initially he sold cosmetics and later he worked with the pharmacist in the dispensary. We believe that it was there that he developed his considerable knowledge of drugs. The information that you gave us about the woman who brought him up and his real father, possibly dying from drugs that Sam may or may not have given them, would seem to fit this disturbing profile."

"Yes, I can understand that, but I still don't see how he manages to appear and disappear. Are you able to tell me?"

Detective Sergeant Wilson continued, "Well, it seems that after Giles Peatwhistle died, Sam really was on his 'uppers'. He was broke and still had Giles' medical and funeral bills to pay. He began to look at easier ways to make money and he quickly realised that his amazing talent was under-used. He already knew that he was good at impersonation, and particularly as a woman. He managed to attract a number of elderly, wealthy men into his life, who seemed unaware that he was in drag, and oddly enough, quite a few of them seemed to die in the process. Whether it was through sheer pleasure or an overdose of drugs we still have to ascertain. However, sufficient to say, the New York Police Department as well as colleagues in California and, we believe, Nevada State Police, are very interested in getting Sam Rivers to help them further with their enquiries. To answer your specific question Mr Young, you must understand that we are telling you far more than we should. You have already been very helpful to us and you deserve an explanation for what you have been through."

"Thank you, I appreciate your frankness," replied James.

"Sam Rivers began to get mixed up with a group of entertainers. They were always on the fringe of petty crime and quickly saw in Sam Rivers a means to a number of ends. Firstly, Sam was a brilliant impersonator of both men and women, he was totally convincing. Secondly, he knew his way around a drugs' counter and knew which drugs could put you to sleep and which would kill with little or no trace. However, his most valuable asset, and as yet under-developed, was that of an escapologist, you know the kind of thing? Being handcuffed and tied down with chains, placed in a tank of water and then escaping within a few minutes. Well, that was something that Sam learned to do very quickly. He was a natural, as we found to our cost when, the other evening, he escaped from his hospital room and came to see you, Mr Young. He was handcuffed to the bed and had two police officers outside his door, but he still got free for a few minutes."

James nodded, "Yes, I heard about that. I thought he was trying to kill me."

Detective Sergeant Wilson continued, "As you will already have noticed, he seems to be made of rubber. He can twist and turn like no one else I've ever known. He's quick, light on his feet and a magnificent athlete. After a period of training with this group of entertainers, Sam became unstoppable, as well as their primary asset. The troop worked in circuses and cabarets in several States until they arrived in Las Vegas. It was there that they found rich pickings from the casinos, and then their real game began."

"This is all unbelievable," gasped James. "But whatever brought him back to England?"

Detective Sergeant Russell then took over the conversation; James really did not like the narrow setting of his eyes and he wondered what Doris would have said if she had been present.

"Well, that's want we want to know as well. Sam Rivers is no fool, he's an extremely intelligent young man and now we also know that he is very dangerous. Something went wrong for him. We believe that he was beginning to over-stretch himself, if you forgive the pun." The older man laughed at his little joke and the younger officer smiled with just a hint of embarrassment, James thought.

He continued, "Maybe he was being blackmailed or was getting into other trouble with the group, who were becoming more daring in their criminal exploits. We really don't know for sure. What we do know is that more or less at the same time that you moved to Prior's Hill with young Tristan Peters, he too appeared on the scene. We had already been alerted by the FBI that he was over here and we were keeping a close eye on him. From our investigations, it seemed that wherever Mr Peters was, or indeed wherever you were, Mr Young, Sam Rivers was never far behind."

"You didn't warn us that he was dangerous?" exclaimed James.

"We didn't know that for certain at the time. We had no evidence and neither did our colleagues in the States. We could only watch what was going on and report back. It was only when Mr Peters was killed in the car crash that we began to take the issue even more seriously!"

"What do you mean? No? My God! Are you suggesting that he killed, Tristan?" exclaimed James.

"No, not at all, but it does remain a possibility that the car may, and I have to stress may, have been tampered with in some way on that fateful day. You see, we believe that Sam Rivers was obsessed with you and that when Tristan Peters died, he believed that he had a chance with you. Both of you being... of similar persuasion, that is!"

"I think the word that you are looking for, Detective Sergeant, is homosexual," snapped James.

"Quite so, sir. Not only that, but he thought that you would be the way that he could stake his claim upon the Peatwhistle Estate."

"He's sick. Sam Rivers is really sick if he believed that!"

"Yes, sir, we believe that he is and that he still does believe that he can get his hands on what he sees as his birthright and is, as he told us, his destiny. His obsessive and destructive behaviour are very clear signs that he is not only very ill, but very dangerous."

"So, I may have spent the last two years with Sam Rivers, Jennifer Miranda or whoever visiting me as a parent, a member of staff from County Hall and indeed anyone sitting in a church service with us! Was anyone real?" exclaimed James.

"You're over-reacting a little, sir. It's difficult to say."

"So you have been putting me in danger to catch your criminal!"

"I wouldn't say that sir. You have been observed and protected at all times."

"Like the other day, when my dog and I were nearly killed. How do I know that?"

"You'll have to take my word for it, sir. One example that springs to mind recently was your birthday celebration at 'The Pantry' a few weeks ago, when Sam Rivers was trying to seduce you."

"Oh my God! Were you there as well?"

"My officers were, sir. He was the one that your dining-partner nearly had a fight with towards the end of the evening. You will no doubt remember the other young couple in the restaurant? They were police officers."

"I just don't believe all this. Why are you giving me all this information?"

Detective Sergeant Russell looked embarrassed and paused. The younger man continued. "As we said, Mr Young. We feel that you have a right to know what has been happening. You've given us a great deal of information and it's in all our interests that we have sufficient information to be able to successfully charge and prosecute. We also believe that there is much more to this story, and our colleagues in the States will attempt to extradite Sam at the earliest opportunity. We need to clear up our end of the crime-wave here first. You can help us to do that."

James nodded and replied slowly, "Yes, I think I understand. What else do you want from me?"

The older man continued, "Thank you, sir. This leads me to why we are here today. Recent events have led us to the conclusion that Sam Rivers is working with an accomplice but, so far, we have been unable to find any trace of this person. Of course, the accused denies any such suggestion. A good example of our difficulty was at the school Carol Service. You may not have realised it at the time, but Sam Rivers was at that service as well. In fact he, or should I say she, was sitting very close to you and your pupils. She really seemed to enjoy joining in with some of the carols!"

"No! I can't believe that. I thought I knew everyone there."

"Well, that's as may be. You see, Mr Young, much of what you have seen is an illusion. The human mind is a strange thing. Things that we think we see sometimes, in our minds, become real to us, even if they are not."

"How do you mean?" asked James, puzzled.

"Well, for example, how do you know that I am not Sam Rivers? You haven't asked to see any identification. You've simply assumed that I am who I say I am. We all do it, but it can be dangerous."

"Well, I know PC Wright and he introduced you to me. Anyway, you don't look a bit like Sam Rivers. It's stretching the imagination too far!"

"But that is hardly proof. You see, Mr Young, we believe what we want to believe. Our minds play tricks on us. We all assume far too much and we all tend to be too trusting. It's in our nature to do so. This was our problem at your Carol Service. As I said, we were following both your movements and those of Sam Rivers very carefully and that led us to the Carol Service. To avoid unnecessary unpleasantness for the children, we decided that we would wait until the service finished and then arrest her quietly as she was leaving. It was the time between the Carol Service and your pupils singing at the Manor House that she disappeared."

"You mean Jennifer Miranda?"

"Yes, that's one of the names that he uses when he's in drag, I believe. We worked on a lead that took us away from watching the Manor House for a short time. When we realised that we had been deliberately led away from the Manor, we went right back and that's when we were aware that you were in serious trouble."

"I see," said James, nodding. "So you think that there's someone else involved?"

"We're not sure if there really is an accomplice, Mr Young, but it's a real possibility. We would like you to think back to all those times when you have been in the company of Sam Rivers, or Jennifer Miranda for that matter, and ask yourself if it could have been anyone else?"

"Impossible," said James. "I would know him anywhere. Apart from his sister, there is no one who looks anything like him?"

"His sister?"

"Yes, I told you yesterday. She's the one who told me about Grant Peters' death. She looks remarkably like Jennifer Miranda I would agree, but that really is Patsy and I've known her for years."

"Have you really, Mr Young? You've seen her every week or so, have you? Could you vouch for her whereabouts? You really do know her that well?"

"What are you intimating? I don't like the sound of this, Detective Sergeant Russell. No, Patsy is certainly not involved. She can't be!"

"In the same way as Sam Rivers could not possibly be me, I think you said earlier, sir?" Detective Sergeant Russell opened his briefcase, and with a forced almost-triumphant smile, took out a number of black-and-white, as well as colour photographs and spread them across the coffee table. Take a careful look at these, Mr Young. Some are better than others, I know."

James gasped as he saw an assortment of colour and black-and-white photographs of a number of women and men looking at him. Some were young and some were old. Some were smart and well-dressed, whilst others looked like 'down-and-outs'. There was an assortment of priests, lorry drivers, lift operators, counter staff and even police officers.

"Take a close look, Mr Young. Don't you think that the handsome man on this one looks a little like me?" Detective Sergeant Russell laughed, showing a little more humour. "These photographs were sent by courier to us by our colleagues in the States a few days ago. If you hadn't already guessed, these people are all Sam Rivers. Believe me Mr Young, we have police departments in at least three States, and maybe more, as well as ourselves over here working on this case."

"Hmm, I see what you mean," murmured James, still looking at the disturbing photographs in front of him. "There's another thing that I've been wondering and worrying about. Where is he living? He must have a base over here."

"Well, that's surprisingly easy to answer, Mr Young," smiled Detective Sergeant Wilson. "Right in Prior's Hill village and not far from your classroom."

"You don't mean in the school?" James gasped.

"No, we wondered about that and we've already searched the school thoroughly. Certainly Sam Rivers has been in there a few times, despite your attempts at changing the locks. You see, locks and bolts will never stop someone like Sam Rivers. You were in hospital and so we asked Sir Toby if we could take a look at the school with our colleagues from the fire service. We found some very disturbing evidence."

"How do you mean?"

"Well, it was thought that the classroom heater was faulty and caused the fire. However, we also found a large quantity of burned clothing, shoes, dresses, make-up and the like. We began to put two and two together and assumed that was where Sam Rivers had his base, in one of the upstairs rooms that is now destroyed."

James began laughing. "I can easily answer that for you. When we took out the old school stage, we found boxes of costumes and stage effects from the Prior's Hill Players that they used to use for their annual pantomime. They never did collect their things from the school and so we stored them in one of the upstairs rooms to get them out of the way. They were not ours and so we could not throw them away, you see." James frowned and added, "This won't cause a problem with our insurance claim, will it?"

The young detective smiled. "No, not at all, sir. The fire was indeed caused by the faulty boiler, but the fact that costumes were stored in the building is of no consequence. You asked where Sam Rivers was based. We've since discovered that he has a large 'den' up on one of Sir Toby's farms. There's a group of cottages near to where you have your temporary barn classroom, Mr Young. It's near there."

"I've never seen or heard anything in the barn," began James.

"No, sir, I said near to the barn. There's one cottage, Apple Tree Cottage, I believe it's called. It has a large loft and the roof space leads along to all the other cottages as well as to one of the other barns. Over the years, and we believe since he was a teenager, Sam Rivers has created a 'den' and built up an enormous collection of men's and women's clothes, shoes, hats, wigs, beards and make-up. All the bits and pieces that performers use. It even has electricity, theatrical make-up mirrors and the like."

"I know Apple Tree Cottage," began James slowly. "That's the one that Tristan and I hoped to rent from the Peatwhistles…"

"Yes, we know that as well, sir. You see, all this is forming quite a clear picture of Sam River's obsession for both yourself and Tristan. It was more or less at that time that Sam Rivers saw himself as being very much part of your lives," said Detective Sergeant Wilson quietly.

Christian, who had never pretended to be a wonderful chef, had done his best to prepare a magnificent Christmas Eve meal for James' first night home after his stay in hospital. Admittedly, he had received considerable assistance from their local branch of Marks & Spencer, but the result was eagerly devoured by James.

"I know I went 'private' in hospital, but this meal far outweighs the hospital food, Christian. Thank you so much."

"I'm not too sure if that was a compliment or not," said Christian seriously, pretending to have hurt feelings, but topping-up James' glass at the same time.

"I didn't mean that. It's delicious, a real treat! You know what I meant!"

"I know, I know. Anyway, you'd better get used to it. All of Christmas is coming from Marks & Spencer's freezer and chilled food cabinets this year. I'm doing the cooking and I've bought lots of treats! Yes, and I've also become vegetarian, as the food looked so good! I've really blown our food budget, but I don't care! It's all in the freezer and you won't have to lift a finger! It's so good to see you alive and getting better, Jay. Happy Christmas!"

"Christian, what are we doing about your aunt and uncle?" asked James later that evening. "I would still love them to come and stay with us. Have you been in touch with them recently?"

"Yes, I have, Jay. They keep calling to ask about you. They were shocked when I told them the news and it really upset Aunt Eleanor. They would love to come over for the New Year period. We needn't have worried about them being alone for Christmas though. Apparently they always go to friends for Christmas Day and that has been going on for years, so they were not available anyway."

"So when are they coming?"

"They'll drive down on New Year's Eve and leave us on the 2nd January, Jay. That will give us a decent time with them and, if you are feeling up to it, we can take them out. Maybe we could even show them your school?"

"Oh no, Christian! It looks terrible at the moment. We took down all the decorations and it always looks so barren at the beginning of term. I'd happily show them around during term time."

"Oh, James, always the perfectionist. You never change, do you? That's one of the things that I love about you," laughed Christian, ruffling James' hair.

"Well, maybe they can see just the outside then," laughed James. "We must tidy up the bedroom a bit and maybe get some new bedding? Ours are not the best quality and I am sure Aunt Eleanor would appreciate that. I saw some nice stuff in town the other week. It may be on sale after Christmas."

"Sorry, James. I didn't tell you. They said that they wouldn't dream of staying with us and Uncle Frank is going to book them into that Country House hotel we went to a few weeks ago. They were coming to stay here with us, but they were horrified when they heard that you'd been shot and they insisted that you sleep in your own bed. I think they're right, Jay, given the circumstances."

"Hmm, maybe, but I'm feeling much better now. They made me so welcome when we stayed there and I wanted to do the same for them."

"Trust me, Jay. They understand. They will still spend most of their time with us and we can go out for meals together. Maybe one evening, I will cook one of my specials."

"Oh, God!" grimaced James. "I really wanted them to come and see us again!"

"Oooh, that was cutting, Jay! You just wait until you are fully better. I'll remember that remark and will sort you out good and proper."

"Yes please! I can't wait," grinned James.

Chapter 21

New Year's Eve

"What time will they be here, Christian?" asked James. "I was wondering what we should get for lunch?"

"I think they are hoping to be here by late morning. I thought that maybe we could have coffee here and then drive over to Coombe to see the cottage. How about lunch at the pub there?" Christian finished drying the remainder of the breakfast dishes and was stacking them neatly back into the cupboards.

"Good idea. What do you think about taking Prince as well? He seems to be walking so much better now. I hate leaving him behind. We've not taken him anywhere recently and he always looks so sad when we close the door and leave him behind."

"Oh, you two softies. It's been for his own good, Jay. Yes, he does look so much better now, doesn't he? Let's take him with us. We're going to visit his new home after all."

"I meant to ask you, any news about the mortgage when you called them yesterday?"

"No, not yet. Everything has closed down for Christmas and New Year and so nothing is moving again yet. We'll have to wait a few more weeks for an answer, I'm afraid, Jay. Don't worry though. It all looks alright."

"I'm really looking forward to moving in. I've so many ideas. It's just been so good to have something positive to think about again." James wiped down the sink and sat down by the kitchen table.

"You look exhausted, Jay. Maybe you shouldn't have washed up those dishes? Remember what the doctor said. It is going to take time to heal and get back to normal. Anyway, you need to save your energy for the bash at the Peatwhistles' tonight. It was very kind of them to ask us over, don't you think, Jay?"

"It's a lovely idea and we can take your aunt and uncle as well, Lady Lotitia said. I think it's the first party they've had in the house since Giles left home all those years ago."

"So what exactly is it all about? I know it's a New Year's Eve Party, but who will be there? Is it some of the old country 'toffs' that they know, their friends or maybe some of the villagers? Will there be music and dancing?" asked Christian.

"Well, I don't think it'll be a disco, if that's what you're wondering, Christian," laughed James. "I'm more worried about what to wear. Maybe smart casual? Nothing was said about dinner jackets and the like."

"Well, that's easy. I don't have such a thing to my name. I'm wearing a smart jacket and trousers. Like it or lump it!"

"Well, I'm looking forward to it, whatever it is. It'll be good to draw a line under this year and to move on. I really enjoyed Christmas and you worked really hard to make it special, Christian. I also know that I have put on weight over the last couple of weeks and just look at Prince. He's huge! We both need to walk some it off as soon as we can."

"Don't you worry, Jay. Once you start dashing around school again, to and from the barn and on that football field, you'll soon start losing weight."

James groaned, "Ugh, football! Do you think I have a reasonable excuse not to do any for a term or two? With me being shot and having to wear this sling, I am sure that I can spin it out until Easter at least!"

"You could, Jay, but before you get carried away with that idea, I will say just one thing to you that will change your mind."

"What's that?"

"Don't you think that your precious kids will be disappointed?"

Aunt Eleanor beamed and gave Christian a big hug and kiss. "We are so pleased to see you again, both of you. James, we were horrified to hear about what happened to you. You are quite a hero now, we hear. Come here!" Aunt Eleanor pulled James towards her and gave him a big hug and kiss as well.

"Ouch!" laughed James, "Sorry, but I am still a bit tender…"

"Good to see you again, my boy, and you too James," said Uncle Frank, shaking hands heartily with James and Christian. "I've left the car on the road outside. Is it safe there?"

"Perfectly," replied James. "There's very little traffic and no parking wardens to worry about. Come and see Prince." James opened the door and the friendly dog went through his usual 'meet and greet' routine. Uncle Frank and Aunt Eleanor made a huge fuss of him and Prince seemed delighted to have more people to play with.

"The poor dog. I can see how worried you must have been. Is he still in pain, do you think?"

"No, we don't think so. He has seemed so much happier since Christmas and after we took off the plastic collar that he had to wear. I think, like James, he just feels uncomfortable where the wound is healing. The vet is very pleased with him. He lost a lot of blood, you know."

Aunt Eleanor gave Prince two large parcels to open. Prince knew exactly what to do with parcels and he opened each of them excitedly. He held the smaller one between his teeth and ripped it open gently. Because of his wound, he had some difficultly in completing the job and James bent down to help him. It was a bag of dog biscuits. Prince tore open the inner bag and started eating them. James grabbed the bag from him and put them on the table, whilst Prince gave him a very disappointed look.

"This dog is such a 'guts'. He'll eat the lot if we're not careful. I'll let him have two and he can eat the rest over the next few days."

"Well, he'll think the other one is a bit boring, but I think he may get to like it," said Aunt Eleanor, as Prince tore open the second, larger parcel. This was much easier to open and Prince soon revealed its contents as being a huge tartan blanket. Prince sniffed it and walked back to his basket in disgust.

"It's perfect," said James, "What a lovely thought. It will go in the new basket that we bought him for Christmas. He's grown so fast that he had to have a new one. This is ideal; nice and thick too. Thank you both very much."

"Now you two will have to wait for your present," beamed Aunt Eleanor. "It was a little too large to bring with us."

"Your presents are by the Christmas tree. Maybe you would like coffee and you can open them then? I thought that after coffee we could go over to what we hope will be our new home. We're so excited about it!"

"We would love to see it, my boy. Maybe the next time we come, we can stay with you there?" said Uncle Frank.

"Yes, I'm sorry that you are not sleeping here this time. How is the hotel, have you checked in yet?" enquired Christian.

"No need, my boy," laughed Uncle Frank. "We had a call from Lady Lotitia Peatwhistle. Apparently, they heard that we were coming down to see you both and they insisted that we stay with them during our time here. It was so very kind of them, but we don't know anything about them, other than that they are friends of yours."

"Know them! I should think so. It was Jay and Prince that saved their lives! Well, that's wonderful, it means that after the party you can stay there. It means you can have a drink as well, Uncle Frank!"

"You too, my boy. I gather that Lady Lotitia has invited you both to stay at the Manor overnight as well!"

Christian's battered old Ford Escort drew to a halt outside Lavender Cottage. Christian had already driven around the village once before lunch so that his aunt and uncle could get their bearings, and he and James had treated Aunt Eleanor and Uncle Frank to a Ploughman's Lunch in the village pub. They talked and laughed so much and, for a brief time, James managed to forget some of the recent issues that were still troubling him. It was always a pleasure to hear Frank, in his broad Irish accent, telling one of his stories. He was always very amusing to listen to and James had laughed so much that it brought back some of the earlier pains that he had in his chest just after the operation. Christian had noticed that James had winced once or twice when he laughed, and decided that it was time to draw the lunchtime session to a halt. After all, they also had a busy evening ahead of them.

"Look, I think James is looking a little tired. Let's move on now and see the cottage, and then he can get some rest before we go out again. It'll be a late night tonight."

Aunt Eleanor, Uncle Frank, James and Christian stood outside the pretty little cottage.

"This is absolutely charming," announced Aunt Eleanor. "Just look at those views. They are priceless. We don't get that in Harrow."

Uncle Frank agreed. "It certainly is, Eleanor. It's a long time since I found myself in such a delightful rural setting. Maybe back when I was a boy in Ireland. Just listen... it's totally silent. Wonderful!"

By now Christian had found the correct key to open the front door and the four of them stood together in the porch.

James opened the front door and was just about to announce the living room when he noticed that in the centre of the room was now a beautifully polished, circular pine table and at the table sat a smiling Lady Lotitia and Sir Toby Peatwhistle.

"What are you doing here?" began James, sounding almost ungracious with the shock of what he was seeing.

"Just paying you a little visit, that's all, James," laughed Lady Lotitia, standing to greet Aunt Eleanor and Uncle Frank. "We are delighted to meet you both, aren't we, Toby? We are so pleased that you can join us for our little get-together this evening. It promises to be much fun, what?"

"Well, I'm shocked, but it is good to see you. What a surprise! How are you both?"

"More to the point, how are you, James?" enquired Sir Toby looking anxiously at James' sling.

"I'm coming on nicely, thank you, Sir Toby. It has been quite a few weeks hasn't it?"

"Well, that certainly is an understatement. How is that handsome dog of yours, Prince? Has he recovered yet?"

"He's coming on well, thank you. He's in the car having a sleep. We took him for a little walk, but he still gets very tired. I think it's the drugs that he's still taking."

"Will you bring him with you as well this evening, James, please? We hope you will all stay with us at the Manor tonight. You will all be our honoured guests and Prince too, of course. That dog and James saved our lives, you know."

"Well, we will leave you to show your guests around now. We will see you all later," smiled Lady Lotitia walking towards the door.

"Before we go, we have a little something for you, both of you," smiled Sir Toby, handing a large, stiff brown envelope to James and a bunch of keys to Christian. "Go on, open it up," he smiled.

James tore open the envelope and inside was an important looking legal document. "I don't understand," he began.

"Well, to save you from reading all of Charles' legal jargon, I will explain. It is simply the deeds to Lavender Cottage, registered in your joint names. You are both now the owners of this property."

For one of the few times in James' life, he was speechless. Christian continued the conversation for him.

"I really don't understand. We've put in an offer, which has been accepted and we are just waiting for the mortgage to come through."

"Which you no longer need," interrupted Lady Lotitia. "It's quite simple really. We wanted to buy you a little something to say 'thank you' for saving our lives. We knew that you wanted to buy this cottage, a very good choice I might say, and then we discovered that the agent handling it was non other than where Christian works, and that your Uncle Frank is a partner in the company that owns the estate agency. What could be simpler?"

"We should also say that your aunt and uncle have paid half of the cost of the cottage, Christian," continued Sir Toby.

"But, but this is far too much!" protested Christian.

"Look, my boy," interrupted Uncle Frank. "You're the closest to a son that we will ever have. We don't like to see you struggling for money and so we thought that this would be the answer for you both, particularly after what you have been through recently."

"Also, Christian, with the money that you will not now be spending on the cottage, we hope that you will put it towards a decent, reliable car and scrap that dreadful thing outside!" added Aunt Eleanor.

"Hear, hear," laughed James. "I keep telling him it's only fit for the scrap-yard."

"I'm rather fond of it," protested Christian, teasing James.

"James, we have brought in a few bits of furniture to help to get you started. They are not special, just some bits and pieces that we had in store, but it will be a beginning. Please feel free to dump them as and when you want to buy replacements more to your taste," said Lady Lotitia.

"Well, if they're anything like this beautiful table, they are staying!" laughed James. "Thank you all, I don't know what else to say, just thank you so much."

"Oh, and James," continued Sir Toby. "This cottage comes without any strings attached. It is yours and Christian's to do with as you please. We know that in time you will want to leave our little community and you must feel free to do so, to sell it and move on, just as you wish."

James looked puzzled. "There's just one thing else I don't understand, Sir Toby. How did you get all the paperwork completed so very quickly? Christian told me that it takes about three months usually."

"And so it does, James," laughed Sir Toby, "but if one pays cash and employs a top notch London lawyer, as well as knowing the partner of the estate agency concerned, you would be amazed at how quickly such a transaction can move!"

"Oh, I nearly forgot. Just look what we have for Prince! Go and get him and come this way," commanded Lady Lotitia.

Christian went to get the sleepy dog from the back of the car and brought him into the living room where a great fuss was made of him. Lady Lotitia led the way to the small garden at the rear of the cottage and pointed proudly to the largest wooden kennel that James and Christian had ever seen. It had a beautiful pitched roof and James could see that it had been lovingly crafted.

"We asked Bert and Eddie to make it," announced Lady Lotitia, proudly. "Look at the engraving too."
A shiny brass plate adorned the front of the magnificent kennel, which proudly proclaimed:

'Prince, A True Prince Amongst Dogs'.

Prince sniffed, walked inside his new kennel and immediately walked out again. He looked at James as if to say that it would be the last thing that he would ever consider living in.

Later than evening, Christian's battered Ford Escort swept into the drive of Prior's Hill Manor House. The large car park at the side of the magnificent, golden yellow stone building was already full of cars, and the house seemed alive with laughter and music. Bright lights shone from the inside as well as outside of the building. Lady Lotitia and Sir Toby Peatwhistle stood welcoming their guests by the main door leading into the impressive hallway, and James was taken aback when he saw the effort that Lady Lotitia had obviously made with her own appearance. Usually, she was happiest in a casual, if not eccentric, range of clothes but, this evening, the straw hat and tweed trousers had disappeared and were replaced by a beautiful blue dress, with a single string of pearls and matching earrings as a tasteful accompaniment. Sir Toby too looked dashing in his dark grey suit and, as James and his party walked up the steps into the hallway, he shook their hands warmly and greeted Aunt Eleanor with a kiss.

Lady Lotitia too greeted each member of the party with a warm handshake and a kiss, and as she took James' hand whispered, "James, this is the first time that I have ever kissed a headmaster, what?" James giggled and felt himself going pink. How he wished that he could stop this annoying habit.

An impressive, beautifully decorated Christmas tree graced the hallway. It was enormous and almost touched the ceiling that was already adorned with two beautiful crystal chandeliers. Although James had seen these before, he had never seen them lit until that evening – they were truly magnificent and glistened and shone as they moved very gently each time the hallway door was opened and closed.

"Good to see you up and about again, Mr Young. I was so sorry to hear what had happened to you and your dog. Are you feeling better now?" It was Peggy, and James was pleased to see her. Although Peggy was carrying a silver tray full of delicately-cut sandwiches, James shook her hand.

"Good to see you again, Peggy. Yes, Prince and I are a lot better now, thank you. It was a nasty business and I'm pleased it's over."

Peggy nodded, "Well I knows he's my nephew and all that, but he's a bad 'un. Always 'as been. He was always a worry to our Rita with his behaviour and, by all accounts, he did her in."

James nodded, "I want to try and forget it this evening. This looks magnificent, Peggy."

"Oh, it will be, sir. We've not had a 'do' like this since Mr Giles left for America, you know. We always used to have 'do's' like this and then they all stopped when he left."

James saw Christian and his aunt and uncle waiting for him by the entrance to the Music Room. "Look, excuse me Peggy. I had better take our guests through to join the others. We'll see you later, I hope."

Peggy nodded, "I'm sure you will, Mr Young. I hopes you has a good evening. By the way, your rooms are all made up and ready for you when you need them. There's fresh towels on the beds."

"Thank you, Peggy, that's very kind of you."

Peggy nodded and gave a small curtsy, a gesture that James always found uncomfortable.

James led Aunt Eleanor, Uncle Frank and Christian into the Music Room. As soon as he walked through the doorway, the music stopped and all the faces in the room turned towards him and they started clapping and cheering loudly. Through tear-filled eyes, James could see all the staff from the school: Bert and Eddie, the Rector and June, Jasmine and Paula. There were many others too including many of his pupils' parents, Jack Sparrow, Les and Jill from the pub, Cedric, Doris and George together with many villagers that James recognised. They were all there cheering and clapping as he, Christian, Aunt Eleanor and Uncle Frank walked into the room.

Eventually, Sir Toby put his hand up to bring the gathering to order.

"James and Christian, welcome to our New Year's Eve Party, and welcome also to Christian's Aunt Eleanor and Uncle Frank. Firstly, you will all no doubt be relieved when I promise that this will not be a long speech. However, as well as a party to celebrate, what we hope will be a better year for all of us, I want to pay tribute on behalf of us all to a remarkable young man, our headmaster, Mr James Young. As well as bringing new vitality and a sense of purpose to our wonderful little school, he has rebuilt its reputation and our confidence in it. He has also won our trust, friendship and, dare I say, our love. We all owe him a great debt of gratitude. Also, as many of you know by now, the Peatwhistle family has been in a state of turmoil in recent years. Recent events culminated in James and his wonderful dog, Prince, saving our lives. James put his own life on the line to save ours and I am not sure how anyone can repay such a debt in this world."

The elderly man's voice trailed away and he brushed a tear or two from his eyes. He tried to resume his composure, but found that he could not speak. Lady Lotitia slipped her hand into her husband's hand and continued speaking for him.

"I have to say that I have in the past been a foolish woman and many of you now know what happened as a result. It is a secret that I have had for far too long, but it is not a secret any more. I feel unburdened at last. I cannot say that I am happy, because my son has done many wicked things and is in prison awaiting to pay the price for his crimes. I also have to tell you that, very sadly, our dear son, Giles, died a few years ago in America. I am sorry that we kept that from you, but we had our reasons at the time. To reassure those of you who may now be feeling anxious about the future of Prior's Hill, there is no need to worry about your homes and your jobs. In the event of Toby's and my own eventual departure from this world, the Peatwhistle Estate will continue, just as it has done for generations, but through another branch of the Peatwhistle family. Toby has made sure that the future of Prior's Hill is secure."

"God bless you both!" came a voice from the back of the room. It was Jack Sparrow. "Three cheers for Sir Toby and Lady Lotitia!" he shouted. There was loud cheering and applause once again and the couple looked both pleased and embarrassed. Sir Toby had now regained his composure and took charge of proceedings once again.

"Thank you everyone. Thank you all, so much." He paused and for a moment seemed overwhelmed by the warmth that was being shown by the assembled gathering. "Lotitia and I have another important announcement, also concerning our headmaster. Sir Toby once again turned to James, who had not resumed his natural colouring from the shade of bright pink, since he had walked into the Music Room. "Thanks to you, our little school is now flourishing once again and, as we all know, is now very short of accommodation. James, you have taken every opportunity to 'bend my ears' and indeed those ears of everyone who will listen to you, to ask for two additional classrooms and a new school hall." There was laughter as the assembled gathering recognised James' determination and single-minded purpose for the school.

"James, I am pleased to tell you that Lotitia and I have decided that rather than to wait until our eventual departure and be prevented in supervising its development, the Peatwhistle Estate will, in the New Year that will soon be upon us, release funds sufficient to pay for two new classrooms, together with a new school hall. Our architect is already drawing up plans in consultation with the diocese and County Hall. The local education authority will, of course, pay for its staffing as well as its general upkeep. This is our gift of gratitude to the people of Prior's Hill."

James beamed and shook Sir Toby's hand vigorously, as well as kissing Lady Lotitia once again. There was more loud cheering and clapping and James beckoned to Doris to come to his side. James whispered in her ear and the little lady nodded and left the room.

"Speech, Speech! It's your turn now, Mr Young," shouted Bert and Eddie from the side of the room. Sir Toby beckoned James to step forward.

"I really don't know what to say," he began.

"Now, that makes a change, James!" shouted Doreen Sparkle, who was promptly nudged in the side by Anne and glared at by Emily.

James laughed, "Yes, I suppose it is. I just wanted to say 'thank you' to you all for being my friends and, if I may say, my family. In the time that I have been at Prior's Hill, you have welcomed me into your community and treated me as one of your own. I am indeed grateful for your support. The events the other evening just happened. I am certainly no hero, I'm not brave, just someone who cares deeply about this community and its pupils. The one we should all really be thanking is my dog, Prince. It really is his evening, because I know that it was Prince who saved our lives. Here he is!"

Doris walked in proudly with Prince at her side. The handsome dog seemed to glow in the light of the chandeliers and seemed unfazed by the loud cheering and clapping. He walked slowly to James' side and sat down looking happily at the sea of faces around him.

Sir Toby once again took charge. "James is right. I have never seen such an incredible dog. Raise your glasses, please! The toast is James and Prince!"

After the sound of clapping and cheering finally died away, James turned to Christian. "I felt so emotional. Did I make a complete 'prat' of myself?"

"No, you didn't and if we were not in public, I would kiss you. You were magnificent!"

"Look Christian, Prince does look tired and I don't want him to overdo it. Would you mind finding which room we are staying in and settling Prince in there. His things are in the car."

"I was thinking the same, James. You have both done very well today, but we must remember that both of you are still in recovery. Don't you overdo it either."

"I'm going to have a word with Lady Lotitia, Christian. Despite all the show, I know she's still very upset about all of this. I just want to have a little chat with her."

"OK, I'll catch up with you later then. By the way, James, when you get back, you really are going to have to speak to Jasmine and Paula. They're both here tonight. You can't leave it any longer.

"Oh no!" grimaced James. "That's all I need tonight."

Chapter 22

The Beginning of the End or the End of the Beginning?

James returned to the Music Room to look for Lady Lotitia, but she was nowhere to be seen. Sir Toby stood in the corner of the ornate room, busily talking to Bert and Eddie, and Christian was deeply engrossed in conversation with Jasmine and Paula. Jasmine waved for him to come over and join them, but James made a gesture pointing urgently to the door and indicating that he was trying to find someone. James managed to escape, for the time being anyway.

James walked into the now deserted hallway and into the breakfast room. He shuddered as the events of that fateful afternoon sprang back into his mind. He stood at the doorway looking at the place where both he and Prince had fallen and he could still hear music and laughter coming from the Music Room. How very different things could have been. He walked over to the patio doors, which were slightly ajar. He now knew where Lady Lotitia would be.

James walked into the Rose Garden. It was no longer covered in heady, scented blooms, and now it was bare. The once impressive rose bushes had been cruelly reduced to a collection of brown, uninteresting twigs. It was now very cold outside the warmth of the Manor House and it felt as if there would be heavy frost the following morning.

In the bright moonlight, James could see the huddled form of Lady Lotitia sitting on one of the ornate garden seats looking at the memorial statues in the centre of the largest bed of sleeping rose bushes. No longer did she look glamorous in her blue dress and pearls, but instead had thrown her trademark corduroy jacket over her shoulders for warmth. As James approached her, she smiled, "Hello again, James. Have you come out for a breath of air too, what?"

"Well, yes, I just wanted to be on my own for a few moments. It's been quite a year hasn't it? Anyway, I thought I would find you here."

"Yes, James, it has been quite a year and not one that I would care to repeat too often, what? When the year started none of us had any idea of what would befall us. It is just as well that we don't know what will happen, isn't it?"

James nodded, "I think it would be impossible to live if we did."

There was silence and after a few moments Lady Lotitia commented, "It was all so much easier when I thought that both my boys were dead and safely asleep with the rose bushes. I thought they were both finally at peace and together."

"Yes, I remember you telling me some time ago."

"You see, James, there was no longer any pain for either of them. Even though Sam has done some wicked things and we are all pleased that he is in prison, he is still my son. When he was born, I handed him over to Rita without a care in the world. I didn't love him, he was merely an inconvenience and I wanted to be rid of him," she added, harshly.

"You didn't have any feelings for him at all?"

"None whatsoever at the time, but later... I missed him dreadfully, James. It was as if part of me had died. You see, I used to see him often, playing in Rita's garden, running to the post office and on his way to and from school. Then he became such good friends with Giles and I had the excuse to see him even more. Toby didn't seem to mind; he had forgiven me long ago, you see. He was always away so much and I was on my own. Forgiveness didn't help me, James; I felt guilty. I always felt so guilty and then, in the end, I turned to my 'best friend' for help – the gin bottle. It is so strange, although I never felt that he was my son in quite the same way that Giles was, he was still very much part of me. I don't suppose that, as a man, you will understand what I am saying, James. Just the nonsensical ramblings of a foolish old woman on New Year's Eve, what?"

"Not at all. I think I do understand what you're saying, but I can only imagine a little of the pain of losing a child for someone else to bring up."

"He was such a handsome boy," she continued. "As he grew up, I could see the village girls admiring and flirting with him. He could be such a charming young man, James. You didn't see that side of him, of course, did you?"

"I think I did," said James. "Yes, he worried and frightened me at times, but there was something about him that I liked... and he looked so much like my Tristan."

"Yes, I know, that is what shocked me when I first saw Tristan. They were uncannily alike. Do you remember when I showed you Apple Tree Cottage, James? I think you wanted to rent it from us and Toby decided that he couldn't possibly let you and Tristan have it?"

"Yes, I do remember. I was a bit upset at the time, but that's all 'water under the bridge' now."

"Surely you can see now why Toby and I couldn't have had Tristan and yourself living in Apple Tree Cottage, James? It would have reminded us of Sam each time we saw him."

"Yes, I do see that now. It doesn't matter anymore, does it?"

"No, I don't expect it does. James, may I tell you something? Just between you and I?"

Lady Lotitia paused and thought for a moment. "The problem for me now that Sam has reappeared into our lives, so shockingly, is that I am now beginning to wonder if Giles is really dead, after all."

"You know he is. Sir Toby had a private detective on the case and it was proved that he died of AIDS, you know that's true."

"I know that is the proven case, but I do just sometimes wonder if both of the caskets buried under those bushes actually contain only tea leaves, as was the case with Sam Rivers'."

"I really don't think so," said James, who was now beginning to shiver in the cold night air. "One thing I do know for certain is that Giles died being loved by someone, who loved him so deeply that he would do anything for him."

"You mean Sam? How can you be so sure of that?"

"He told me, several times. I really do believe that Giles and Sam had something so very special between them that few can ever replicate in their own lives."

"Like you and Tristan, James?"

"Yes, just like Tristan and I."

Lady Lotitia shivered. "My goodness it is getting cold. Eleven o'clock, James," she said looking at her watch. "We had better soon go in or we will be missed. I am supposed to be the hostess, after all!"

"Before we go in, may I ask a very personal question?"

"You may, James, but I cannot guarantee that I will answer it. Try me, what?"

"Who was Sam Rivers' real father?"

Lady Lotitia answered slowly, "I always promised that I would take that secret to my grave, James. I cannot possibly tell you."

"Look, I don't want this to be too painful for you, but I think people have already guessed. Was it Grant Peters?"

Lady Lotitia gasped. "How did you find that out?"

"I think you will find that the police already know. You see, my Tristan was also Grant Peters' son. I now know that he and Sam were half-brothers."

Lady Lotitia thought for a moment.

"Yes, James. What you say does make sense. I have often wondered about the amazing similarity between the two of them. When I first met young Tristan I wondered if it could be a possibility and then I dismissed it as highly unlikely, indeed, impossible. Did the police tell you?"

"Do you remember a small girl that Grant Peters used to bring to Abbotsford when he came to see you."

Lady Lotitia smiled, "Why, yes, I do. A pretty little thing, but I cannot remember her name now. It was so long ago."

"Her name was Patsy. She called you Aunt Lolly, remember? She was Tristan's sister and, of course, Sam's half-sister. She came to see me the other day and the pieces of the jigsaw suddenly fitted together at last."

James walked over to Christian who was still engaged in an animated conversation with Jasmine and Paula. Christian smiled, James thought 'between gritted teeth', when he saw him and promptly made an excuse to move on.

"Lovely to see you both again. I must go and have a word with Jack Sparrow. I know he wants to talk to me. Catch up with you at midnight, Jay!"

"Good evening, James. I was beginning to think that you were trying to avoid us," purred Jasmine De Valle.

"No, not at all, Jasmine," lied James. "It's lovely to see you both again."

Paula kissed him. "We're so proud to know you, James. You're very brave even though your bravery did us out of two corpses last week," she smiled and winked wickedly at James.

James picked up on the joke and laughed, "Ugh, that's an awful thing to say, Paula, but I gather that business is brisk for you at the moment?"

"It certainly is, James. It's always a good time of the year for us, Christmas and the New Year always brings the 'stiffs' rolling in. As well as heart attacks and strokes, we usually do well with car accidents too."

"Oh really, Paul, do you have to? I know it's your business, but that's a horrible thing to say! Look, James, I know that Christian mentioned our little problem to you. We would be so grateful if you would oblige," beamed the librarian.

"You see, James. We have done a lot of research recently, and we have come to the conclusion that with your boyish good looks and undoubted intelligence..."

"And bravery. Don't forget the bravery," purred Jasmine.

"And bravery," added Paula. "These attributes of yours, as well as Jasmine's natural effervescence and charm, not forgetting her musical and literary talent, would create the most wonderful combination of genes that any child could wish for. You're a healthy vegetarian and drink very little as far as we can see. It's a truly wondrous combination," Paula gushed happily.

"Look, ladies, I'm really flattered to be asked but..."

"Of course, you don't have to sleep with me, if you don't want to, James. It can all be done by test tubes and syringes nowadays, but you may prefer the natural way, of course. Paul won't mind, will you, Paul?"

Paula was just about to open her mouth to respond when James swiftly intervened.

"The answer is no. Not in a million years, ladies. I'm sorry," he said sharply, giving what Doris would have called his 'Paddington Bear look'.

"Oh, that really that is a little harsh of you, James."

"Look, I don't mean to be unkind, but we're not trying to breed a pedigree dog or cow here. I would love a child, of course, but it doesn't end with selecting the right genes does it?"

"Oh you mean, looking after the little thing, don't you. Well, he or she would have two mothers and two fathers, what could be better than that?"

"I didn't mean that. I meant that I wouldn't be there to bring the child up. I would want my child to know me as his father and to know that he is loved."

"Or her," added Jasmine.

"It wouldn't work, Jasmine, and I wouldn't want to be party to anything that would cause confusion or unhappiness for the child in the future. As a gay man, I know that some doors are closed to me and one of those is having a child of my own, as much as I would love to be a father."

"You would be a good one," added Paula.

"Oh, isn't he passionate about things? I do so love that in a man," gushed Jasmine.

"So you will think about it then and let us know?" asked Paula, anxiously.

"My God, don't you women ever listen? I said, no, not in a million years! As much as I would have liked to be a father, I will just have to content myself with teaching other people's kids. That, ladies, is my final word on the subject."

With that James stormed off leaving Christian, who was listening to and watching the conversation from only a short distance away, creased up in helpless, yet silent, laughter.

The chimes of Big Ben could be heard on the radio. The assembled crowd gathered together in the Music Room and cheered as the familiar chimes struck midnight.

"Happy New Year Everyone!" boomed Sir Toby.

Glasses were raised and toasts were made. The gathering put down their glasses, joined hands and began to sing a lusty rendering of *Auld Lang Syne*, a song that James thoroughly detested, along with bagpipes and kilts.

"Come over here, Jay," whispered Christian, pulling him to the side of the Music Room. "I want to say Happy New Year to you properly. Come into this room quickly!"

James and Christian dived into the adjoining lobby. "Happy New Year, Jay. I love you and want to be with you always," said Christian holding James hands tightly. "I know I can't marry you properly, but I have this for you."

Christian gave James a small box, which when opened revealed a simple gold ring.

Tears flooded down James' face and he held Christian close.

"Thank you," replied James softly, slipping on the ring. "I love you so very much, Christian. You're all that I need and you are my reason for living."

The two young men kissed in the darkened room, lit only by the light of the waning moon.

If James and Christian had not been so preoccupied with passion, they would have seen a small white van stop for a moment at the bottom of the driveway and a young woman, dressed as a maid, scurry down the stony driveway, through the gate and climb into the passenger seat. Together, the driver of the vehicle and the maid sped out of the village.